P9-CQB-159

Daughter of the Bride

Francesca Segrè

BERKLEY BOOKS, NEW YORK

THE BERKLEY PUBLISHING GROUP
Published by the Penguin Group
Penguin Group (USA) Inc.
375 Hudson Street, New York, New York 10014, USA
Penguin Group (Canada), 90 Eglinton Avenue East, Suite 700, Toronto, Ontario M4P 2Y3, Canada
(a division of Pearson Penguin Canada Inc.)
Penguin Books Ltd., 80 Strand, London WC2R 0RL, England
Penguin Group Ireland, 25 St. Stephen's Green, Dublin 2, Ireland (a division of Penguin Books Ltd.)
Penguin Group (Australia), 250 Camberwell Road, Camberwell, Victoria 3124, Australia
(a division of Pearson Australia Group Pty. Ltd.)
Penguin Books India Pvt. Ltd., 11 Community Centre, Panchsheel Park, New Delhi—110 017, India
Penguin Group (NZ), Cnr. Airborne and Rosedale Roads, Albany, Auckland 1310, New Zealand
(a division of Pearson New Zealand Ltd.)
Penguin Books (South Africa) (Pty.) Ltd., 24 Sturdee Avenue, Rosebank, Johannesburg 2196,
South Africa

Penguin Books Ltd., Registered Offices: 80 Strand, London WC2R 0RL, England

This book is an original publication of The Berkley Publishing Group.

This is a work of fiction. Names, characters, places, and incidents either are the product of the author's imagination or are used fictitiously, and any resemblance to actual persons, living or dead, business establishments, events, or locales is entirely coincidental. The publisher does not have any control over and does not assume any responsibility for author or third-party websites or their content.

PRINTING HISTORY
Berkley trade paperback edition / March 2006

Library of Congress Cataloging-in-Publication Data

Segrè, Francesca.
Daughter of the bride / Francesca Segrè.
p. cm.
ISBN 0-425-20880-X (trade pbk.)
1. Remarriage—Fiction.   2. Mothers and daughters—Fiction.   I. Title.

PS3619.E377D38   2006
813'.6—dc22   2005057028

PRINTED IN THE UNITED STATES OF AMERICA

10 9 8 7 6 5 4 3 2 1

For Papa

Acknowledgments

Peggy Hackman launched my writing career, and this book, when she published my "Daughter of the Bride" personal essay in the *Washington Post*.

Laurie Horowitz read that essay and immediately sold Hollywood on the idea. Laurie encouraged me to write a book based on my experience, served as my first editor on the novel, and contiunes to generously provide me with great guidance, friendship, and abundant shared laughter.

Stéphanie Abou, my literary agent, helped give this book its *oomph*, convinced others of its worth, and together with the help of everyone at Global Literary Management, deftly combined good business with good times.

Leona Nevler, my editor at Berkley Books, took a risk with me, guided me with the confidence of experience and, with the entire Berkley team, whipped this novel into shape.

Maria Miles and Steven Beer, my lawyers, are skilled, good-humored professionals who did not balk at all the hand-holding I requested.

Shana Aelony, Sabrina Cohen, Stephanie Ericson, Kyoko Gasha, Emily Gordon, Kathleen Hanna, Orit Harpaz, Rebecca Klein, Rachel

Masters, Tomo Moriwaki, Bobbi Rebell, Sarah Rose, and Maxine Teller are among many friends who made precious, pertinent, and clever contributions to this book.

Bernard Chen, my patient, stalwart supporter, provided me with priceless comic relief and relief in general.

My family, Amanda Weinstein, Marvin Weinstein, Kate Gordon, Gino Segrè, Joel Segrè, and Elizabeth Segrè, inspired me with their story, helped me write it, and then trusted me with it. And we're still talking.

Thank you all.

One

The New York Stock Exchange reeks of testosterone. The scent assaults me each time I burst through the swinging doors onto the NYSE floor. I inhale it. Accept it. Can't fight it. I walk quickly, deliberately, shielding myself with my clipboard as I push and snake through the swarms of shouting, sweating traders. It's like I'm the sperm swimming upstream in a fierce battle for the egg. Only at the NYSE, I'm the egg doing the sperm work, and there's no chance of conception at the end.

"How's I-beam?" One trader yells across me.

"Five cents for fifty thousand, twenty-five thousand at ten cents," another trader shouts back.

"Ten thousand at six cents."

"Take him!"

Ventura, a trader with salt and pepper hair and a dirty smile, is at his post on my left. He gives me the once-over as I rush past. I make friendly eye contact but don't slow down. Sure, he's got the best scoop of any trader on the floor, but right now his inside information isn't worth his ogling. And there's no time for games. The trading day is seconds away from evaporating. I race past Pacelli and Ryan and "the Murphy man." They're looking at their screens intently, frantically trying to lock in deals before the closing bell rings.

I arrive at my camera position, flick on my microphone, flick on my earpiece, and tune out the frenzy. Focus. Face composed, body poised, I smooth down my red skirt suit and glance at the notes on my clipboard. The men jostle me, but I hold my position, imagining my high heels superglued to the hardwood floor. Breathe in. Breathe out. Lighten up.

The closing bell rings, I look up into the camera, three-two-one and I'm live with a smile. My lips move automatically, as if someone flicked a switch to turn me on. I speak gently but authoritatively to the remote-controlled camera like it's a sensitive person eager and craning to hear every bit of market news streaming from my mouth.

"Blue chips rally . . ." "Tech selling off . . ." "Quarterly earnings missing expectations . . ."

Up or down arrows I've drawn in the margins of my notes remind me whether the stock I'm talking about closed higher or lower. I turn up a cheery smile or drop my voice with gravitas depending on the arrow's direction. Two minutes later I sign off with a finishing smile. "And that's a wrap of trading action on Wall Street, Tony, back to you."

"You're clear," the producer says in my earpiece. "Have a good night."

I will. I give him the thumbs-up. I have a special night planned. I switch off my microphone, switch off my earpiece, and gird myself for the exit push. The trader traffic is now surging toward the swinging doors, where it's backing up. I squeeze my way into the moving mass as the guys give each other friendly swats on the back and grunt about the next train home to Jersey. Some wave me good-bye. I do the buddy-buddy wink and nod back. I slither and bump my way through the crowd, the swinging doors, the turnstile. Finally I'm in the cool air of the NYSE lobby.

I take a deep breath through my nose and feel my lungs filling up. I've held my ground for another day inside this bastion of male power. And I've managed to sound convincing with all the stock market talk, even though I'm no good with numbers. I'm a "money honey," aka a female financial news broadcaster, and a typical day like this does not come cheap.

I hurry up the back staircase to the cramped BizNews office and untangle myself from the microphone and earpiece wires. I'm packing up to leave, when I do a double-take of my makeup-caked face in the mirror.

Clown! I think.

I've spent so many precious minutes of my life staring at my face in the mirror, carefully applying TV makeup, hoping that my painstaking efforts to precisely outline my lips, shadow my lids, and bronze my cheeks would help advance my career. Why do I submit to the fifteen-minute makeup-hair routine five times a day as if it were integral to the news itself? This question does not deserve any more attention.

I remember getting into this glamorous career ten years ago. It started with the overnight shift at a no-name station in a tiny town for a paycheck that gained me poverty status. In those days, I shopped at the Salvation Army for the blazers I wore at the anchor desk. Egotistical, insecure bosses have harassed me each step of the way as I've leapfrogged from small town to bigger town, trying to make it to New York. Along the way, I've collected a library of job rejection letters. "Wrong voice."

"Wrong hair." "You're just not what we had in mind." I've never worked so hard for anything in my life. I never wanted anything so much. And now, here I am. I've got it. The international news spotlight. And now I'm searching for something, somebody else.

"Can't work late tonight, gotta run, bye," I say to no one in particular. I lock the office door and dash out onto Wall Street. I squeeze into an uptown train, and twenty minutes later emerge from the subway, flooding back out onto my neighborhood streets with the masses. It's a crisp, fall afternoon, and the sky is clear. I swerve quickly and purposefully through the packed pedestrian traffic. It's the same skill I use to navigate the floor of the NYSE. I avoid making eye contact with my friendly neighbors on the way home. I don't mean to be rude. But no time for small talk tonight. I have a date with me.

Alone in my apartment there will be no more eyes on me, no more voices surrounding me, and no more expectations of me. No need to put on a candy-ass smile. I reach my apartment building and hurry up the five flights of stairs to the prized peacefulness of my cozy home on top.

Unlock the bolts, shoulder shove the door open, drop my bags, kick off my heels. I tune out the sirening car alarms on the street below and keep the lights turned off. In the bathroom, I wash the day off my face. I know I'm streaking brown and reddish lines of makeup across my towel, but I do it anyway.

I shed the suit and grope for Dad's old, long-sleeved, pale yellow T-shirt. It's my favorite T-shirt. I only wear it on special occasions. Fifteen years ago, when I was fourteen, my dad and I got the matching yellow T-shirts at the finish line of a race we ran together. I lost mine; he gave me his. It's worn tissue thin, and it's see-through in many places. Conveniently, a pair of threadbare cotton sweatpants is on the floor where I dropped my skirt.

They, too, are comfortable and comforting. I pull on thick socks and light a lavender aromatherapy candle on my windowsill.

I'm tempted to uncork a bottle of wine, but that's just pathetic. What kind of a person drinks alone? I pour myself a glass of water and collapse into my oversized, overstuffed chair.

I'm long overdue for this date with myself. I've postponed and rescheduled it for months. If I didn't insist on this alone time now, I would've inevitably ended up at a loud bar, a pretentious art opening, a work function, a dinner. Or forcing a smile—but revealing a blank stare—at a cocktail party when a colleague enthusiastically explains the ever-fascinating world of the disinverted bond-yield curve.

Worse? I would have been out on a date with another Mr. Not Quite Right. Sometimes he is polite and charming. Other times his relation to his knuckle-dragging ancestors is painfully obvious. Inevitably he bores me, ignores me, or offends me.

Truth? I don't carve out too much time to be alone, because I get lonely.

But tonight is different. Tonight I'm relishing my alone time, not fearing it. The dark is refreshing. I am not working, I am not worrying, I am luxuriating. It feels so good to rest my head back and shut my eyes.

BEEP.

Huh?

BEEP. BEEP.

Uggh.

BEEP. BEEP. BEEP.

My cell phone, shrill and insistent, is beckoning an urgent response. Someone's horning in on my "me date" already?

BEEP.

"UNIDENTIFIED CALLER" the screen reads.

If I were on a regular date, I would not answer.

BEEP.

It's probably Richard, that terribly handsome, but equally arrogant lawyer I met for Greek food in Midtown last night. Or maybe it's "Jon the banker," a genuinely sweet but hopelessly dull friend-of-a-friend blind date from last weekend.

BEEP.

It can't be Ruben. He's at a meteorological conference in Dallas. To answer or not to answer: that is the question.

Not answer. I will not be interrupted tonight. Not even if it were NBC offering me Katie Couric's spot or Bono serenading me. Mercifully, the voice mail picks up. I'm not even going to dignify that interruption by checking the message.

Wine. Yup. I'm that kind of a person. In the kitchen area, I pop the cork on a bottle of Riesling that I've been saving to share with a special someone. I pour until the glass is half-full. Wine in hand, I go back to the chair and the depression in it that my body so deliberately formed a few minutes ago.

I have a good life. Great family, fab friends, a high-profile job, and I don't lack for male attention. I have the luxury of searching tirelessly for the best jobs and the best man, without compromising much. The list of options grows every day. But where has all this freedom left me? It's left me continually raising the bar of what fulfillment means. Increasingly, satisfaction seems out of reach, and tonight I am alone.

Tonight though, I will focus on the perks of my life. Tonight is my opportunity to appreciate how lucky I am. My apartment is warm, and the candle is soothing. The wine is dry, fruity, cool. Alone is beautiful. I set the wine down and rest my eyelids. At last.

BEEP.

I'm startled from my snooze.

BEEP.

I meant to turn that thing off!

BEEP.

The nerve! This better be the commander in chief, God, or a more powerful being for me to pick up. The screen on the phone reads "Momobile." I have to pick up.

BEEP.

I hesitate. My mom is anything but relaxing. She's high-strung, exhaustingly energetic, and she pries. She's one of those trim, perfectly put together ladies. Her short, light brown hair always coiffed. Her makeup minimal, perfect. She knows how to wear scarves and does. She's probably squeezing this call in while she clicks in her heels at lightning speed across campus. Maybe she's rushing to class to teach her nineteenth-century French literature course. Or maybe she's running late for a lunch appointment. It's always something. It's always high pressure.

BEEP.

I don't want to pick up. Of course I love her. But she can be such a royal pain sometimes.

BEEP.

Just one more minute of serenity.

BEEP.

Quick sip of wine, and I relent. The gods of relaxation are not with me tonight. My best plans for QT with me, foiled.

"Hi, Mom," I muster.

"Hi, Cookie!" she exclaims. "I'm just driving up 880 home. How are you? How was your day? What are you doing? I miss you. Oh! Hold on! Let me pass this guy. Dammit. Jerk. Cookie?"

"Yes? I'm here." I'm already exhausted.

"What's wrong? Why didn't you answer sooner? I was beginning to get worried. How was your day? Meet anyone interesting?"

"I'm tired," I grumble. I want to say, "and I'm not in the

mood to chat right now." But I don't. Something's up. Her pitch is high. I've never heard this edgy nervous soprano tone from her fast-moving mouth before, and believe me, I've heard plenty from her.

I put down the wine, pry myself from the chair, flick on the lights. From three thousand miles away in California, she's crashed my carefully crafted calm.

She's driving her white Honda home toward Berkeley from her boyfriend's house in Palo Alto. I imagine her brown eyes wide, scanning the road, compulsively looking for dangers. I can just see her hands tightly gripping the steering wheel. Her right foot pressing the gas hard, and even though it's an automatic car, her left foot is cocked at an awkward, upright angle, ready to slam on the brakes at any moment. Two feet "gives me more control," she always says.

Suddenly, I'm uneasy. She's driving fast, talking on the phone, and there's this untamed, teenage excitement teeming in her voice. I think I know what's on her mind. But I half-hope I'm wrong. The other half of me knows I'm right and is curious. But it's not the good kind of curious. It's the kind of curious that makes you want to stare at that crazy person on the subway who's in a deep, animated conversation with no one. Why is she stalling?

"Mom, I'm tired. What's up?"

Her chatter speeds up as if she's suddenly under a deadline. Her pitch gets higher and higher. I fear her foot is pressing harder and harder on the gas with each octave. I'm pacing now, phone pressed to my ear, bracing for the imminent bombshell. She hems, haws, chatters, and stalls. She yells at other drivers. Then, uncharacteristically, she falls silent.

I imagine she's biting her lip. A last-ditch effort to seal a dam cracking from the pressures of holding back a great secret. Then, she breaks.

"We're doing it!" she blurts out and erupts in laughter.

I take a deep breath. "Congratulations," I exhale.

I'm not sure she's heard me. She's laughing wildly like a schoolgirl. My dam breaks now, too, and I smile.

But then the words "gown" and "band" and "caterer" start flying out of her mouth. Words I've never heard her say before.

"Mom? Mommy?" Is it really her or is it just some twisted dream?

"Yes, Cookie? Isn't it *so* exciting?"

I hear a car horn blaring.

"Creep! Learn how to drive!" she yells. Yep, it's Mom.

But then she carries on in this jibberish tongue of wedding talk. "Wedding colors," and "Vera Wang," and "flower arrangements."

I tune out. I don't recognize this woman spinning a fairy-tale wedding dream. It's not like her. She always told me to focus on career and personal development and ignore frilly, girly distractions. And if anyone's going to be dropping big news and bandying these words about, shouldn't it be me? I'm almost thirty years old! She's going to do it again, and I haven't even done it once?

Then it hits me. She's moving on.

What about Dad? What would he think? Would he be hurt? I hardly know Stanley, but I know he's incredibly different from Dad. Stanley. Name reminds me of a tool. Does Stanley really love Mom? Has he any clue what a handful Mom can be? Where will she live? Will our families get along? What will my brothers think? Who will walk her down the aisle?

As she chatters on, the worries take me hostage, and my

mind starts spinning, spiraling down toward a dark, unpleasant, unknown. Will I ever get married? With Dad gone, who will walk me down the aisle?

"Cookie, Cookie . . . so can you come?" I hear her voice through the fog of my thoughts.

"Come? Come where?"

"Dress shopping. The lady at the boutique said I need to choose a dress by next weekend or it won't be ready in time for the wedding and I have no idea what looks good on me or what a woman my age should wear and I've never chosen a wedding dress before and I'm not so young and I can't ask the boys for help and I can't ask Stanley and I can't . . . You won't tell the boys . . . will you? I want to surprise them . . ."

"Mom?" I interrupt. "A dress?"

"A dress," she repeats. "Next weekend. Help. Please?"

"Help?" I answer, "Yes." Help!

Two

I need help. I've got a dozen friends I can call, but I don't want to bother anyone. And who's home anyway on a Friday night? Plus, it's not like I'm proud of the way I'm feeling. Mom's getting married; I should be happy. Yet, I can't seem to get over myself enough to celebrate. Instead, I'm disoriented. If she's getting married again, what does that say about me being single still? Embarrassingly, I feel alone and sorry for myself. She is so lucky.

I can understand that she wants to get remarried. To have companionship again after being alone for so long. But a white-dress-and-frills wedding? It doesn't make sense. She was one of those "zap action" Berkeley feminists of the sixties—the ones who ripped off their bras, girdles, and repressions and threw them in the trash. She used to love telling me about how she marched on Washington with thousands of other women demanding equal rights and respect for women. She always insisted that she be respected for her brain, not just her beauty.

What does it mean if women of the sixties, now sixty, are embracing frills, lace, and tradition? I thought I was doing my part to advance feminism by focusing on my career and penetrating the male-dominated financial world. Did Mom make inroads to the working world only to decide now that careers are overrated and dressing up like a princess is more worthy? Holy backlash Batman, err, Wonder Woman. This whole girly white wedding for Mom seems so anachronistic. And there's a part of me, a little part, that feels betrayed.

I want to call my brothers right away, but I promised I'd wait till tomorrow so she could tell them in person first.

Who can I call? Ruben is at that meteorology conference. Jackie will be sympathetic at first, but then we'll just end up talking about her divorce. Maybe Maxine, my college roommate, will help. She's stable. Rational. It's worth a shot.

"Maxine? Daniella."

"Hi!" She sounds surprised. "What's wrong? Why aren't you out? It's Friday night."

"Nothing, really. It's just that . . ."

"What?"

"My mom's doin' it."

"What?"

"She's getting hitched. Tying the knot. Saying 'I do.'"

"Congratulations! That's great!"

"Yes, but . . ."

"But what? You like the guy, right?"

"Right. It's just that . . . well . . . I'm happy for her, but it's a bit unnerving. I mean my mom's on number two, and I can't even find number one? What's wrong with me?"

Maxine sighs. "Daniella. Nothing's wrong with you. You just haven't found the right guy," she tells me as she's told me so many times before. "And anyway, you're doing so well with your career, and you have such a great social life, just keep at it. Don't sweat it. Be patient. He'll come."

"Right." I roll my eyes. Easy for her to say. "I've been patient. Twenty-nine years patient. And yes, my career's great and friends are great, but HE is missing. Something's wrong with me. And forget about me for a minute. What would my dad think of my mom getting remarried? It hasn't really been that long."

"Oh, Daniella. I know it's hard. But it'll be good for her. And you want what's good for her, right?"

"Right," I say. "But, you're my friend, would you please tell me what is wrong with me? Too career-driven? Too picky? Something about the way I look? And explain to me, please, why does she need to be princess for the day after raising me to be an ardent feminist?"

"Daniella, whoah. Getting married and being a strong woman are not mutually exclusive. And nothing's wrong with you. Just be patient," Maxine repeats. "It's a lot to take in. You're probably tired. Had a long week?"

"Yes," I say, resigned. I hear her two-year-old daughter screeching in the background.

"Do you want to come over?" she asks. "I'd come to you, but Jon's out for the night, and it's just me and the baby."

"Thanks, but I think I'm just gonna stay home."

"Why not get out? At least pop over to Fairway and pick up something nice to eat. Soup? Tea? Ice cream? Might make you feel better," she says. "Fairway's such an awesome market."

Maxine knows I never have food at home. For her, an empty fridge is equivalent to an empty life.

"Thanks, Maxine. Thanks for being there," I say, hanging up. Food is not going to make this news easier to swallow.

Maybe I'll call my brothers after all. I could just hint at the news to come without revealing all. Warn them. It's my sisterly duty. Right? I really shouldn't call. I'll spill it all.

I'm pacing in my apartment in circles. Perhaps Maxine is right. Something to eat to calm my nerves. I open the refrigerator. It's condiment central. Ketchup, mayo, peanut butter. I also have five beer bottles and some frozen chicken soup a friend made six months ago. Lovely. I am a living bachelorette caricature. How embarrassing.

Maybe this is a sign. Time for me to start acting like a responsible adult. A grown woman. Maybe Maxine's onto something with that whole retro-housewife thing. A trip to the grocery store might be a good idea. What if filling my fridge helps fill my life with substance, meaning, and love? Who knows? I bet feng shui experts would support the full-fridge theory. Anyway, I'm not in any position to pass up an opportunity for happiness. And who knows? A trip to the store might help me appreciate and celebrate Mom's big news. I'm jealous, pathetic, and lonely. I'm not proud.

Jeans, a fleece, and boots outfit me for the trip to the neighborhood grocery store, Fairway.

"I'm walking to Fairway at ten o'clock on a Friday night," I grumble to myself as I shuffle to the store through the brisk autumn wind. Now I'm one of those people talking out loud to myself. I hate shopping, especially for food, just like my mom. Shopping is the anti–me date. It's irritating. It's stressful.

And Fairway is anything but a fairway. It's like a crowded war zone. I'm wearing urban combat boots, because, among other things, exposed toes are entirely too vulnerable there. People run over feet with carts and don't even turn to see the casualties. Wise shoppers cover as many body parts as possible: the freezer section is biting cold, and the hot food section can feel like a sauna. Most importantly, a savvy shopper brings her thick skin and razor-sharp elbows to navigate through the hordes of people packed into the store's twisting aisles. Fairway reminds me of the New York Stock Exchange—just more hazardous. Fairway shoppers stop at nothing to get to their Japanese eggplants or end-of-summer heirloom tomatoes. And mercy be with you if you dare get in the way. Fairway is a food Mecca for New Yorkers. People make pilgrimages to get there. And as Sinatra said of New York, I say of Fairway. "If you can make it there, you can make it anywhere."

I take a deep breath, reach for a basket, and psych myself up to enter the store. I advance, basket shield first. Forward march! I bump and swerve through the people in produce, toss a box of tea into my basket, dart past the olive bins, scoop up a tranche of Camembert cheese, swipe a container of matzo ball soup off the shelf, graze the corner of the frozen fish counter at top speed, and arrive in my comfort food zone. The ice cream freezer. I stand before the freezer as if before a shrine, basking in its fluorescent glow. I'm deep in thought, debating: a pint of Ben & Jerry's Mint Chocolate Cookie or Chocolate Fudge Brownie? Ice cream or low-fat yogurt? People are opening and slamming shut the freezer doors. Finally, I make up my mind. Mint Chocolate Cookie ice cream. I lunge for the freezer, swing open the door, and just as I'm snatching my pint, a deep voice booms, "Hey-hey!"

I freeze. Should I drop the ice cream and hold up my hands? Did I break a Fairway rule of etiquette? I whip around, holding the ice cream evidence above my head.

It's Leif, smiling at me. I lower my ice cream.

Leif.

Leif is the priceless, unpredictable bonus in coming to Fairway. He's the store manager. He's usually using his heavy voice to direct shopping cart traffic and corral customers in lines for the cashiers. He's tall and broad-shouldered, easy on the eyes. He has this way of constantly flipping his long, dirty-blond hair back, out of his eyes—that is just so sexy.

"What brings someone like you to the emergency aisle on a Friday night?" Leif starts to flirt immediately. It goes this way every time I run into him.

"Oh. Long story. How're you?" I try to deflect. "How's business? What brings you to this part of the store?"

"Thieving old ladies." He takes my bait, flips his hair back.

"What?" I ask.

"Thieving old ladies," he repeats. "They tend to come over here to the frozen foods area and try to steal fish. They always go for these frozen jumbo shrimp." He takes a pack and lightly tosses it in the air. "It costs $21.99, and since it's pretty small, they have a nasty habit of shoving it in their pockets or purses. We lose more money on these little crustaceans than on anything else in the store."

I look at Leif incredulously.

"No, really," he insists. "So, I'm just hangin' out here for a bit. Deterrence. You know?"

Leif's strong build and booming voice may be a deterrent to those ladies, but more likely, he's a magnet.

"They just go for the shrimp?" I ask. "Any other stealing specialties?"

"Ahhh, they love this corner. They feel like no one can see them behind the freezer shelves. This one lady, she once stuffed a full fish down her blouse."

"No way!"

"Yeah, better believe it. This well-dressed middle-aged woman got this floppy full salmon, and slid it right down the front of her silk blouse, a flower print." Leif smiles as he reminisces.

"We stopped her on the way out. She said she forgot to pay for it."

"Wow. How slick. "

Leif cracks a smile.

And I thought I couldn't be surprised by much anymore.

The story fits right in with the bizarro night I'm having.

"Hey, so you didn't answer my question," Leif prods. "What's a saucy cat like you doing here on a night like this?"

"Just buying some ice cream, uh, and some other stuff. You know, food for the house."

"Uh-huh," he says. He's not buying my story.

"Well, truth is . . ." I put down my basket, and push down the sleeves on my fleece. I'm freezing. "I just found out some big family news."

He doesn't say anything, just nods. His gray eyes look concerned.

"There's going to be a wedding in the family," I say gravely.

"Why so blue?" he asks, flips his hair from his forehead. "The way you looked, I thought someone died."

"Oh! Me? Blue? No way. Just kind of taking it all in. Ya know, processing. It's just kind of different."

"Different?" he asks.

"Well, it's my mom. She's the one getting married. And she's known him less than a year. I'm happy for her. And I'm not really all that surprised. It's just that it seems kind of abrupt. My dad died a few years back, but it seems like yesterday. Ya know? I mean, the new guy is nice enough. And he's good to her. But she's still pretty fragile. And I hope he's not taking advantage of her vulnerable state. And I'm just sort of freaked out. I hadn't counted on having a stepfather. Am I like, part of some modern-day Brady Bunch?" I lean my back against a freezer, exhausted by the ideas running trenches through my head.

"Hmm. So, your mom's getting married." Leif smiles. "That's not so bizarre. My dad's remarried. Why are you so bugged out? How's your love life?"

Ouch. I am so transparent. I roll over and lean my forehead against the freezer. Then I push myself away from the freezer and turn and face him. Every time I see Leif, he asks me about my love life, but this time, the question seems particularly raw.

"My love life? Good. Fine. Okay. Same ol' same ol'," I stumble over my words. "You know Ruben. The weather guy on Channel 5? We're still seeing each other," I say, slightly bored.

"That good, eh?" Leif asks.

"Yes," I answer defensively. "We have a lot of fun together. The parties, the friends, TV work in common."

I'm unconvincing; I know it.

"What about you? Still with that lovely doctor? Shelly?"

"Sure am," he answers. "She wants to get married." He runs his hand through his hair and sighs. "We've been together like six years. But I can't really see the hurry." He straightens up a pile of fish sauces.

I look at Leif. He's at least thirty-five. Tall. Rugged. Handsome. Parties like a rock star. Smart enough to do anything, not motivated to do more than this.

He looks up at me. "Hey. D'ya think we'd hang out more if you weren't with that weather guy, and I weren't with Shelly?"

"Sure," I answer, surprising myself. "But neither of us should be thinking that way."

"Yeah, I know, but . . . I'll just lay it out there for you. I've always thought you were hot. And, I just wanted to tell you. Someone gave me a compliment this morning, and it made me feel good all day. So why shouldn't I give you a compliment? You look like you could use one."

"Uh. Thank you?" How does one respond to flattery born of pity?

"Yeah. Well, congrats," Leif says. "Let me know if you need help with the wedding catering. I know my layer cakes."

"Thanks," I answer. "I should go."

"Yeah. Oh, hey," he says. "Take it easy, there. Remember, it's a wedding, not a funeral."

"Right." I pause, get my bearings, then turn to leave. I head toward the checkout counter with my head down. I can't process all these experiences at once. At the cashier, I realize I've left my basket of tea, cheese, and soup over by the freezers. I have nothing I came for. Go back? No way. I don't want to face him again. I'll just go home empty-handed.

"Hey!" Leif booms from behind. I spin around. "Your stuff." He's moving toward me at a rapid clip. He hands me the basket. Mint-choc-cookie ice cream, too. "You missed out on our olive oil special."

"Thanks," I say, blushing with embarrassment.

"See you around," he says. "Gotta run, marinara sauce spill, aisle two." He smiles, winks, and turns away.

Outside, away from the fluorescent glare of the store, I replay the events of the evening in my mind. I'm carrying a bag of random food. My mom's getting married. My brothers don't know. My pseudo-boyfriend doesn't know. And I just spilled my guts to the sexy protector of frozen fish at Fairway.

Three

Last night I dreamt that Leif and I were getting married. I wore a flowing, white gown and cradled a limp, stinky fish in my arms as I walked down the aisle. The guests were clutching cans of asparagus and yams. He wore a dirty apron. That's it. Lovely.

So far, my awake time this Saturday morning is not much of an improvement over that confusing fish dream. The morning is dragging on like eternity. I orbit around my apartment, alternately cleaning up, flipping through the paper, and playing music off the Internet. Unable to concentrate. I'm waiting to call my brothers, who both live in Berkeley, California. I promised Mom I'd wait till at least 10 A.M. West Coast time before calling. Presumably, it would give us "kids" a chance to sleep on the news before launching into a sibling powwow. I already tried calling Ruben for consolation, but I got his voice mail. And, no way am I calling Maxine again. I'll pass on the fast-food fixes.

I should relax. My brothers and I, we're a team. We're going to glide right through this family drama. We've dealt with much, much worse. We made it through Dad's death together. Anything else will be easy by comparison. The clock creeps forward until finally, I'm clear to call. First, I try my younger brother, Max, at home. He doesn't answer. I try his cell.

The cell rings and rings. There's static. Finally, he picks up.

"Hey, brotha!" I try to act cool, like one of his twenty-two-year-old peers might.

"Yo, Sista-Sista!" Max catches his breath. "I'm in the bay right now. Windsurfing. Good thing you caught me. I'm taking a break. This wind is epic!"

His youthfulness breezes through the phone. He's the baby in the family, and my older brother, my mom, and I encourage his adventurousness. We're inspired by it. We feed off his energy, his high risk tolerance, his sense of humor. Max taught English in Costa Rica for a summer. He's spent a large part of his college career helping build a solar car. He's a windsurfing addict. We help him stave off the burdens of adulthood. He was fourteen years old when Dad died.

"This wind is ep-ic!" Max repeats. He sounds ecstatic. Guess he isn't too worked up over Mom's wedding. I know he windsurfs in the San Francisco Bay a lot, but I've never actually caught him on the phone while he's on the water.

"How are you answering your cell phone?" I ask.

"Oh, just keep it in a waterproof pouch in my wet suit. No biggie. What's the story, Sista?" Max prods. He's obviously not interested in discussing the intricacies of how he, like any ordinary Silicon Valley technophile, meshes technology and recreation seamlessly.

"Mom," I say.

"Oh, yeah. That," he says in an offhanded tone. "Whatever."

He sounds aloof, as if it just rolls like water off his wet suit. Like he isn't bothered at all. Have we coddled him so much that he doesn't know when to get worked up?

"Well, don't you want to talk about it? I mean, do you even know him? Do you like him?" I ask.

I hear the scratching sound of wind crashing and blowing into his phone, then, ". . . ins ok . . . we . . . ve pow . . . er?"

"What?" I ask.

"Stanley's okay. Can we have this powwow later?" he manages to get through.

"Yeah. Fine. Sure." I'm not hiding my disappointment. "Later? Why not? This is just going to change our lives forever."

Nothing.

"Max? Max?"

The phone line's dead.

"Can we have this powwow later?" What kind of a question is that? He treated the call like I was trying to coordinate vacation dates with him or perform some other mundane familial task. What nerve! I'd be more angry, but he's so young. He's probably just trying to cloak his ambivalence in a veil of what he considers to be mature indifference. Or maybe he really is that laid back. I'll let it go. This time. And who knows? Maybe he's onto something. Maybe I should learn from him. Maybe I should try his nonchalant approach.

Right.

I call my older brother, Enrico, at home. He's responsible, mellow, mature. The firstborn. He had the tenacity to slog through and finish his Ph.D. in physics. He now works as a scientist at a biotech company—a brainy job with benefits. After Dad died, he managed our family's finances, meticulously researching every decision we needed to make, usually advising the most low-risk, conservative option. Enrico will understand the gravity of Mom's decision to remarry. He'll be as worried about all this as I am. I speed dial his home number.

"Hello?" a woman answers.

"Oh, sorry, I must have the wrong number," I say.

"Daniella?"

"Yes."

"It's Leslie."

Leslie? Oh Leslie. Leslie. Enrico's girlfriend. They've been dating a few months and already she's answering his home phone?

"Hi. Sorry to bother. I was just looking for Enrico."

"He's out food shopping," Leslie says. "Everything okay?"

"Fine. Everything's fine. Just need to talk to him about some family stuff."

"Oh, yeah! Congratulations on your mom! That is so, so great!" she says.

"Thanks," I say halfheartedly. Just what I need. "So, so great!" The word of Mom's wedding is spreading quickly, and we kids haven't had a chance to weigh in on whether we approve (as if it would make any difference).

"You know, Daniella, my parents split when I was much younger. It was really hard at first. My dad got remarried, his wife brought her family into the mix . . . it was tricky . . . but hey, I'm still here to tell the tale. In the end, it was good for my dad."

"Thanks."

"No problem."

"I'm just going to try Enrico's cell now."

"Hey, Sister," Enrico chirps. "Nice to hear from you at this early hour. I'm at the Berkeley Bowl—you know—the organic market? Beautiful Chilean grapes. Mmm. Firm Japanese eggplants. Anything urgent?"

What's with this cross-continental obsession with eggplants? First at Fairway and now at Berkeley Bowl?

"No. Nothing urgent. Just the Mom news." I'm sarcastic.

"Yeah, well, it's what she wants." He sounds nonplussed. "Listen, can I call you later? I'm just trying to get though the store before the crowds come."

Is he for real? What is wrong with my brothers? They choose fruits over feelings? It's only our mother's future, and we're going to have to live with it.

"Okay. Sure. Fine," I say. "Call me in an hour and get Max on the phone, too?"

"Yeah, sure," he sounds distracted. "Three-way conference call in a couple of hours . . . Hey! Excuse me! That was my eggplant!" he barks at another shopper. "Daniella, gotta go."

I cannot believe my brothers. They're so absorbed in the minutiae of their own lives they can't even recognize the massive, long-term implications of our mother's decision. I thought we'd rally together and tackle this news. Digest it as a team. No such luck. Maybe I'm just overreacting. Wouldn't be the first time.

I'll have to work this out on foot. I'll pound pavement until my brothers are done with their top-priority windsurfing and eggplant squeezing. I put on another one of my dad's old T-shirts, pull on a pair of black running tights, and lace up my running shoes tight for a jog in Central Park.

The park is chilly, sunny, inviting. I head straight for the reservoir, an oasis of calm in this frantic city. It's elevated and therefore has the most spectacular, unobstructed view of the Manhattan skyline. It's known as the Jackie Onassis Reservoir, but I think of it as my personal pond. Here, no advertisements or city sounds disturb me. I only hear birds, wind, and the soothing, repetitive, crunch, crunch, crunch of the track beneath my shoes.

My dad was the one who got me into running. He taught me to use the rhythm of my jogging stride as a foundation for clear thinking. His strides were always much longer than mine, considering he was six feet tall and I peaked at five five. When I was a teenager, we used to go on early morning jogs around Town Lake in Austin, Texas, together. It was during those father-daughter runs that I learned most about his outlook on life. I remember one loop around the lake in particular. We were jogging, sweating, and pushing ourselves further than normal under the scorching Texas sun. We finally stopped, earlier than planned, breathless. He bent over, hands on knees, sweat beads dripping from his nose and brow onto the dirt path below. His graying head of hair wet with humidity.

"Less is more, more or less," he panted and looked up at me with his green eyes and smiled.

As we walked back to the car he explained that "less" in terms of material things can often lead to a simpler, more meaningful existence. I know that our shorter or "lesser" run that day meant more, because it gave me time to learn one of his core personal philosophies. Unfortunately, his proverb didn't apply universally. I wish he would have had more time alive, not less.

He had been out jogging in the Berkeley Hills one evening eight years ago when he collapsed. Heart attack. A neighbor saw him fall. That was it. Over. Fifty-eight years old. I remember the sober message Enrico left on my answering machine, telling me nothing other than to call the hospital. The emergency room doctor who answered asked me to sit down. The rest was a full body and mind blow.

At first, I couldn't accept it. I rushed back to be with my family in Berkeley. There, my mind played tricks on me. I kept thinking I saw my dad's lanky figure and full head of white hair walking down the street. Or I thought I heard his soft but firm voice in our house. I kept wishing I were in the worst kind of nightmare and would eventually wake up. How could we carry on without him? Who else could provide us with the unconditional cheerleading he gave us? What would we do without our even-tempered anchor?

Even the most ordinary moments were unbearably sad. Cooking, walking, brushing my teeth. Nothing seemed the same. We missed his calming presence. We missed his soothing voice. We missed his dry, quiet sense of humor. Without him, who would tell us everything would be okay? With each passing day, the reality became more apparent, and our smaller family pressed on with the gaping void. Eventually, our innocence defeated, I went back to work, and my brothers, back to school. But my mom was inconsolable. Despondent.

Each day was a struggle for her, especially that first year. Some mornings were easier than others. She'd get up, get ready, and go out to meet life's demands. Other days, it was more than she could muster. She stayed home and sobbed. For me and my brothers, it was a constant responsibility trying to encourage her, entertain her, and distract her enough so that she could carry on. It was disorienting and unsettling to see Mom as a mere shell of the tough, proud, vivacious woman who raised us.

About seven years after our father died, including six years of torturous dating for Mom, Stanley exploded onto the scene with his booming voice and loud, full-bodied laughter. Immediately, she was gushing about Stanley. She was enthralled with the stories that this brash, boisterous, Brooklyn know-it-all told. She was enchanted with his intelligence and appreciation for living large. He kept her laughing and smiling in a way we hadn't seen in years. He revived her.

With Stanley, she began to focus less on loss and more on possibilities. And they understood each other. He, too, was a widower. At first, we were skeptical of Mom's sudden emotional shift, but we welcomed the change anyway, even if it was only a distraction.

As I come to the end of my usual forty-minute circuit, I slow down, leaving the pond and the crunch, crunch, crunch therapy behind. I wonder what Dad would say about Mom marrying Stanley. Stanley is a good guy, but no one can replace Dad. And I really do think Mom could cut me some slack. I've already lost one parent. Do I need to lose her, too? Without my mom at the helm, what will happen to our tight-knit family of four?

On a park bench just outside Strawberry Fields, I sit and clutch my cell phone, waiting for the sibling conference call to start. The Beatles sang the song "Strawberry Fields," and Yoko Ono dedicated this parkland as a memorial to John Lennon. How tragically romantic. A pair of Beatles fans walks into the Strawberry Fields grove, hand in hand, gazing around as if in a slow-motion movie of aliens visiting earth for the first time. Another couple walks briskly by, but both have their arms folded, an angry silence cutting the air between them.

Beep.

It's Ruben. Good to hear from him, bad timing.

"Hi, Ruben. How's the weather conference going?"

"Hi, babe," he answers in the deep, sexy voice that has a reputation for sending housewives watching him on morning TV news into a tizzy.

"The conference is good." He sounds tired. "I sat up on the stage for dinner—the dais—because they gave me that forecasting award. I'm now the brand-new owner of a gold-plated sunshine medallion on a ribbon. Where are you, Mo-Hon?"

"In the park—" I start.

Beep.

Green LCD screen reads, "Enrico."

"Ruben, hey listen, I'm sorry, my brothers are on the other line. Big family news," I say. "Can I call you back?"

Beep.

"Okay, Miss Cliffhanger." He's disappointed. "Nice talking to you."

Beep.

"Great, sorry, thanks," I tell him, and press the button to switch over to my brothers.

"Hello?" I answer.

"What took you so long to pick up the phone?" Enrico teases. It's a tricky question. I haven't told anyone in my family that Ruben exists, despite the fact that we've been seeing each other for four months. I really haven't wanted to explain Ruben to anyone yet. More on that later.

"What took you so long to call me back?" I taunt in return. "Two hours later we're discussing the late-breaking Mom news? Men, we might have missed our deadline."

"Oh, it's never too late to tell her what to do," Enrico says confidently. My brothers are together, on speakerphone, calling from Enrico's apartment in Berkeley. I can hear pots clanging as Enrico messes around in his kitchen.

"So what's on your mind, Sista?" Max asks in a mock-serious voice. I hear a refreshing levity in his tone. Helps me relax a bit. *Get a grip, Daniella*, I say to myself. *Remember what Leif said at the grocery store? "It's a wedding, not a funeral."*

"Well, so, whaddaya think about Stanley and Mom getting hitched?" I ask.

"Bummer," Max answers in a wry tone. "It means we won't have fresh material for the Mock Mom's Dates show."

I smile. This, I hadn't considered.

Over the past few years, Max perfected the art of impersonating the men Mom dated. Unfortunately for Mom, fortunately for the show, the men Mom dated were colorful and plentiful. With each new man, Max created new, miniskit spoofs loosely based, and I mean loosely, on that sixties game show, *The Dating Game*. Max's caricatures inevitably sent us into convulsions of laughter. We got so into it that we'd encourage Mom to go out on hopeless dates just so we could have new material. It was vicious, but it was fun. It was our way of coping with, or denying that, she was moving on.

Max immediately beats his chest in a drum roll, then hums the theme song from *The Dating Game* and, in his cheesiest, deepest announcer voice announces, "Heeeeeere they AAAAAAAAre. Behind the curtain, Contestant Number One: Missssssssssster Garden Supply!"

I can hear Enrico sighing a smile.

"Wait!" I stop the show. "I want front row seats for the grand finale. Please? I'll be in California in a few days. Can the show go on then?"

"Aw, man!" Max says, disappointed. "I was just getting going."

"Please?"

"Ohhh-kaaay," Max concedes.

"Thank you, Max, you're a good performer and a good brother. But men, come on. Can we talk seriously about this for a minute?"

"Sure," the guys answer.

"Are we okay with them getting married? I mean, do they even know each other well enough?"

"Yeah," Max says.

"It's okay," Enrico answers, maintaining an air of indifference.

"Yeah? Okay? Is that it? Aren't you worried that Mom might be feeling vulnerable? That she's making a rash decision? Don't you think it's a little soon? Does she even know what she's getting into? Does he?"

"Hey, Daniella . . . just one question for you . . . do you think she's better off with Stanley in the picture?" Enrico asks.

"Yes," I concede.

"Do you think we're better off with him in the picture?" Max asks.

"Yes," Enrico responds.

"Do you think he can handle our precious live wire?" I ask.

"Yes," Enrico and Max respond.

"Then he's fine for the job," Max says. "And anyway, what can we do to stop it?"

Four

"It's the grand finale of the Mock Mom's Dates show, take two." Max shoots me a blaming stare for delaying the show, then smiles. I've just flown in to California after a hectic week in New York. My brothers and I are in the living room at Mom's house in Berkeley, reverting to our juvenile tendencies of poking and joking, as we wait for Mom's return. Mom's living room, complete with her Kilim rugs, Israeli collages, and plants and books, is familiar. It's good to be home.

Max, my younger brother, clears his throat dramatically.

"The grand finale of the Mock Mom's Dates show," he repeats in the announcer's voice.

Enrico and I, the sibling audience, sit at attention on the couch. Max stands in the center of the room beating his chest in a drum roll. He hums the theme song from *The Dating Game.*

In his practiced announcer voice he says, "Heeeeeere they AAAAAAAAre. Behind the curtain, Contestant Number One: Missssssssssster Garden Supply!"

"Mr. Garden Supply: tan, toned and forty-something, will walk right into your yard and tell you about plant survival and communication. He'll suggest in a deep Elvis-like voice, that 'You baby, could use some tender loving care, too.'"

"Too bad Mr. Garden Supply wasn't the sharpest tool in the shed." Enrico breaks into the performance. "Mom never should've left the garden with him. Remember? They went to dinner, and his limited vocabulary and limitless grammatical mistakes turned our literature professor mother off."

"But give Mom some credit. She did try," Max says. "Too bad it was such a fabulous failure. Giving him a French and English copy of *Madame Bovary* to spice up the conversation was not quite the right move on her part."

"Take your book and shovel it," G. Gardèn had said, insulted.

"At least he got the last word," Enrico smirks. Max and I sigh with pleasure.

Max does another drum roll and chest beating and switches back into the announcer's voice, "Heeeeeeeeereeeeeee we arrrrrrrrre. Contestant Number Two! Missssssssster Millionaire! Mr. Millionaire will strut right into your house as if he's doing everyone a favor by showing up. He'll talk and talk about his private jet and mega yacht. He's got a shiny red nose and a hides-nothing comb-over."

"And one nasty case of halitosis. Just call me Hal," Enrico adds.

"Oh, Hal!" I hold my nose dramatically.

"Each time Mom backed away from him, Hal Millionaire stepped closer and spoke louder. 'My plane, my boat, my car, my money . . .' he insisted, his pungent breath contaminating each crevice in the room. Mom couldn't get away soon enough."

"Eeeeeewwww!" I cringe.

"Mom wasn't impressed with all the money talk," Enrico says. "But remember Pompous Ass? Do Pompous Ass. Mom *was* impressed with him."

"Sure," Max says, chomping at the bit to tell one of his favorites.

"Heeeeeeeeerrrreeeeeeeee heeee isssssssss," says Max the announcer. "Contestant numero tres. Pompous Ass. He'll bring an autographed copy of his own book as a gift on the first date. He'll tell you how the *New York Times* calls him 'all the time' for quotes.

"How old are you?" Max impersonates Mom. She didn't want another man to croak on her.

"Aha! Wouldn't you like to know?" Pompous Ass had responded. "First, my dear, let's get to know each other better."

I wince at what comes next.

Enrico, animated, jumps off the couch. "One dinner with Pompous Ass, great. Two dinners, fascinating. The third dinner? Disaster."

I'm giddy with anticipation.

Max the narrator swoops in for the punch line. "He picks her up for dinner, regaling her with fascinating stories. Then as they approach the restaurant, he turns around to go home. Apologizes. He had forgotten his dentures."

If he was old enough to need dentures *and* forget them, he wasn't right for Mom.

Oh, Mom. She endured a lot in her search for a new companion. Sometimes I thought she was on the brink of giving up, but she didn't.

"Remember the good ol' days when she first started dating?" Max asks. "In the beginning, she'd only agree to lunches that her friends arranged. Then, as she got more confident, she met men on campus and at lectures. As a last resort, she took the plunge into online dating. I still can't believe she did that! She ended up placing and answering ads on the *Jewish Bulletin* Web site as if it was the most ordinary thing in the world."

"What did she expect? Prince Yehudah Charming?" I quip while wondering if she might have been on to something.

My brothers and I nostalgically remember the online ads she told us about. One man wrote, "Hunchback with lazy eye seeks nurse to change drool cup." Another man wrote, "Scientist seeks woman to share chemistry, maybe even physics."

Despite her best efforts, no one was a good fit. And, as much as we laughed, it was hard to watch Mom struggle. The expectations and disappointments were exhausting for her. She used to get dressed up and go to the singles folk dancing events, Jewish Museum art openings, public radio fund-raisers, only to come home disillusioned.

"I must admit, I was a bit jealous," Max says. He's sitting Indian style on the floor by now. "Mom had a more active social life than I did. I remember racing home to beat curfew, only to find that Mom was still out on a date. On those nights, I had a whole routine. Brush teeth. Lock bedroom door. Turn on music. I didn't want to hear anything if Mom invited the date inside for tea."

"Ewww!" I wince in my girliest voice.

Just when we thought the curtain had been called on the Mock Mom's Dates show, Max pops up and launches into the final act, the act that will stay with us. The final contestant. One Stanley Weinberg.

Max the announcer, "Heeeeeeeeeeerrrrrrrrrrre heeeeee issssss folks. The final contestant. Mr. E-Romeo, master of cyber mush."

"Can I just send him an e-mail?" Enrico impersonates Mom.

"No." Max glares at Enrico and his interruption. "Our E–Romeo was fine in the virtual world," Max returns to the narrator's tone. "But take the *E* out of E-Romeo, and Romeo disappears, too. The final contestant, also known as Staaaanleeee, makes a deafeningly loud first impression. He's been known to laugh and talk with such sheer volume that the air pressure in rooms seems to pump up till it almost bursts."

"I remember the first night we met him." Enrico smiles. "It wasn't just the air that seemed pressured. His pants were so tight, it looked like he was going to burst!"

A round of snickers and cackles. Enrico and Max had been here on the same couch in this living room when Stanley first appeared. I was in New York. Max sized Stanley up quickly and immediately saw wonderful cartoonish Mock-show material. It was funny, but I also remember my brothers telling me that despite the noise and tight pants, Stanley made a good first impression. Stanley immediately read the Hebrew writing on one of Mom's Israeli collages. He made eye contact with Max and asked him about school. He knew Enrico's colleagues. He offered to make Mom dinner. He was ready to care for her personally, rather than relying on money or status.

Enrico's face turns semiserious. "Do you think Mom and Stanley know each other well enough?" Enrico asks. "Maybe she's flinging herself at him because she's vulnerable."

Now my brothers want to have a serious conversation?

"Mom, vulnerable? Come on!" Max says. "She was the one breaking curfews and sending men away with their tail between their legs."

"Do you think they're rushing it?" Enrico tries again.

"Rushing it? If they wait any longer they'll be in a nursing home," Max jeers. We bond in our laughter and shared responsibility for her. I wipe the tears from my eyes.

Then the front door swings open, and Mom bursts into the room—a tornado of energy, enthusiasm, and gushing hugs and kisses. Her eyes are shining, and her hair is frizzy with energy. She's put together neatly and totally charged up.

"How was your flight? Thank you so much for coming! What's so funny? Kids, get your feet off the couch! Why'd you park that way in front? Dress shopping is going to be great!"

My brothers and I look at each other. She is beyond our control. The Mock Mom's Dates show may be ending, but we can always count on Mom to provide us with material for a new show.

Five

The next morning, I'm sitting in an ornate throne-chair in a small bridal boutique in Oakland. A dressmaker's shop must have looked like this at the turn of the century. The walls are covered in faint, textured, gold-colored wallpaper. Measuring tapes, lace, and elaborate handmade wedding dresses hang from brass hooks on the walls. An assortment of white sequins, beads, and threads are scattered about on the washed-out rose-colored carpet.

It's Mom's second appointment here, and she was so excited to show me "this one dress," she practically skipped in the front door. The boutique is empty except for the designer-owner, who must be thinking, *Now here's a mother-daughter role reversal I don't see too often.*

Mom pushes open the swinging, fitting room doors, and steps out with an enormous smile. Her big brown eyes are wider than usual, and her short light brown hair, which is usually perfectly coiffed, is a bit tousled. She's wearing a strapless, cream-colored, silk-satin gown with a full, sweeping skirt. It's a strange sight, really. She doesn't look like a bride. She looks like Mom dressed like a bride. I'm disoriented. I've only seen her once in a formal dress, and that was thanks to a freak invitation to a debutante ball in Texas. She usually wears classic, neutral-colored business suits or gardening clothes.

Now she stands before the mirror looking at herself in this princess dress. The bodice, which hugs her trim torso neatly, is impeccably embroidered with a white gold–colored delicate vine of intertwining leaves and flowers. A column of tiny buttons traces her spine from her lower back down the chapel-length train. A matching vine of embroidered leaves and flowers gracefully follows the hem of her dress.

Designer-owner and I both admire the work of art that is my mother in this dress.

"How much is it?" I whisper to Mom when designer-owner glances away for a moment.

"Too much." Her grin turns to a frown.

Mom turns back to the mirror, fidgets with the back buttons, smooths down the skirt. She makes a few comments about how beautiful the gown is, why it doesn't look right, and how she'll have to think about it. Then she disappears back into the dressing room, designer-owner following to help her off with the dress.

I scan the bridal salon again. Now I'm really curious about the price. How much could it be? These dresses are all unique and handmade. Besides the couture dresses at fashion shows in New York, these are easily the most beautifully crafted dresses I've ever seen. I sneak over to an Alençon-lace gown with Shakespearean full sleeves. I look over my shoulder to make sure I'm not being watched and plunge my hand into the deep neckline to pull out the price tag. Two thousand two hundred twenty dollars! Wow, these wonders aren't cheap. Next to the lace dress is a satin fishtail dress with a scalloped neckline and trim. Four thousand three hundred seventy-five dollars! No way! How about this silk organza ball gown with bell sleeves? A bargain at $5,750. How could Mom even consider this? One dress. One day. More than five grand? Outrageous.

The Mom I know used to parrot my father's expression: "Less is more, more or less," when talking about price in clothing. She repeated this mantra often, especially when I was a teenager demanding designer jeans. Now she's considering a wildly expensive dress, and she's only working part-time? I thought my mom was a great saver, not spender. It's enough that she's having a big wedding, but spending like this would fly in the face of twenty-nine years of implicit lessons about the value of money. I thought she said women should spend money on things that help us develop ourselves, not objectify ourselves. Cultural events, educational experiences, and little indulgences were on the list of valuable expenses. Overpriced wedding dresses were not.

And anyway, shouldn't she be more frugal in her quasi-retirement? Doesn't she need to plan ahead? She's acting as if she were a teenager, reckless with someone else's credit card. Do I need to rein in my mother? We leave the store. I say encouraging nothings, and say nothing about price.

"There's a beautiful silk in the fabric store around the corner," she explains. "It'd make a great dress. We could sew it."

Now she's sounding more familiar. This is the creative, resourceful, do-it-yourself mother I know. The one who helped me make my teal-colored taffeta dress for the prom. Ever the teacher, she thought making a dress would be a good learning experience for me. Come to think of it, I shed a lot of tears making that dress. Screwing up. Cutting the fabric the wrong way. Fighting with Mom. Struggling with a temperamental sewing machine. Swearing I would never make a dress again. Suddenly, the prospect of sewing a wedding dress with Mom makes buying one of the gowns we just saw appear much more reasonable.

"Oh, Mom. Just buy a dress, let a tailor make alterations," I say. "It's your wedding. Who wants the hassle?"

On the car ride across the Bay Bridge to San Francisco, Mom explains that Stanley and his daughter Erica are both away at physics conferences this weekend. How cute. Stanley in Los Angeles, Erica in Chicago. It's too bad they're away, but I must admit, I'm relieved. Dress shopping is proving demanding enough without facing the uber-brainy stepfather-to-be and his uber-brainy daughter.

An hour later, Mom and I are still in the car, arguing about where to park on Union Street in San Francisco. Honks and loops later, we squeeze into a spot. Motor off, meter paid, nerves frayed, we agree to eat. Mom is jumpy, and food may prevent us both from getting cranky. We sit down outside at a sidewalk café. We order soup and salad.

I look up. Sky? Blue. Sun? Shining. Temperature? Perfect California seventies. Maybe this "emergency" trip to California wasn't such a bad idea after all. The weather is already getting nippy in New York. That I can wear my sunglasses at all is reason enough to celebrate. I might even enjoy this dress process.

"So. Meet anyone interesting lately?" Mom asks. Bye-bye pleasant dress shopping. Of course I've met a lot of interesting people, that's my job. But have I met *the anyone* she's always asking about? No. Not yet. I haven't told her about Ruben, either, because I don't know how much of a someone he is to me yet. I'm sure she sees this dress excursion as prime "get to know your daughter time." But I prefer privacy. I know mothers and daughters are expected to be best friends, but that's just unrealistic for us.

"Nope, no one interesting," I deflect. Unless I bring up another subject immediately, she's going to hammer me with questions about my love life. So, I take a risk, even though it makes me squeamish, "You haven't told me about the engagement. How'd it happen?"

"You really want to know?" she asks.

"Sure," I choke on a bit of salad.

"Well"— she's delighted —"I thought you'd never ask. But of course I'll tell you . . . from the beginning."

Great.

"You know how much I was dating," she starts. "It was so discouraging. Gosh, Cookie, it was probably a bit like your dating life."

I hope not.

"Mediocre men, with problems," she continues. "Cookie, you date guys who've just broken up with girlfriends. I met men who were wrapping up a divorce, or a second divorce, or recovering from some terrible ailment. One guy talked nonstop about his men's emotional support group and his four weekly appointments with his shrink. It was so depressing." She picks at her salad. "But at least it was comforting to know that everyone's a little broken."

I drink some iced tea. I remember these men. The ones who, at age sixty, had never married, and the reasons were painfully obvious. Among them, a good-looking, gentle doctor who kept inviting Mom to dinner. He was full of good conversation, but his flailing wrists and effeminate manner were "a bit distracting," she had reported. It wasn't until the third dinner that Mom realized she'd been going out on dates with a gay man, or "gates."

"My friends warned me, 'for my own good,' that the odds

were against my getting remarried," she recalls. "They said I should keep my expectations low."

In her dark spells, she resigned herself to the prospect of living life out as a widow. But more often than not, she rejected the conventional wisdom and the lonely life it promised. Instead, she kept dreaming and searching for another fit.

"The first time I met Stanley, Stanley was with his wife, Miriam," Mom tells.

They were? She met the wife? Has she no shame?

"Now, don't think I was eyeing him, because I wasn't." Mom looks at me seriously. "They were at Bob and Dinah's house for a Hanukkah party. Miriam seemed to be enjoying herself, but she was already sick. Cancer. You could just see the chemo tearing her apart. Stanley told jokes to try and lighten the situation, but Miriam's frailty was palpable. I saw Stanley as part of a couple so strong that they would surely overcome this.

"A year later, I saw Stanley again at Bob and Dinah's house. Bob's sixtieth birthday party. This time, Stanley came with his daughter, Erica. Miriam had succumbed to the brain tumor over the course of what had been an agonizing year. Stanley was still grieving deeply, but Erica had encouraged him to get out of the house and visit with friends. Dinah reintroduced me to Stanley, but he was still too raw to register my presence. I thought I could comfort him as a fellow widow. But when I tried to talk to him, he seemed to turn away. I was still reeling from Dad's death and I felt totally dejected. Then, I found myself in a long conversation with Stanley's daughter Erica, who said, 'No one will ever replace my mother.'"

Erica, I hear you.

"By the time I saw him at another Bob and Dinah party a year later," Mom continued, "I wouldn't even talk to him. We were all in a synagogue reception room for a Bat Mitzvah party, and I figured if there was no traction or attraction last time, there was no use subjecting myself to rejection again."

Mom looks lost in thought, then smiles.

"But Bob and Dinah had other ideas. Dinah suggested I go talk to Stanley. I resisted. Dinah promised that he was much more open now than he had been the year before. I refused.

But Dinah persisted, dragging me across the reception room to where Stanley was holding court with a group of friends. He was talking about refinancing home mortgages," Mom reminisces. "I was immediately smitten."

Funny, I may work on Wall Street, but I don't think *refinancing* and *smitten* will ever make it in the same sentence in my love story.

"Anyway," Mom continues, "we exchanged a few words, and as the party was breaking up, he asked if I might like a ride to the far parking lot where my car was. [How very California.] Well, considering I was a naive dater and fundamentally a feminist, I declined. Why would I need a ride? Did I not look perfectly capable and healthy?"

Mom laughs. "I totally missed the cue. I stopped his modern-day chivalry dead in its tracks. He then offered to walk me to my car. I accepted."

"He lightly touched the small of my back to guide me out of the building, and immediately, I whipped up a frenzy of possibilities: retirement trips together, a shared home in the South," she recalls. "I felt like I was in grade school. Did he like me? I was covered in goose bumps."

"On the way out to the car he mimicked some story in his best Russian accent that sent me into a giggle fit."

Whatever floats your boat, Mom.

He helped me into the car, closed the door, and said, 'Bye, nice meeting you.' He didn't ask for my number. Nor did he suggest we get together again. Was he just setting me up to reject me again?

"Oh, no he wouldn't," Mom remembers. "I wasn't going to let him turn me away again! I rolled down my window and asked, 'Do you ever come up to Berkeley?'

"He thought about it, and answered truthfully, 'Rarely. Bye!' then turned and walked away.

"The nerve! I was shocked. Why did he just put his hand on my back and walk me to the car if he wasn't interested? Did I say something wrong?

"That night, I called Dinah like a gossipy high school girl. I told Dinah every detail about our encounter and wanted to know if Stanley had said anything about me to her or Bob.

"'Not yet,' Dinah said, 'the party only ended a few hours ago. But Bob and Stanley are having lunch together in a couple of weeks. I can get the scoop then.'

"Two weeks? Too long," Mom said. "I hung up, got online, and tracked down an e-mail address that looked like it belonged to him.

"I immediately fired off a note.

"'*Are you the Stanley Weinberg I met at the Rosen Bat Mitzvah party? I'm still laughing about how well you fake a Russian accent. Would you like to come to Berkeley to hear an anthropology professor lecture on oral histories as sources for the Bible? Maya.'*

"He e-mailed back immediately.

"'*You found me. I am the one, Stanley Weinberg, who can wax in a Russian accent about anything, including home refinancing. Unfortunately, I can not come for the talk, but how about dinner Saturday?'*

"I hit Reply and typed, '*Yes.*'

"I would have gone on a date with him that night, but he was busy," Mom said.

I had no idea my mom could be so aggressive in matters of the heart.

"The night of the first date I wore a form-revealing outfit," Mom tells me with a mischievous sparkle in her eye. "Stanley took the bait, his hands tickled up and down my back . . ."

"Okay, okay I get it." I cut my mother off.

"Oh, sorry," Mom continues. "But honestly, I was so exhilarated after that first date, I had to be scraped off the ceiling. I called him the next morning to thank him and see if he wanted to get together again.

"'Hello?'" he answered.

"'Hi,' I said. 'I was just wondering, would . . . ?'

"'Absolutely!' he answered before I had a chance to finish," Mom says, smiling to herself.

My brothers and I remember when they started dating. A dinner here, a walk there. The occasional e-mail or instant message. But when Mom insisted on switching from dial-up to DSL, we knew this relationship had a level of urgency and intensity that was different from the rest. Almost overnight, Mom, who had been reluctantly computer literate, morphed into an impatient tech enthusiast. More accurately, an e-mail addict.

Soon the clever e-mails and IMs they exchanged turned mushy, and their relationship took a disruptive turn. My brothers told me they'd be out with Mom running errands or having a meal, and she would hurry them to finish so she could get home. She *needed* to check her e-mail. And if, God forbid, her computer was having trouble, our modern-day damsel in distress immediately called Stanley for help. He was happy to make house calls, knocking at the door, announcing, "At your tech and call." Hello corny! Of course my brothers could have solved just about any computer problem and spared him the inconvenient trip to Mom's house, but it was Stanley's help she wanted.

Their relationship soon blossomed beyond the virtual world, and eventually she started to spend nights at his house. Oh, the excuses she'd create to justify her overnight visits.

"I'm just staying over because I don't want to drive back in the dark," she would say. She was bashful, fearing her children would criticize her for less-than-correct behavior. Or worse, imitate her behavior. Soon enough, Mom and Stanley were spending entire weekends together. Max, who was away at college, would occasionally come home on a Friday night wondering where his mom had run off to.

Then Mom and Stanley actually did run off together. To Italy. My father's homeland.

"Mom, tell me about the proposal," I say. "The engagement."

"So, he was going to a physics conference in Italy, and he invited me along. Spring in Italy? *Certamente!* But of course! After the conference in Venice, we went to Tuscany and poked around in tiny hilltop towns. Night after night, we dined in fine, romantic restaurants. In the back of my mind, I kept expecting he might propose, but he didn't.

"Then, the night before we were to return to the States, he still hadn't brought it up. We were in a tiny medieval village near Siena, sharing an intimate dinner. It was a cozy restaurant. A stone dining room with vaulted ceilings. It was on a cliff, but not a dangerous cliff. It was like there was no one else in the world but us," Mom said. "In fact, we were the only ones in the dining room. Everyone else had left long ago. We kept holding hands across the table between bites of food, so the meal was taking forever. Even so, the waiters didn't interrupt. Finally, one waiter just brought us dessert, and I realized time was running out. I looked him straight in the eye and asked, 'When?'

"'When what?' he taunted.

"'When you know what,' I teased back.

"'When are you going to move in with me?' he asked.

"'Before that,' I teased back.

"'What?' he goaded me on.

"I took a sip of champagne and smiled.

"'You know what,' I responded.

"He played along, providing more oblique conversation, but he didn't propose. I began to think he wouldn't ask, never mind offer me a ring to mark the occasion. But it did not matter, I was blinded by love. I figured here we were, two adults, experienced in marriage, wanting to do it again, but too bashful to admit it out loud.

"Finally, I asked, 'Will?'

"He said, 'You?' He pointed at me and shrugged his shoulders in feigned confusion.

"I laughed. 'Marry?'

"'Me?' He pointed at himself and looked around the room as if I might be referring to someone else.

"And we laughed and laughed together. We didn't need to say anything. We just understood each other."

"That's great, Mom."

"And you know what, Cookie? The funniest thing about it? His first wife popped the question on him, too."

I guess the plump, disheveled professor had a way of convincing women to take charge. Or the women just grew impatient with him.

"And no ring? You're still wearing Dad's engagement ring?" I ask Mom.

"Yes," she looks at her hand as she twists the diamond around her finger. "I'm not ready to give this up yet. I may never be."

She stares at the stone, now lost in her own private thoughts. I can tell she's not ready to talk more about that, and neither am I. Maybe later.

"I'm really happy for you," I tell Mom softly. And I really am. If we were in a movie, I'd probably hug her right now, but I don't really want to get too emotional. It'd be overload.

"I hope that didn't make you uncomfortable," she says.

"No, it's fine. I asked," I say. "Now, how about that dress?"

Six

"This is it." Mom points to a bridal salon with a sunken entrance on Union Street.

We duck inside and immediately, a young, smiling saleslady looks me straight in the eye and asks, "Looking for a gown?"

I'm blindsided. Totally unprepared. I just look at her.

An awkward silent moment.

"I'm the bride," Mom leans in and whispers.

The saleslady's perky expression turns confused.

Then, just as another silence teeters on the brink of unbearable awkwardness, the saleslady recovers. "Bridal party here to the right, gowns to the left." She's smiling now, relieved that her directives still apply despite the mix-up.

Mom, also unnerved, turns magnetically bridal-party right. She's not ready to face the wedding gowns yet. And she's drawn to a classy woman her age searching the mother-of-the-bride and bridesmaids dresses. I follow in a daze.

"So hard to find the right mother-of-the-bride dress," the coiffed silver-haired shopper says.

"Yes," Mom says, bewildered.

Mom immediately dives into the dresses, pushing a blurry rainbow of pastel dresses down the rack in rhythmic three-second intervals: examine, reject, slide; examine, reject, slide; examine, reject, slide. I'm entranced by the mechanical nature of the dress mission.

"Cookie. Cookie!" Mom snaps me out of my stupor.

"Huh?"

She's pulled a floor-length, long-sleeved, silvery gray taffeta ball gown off the rack.

"That?" I cry as if she's just asked me to eat live rat.

"It's not bad," Mom defends. "Maybe they can make it in white?"

"Now why would you want that?" the silver-haired lady butts in. "White is for the bride. Silver is perfectly nice for the mother of the bride."

"Right," Mom answers and hangs the silvery gray whale suit back on the rack.

Mrs. Know-It-All pretends to return to her shopping, but she's obviously trying to size me and Mom up. Watching us out of the corner of her eye, sensing we might provide her with an outrageous story to tell her partners at the Marina Bridge Club.

I can see Mrs. Know-It-All now: *And there was this lady, our age, talking about wearing a white gown to her daughter's wedding, a white gown!* Her bridge club partners shaking their heads in disapproval, as Mrs. Know-It-All puts down an ace of hearts.

"Nothing here," Mom says.

Good. I don't want to give Mrs. Know-It-All any more material.

Mom stiffens her posture, girding herself as she aims for the gown section.

I follow dutifully.

The gown section is much busier. Giggles and whispers of excitement emanate from the women twittering about. Shoulder-to-shoulder with other mother-daughter pairs, we begin searching through the racks of white chiffon, lace, and silk. Mom looks at each dress discerningly, at least six seconds, before shifting them down the rack: examine, reject, slide; examine, reject, slide. She gains confidence and momentum as we move down the rack. She even breaks the rhythm a couple of times to pull a dress off the rack, hold it against her, and look to me for approval. I give three gowns the nod. The saleslady is now standing self-consciously off to the side, uncertain how, or if, to approach us. Mom takes the three hangers, lifts her arm straight above her head so the dresses won't drag, turns, and, as if participating in a silent military formation, marches into the dressing room. She snaps the dressing room curtain closed behind her.

The room now seems blindingly white, spinning with bridal buzz. I am light-headed. I move to the center of the room and sit down on the velvet divan. I put my elbows on my knees, hold my head, and close my eyes. Breathe.

When I open my eyes and look around, I see that I'm sandwiched between mothers of brides on the divan. The mother on my right is wearing pressed slacks and Ferragamo bow flats. Through stylish reading glasses, she's studying the bridal magazine in her manicured hands. The mother on my left has legs like polyester sausages stuffed into cheap, tight shoes. Her eyes are darting around the store, and she's nervously peeling off her nail polish.

"Isn't it just great?" the mother to my left says. "I mean all your life you dream of this moment, and you've finally found him, the one," she continues. "To be honest, I was getting worried about Esther, and now look at her—trying on a Vera gown." The mother gushes. "I didn't even know who Vera Wang was until a few weeks ago."

Really? You fooled me.

Then she looks around and leans in and whispers to me, "Esther's thirty-five. She's a very successful accountant, but she hadn't had a serious boyfriend in years. Just a serial dater—ya know? Then she met Blake on the computer. And I thought, oh, this is bad news—especially since he didn't have a job, but he kept talking about his idea for a dot-com start-up. Anyway, they exchanged e-mails and started dating, and it turns out he's all right. Anyway, what can you do? It's love." A misty, distant look clouds her eyes.

"What about you, honey? What's the story?" she asks. "You must be thrilled." Then in a singsong voice she presses, "What's his name?"

This can not be happening to me. Am I wearing a Talk to Me button?

"Stanley."

"Stanley?" she asks.

"Stanley," I repeat.

"That's an unusual name these days. How old is he, dear? If you don't mind me asking."

"Sixty."

"Sixty?"

"I'm not marrying him."

"You're not."

"My mother is."

"Your mother is."

"Right."

"Right."

"Oh, sorry," she apologizes. "I didn't mean to be presumptuous. I just figured . . ." she trails off. Then, upon reflection, she says, "How wonderful! Nothing like new love for your mom to erase memories of a nasty divorce."

"She's a widow," I say.

"Oh dear. I am so sorry honey. There I go again. My ex-husband used to say I was too nosy. I am so sorry," she pleads.

"Mom? Mom!" It's Esther stuffed into a dress the way her mom is stuffed into those poly pants. "Come here. What do you think?" Esther's mom jumps to attention and waddles over to her daughter. I'm liking Esther right about now.

I sift through the bridal magazines on the coffee table. The magazines: *Modern Bride*, *Brides*, and *San Francisco Weddings* are dog-eared and tattered from nervous brides planning every last detail of their dream day. On the slick, heavy pages, brides in their twenties are radiant in their cream or ivory or white gowns. None look like they'd be my friends; too perfect, too carefree. And they certainly wouldn't be Mom's friends, especially the ones wearing tiaras.

But I've got to wonder why these magazines, which are so successful at marketing romance to young dreamers, don't tap the older market. Judging from my mother, older brides are spending like mad to create a fantasy, and they have deeper pockets to do so. Did the editors of these mags just overlook the fête Barbra Streisand threw a couple years back when she got hitched? In this pile of fairy tales, there aren't even pictures of mothers of brides, let alone senior brides.

There aren't any pictures for me, the daughter of the bride, either. What am I supposed to wear to the nuptials? I look up from the magazines to scan the store for a daughter of the bride dress section. Now there's a fantasy. Maybe someday daughters of the bride will become so common they will eclipse the role of mother of the bride. Maybe the idea of marriage will become so old-fashioned that only the fifty-and-over crowd will do it, and a young bride will be nearly obsolete. Someone could make some nice pocket change writing a daughter-of-the-bride guide.

I drop the fairy-tale guides and walk over to the dressing room.

"What's going on in there?" I ask.

"Shhh." Mom says.

I look at the curtain, listen to the rustling and grunting behind it.

"Want help?" I ask.

"SHHHH," she says much more audibly.

Then she pokes her face out. The curtain is wrapped in a C shape over the crown of her head and around her neck, hiding her hair and body.

"It doesn't fit." She whispers. "I feel weird. Don't want to come out."

"Want me to come in?"

"No!" she snaps the curtain shut.

Okay. Cool. Glad to help.

Back I go to the burgundy divan, the magazines, and now, understanding looks from mothers of brides. We all know our brides are princesses: emotional, temperamental, and not entirely rational. Our job is to smile, be patient, supportive, and gently-so-gently honest. Esther's mom glances my direction but looks away, uncomfortable.

Eventually, Mom emerges from the dressing room. She looks at me bashfully, then scans the room full of mothers and brides. A self-conscious expression flashes across her face, then she straightens her posture, nods, and smiles elegantly. She is beautiful in the ivory, spaghetti-strapped, sweetheart-neck, taffeta gown. She glides gracefully by me, toward a standing, oval, full-length mirror. A cascade of bustles tumbles down the lengthy train that follows her. She's facing the mirror, and from behind she has the figure of a trim young woman: toned slender arms, sculpted back, a long, graceful neck. The twittering in the room silences. She's looking at her reflection in the mirror; the brides and mothers stop to gaze at my mom the bride. She looks radiant and confident. I move toward her.

"Nope!" Mom shatters the dreamy, romantic silence of the moment.

The other ladies in the room quickly turn back to what they were doing.

"But you look beautiful," I protest.

She starts to pull at the top, twist at the waist, and tug at the skirt.

"It's just not right. Doesn't fit."

"It's just a sample," I say. "Your dress will be tailored to fit."

"I don't know."

"Look how flattering the dropped waist is on you. These straps are so thin and graceful, call them vermicelli straps. It's lovely," I encourage.

"Yes, but the bustles are gaudy, the cathedral train is too much, and I'm not twenty-five, you know," she growls.

I look again. She has a point. The dress is pretty busy. The beading and sequins around the bodice. The scalloped skirt. The half-dozen bustles. Yes, it's a bit much.

"You'll know when you find the right dress." The saleslady suddenly reappears. "I've seen lots of brides come through here," she explains. "And when you know, you know. It's like finding the right man to marry. Once you see him, you don't need to look any further."

Is that so, Miss Twenty-five-Year-Old Saleslady Authority? Five minutes ago I overheard her tell the other saleslady, "If I get married, I'm going to elope. Weddings are too much hassle, too much money."

I turn to Mom. "Yeah, you'll know the right one when you see it."

Ten minutes later, we're in the car and on to the next store.

Seven

Back in the car, we're racing up and down the hills of San Francisco, trying to get to one more store before it closes. I'd probably be carsick were it not for the fact that the city's peaks and valleys harmonize with my roller-coaster emotions. I'm happy that Mom has a new companion. I really am. But this big wedding to-do is so disorienting. Big showy parties were not the kind of thing I was raised to respect. The way Mom and Dad got married was much more low-key.

It was the sixties, and my parents were students at the University of California, Berkeley. My father's parents were hosting a Thanksgiving dinner and needed more women to balance out a table full of male students. My father's sister, Aunt Amelie, invited my mom, and Mom accepted. Mom and Dad were curious about each other from the moment they sat down across the formal table from each other. After dinner, when the other guests were captivated by a game of chess, Mom and Dad shared a lack of interest in chess and a joint desire to talk about literature, languages, and laughing. They began seeing each other the next week.

They dated on and off for about three years, until late one summer afternoon, as they were driving back to the Bay Area from Los Angeles, Dad stopped his convertible on the edge of a cliff overlooking the ocean. My parents-to-be held hands and watched as the waves crashed below. The ocean sunset provided a spectacular, misty view.

"What would you say if I were to ask you to marry me?" Dad asked.

"You'd have to ask," Mom said.

He screwed up his courage, and right there on the cliff, proposed.

"Yes," she immediately responded, and they held each other in an embrace that would last a lifetime.

They were elated, and their parents were pleased with the decision, in an understated old European kind of way.

Dad didn't have a proper engagement ring for her at first. Instead, he gave her a green daisy ring out of a Woolworth's gumball machine. A place holder, if you will. She thought it was funny. It had never occurred to her to want a ring. Then, a few weeks later at a San Francisco café, he said, "Close your eyes and give me your left hand."

He slipped a sparkling diamond ring onto the fourth finger.

"I was so overwhelmed by it," Mom had told me. "Its size. Its brilliance. I was afraid I'd be mugged for it. Later I grew self-conscious about making my private life so public with the ring."

Eventually, Mom got comfortable with the ring and with the planned wedding. But Dad did not.

One month before the wedding, Dad came over to Mom's

house. "I can't go through with the wedding," he told Mom. He was shivering and sweating.

Mom, in her budding take-charge manner, decided he could go through with it. He just needed a good night's sleep. She coaxed him into her bed, tucked him in, brought him soup, talked to him about his fears, and then left him to sleep. She immediately went over to a friend's house for consolation.

"A man with cold feet is not exactly new," the friend said.

The next morning, Dad felt somewhat better.

"Well okay, I guess we can do it," my mom remembers him saying.

Not good enough, she thought. She wanted more conviction from him in this lifelong decision. She suggested he take a walk around the block. Fifteen minutes later, he was back.

"Get in the car," he said. "We're going to Reno."

She hopped in the convertible with her German shepherd, Mika, and off they went.

In a tiny, tacky chapel in Nevada, they exchanged vows in the most private of ceremonies. Only Mika and a nearby vagrant bore witness. Mom was twenty-three years old. Dad, thirty.

Now, some thirty-odd years later, Mom is getting married again.

The engagement diamond ring Dad gave her reflects a spectrum of colors around the car as Mom cranks the wheel into a parallel parking spot. I wonder where she put the wedding band Dad gave her.

"Hurry!" Mom says as we rush up to the second floor of the arboretum mall and into the boutique. The store is empty except for the cheery husband-wife shop owners who greet us.

"Take your time," they tell us, "we'll wait."

Great. Just what I wanted. An invitation to shop all night.

They are a comforting pair in their mid-sixties with matching bright blue eyes. How long have they been married? Forty years? Is this the only love they've ever known? Are they just starting a second marriage? The husband is chatty, the wife keeps busy behind the counter. The husband explains the sizing, the tailoring, and the various options for ordering dresses. Mom's probably thinking, *Okay, mister, let's just see what you've got before we make any big plans.*

The husband gets the vibe, and returns to his wife's side by the register. Opera music is playing overhead. I'm drawn to the framed pictures on the walls. They do not look like the pictures in the magazines I was just flipping through. Instead, these are pictures of real families and real weddings. Some of the brides are childishly young, and some are of a certain age. The bridesmaids are different sizes and shapes, and not all the men are as groomed as groomsmen should be. Will the happiness captured in these pictures last? Were these pictures of joy tempered by prior sadness? Did any of the happy couples lose a former spouse to divorce or death? How will our family wedding portrait look? Will people be able to see the loss we suffered if they look closely enough?

"Cookie! Cookie!" Mom waves me over to her side. Her wide Julia Roberts smile shows she's got great expectations for the dresses she's found. At first glance, it's obvious the two gowns she's discovered have cleaner lines and more elegant shapes than the others we've seen. These dresses are original, sophisticated, and meticulously crafted. I immediately nod approvingly, and Mom heads straight for the dressing room.

The first dress, a narrow, ivory, silk, georgette dress with a plunging neckline is trim and refined. Mom looks like a fabulous flapper from the 1920s in it. She smiles sassy, looks in the mirror, and says, "It's fun, but too racy," and she Charleston-steps back into the dressing room, waving her hands and flashing a smile before the curtain closes.

Cute.

The store owners come out from behind the counter to help. I sit in the chair outside the dressing room and wait. Within minutes, Mom bursts out of the dressing room with renewed energy. This time she's wearing a dress I do not recognize. She must have found it in the fitting room. It's strapless and taffeta with a drop waist and full skirt. It's striking. It fits magnificently. It's light pink.

"Pink?" I ask.

"Why not?" she smiles back.

The shopkeepers shrug and nod in unison.

Pink. The pastel shade is more suitable for a senior prom than a senior wedding, that's why not. But, then again, Mom has been acting like a schoolgirl in love since she met Stanley, and the color doesn't seem wholly inappropriate.

"We can get it in any color you want," says the chatty husband.

"Oh?" she asks.

"Yes," he assures. And they launch into a long conversation about other dress colors and how soon a gown could be ready.

Meanwhile, I'm having an existential moment. I'm dressed head to toe in my uniform New York black, and Mom is pirouetting in front of me considering a pale pink wedding dress? What are the implications of this? Is my future dark? Is hers one of eternal girlishness?

"Just one more to try on," Mom chirps and slips back into the dressing room.

I slouch back into the chair and hold my head.

Within minutes Mom glides out of the dressing room again,

and I pop up at attention, bracing for her next surprise. This time, the surprise is that she looks calm.

My eyes drop to see her wearing an exquisite A-line, ivory, satin gown with a drop waist and delicate, vermicelli straps. The fabric's subtle shimmer casts a celestial glow on her face. She turns, and I pull taut the wide, flat, satin ribbon that crisscross laces down her back. The bodice is snug now, and the skirt poufs out, highlighting her tiny waist. She spins around to face me.

I take a deep breath.

Mom takes a deep breath.

"Sublime," I say. "Like it was made just for you."

"You think?" A look of satisfaction has already settled comfortably on her face.

"Yes," I say softly.

Mom is beaming, like there's music in her head making her eyes dance. She pirouettes in front of the three-paneled mirror. Her satin skirt rustles in a hushed way. She looks at one side. Then the other side. Then the back side. The front again. A little curtsy. Her smile reflects in triplicate. Her calm aura is now one of giddy confidence, and she is steady.

The shopkeepers stand with their hands over their mouths. Mom floats around, continuing the mirror dance, looking at her back, turning, smoothing down the front. Looking from the side. She gives the bones in the bodice a light tug to make sure it's a snug fit. I slide a finger gently under the vermicelli straps and tell Mom to stand up straight. She obeys.

"So?" She straightens her posture and smiles wider.

"I love it," I say. "I think we've found it." And somehow, a lump swells in my throat. I swallow hard and smile.

"Some things are just the right fit." She looks at me.

"Yup," I say.

"Uh-huh," the shopkeepers nod in unison.

"Good then," she says, "then this is it." One last glance in the mirror, and she disappears to change out of the dress. I crumple into the chair outside the dressing room again.

Deep breath. The search is over. Finally, I can relax. Just as I'm exhaling, I hear what sounds like sniffling in the dressing room. I can barely make it out over the Italian opera music, which now seems much louder than before. They're playing *La Bohème*, and it's achingly romantic. I hear sniffles and sighs again. It is unmistakably Mom. The singer wails in Italian, Dad's native tongue. His voice rises and falls with emotion as he sings of love and loss. I'm immobilized. The music must remind Mom, as it reminds me, of Dad and the life she had with him, with us. Mom's transformation from widow to bride is taking place behind the changing room door.

What should I do? Console her? Let her alone to remember her love for Dad? Encourage her to focus on the happiness ahead? Dad would have said, "Do the best you can."

I get up to check on her, but she's already coming out of the changing room, wiping her eyes. Her face is sad, but she's smiling. We look at each other, hesitate, hug, and then start to cry into each other's necks. Dad is still such a force in our lives. The shopkeepers are silent, watching. Eventually, Mom pulls away from me, hands me a tissue from her purse, and dabs her eyes with another one. Then she studies me in my black turtleneck and black pants.

"Try on the dress," she says.

"I don't think so."

She insists.

I refuse.

She thrusts the dress at me. "You might want to wear this

when you get married," she says, gracefully twisting tradition. "Please?"

I relent, and within minutes I'm staring red-eyed into the mirror, in Mom's bridal gown. It fits me perfectly.

She may be the bride, but I am still the daughter.

Eight

My throat burns cold as I suck in the freezing New York air and scan the traffic outside Terminal A at JFK. The late-afternoon winter sun is coming down. Cars are honking. Police are directing traffic with their whistles. A soft, warm voice comes up from behind and whispers in my ear, "Welcome home." Ruben wraps me in a strong, warm, embrace. Wow. This is nice. It's been so long since I've seen him. He picks up my bags and leads me to his car. He's wearing a long, black winter coat and his gray cashmere scarf. His pale green eyes look surprisingly rested, especially given the odd hours he works. His jet-black hair is slicked back. His El Salvadoran olive-dark skin and high cheeks are red from the cold.

He's the perfect antidote to my exhausting trip to California. Suddenly I can't remember why I have doubts about him. Why do I feel noncommittal? I am so lucky. Look at this man!

I'm emotionally spent, and I'm probably looking that way,

too. He probably looks as good as I look bad. It's amazing how much energy it takes to accept the fact that my mother is moving on. Ruben smiles at me and squeezes my hand. I love his dimples.

I've been a sucker for his dimples since we first met last summer at a professional TV news conference in Atlantic City. I recognized him, as so many people do, from the Channel 5 morning show. He's the weather guy. At the conference, the panel was having an animated discussion on "Information or Infotainment? The Future of News." I was about to raise my hand to ask a question, when he put a note in my palm.

"What's a broad-caster like you, doing in a place like this? We could create our own headlines outside, on the beach," it read.

I fake-smiled at him. Flattering, but too forward. I dismissed him. I, for one, wanted to learn something from the panel. I was not here for a hookup. Anyway, what would a meteorologist talk about over dinner? The weather? No thanks. I need more than that.

But Ruben was relentless. During the coffee breaks and break-out sessions he flirted with me and told me bits of trivia that I actually found interesting.

"Did you know that the Empire State Building is struck by lightning an average of twenty times per year?" He smiled with his deep dimples.

I resisted, but I got to know him better in the process of trying to avoid him. I found out that he was forty-two years old, thirteen years older than me. He was Catholic; I'm Jewish. He was an aspiring politician; I don't like politicians. What could we possibly have in common? What's more, I bristled at the way he called me a "money honey" instead of a financial news reporter. *Money Honey* seems so patronizing.

But he persisted, enchanting me with his deep voice, his signature dry, self-deprecating humor, and his outgoing nature.

He revealed an encyclopedic knowledge of history and a breadth of interests spanning far beyond the year's rainfall totals. I had underestimated him.

By the closing session of the weekend conference, he had me laughing until my stomach hurt. Not only that, instead of calling me Money Honey, he was calling me Mo-Hon, and I thought it was cute, not offensive. On the last night of the conference, he coaxed me out to the boardwalk for a sunset walk and said, "Come on, Mo-Hon, open up your mind. Give me a chance." He wrapped his arm around my shoulder, much the way a father would protect his only daughter. He would take care of me, and I liked that. We've been seeing each other ever since.

"So, how was California?" he asks, eyes focused on the road as he deftly cuts across three lanes of traffic.

"Uh, fine," I answer.

He looks at me. Eyes back on the road.

"I'm happy for her. Especially given the circumstances. It's just bizarre."

He looks at me again. He can probably tell that I don't want to talk about it. I want to enjoy tonight. I want to think about us, not my mom.

He's taking me to Little Italy where some of his biggest fans, who own a restaurant, have invited him to dinner. It will be fun. It will probably be one of our signature magical New York nights: zipping around the city, enjoying red-carpet treatment, delighting in Ruben's celebrity status.

When we go out, he's always the top comic and center of attention. Usually, I'm just happy to bask in his glow. But I must admit, sometimes it's frustrating that everyone knows him, and only a few people recognize me. Occasionally, a derivatives trader or bond dealer looks at me as if I'm familiar but can't quite place me. If that trader manages to figure out who I am, and approaches me, we inevitably end up talking about what the Fed will do next with interest rates. "Will they raise rates half a point or a quarter point?" Fascinating.

Ruben attracts a different crowd, and it is a crowd. Everyone gravitates to him. I wouldn't be surprised if the Masai warriors in Kenya recognize Ruben from satellite TV. At the restaurant in Little Italy, an army of waiters and Salvatore, the owner, greet us warmly. Salvatore is a short, muscular man with a jaded and paternal face. He gives Ruben a bear hug and heavy pats on the back. He kisses my hand. He shows us to a cozy, candlelit table in the back corner he's reserved just for us. The setting has all the trappings of being an intimate night, but I know we will not have privacy. Salvatore told his family that Ruben was coming, and they've crowded into the restaurant and the kitchen, twittering over the celebrity among them. One by one, and in groups, they come to say hello, setting dishes upon dishes of antipasto, pasta, and salads on the red and white checkered tablecloth. So this must be what it feels like to get special protection from a Mafia family.

At one point, about fifteen members of Sal's family gather around the table, engrossed in one of Ruben's terrifically terrifying stories of flying into the eye of a hurricane. Ruben tells the story, stopping only for dramatic pauses and to imitate the hurricane's wooshing and sucking sounds. At the end, he signs off, "I'm Ruben Mayorga, Live on Five." Sal's family cheers with delight.

I'm perfectly content to sit in the shadows and keep quiet. We'll get some time to talk privately later. I've grown quite attached to Ruben since we first met. He is so incredibly genuine. He hasn't turned out to be the great protector I expected, but he does show the occasional sign of being a nurturer. He also has a disarming way of making fun of himself while making fun of the universal, mundane aspects of daily life. No wonder he's so popular on TV. His down-to-earth aura reaches out through TV screens and touches people. I've seen complete strangers come up to him on the street and hug him as if they've been best friends since grade school. He's got this guy-next-door accessibility.

But few people know his private, lofty aspirations and profound frustrations. I feel privileged to have access to the intimate, if troubled, Ruben. He's set his sights higher than the New York City skyline. In addition to reporting the comings and goings of weather systems, he's busy building a foundation to launch a political career. He's passionate about environmental protection, better education, and yes, emergency (weather) preparedness. He's finishing up his dissertation for his Ph.D. in political science. He spends evenings at city council meetings weighing in on everything from stoplights to septic systems. He hopes his academic background, his local political action, and his celebrity status will eventually help him gain political recognition. I support him. I believe in him. I want him to succeed.

But convincing others to take him seriously is another feat altogether. Most can't get past the fact that he is the weather guy. They just want to chum around with him and tease him about an inaccurate forecast. Rarely, if ever, do they ask him his political opinions or personal philosophies, unless it has to do with the environment. He goes along with it, joking cheerfully, but I know the constant pigeonholing frustrates him. Sometimes he gets so discouraged by the public's narrow perception of him, he threatens to give up the whole political project and just do weather forever. "So what if I live my life in Storm Center 5?" he asks. When he gets dispirited, I try to cheer him up and encourage him. Sometimes it works. Other times I just leave him alone to find a way out of his own funk. Sometimes he disappears for days at a time.

As for those differences I was concerned about when we first met? That pesky age bit, and religion part? I'm working on it. I've come to see the age gap between us as an asset, not a liability. His thirteen-year lead on me enables him to frame comments or observations in historical contexts, and he's always referencing books he's read and thinks I should, too. I learn from him. I love that. But I'm not so naive to overlook the teacher-student, father-daughter roles we're playing in this relationship. And in terms of the religious issues? Well, he is Catholic and I am Jewish. Yes, I've always said I would prefer to be with someone who shares my traditions and culture, but just because we're different doesn't mean we're incompatible. Anyway, who am I to bow to social constructs? This is the twenty-first century after all, and I'm more evolved than to doubt mixed couplehood.

All this wedding talk for my mom has made me think more seriously about getting married. I wonder if it's putting pressure on him to propose to me? I hope not. We aren't ready for that. But what if he did? What would it be like? Would he totally catch me off guard?

Perhaps he would call me on the phone at five in the morning, rousing me from a very deep sleep.

"Good Morning Mo-Hon," he would say. "Take a look outside . . . there's been a blizzard."

I open the shades to see bright white blanketing the city.

"Mo-Hon, isn't it romantic?" he would ask.

"Yes, very romantic. You forecasted it three days ago. Congratulations."

"Why don't you come meet me in Central Park? It's stunning. I'm doing live shots here all morning."

"Uh, I'd love to, but it's kinda cold outside."

"*Please? I actually need a favor, kinda fast. I forgot my makeup, and I need to be on air in half an hour. I think I left it at your place.*"

"*Oh boy. Of course. How can I keep a man from his makeup at a time like this?*"

He gives me his location, I throw on some clothes and a parka over my pajamas, pull on my snow boots, hat, gloves, scarf, and put his powder makeup deep in my pocket and race out the door.

The snow is thick, and as I trudge through Central Park, a place I pride myself on knowing well, I get a bit disoriented and delayed. But I hurry and push through the deep snow, the cold burning my nostrils even as I'm sweating beneath my layers and parka. Eventually, I find Ruben underneath the bright lights near the microwave truck.

The cameraman and truck operator clap as I arrive with the makeup. Strange. A small crowd has gathered to watch Ruben do his weather report live. They seem to be watching my every move, and I am suddenly self-conscious. I don't have my TV makeup on. All I've got are red eyes and a red nose.

I make sure that the program is in a commercial break before stepping in front of the camera to hand Ruben the makeup and give him a morning hug and kiss. But as I approach, I see he already has makeup on.

"*Ruben?*"

"*Mo-Hon, come here,*" *he wraps me in a big bear hug.* "*I have something to ask you.*"

I try to pull away, but he's got my gloved hands in his gloved hands, and he seems to be kneeling down in the snow for some reason. In my peripheral vision, I see the red light of the camera go on, and Ruben is waist deep in snow. He starts declaring his love for me, and I realize he's proposing to me live on TV with thousands of people watching.

"Daniella. Daniella? Anyone home?" Ruben is grabbing my knee beneath the table. "Something wrong with your food?" he whispers in my ear.

He's not wearing foundation makeup. I look at my picked-over plate. I look at the lively and warm Italian restaurant.

"No. Everything's great. Great!" I say. "Sorry."

"Want to leave?" he asks, concerned.

"No. It's okay. Just more wine, please," I say. I plant a kiss on his rosy cheek. "I'll be fine." I smile. He's a good person, and he's good to me. The least I can do for him is crawl out of my brain and engage with the festive bunch at the table. I raise my glass of wine. "To Salvatore, Il Fornaio, and the man who brought us all here together, Ruben. *Salute*," I toast, throwing in one of my few Italian vocabulary words.

"*Salute, bravo!*" they chime in and chink their glasses.

Salvatore then gets up and says, in a heavy Bronx accent, "To Ruben Mayorga and the Live on Five weather team. We'd be all wet without you."

Louder cheers and "*Salute*" all around.

"Or we'd be cold," says Salvatore's teenage son.

"Yeah, but we've got the Eye in the Sky, Live on Five Doppler weathercaster to look after us," Salvatore continues. "Unless he gets it wrong."

Ruben is laughing and smiling, but he won't be later. His tolerance for unoriginal weather humor is wearing thin.

In the car back uptown to my apartment, Ruben looks at me. "Daniella, I'm worried about you. How are you? Is there anything I can do to help?" he asks sincerely. Then, continuing with the straight face, "If you don't like your mom's fiancé, Salvatore and his boys could probably take him out."

Ha! Ruben helps me laugh at myself. But I still don't want to talk about Mom. It's time to give it a rest. Ruben's sensitivity and concern does make me feel better. What's more, he's not noticeably bothered by the weather forecasting comments. What a relief! He carries my bags up the five flights to my apartment, and we kiss and get carried away in each other, shutting the rest of the world out.

By morning, Ruben's world is back and blue. The comments from last night have caught up with him. He's grumbling about how even he is sick of talking about the weather. I try, in vain, to cheer him up, mothering him emotionally.

"I just need to work this out on my own," he says as he leaves my apartment. "I'm sorry I'm so down. I wish I could be here for you, but I can't. I'm sorry."

"It's okay." I kiss him good-bye. "Really." I hope the kiss will penetrate down to his core and make him feel better. The surprise shift in my job doesn't help.

Nine

I've just woken up from a nap on my keyboard. I look in the makeup mirror and try to make out whether the letter indentation in my forehead is a p or a q. It's Monday afternoon, three o'clock in my shoebox sized "office" at the New York Stock Exchange.

It's been a dreadfully slow day on the markets. I've retold, rebroadcast, and regurgitated the same three pieces of business news multiple times, and now I'm just waiting for four o'clock and my final closing bell report. The second hand on the clock is moving so slowly.

I should take this time to call my friends back. They've left me messages over the weekend, curious about how the dress shopping expedition in California went, how things are going with Ruben. I'd like to call them and invite them to the wedding. It would make everything much more fun. Maybe I can. If the roles were reversed, Mom would surely invite her friends.

Maybe I should insist that my friends get added to Mom and Stanley's wedding guest list. That way I can prove what a good job I've done raising my mother. But even if I could invite them, my friends would probably decline. Call me crazy, but they might have things to do other than attend a wedding of AARP members.

I wonder what the invitations are going to say. What kind of paper is appropriate for a senior wedding? Antique linen? Are we, the children, expected to foot the bill for the whole affair? Sorry, Mom. No way. Especially if we can't invite our friends. On second thought, since the children are the ones who are gainfully employed now and Mom is on the brink of retirement, maybe we should be paying for it. Mom and Dad paid for so much in our lives. But if we do foot the bill for the wedding, we should also get to craft the wording on the invitation. What would we write? It's not like the folks in the stationery stores have a pile of sample invitations with wording to suit our needs.

Invitation wording could be interesting. Would it be *"Enrico, Max, and Daniella Finzi and Erica Weinberg request the honor of your presence at the marriage of their parents Maya Finzi to Stanley Weinberg."* Too wordy. *"The kids of Maya Finzi and Stanley Weinberg invite you to the wedding of their 'rents."* Boring. *"The kids of the superheroes Ta-da Ma-Ya and Stupendous Stanley invite you to their parents' big zip-bang of a wedding."* Cheesy. *"Our parents are getting hitched, and there's nothing we can do about it. Please come."* Appropriate.

The office phone ringing snaps me out of my daydreaming.

"BizNews," I answer.

"Hello, Daniella, it's Tom."

Tom. My boss.

"Oh, hi."

"Good afternoon." he says. "Can you come into the Times

Square office first thing tomorrow morning? I'd like to have a chat."

Oh no. In my experience, "chats" are never good when coming from a Brit. Did someone tell him I was snoozing on my keyboard? Maybe I said "million" instead of "billion" in that merger report this morning? Or did I say "secretary of labor" when I meant "secretary of commerce?" What if I calculated the conversions wrong in that dollar-yen currency segment? Tom knows I'm no good with number crunching, even when I double-check my calculations. The question is not if I screwed up, but how. The possibilities are endless.

"A chat? Sure," I squeak.

"Nine-thirty?"

"Okay."

"Cheers," Tom says and hangs up.

Okay. Calm. Emergency. He's going to fire me. I need a game plan. When Tom tells me how disappointed he's been in my work lately, I'll just tell him the straight story: "I've been preoccupied with some family business, and I haven't been as attentive as I need to be. I'll work on that. I won't let this happen again. I promise. I'm sorry."

Lying in bed that night, my creativity and paranoia work in terrifying synchronicity. Has a younger, smarter, prettier reporter been hired? Did I incriminate someone by misspeaking in one of my reports? I envision my boss yelling at me, as I flee the building, running out the fire escape route.

I get so anxious, I can't sleep. I wonder what time it is. I know it's some wee morning hour, but I'm afraid to look at the clock. What does it matter? I already know that I'll be fully dysfunctional and overly emotional tomorrow.

I'll just apologize. What else can I do? I can't lose this job. My job and my identity are so intertwined. Where would I be without my career? It'd be like losing my left leg. I need it to stand on and move forward. The job has been a steady area of growth in my life. It balances out my personal life, which is chock-full of fits and starts.

Tuesday morning finally comes, and my heart is pounding as I slide open the glass door to Tom's office. The lady from Human Resources, who has to be present at any firing, isn't here. Yet.

"Sit down, please." My boss smiles.

Can he see the terror in my eyes?

"Daniella," he begins, "we've been reviewing your work over the past few months, and . . ."

He's going to fire me. Why didn't he warn me? I could have made changes if only I had known. I can not, not handle losing my job right now. I must have at least one constant in my life. I can't plan Mom's wedding and look for a job. He can't fire me without the lady from HR being here. It's against union rules! I'll just tell him I'm sorry.

"And," he continues, "we'd like to know if you'd be interested in stepping up your role here at BizNews."

I look at him, dumbfounded, confused.

"We're going to launch a new, fast-paced, no-nonsense, half-hour program, *Pulse*, as in, 'We've got our fingers on the pulse of Wall Street.' It'll run from four to four-thirty p.m., right after the closing bell and *Market Wrap*. I'd like you to be our chief live correspondent for the show."

"I'm sorry?" The apology I rehearsed comes out in the form of a question.

"We've been watching your market reports from the New York Stock Exchange and the NASDAQ over the past few months, and we think you're the best fit for the job. Your primary responsibilities will remain reporting from the exchanges, but I want you to ramp it up, especially during the *Pulse* program. Pepper the reports with more analysis. Get more scoops from traders. Add in political context, too. You'll still have a minute thirty for each report, and we'll give you an extra thirty seconds for Q and A at the end. Got it?"

"Yep." I only half-register what he's saying.

"Separately, and equally important, we want you to conduct our high-profile interviews. We've got a lot of big names coming up soon, Gates, Soros, Greenspan. They'll be taped, one-on-one, sit-down interviews. I want you to be the face of BizNews. We need you to break news in your interviews."

Am I hearing this correctly? I can hardly contain my excitement. This is just the kind of job I've always dreamt of! Grilling the world's heavyweights and making a difference. Educating and informing the public.

"Right," I say, mimicking his British accent.

"Right. We'll get you the details shortly about the new show. But just to get you started, we've got Bono at the UN today talking about debt relief. We need you to be there in an hour for a one-on-one. Any questions?" Tom asks.

"Um . . ."

He stands up, "Good then."

I stand up to leave. "Thank you."

"Cheers," he says.

"Cheers," I say and step backwards out of his office.

Promotion? New show? Bono from U2? I have to pinch myself. This is too good! This is too much! I don't have much time to register it all, I just run with it. Within an hour, I'm sitting down, bags under my eyes, with one of the world's biggest rock stars talking about emerging markets and the economics of the developing world.

That night Ruben takes me out for a special celebratory dinner at a sleek modern restaurant in midtown. We're waiting at the green glass bar for a table when the bartender says to Ruben, "Hey, don't I recognize you from somewhere?"

Ruben, polite as always, says, "Yes, I work for Channel 5. But here's the real star." Ruben points to me and urges me to tell my story. I smile graciously, accept the Kir Royale on the house, and start talking about my day. The bartender's interested when I say "Bono," but the moment I mention "debt relief" he looks around the bar for another customer to serve.

When we sit down for dinner, Ruben toasts to my promotion with champagne. He wants more details about my new responsibilities. I tell him I'm expected to interview big shots, pump traders for news scoops, and put more analysis into my reports.

I hesitate to tell him about the "political context" Tom wants me to add to my reports. I'm afraid I'll be treading on Ruben's carefully cultivated political turf. But then again, this may be just the nudge Ruben needs to keep his political ambition strong and sharpen his competitive edge. Maybe he'll begin to do things for himself again, rather than continuing to blame others for his unrealized ambitions.

"And," I take a deep breath, "Tom wants me to weave 'political context' into the stories. Maybe with all your political background, you can help me?"

"Of course." Ruben smiles, but I can see he's hurt. He probably wants my new job more than I do.

That night, Ruben takes me home but doesn't come upstairs. "Sorry. I'm just not up to it. But congratulations." He gives me a peck on the cheek good night.

Since then, we haven't seen each other much. I've been consumed with my new job, and he with his old job. I might be more concerned about our distance, but I'm distracted with work.

I talk to George Soros about how economic reform can help education and human rights initiatives. I get a scoop on interest rates from Greenspan's people. The job is demanding, and I love it. Most of the interviewees are interesting, but some are just smooth-talking CEOs in suits. Not that I'm complaining. But sometimes my mind wanders at inopportune moments.

More than once, I find myself in a luxurious meeting room at the top of some swank midtown office building, preparing to interview some top CEO. The cameras are positioned, I'm poised, and the CEO comes in, his public relations person nipping at his heels. We all shake hands, quick introductions, and then he sits down across the corner of a shiny wide mahogany table from me. Inevitably, he's super smart, suave, and pressed for time. I give him a quick brief of the topics I plan to cover while my cameraman clips the microphone on his suit and adjusts the lights. The public relations flak hovers in the back of the room behind me, ready to make faces and hand motions to the CEO should he veer off message or stumble during the interview.

As the CEO settles into his chair and prepares to spin his tale, I look at my list of questions. I look at him. He's invariably close to Mom's age. I smile. Often, he's not wearing a wedding band. I want to ask him about his personal life, not his company milestones. I know it's not fair, but I often presume the worst when it comes to a CEO's personal story. If I had my way, I'd conduct the interview something like this.

"Mr. Titan of Industry, two years ago you merged with Acme Fortune 50 company. Today, you're announcing two more major acquisitions. [I am confident, looking at him seriously.] You obviously do not shy away from corporate weddings, ha-ha.

But [I look at him hard, straight in the eye, the camera zooms in] what happened to your personal mergers? Why aren't you wearing a wedding ring? Did your first wife spin off from you? Were the two people in the merger-marriage unable to make the kind of sacrifice necessary to make the deal work? Did you neglect your former wife too much? Bore her away? Mr. Titan, did you just find a younger, blonder woman who'd put up with things your first wife wouldn't? Is that younger woman close to, say, my age or your daughter's age? What kind of role model is that for your daughter? Did your first wife leave with the houses? The boats? The kids?"

In reality, I say, "Congratulations on your new acquisitions. What will the new business do for your company's growth? What is your full-year outlook? Are there more acquisitions in the pipeline?" Blah, blah, blah.

While he's talking, I wonder how the world would look if every man who was at fault in a divorce had to wear a ring on his right hand to signify the split. One band for each divorce, and he just stacks them up. Different colors for cheating and neglect. Then there are the types like Donald Trump, where you already know what happened in his marriages; the question is, what's happening with his hair?

This in mind, I begin to feel grateful. Even if it is awkward to watch Mom get remarried, at least she didn't pick a sleazy CEO who makes "accounting errors" and suffers from a wandering eye. He probably wouldn't have picked her either: anyone within ten years of his age would likely be too old.

The other part of my job, reporting live from the stock markets, doesn't allow my mind to stray toward neurosis. There isn't any extra space. I'm too focused on squeezing political and economic analysis into my minute and a half report.

But when the lights come down and the makeup comes off, I'm haunted by one question. Why is it that just as I'm achieving the professional dreams I've aspired to for years, I feel so empty? I know I should be reveling in how lucky I am: I have a terrific job, a great boyfriend, and a wonderful family. But still I'm not satisfied? What is it going to take, self? Are my expectations too high? Am I just setting myself up for disappointment?

Back in college, I wrote in my diary that in ten years, I wanted to be an international news correspondent reporting on important stories. I wrote down a career plan, mapped each step, and checked the goals off my list, one by one, as I accomplished them. Well, I'm here. Plan worked.

But it never crossed my mind to sketch out personal goals. Why bother? I just figured Mister Man would magically appear, and the rest would work out. Anyway, who can plan for love and emotional symbiosis? By now, my priorities have shifted, and the professional goals I used to place on a pedestal are now serving as glamorized place holders until I can sort out my personal dreams.

If only I could find the right man the way I found the good job: hard work, perseverance, and a great video résumé.

Ten

Ruben and I are holding hands, strolling through the streets of downtown Chicago, laughing, kissing each time we stop. We've come to the Windy City for Jen and Jason's wedding, friends of mine from college.

In our time apart, Ruben and I realized how much we missed each other. And we've decided to give our relationship more respect. We've also agreed to not talk shop anymore.

Meanwhile, Mom's engagement has made me think I should get more serious about serious relationships. Inviting Ruben to Jen and Jason's wedding might help me figure out if he's marriage material. If nothing else, it'll help me determine whether to invite him to Mom's wedding.

Jen crowned me with the honorable burden of maid of honor one year ago. At the time, I protested, saying, "But I've never been a maid of honor." She responded, "I've never been a bride."

With that, I began organizing a bridal shower, planning the

bachelorette party, and ensuring that all the dresses, shoes, and bridesmaids would be prepped and ready on W-day. Admittedly, I have the experience to do the job; I've been a bridesmaid multiple times. But I've never been elevated to the stature of "maid of honor" before. I don't really mind being a bridesmaid. The parties and gatherings leading up to the weddings can be fun. It's just that the weddings themselves are so publicly intimate; they end up being such a display of status: single or married? And they force the cliché question: Who's next? And, of course, the spotlight is harshest on the maid of honor. Ruben by my side will help.

The rehearsal dinner is on a cruise boat in Lake Michigan. It's remarkably warm, but breezy for a late-autumn night. More than one hundred of us board at the Navy Pier. The Chicago skyline is golden in the late-afternoon sun. I'm ready to be inspired this weekend by Jen and Jason's love and commitment, hoping it will rub off on me and Ruben.

After the sunset, cocktail hour, and buffet dinner, the cruise director announces, "It's time to roast the bride and groom. Everybody to the top deck!" Up top, Ruben and I sit down with other guests on white fold-out chairs arranged in concentric semicircles. Behind us, the rowdier crowd stands and sways, drinks in hand. One guy in the back is lightly tapping on a toy drum someone hung around his neck. Next to him, a woman is standing, delighted, as she gently claps the cymbals she's been handed. Jen and Jason sit in the middle of the semicircle, clutching each others' hands, laughing nervously.

The drummer boy rolls a welcome, and Jason's best man, Nate, a plump guy with alcohol-induced rosy cheeks, steps into the center of the ring and takes the microphone.

"I've known Jason since high school," Nate says. "I am highly qualified to discuss Jay's sordid past."

Jason hangs his head and shades his eyes as the incriminating, embarrassing stories flow out of Nate's mouth like a spigot with an everlasting source. Drunk cymbal girl sometimes claps her instrument right after the punch line, sometimes during the punch line. Jen acts offended and angry. Maybe she's not acting. Finally, Nate runs out of material, and cymbal girl claps her instrument enthusiastically.

Drummer boy improves his roll with each new roaster. Cymbal girl, increasingly drunk, claps her instrument at random. The comments are cutting, witty, and warm. The crowd laughs heartily, with the more inebriated friends shouting additions to the stories from the back of the semicircle. We know we've done well as a roasting team when Jason pretends he's going to hurl himself off the side of the boat and Jen offers to give him a push.

As the joking carries on, I think this is the kind of humorous approach to a wedding I want: if and when. Ruben would shine in circumstances like this. Tonight, he's been shouting out occasional one-liners that keep the party rolling with laughter. It's as if Ruben has known this crowd all his life.

Oh no! A wave of panic washes over me. Are we going to roast Mom and Stanley? Please, no, spare us. That would be pure hell. It's one thing to make fun of her privately, but the prospect of a public roasting with too much information makes me cringe. I don't want to hear about Mom's ex-boyfriends. If she ever landed in an embarrassing sexual situation, I don't want to hear it. If he ever, I mean ever, in his entire life, went on drunken carousing strip club trips, I don't want to know. I want them to be asexual prudes. I'm putting my foot down; there will be no roasting at Mom's wedding. If she so much as breathes a word of it, I will not come. I mean it.

I should really calm down. Have a nice sip-sip of champagne and relax. Breathe. I'm sounding awfully severe. In fact, I sound a lot like Mom. Scary. My brothers always tease me that I suffer from matriphobia, a fear of growing up to be like your mother.

Mom won't want roasting. She's too refined for that. She's a toasting kind of woman. And toasting could be really fun: sweet, harmless, G-rated. In fact, I think toasts are the best parts of weddings. So tender and telling. Believe it or not, I'd even like to toast Mom at her wedding.

The cymbals clap. Ruben pokes me. "You going to join the party any time soon? It's your turn to roast, fair maiden of honor."

I jump up out of my chair and grab my roast notes. Drum roll, clap, bang of the cymbals, I'm standing in the center of the semicircle. I look at Ruben. He helped me write this and practice it last night in the hotel room. I hope it isn't too raw. I hope Jen doesn't divorce me as a friend after this. Ruben gives me an encouraging nod, and in my best TV voice and poise, I say:

"Topping the headlines tonight in the Windy City . . . traffic has screeched to a standstill. Pedestrians are stopping in their tracks as word spreads that Jen Tessler, one of Chicago's most celebrated bachelorettes, is getting married. Authorities say that after years of investigating and searching for Mr. Right, Tessler has found someone to call hubby. Sources close to Tessler say they are 'shocked' and 'relieved' that Jason Klein, a man she's known for ten years, will wed this legendary woman.

"You'll remember Tessler grabbed national headlines during her senior year at Brandeis University in Waltham, Massachusetts. She dispatched an entire search team to a Waltham Burger King. Their mission? To retrieve her one-hundred-twenty-page thesis on 'Andy Warhol's Use of Camp Culture to Open the Closet for Gay Men in Mass Culture.' Tessler had worked on the project for more than a year and then left it at the big BK by accident amid a revelry of French fries and milk shakes. It was Jason, one of the brave rescuers, who recovered the priceless document."

The crowd is smiling and chuckling.

"Jen made news a few years earlier when she invented the cafeteria tray snow sled on the hills of the university campus. Little did she know she was sitting on an invention that would soon become a phenomenon throughout the snow-covered world, bringing joy to children and immature adults everywhere. Again, Jason was there: sledding alongside her, but not yet with her."

People in the crowd who remember the cafeteria trays whisper—the trays were a good idea.

I take a deep breath. Here comes the part I considered cutting out. "And just when we thought this one woman couldn't possibly impress us any more, she unleashed her bare body, shall we say, 'artistically' for the students in oil painting 301. No other naked model has ever caused such a stir in the university art department. Enrollment in the course overflowed, and students fought to get into the course, with or without paint."

Jen turns scarlet, then protests, "I was not completely nude!"

"Ooh-ooh-ooh!" The folks in the back hoot and clap.

Jason looks at her like it's the first he's heard this. Jen's parents look more embarrassed than Jen.

"Go, Jen!" the crowd eggs the controversy on.

"And, lest Chicago forget the other precious Jen stories. There was the fling with Vladimir, the Russian literature teaching assistant." Jen curls her neck down and shadows her brow. "And the case of Jen's mysteriously disappearing bras."

Jen motions to me that she's going to push me overboard, but I continue.

"Tomorrow Miss Tessler will get hitched to one lucky Jason Klein. Chicago, get ready to say good-bye to your bachelorette sweetheart. Jason, don't tell us we didn't warn you. That's it for this edition of roasting Jen. Now, back to you."

The cymbals clap, the drummer rumbles, there's a round of applause and hoots, and it's onto the next roaster. I check Jen's face to make sure she's not too angry. She gives me a friendly glare. Ruben presses a wet kiss into my cheek when I sit down next to him. "Excellent performance, my dear," he says. "You and I, we're a good team." I squeeze his thigh and smile.

As we make our way back to the hotel room that night, Ruben's mood turns inexplicably dark. Why? He doesn't want to talk about it. He mumbles something about extravagance, gaudiness, materialism replacing love, and bad fish.

Moments like these, I question what we're doing together. These bouts with darkness do not inspire great calm. And yet, I'm still drawn to Ruben's intensity. I'm intrigued by his constant critique of the human condition. His tendency to put each experience into a broader context fascinates me. I care for and respect him, but I also have a hard time envisioning marrying him. Do I want to spend my life negotiating his inherent cynicism and unpredictable dark patches? Would I be more optimistic if he were Jewish like me? More patient? Jen certainly doesn't seem to have doubts about Jason. And, if Mom has any questions about Stanley, it isn't apparent. Am I the only one with a difficult relationship, or does everyone have trouble and hide it?

Eleven

I'm with Jen and the bridesmaids (sounds like a bad name for a rock group) in the "bridal ready room." Ruben is off on his own, finding his center, working things out. Whatever. The ready room is one of those plush hotel rooms in Chicago's famous Standard Club downtown. The club is one of those stiff, conservative spaces with history. The ceremony will take place in the club's ballroom.

The five of us bridesmaids are rustling around in our matching light-raspberry-colored taffeta dresses. Bridesmaids' dresses are inevitably tacky, and these are no exception. At least these dresses are straight to the floor with simple, off-the-shoulder tops. They could be worse, i.e., tangerine-colored iridescent taffeta with lime ruffles.

I'm half-sitting, half-lying down on the divan. It's strange to think how bridesmaids' dresses have evolved. (Yes, as maid of honor, I've looked into it.) The whole "wear the same dress" tradition began as Roman law, when bridesmaids dressed similarly to the bride to confuse evil spirits who presumably wouldn't be able to pick the bride out of the crowd. Nowadays, women avoid wearing white to a wedding so that the bride stands out.

I have to wonder, though, how come the bride always manages to pick a classy gown for herself and tasteless dresses for her bridesmaids? Maybe it's all part of a ploy to make the bride look better. Maybe the bridesmaids' dresses are designed to be so ugly that they frighten off evil spirits.

I look around the room. My closest college girlfriends are all here. Maxine is at the mirror, smudging in her eyeliner. Shana is pressing her hair into place. Becca is messing with her panty hose, while Rachel is digging through her bag of jewelry. I gave up trying to perfect my appearance; it felt too much like work.

When bridesmaids were invented, they did more than primp and wear awful dresses. They cooked food, helped sew the bride's gown, or decorated for the reception. I only feel worthy of my maid of honor title when someone knocks unexpectedly on the door of the bridal ready room. I jump up from the divan and swish over to the door. Jen and the bridesmaids twitter and giggle—who could it be? It's a waiter carrying a tray with an open bottle of red wine and glasses on it. The outrage! I stop him at the door and body block him from entering.

"Please give our thanks to whoever sent the bottle," I say, "but unfortunately, I can't let it come past the threshold. Don't want it to spill on Jen's dress. You understand, no?"

He looks embarrassed. He should've known better.

"Please, come back only if you've got white wine or some other clear liquid." The bridesmaids nod in agreement. I'm proud to have averted potential disaster, but thirst for what would have been a well-timed glass of wine.

Jen isn't riled by the wine threat, nor does she seem worried by much else. In fact, I've never seen her so confident and relaxed. She's sitting with perfect posture on a stool before the vanity: a model of poise and grace. Zen Jen is a tad disappointed that the rose bouquets are a darker shade of pink than she wanted, and that the violinist is running late, but overall, she has an aura of serenity that I've never witnessed before. I aspire to her calm on my wedding day, but I think it may be unattainable for me. Unless of course, Mr. Perfect magically appears.

Mr. Perfect wouldn't be perfect, but he'd be perfect for me. He'd be all those things you see listed in a personals ad: smart, funny, handsome, honest, and ambitious. Beyond that, he'd be adventurous, emotionally intelligent, and Jewish. He'd be tall and dark and muscular. No, it's not original, but I like it. He'd say all the right things, in all the right ways, at all the right times. He would delight me with his wit, charm, and sensitivity. This guy, we'll call him Imaginary Boyfriend, or IB for short, would shed his suit on a hot summer day and follow me into a Central Park fountain. He would convince me that his idea of tearing up the streets of Manhattan and replacing them with gardens is feasible. He would bring me two roses. He would tickle me. He would cook. He would know how to whistle.

He would propose to me in the most wonderful way.

We're in the Adirondacks, camping on one of those fresh, brisk, fall nights. You know the kind: chilly with an occasional frosty breeze blowing gently through the mountain valleys. The leaves rustle in the trees with each gust, and I feel totally at peace. Mother Nature embraces me, and so does my oh-so-strong and manly IB. We go fishing late in the afternoon, and while I am reading a book, he comes back with a broad smile to show me the big, beautiful bass he caught in the lake. It's the kind of fish that only an outdoorsy, skilled, strong man can catch.

Back at the campsite, IB lights a fire in the most primordial way: gathering logs, building a pyramid with them, and then gently blowing on the fire until great flames jump and crackle. We cook the fish in foil on the campfire, just a squeeze of lemon, and drink the wine he insisted on carrying all the way from the car to the campsite. After dinner, we sit, snuggle, and nuzzle under one plaid wool blanket that's a touch too small.

We watch as an enormous full moon creeps up ever so slowly from behind the mountain range. The fire flickers in the foreground. I feel IB's biceps hard around my shoulders as we giggle and recount messy childhood stories of roasting marshmallows to make s'mores. Then he unwinds himself from the blanket and wraps me up in it, like a burrito, with only my left hand revealed. I pull my hand back under the blanket to stay warm. He kneels in front of me, his back to the fire, the glistening lake, and the golden-bright moon. He fishes for my hand under the blanket, finds it, and holds it.

He says, "Daniella, I have loved you since the moment we met. I want to be by your side so long as the moon rises above the earth. I want to be with you longer than eternity." I blink, wondering why this gorgeous man is kneeling in front of me, saying these beautiful things. I want to say, "Yeah, me, too. That's how I feel."

But he continues. He digs into his pocket and produces a sparkling ring. (Of course he assures me it's a certified conflict-free, politically correct diamond that was not sold to fund rebel forces in Africa.) He squeezes my hand firmly, and with the most sincere eyes ever invented, asks, "Daniella. Will you marry me?"

I can't breathe. Is this really happening to me? The love of my life proposing we spend forever together? I can't speak. I nod and smile, holding back the tears.

"Daniella?" he asks.

"Yes," I squeal. "Yes!" He slips the ring on my finger. We talk about our future together, and that night we don't go into the tent. We burrow into the two-person sleeping bag outside, listen to the crickets, smell the lake water lapping up against the rock shore, and ponder "forever."

Reality? No IB. No ring on my finger. And no clue what to expect from Ruben's mood tonight.

Twelve

Jen and Jason's W-hour is ticking closer, and I'm the one with butterflies fluttering. Really, I shouldn't be surprised. Each time I go to a wedding, I get knotted up as if I were the one tying the knot. I went to a wedding once with my ex-boyfriend from Brooklyn, where I didn't know the bride or groom. My only responsibility that night was to sit in the audience, and I almost failed to do that properly. But, in my defense, I wasn't sitting just anywhere with just anyone. I was sitting in the grand ballroom of The Pierre, one of New York's most expensive and lavish hotels, amid some of the world's most famous and powerful people. Yep, there I was with Henry Kissinger, Barbara Walters, and Yo-Yo Ma. New York Attorney General Eliot Spitzer was the best man. You get the idea. The power of the people in the room, combined with the security guards lurking about, infused the room with infectious nervous energy. Before the ceremony, I visited the ladies' room twice.

I didn't know the bride and groom well enough to sense whether it was a good match. But as they took their vows before the crowd, it was obvious there was a lot of pressure on the couple to be perfect. The way the justice of the peace spoke so assuredly about the intangibles of love, God, and forever made me gasp for air. Were these concepts all so apparent and easy for everyone but me? My boyfriend kept caressing my hand sweetly during the ceremony, as if patting a dog so it won't yelp. Finally, the bride and groom exchanged vows, and I returned to full breaths, not gasps.

Jen's ceremony won't be nearly that stressful. The people here are friends, not policy makers, celebrities, and strangers. Plus, there's a bonus for me in being the maid of honor: I'm to walk down the aisle with Ben, Jen's older brother. I've always had a crush on him. Ben went to college with us. He's an outdoorsy, crunchy type, with ringlets of long dirty-blond hair, who's doing his residency in pediatric emergency care at the University of Chicago. We've often flirted, but he's been in Illinois, and I've been in New York. That's why, I convince myself, nothing ever happened. And anyway, I'm here with Ruben. I should not even think about Ben. He's just my escort down the aisle. Who am I to be critical of CEOs with wandering eyes when I have a wandering mind?

Jen's big W moment finally arrives. We all line up, bridesmaids, groomsmen, parents, and Jen and Jason outside the Standard Club's ballroom. We're all a bit jumpy except for Jen, who is calm and focused. The guests are seated, the flute and harp duo starts, and the procession begins. First, Jason starts down the aisle with his mom linked on one arm and his dad on the other. Then Jen's mom starts down the aisle proudly with her second husband.

The butterflies in my stomach pick up speed—they're bat-

ting against my intestines. I watch from behind as one after another, Maxine, Becca, Shana, and Rachel walk gracefully, arm in
arm with their paired match, down the aisle. Despite the soothing music, my heart is pounding. Why is all the TV composure
I use daily to deliver news escaping me today? This nervousness
makes no sense. No sense at all. This isn't my wedding. I'm not
committing to anything. All I have to do is walk, and I've been
doing that for twenty-nine years.

Ben sees the terror in me and pokes me in the butterflies. I
jump and squeal and clap my hand over my mouth. This is not
good. I turn around, looking for an exit, and see Jen smiling behind her veil, her hand wrapped around her father's strong arm.
Ben links my arm with his and starts to move forward. My feet
turn to lead. Ben gives me a little tug. I can't move. Then he
puts his hand on my arm and begins to pull. With all my might,
I lift one heavy leg and then the other. Right then left. Smile,
Daniella. Yes, smile. Right. Left. I self-coach. The audience is
turning to watch as Ben pulls me down the aisle. He walks me
to the end of what seems like a marathon and guides me directly
to my spot next to the chuppah, the Jewish wedding canopy. I
teeter on my heels and clutch my flower bouquet for dear life.
Ben lets go, and remarkably, I'm still standing. I search the
crowd for Ruben's face, something to focus on for reassurance.
He catches my panicked glance and smiles.

Just then, the harp and the flute start playing Pachelbel's
Canon, and Jen appears. She's glowing, confident, and polished.
Her father guides her down the aisle. I'd like to take notes on
how she does it. Oh yes, there will be a video; I can play it later.
Play, rewind, play, pause, play. Her father's face shows a mix of
loss and pride as he walks her step, step, step, down the aisle.
With Dad gone, who will walk me down the aisle?

What about Mom's wedding? Who will give her away? Me?

My brothers? I'm anxious. If I'm any more nervous for Mom's wedding, it could be ugly. I try to hide my panic with a candy smile, which I maintain until Jen and Jason finish the traditional Jewish ceremony with the crunch of a wineglass beneath their feet.

Ruben greets me immediately after the ceremony with a glass of champagne.

"You did a wonderful job, Mo-Hon. And you look beautiful. But you're so nervous. What's up?" he asks.

"Just wedding jitters." I knock back a flute of bubbly.

"You know what these weddings need?" Ruben laughs. "Good forecasters who can predict which guests will be most leaky during the ceremony."

I crack a smile.

"Lighten up, Mo-Hon!" insists the closet heavy thinker. Within minutes, he's cranked up his charm factor to high, and a group of guests has gathered around us, laughing as Ruben says that 85 percent of people killed by lightning are men.

"Coincidence or conspiracy?" He raises his eyebrows skeptically.

Soon, we're herded into the dining room, where tuxedoed waiters serve us dinner. The Caesar salad and chicken piccata is fine, but not great. The band, however, is incredible! From the head-thrashing drummer down to the self-proclaimed "guit-artist" who is jumping and sliding all over the stage, we can't help but let loose dancing. Plus, we're drinking champagne like water. At one point, the bridesmaids and I all line up on stage next to Jen, just as we did in college for a lip-sync contest. We sing along to Madonna's "Respect Yourself," complete with our once well-rehearsed, but now embarrassingly bad, dance moves. We're a vision in unsynchronized raspberry taffeta.

The band jams out a rockin' interpretation of "Hava Nagila" complete with electric guitar. Dozens of us clasp hands in the hora, the traditional Jewish dance, and form a giant circle that slowly rotates around the dance floor. The band steadily speeds up the beat, and we keep pace until the band cranks up the tempo to such a frenzied pace that we're dancing wildly around in the circle with our heads spinning and our grins hurting.

But the band won't let us rest. Once "Hava Nagila" ends, they keep the party pulsing, and the "guit-artist" encourages guys on the dance floor to lift Jen and Jason up, while they are seated in chairs. In typical Jewish tradition, the men lift Jen, in her flowing white gown, above their heads, bouncing her around. She screeches with delight. Another group of men lift Jason up in a different chair and dance with him in the air. We clap in sync in a circle around the king and queen for the night, clapping and singing. Then the chair carriers bring the newlyweds close enough together that they can connect by grabbing at separate ends of a white cloth napkin. The chair carriers whirl and spin them like a pinwheel. I'm smiling and clapping so much it hurts. I'm jumping up and down. All of the dancing has spun my anxiety into delight.

Just as the men gently place Jen's chair on the dance floor, and she's about to stand up, Jason pushes her gently back into the chair. There will be no rest. The band strikes up some sexy stripper kind of music. That's right. It's time for the ol' garter ritual. Not my favorite. In fact, it's my least favorite part. It suggests that a woman's greatest value is found between her legs. Have we not evolved at all?

Jason kneels before Jen and slowly peels back the tulle layers of her dress, revealing her leg beneath. We squeal as Jason kisses her ankle, then her shin, then her knee. The band gives a proper drum roll (not like the kind we heard last night), and Jason's head disappears beneath her tulle layers. Seconds later he reappears, biting the garter with his front teeth. The cymbals clap and the music returns to sexy tunes as Jason slides the light blue and white garter down over her knee, down her calf, and over her high-heeled white shoe. Another cymbal clap. Jason raises the garter above his head, as if the victor holding a trophy.

By now, the single men, Ruben included, have gathered behind Jason like a pack of wolves. They're hooting and whistling. The drummer rolls the drums again, a cymbal clap, Jason throws the garter. A teenager with budding facial hair catches it, discovering only after he's got it, that it means he'll be next to marry.

It's all good fun until I envision Mom and Stanley doing a garter show. I really don't want to see Stanley's mouth climbing up Mom's leg to grab her garter. I don't even want Mom to wear a garter. She's too old to be that sexy. Heck, I've never even worn a garter. The thought of watching elderly single men with bifocals fight for Mom's garter makes my stomach turn.

But the band is so good, it makes everything okay. This band could really rock Mom's wedding! When the musicians finally take a break, I slide over to the "guit-artist" who's standing by the speakers, which are blasting recorded music.

"Hey!" I shout. "Great tunes!"

"Thanks!" he shouts back over the music.

"You do weddings in California?" I ask.

"Sure do!" he shouts back. "When are you getting married?" The music is blaring in our ears.

"It's my mom. Her wedding. June. Have to ask her . . ." I shout back.

"It's your wedding darling! Your day. Don't worry about your mom," the "guit-artist" says. "When is it?"

"Her wedding. She's getting married." I shout back.

He looks confused.

I give up.

"Card! Can I have your card?" I ask, using my fingers to make a C shape the size of a business card.

He digs into his pocket, produces a card, holds it up at eye level, smiles, then presses it into my palm. It reads Big Rick and the Dyno-mites.

This card could be the ticket to a very entertaining wedding for Mom. I can just see it now.

The senior crowd, gathered for Mom and Stanley's wedding, expects a sedate evening of being served, talking about the newlyweds, and debating elements of physics. But then Big Rick and the Dyno-mites burst onstage and belt out James Brown's "I Feel Good." The ladies with white hair (colored blond) jump up out of their chairs as if the seats were on fire and start dancing wildly. They drag their crotchety husbands out onto the dance floor with them. They're all shouting, "I feel good, I knew that I would, so good, so good, I got you waa, waa, waa, waaa!"

Then the band plays "Born to Be Wild," and the closet white-haired air guit-artists fall to their knees, leaning back with their imaginary electric guitars, as if onstage.

Just when you thought it couldn't get any more wild, Big Rick calls on the waitstaff to stop serving food, and "come on out to the dance floor to lift the newlyweds up above the crowd in two chairs." (The Dyno-mites forewarned the caterers about their additional job responsibilities because Big Rick didn't want a lawsuit on his hands if the older guests tried to lift the bride and groom and ended up with hernias or heart attacks.)

Mom looks panicked. Stanley looks pissed. The waiters are tickled. Mom shakes her head wildly. "No, no, non!" (her French slips out) as she's lifted in the air above the crowd. Stanley, the bril-

liant professor, suddenly looks like a mad professor. He wants out,
but it's too late, he's already floating in the chair above the dance
floor. Mom is terrified. "I'm scared! I'm scared! I'm afraid of
heights!" And Stanley, squirming in the chair shouting, "It's go-
ing to break, I'm going to break! I'm going to fall!" The waiters'
faces turn from amusement to annoyance as they strain under
the weight of the squirming, shrieking bride and groom.

Okay, so maybe it's not such a great idea to call Big Rick for
Mom's wedding. Instead, I'll just keep the card for myself,
should I ever need it. Maybe a calm chamber music quartet is
better for Mom's wedding. No matter what, I'm going to make
sure that Mom's friend, Dr. Rosenfeld, an ER doctor, makes it
onto the guest list. Just in case.

The Dyno-mites step back onto the stage at Jen and Jason's
wedding, and Big Rick takes the microphone. The band starts
playing some soft sort of background jazz music as Big Rick announces, "It's time for another toast."

"Now we'll hear from the maid of honor, Daniella!" What?
No one told me I was doing a toast! I just did last night's roast!
I shove Big Rick's card into my bag, and he hands me the mi-
crophone. My mind is blank.

Under normal circumstances, a microphone in hand makes
me feel comfortable, as if I'm at work. But standing before the
expectant crowd without any notes wearing a raspberry taffeta
dress, I'm discombobulated. I take a deep breath, and, just like
my broadcast voice coach said, I envision my feet superglued to
the dance floor for grounding. I've pulled off TV reports with
less preparation than this. I just need to focus and believe that
all my ad-libbing experience will come through. *Trust yourself,*
Daniella. Inhale. Exhale. Go.

"Love is transcendent," I start, my eyes searching around the room, making eye contact with Jen, Jason, their parents. "With love, two people who previously operated in their own individual worlds now share one universe. And not just any two people can share the same, unique universe. These two must be soul mates. The kind of people whose inner spirits draw them together like magnets. They understand each other without having to explain much because fundamentally, they see the world from a shared perspective. Tonight we are celebrating the miracle that Jen and Jason managed to find each other in this vast world. A union like this makes the world a better place because it helps build community. It shows us how wonderful and transformative one person can be for another." I raise my glass. "To Jen and Jason for finding the meaning of life: love. Mazel tov."

I take a swig of champagne and breathe a deep sigh of relief. Thank you ad-lib training! The band picks up again, and people start dancing. I'm surprised that these romantic notions came out of my mouth so easily. It's as if they've been sitting there on the tip of my tongue for years waiting to be uttered. Perhaps it's all this stubborn idealism about how perfect love can be that's actually preventing me from appreciating the good love I've got.

The microphone in my right hand is soon replaced with Ruben's hand. He leads me to a darker corner of the dance floor and says with his pale green eyes, *You were wonderful.* He gives me a peck on the cheek and squeezes my hand. Does he really understand what I want in love? I give him a guilty hug. Can we have a profound love? As he swings me gently around the dance floor, I wonder, is Ruben my soul mate? Could he become my soul mate? Maybe I'm overanalyzing. Maybe I'm asking too much. I need to relax. I rest my head on Ruben's broad shoulder. Nice. Nice shoulder.

Just as I'm settling into the crook of Ruben's neck, someone taps my shoulder.

"May I cut in?" My friend Rachel grabs my hand, yanks me from his arms, and drags me to the center of the dance floor for the ol' bouquet toss. Yuck. A gaggle of squealing, giggling girls surround me. I smile and laugh along. The drum rolls, the cymbals clap, Jen throws the bouquet over her shoulder. It sails through the air toward me.

I dodge it.

Thirteen

It's the day before Thanksgiving. I'm walking down the aisle. No, not that kind of an aisle. The aisle of an airplane. I wrap up the last work-related call for three days, snap my cell phone shut, and smile at the unwelcoming, chubby man squashed into the aisle seat of my row. He reluctantly peels himself out of his seat so I can squeeze in next to the window. Thanks.

My new responsibilities at work have become increasingly stressful. Chasing people, chasing video, racing for deadlines. Elbowing my way through packs of journalists at press conferences. Jousting with corporate titans. Wrestling with my boss over writing style and story content. But the hardest work lies ahead. Touchdown San Francisco will mean my first formal gathering of *la nouvelle famille*. Thinking of things, like "the new family," in French takes some of the edge off of it. Mom taught me that trick when she taught me French.

The pilot announces, "We've reached our cruising altitude of thirty-five thousand feet," and I'm relieved to leave my work and Ruben behind for the long weekend. Ruben and I had a good time at Jen and Jason's wedding. We did. But overall we're still not steady. We're apart often, often blaming work. We're trying to make this relationship work, but we're struggling, struggling.

Ever since that Chicago wedding, Ruben's dark, tortured side has been rearing its head more often. I can tolerate and sometimes even empathize with his sweeping social criticisms. But the Mr. Fix-It part of him, that unbridled ambition that attracted me to him in the first place, is gone now. He's stopped saying, "I'm going to the council meeting tonight to tell them what they should do." Instead, he's just given up, content to say things like, "Trucking Manhattan's garbage out of the city won't work for long; they've got to think of something better." That's it. The end. No innovative resolutions. No alternative ideas for planning or reducing trash. None of that fresh thinking that so intrigued me when we first met. By now if he even has any new ideas, he's stopped expressing them.

I try my best to draw him out, but I'm simultaneously building emotional barriers, trying to protect myself from disappointment if the relationship collapses. No doubt this relationship is ailing and needs rest. So I'm on my own for this trip. Not ready to introduce my angst-ridden, older, Catholic, weather-reporting boyfriend to my new, perky, academically overqualified family.

My brothers pick me up from the San Francisco airport in Max's new electric hybrid car. I spend most of the ride listening to them talk about the engineering and efficiencies of the car; never mind how we're doing, or that we are driving to Stanley's house instead of Mom's house for Thanksgiving dinner. If my brothers are nervous about the upcoming dinner, there's no hint of it.

We arrive at Stanley's house, and Mom bursts out of the front door. She hugs me. "You look so beautiful! I've missed you! Are you losing weight again? Come inside."

The speed at which she darts out the door and the pace at which she pulls me toward the house shows me she's jumpier than usual. Frightening. Her nervous energy propels her at speeds that would trump any Wall Street trader trying to make a transaction on the floor of the Exchange. I take a deep breath and look longingly back at my brothers who, still outside, are tinkering with something under the hood, still deeply engrossed in the details of the drive train. Mom meanwhile is dragging me up the stairs and in.

Stanley greets me with a big bear hug and his signature loud laugh. Why is he wearing a maroon polyester blazer? He introduces me to his daughter, Erica, who greets me with an awkward hug and a complementary nervous laugh. She's about as tall as I am, and she's pretty. She has bright green eyes, curly long brown hair, and a warm, sincere smile. Presto! Insta-sista.

My brothers, in their own time, casually walk in the front door and head straight for the kitchen. Within seconds, we're all flitting about, stirring, cutting, and squabbling. I'm surprised by how natural the whole exchange feels. It feels particularly homey when my brothers' and Stanley's conversation about the turkey turns into a spirited debate about the physics of cooking a turkey.

"How long will it take to cook the turkey?" Stanley the physicist gives the students gathered in his kitchen a problem to work out.

"You would have to know the heat capacity of the bird," Enrico says, digging up concepts of thermodynamics he researched in his physics dissertation.

"Well, you can't really know that," Max says. He just graduated college with a degree in engineering and speaks with conviction.

Mom and I quietly fold napkins, count out silverware for six, and try in vain to follow the discussion.

The men's voices rise in hearty, academic debate.

"So you could just approximate using the heat capacity of water. Just use a simplifying assumption," Erica says.

The men silently digest her comment. Enrico looks at the ground. Max looks at the ceiling. Stanley looks at his daughter. Mom and I freeze.

Erica stirs.

The men think.

Mom and I stare.

Lest anyone dare forget, Erica is midway through her doctoral work in physics.

"Water's not a good enough approximation." Max eggs the debate on.

And off they go again.

Soon, we're standing around the table as *la nouvelle famille*. I'm waiting for someone to say something before we sit down and eat. Something like, "We are thankful to be here today, to meet each other blah, blah." But no. Not a peep. Everyone clams up on emotional matters. Talk physics, and they can't cork it.

I follow everyone else's cue and just sit down. My spot is between Erica and Mom. The inquisitive journalist in me kicks in right away. I'll ask Erica a simple question, and then take it from there.

"So, I'm not a scientist or anything. But what are you working on at the lab? Anything a layperson like me could understand?" I ask.

She smiles, then starts off slowly with her answer. "I study the fundamental structure of the universe."

Oh, is that all?

"I'm trying to figure out which particles make up the universe and what the forces and interactions are that govern how they behave," she continues.

I smile and nod as she carries on nonstop for ten minutes. I'm utterly clueless about what she's saying. Evidently she doesn't inhabit my media world of fifteen-second sound bites. She hasn't taken a breath or a bite since she started talking.

She's very animated, and her voice rises and falls with intensity as she continues to explain her work. She's bubbly, brainy, and beautiful, and I wonder if she has some genius boyfriend back at the lab. I'm curious and feeling a touch competitive. I look for a way to guide the conversation away from particles to personal. She doesn't let up though, and I feel a headache coming on.

Just then Enrico, overhearing the conversation asks, "Well have you tried . . ."

"Yeah," Max says.

Stanley says, "Better yet . . ."

And, off they go again, a table full of know-it-all scientists, each vying for the top spot of biggest brain at the table.

Mom gives me a knowing glance: we are both grateful to be left out of this brainiac competition. If IB were here, he'd follow the conversation, adding enough insight to be polite, but not enough to be competitive. He'd be above childish brain sparring.

I wonder how Erica feels about this brand-new sibling rivalry. Just three years ago she was an only child who had the constant, adoring approval of her mother and father. Now boom! She's without Mom and on the brink of having a high-maintenance stepmom and three provocative "siblings."

If Erica is giving up her spot as an only child, should I prepare to give up my spot as only daughter? Will Erica start calling Mom, "Mom"? Or will she call her Maya? Maya? Both sound bizarre. Will Mom and her two "daughters" go out shopping? What should I be calling Stanley? Dad? Stepdad? No. Stan? Hardly.

Come to think of it, our families could be even closer. It might sound ridiculous, but one of my brothers could marry Erica. For example, if Enrico and Erica got married, he could call her, "my wife" or "my stepsister." Max and I could call her "my stepsister/sister-in-law." Yikes! On the bright side, the kids would only have one set of grandparents and no one could complain about the in-laws.

I take another serving of turkey and cranberry sauce. Does Erica see us as invaders? If she does, she's polite enough to keep it to herself. I hope she sees us as add-ons, not replacements for the cozy family she once had. I scan the house she grew up in. It's inviting but clearly foreign turf. Our house growing up was full of muted, neutral colors and eclectic textiles. This house is full of vibrant reds, blues, old-fashioned decorations, and formal china.

Suddenly, it hits me. Does Mom plan to move into this house with Stanley before marriage? I don't approve. Why should I? Mom's never even let a boyfriend of mine stay the night "under her roof." Maybe I can insist that similar rules apply. "No fiancé of yours can stay the night with you under his roof." Nah, it doesn't quite roll off the tongue, does it? Aha! But Erica could enforce rules. She could say, "Not so long as you're in my mother's house." Maybe Erica and I could team up and force them to live apart. C'mon Daniella. That's silly. You're happy for them. You are.

Anyway, I'm in no position to protest if they decide to move in together before they get married. I made the pitfalls of "living in sin" abundantly clear with my own mistake less than a year ago.

In fact, the first time I met Stanley, I was at the end of my mistake. I was breaking up with my longtime boyfriend David and moving out of the Brooklyn apartment we shared. I hadn't slept the night before as David tried to talk me out of leaving. I cried all night, but I stuck to my guns. By morning, David had given up and left the apartment so I could pack.

I started to collect my things. The framed pictures of us as a couple. The books we bought together. The blankets we used to snuggle under. It was a couple of hours into sobbing and packing that Stanley and Mom knocked on the door. I opened it, and through wet eyes, I saw my mom and Stanley. Stanley looked like a jolly man with a Santa belly and shock of silver-gray hair. I awkwardly put out my hand to shake his. His hands were full of work gloves and packing tape, so instead of shaking my hand, he wrapped me in a strong, reassuring hug. I cried harder.

They had come from California to New York for the weekend to go to a wedding and do some sightseeing. They did go to the wedding, but aside from that, the only sites Mom and Stanley saw that weekend were the inside of my moving boxes. That weekend, Mom and Stanley helped pack up my stuff in the Brooklyn apartment, and then unpack it in my Manhattan studio. Stanley didn't complain. In my new apartment, he installed locks on the door. He attached my bookcases to the wall. He introduced himself to the superintendent.

He took Mom and me to dinner at a small Italian trattoria in my new neighborhood, the Upper West Side. He kept my glass of red wine full all evening and showed great empathy without prying into the details of the breakup. Stanley's no-pry approach also prevented Mom from launching into her typical crowbar approach to getting information, and I was grateful. Both Mom and Stanley seemed especially sensitive to my breakup. They kept repeating that it would get easier with time. I had to believe them. They both survived much heavier losses.

I told Stanley how David and I had moved to New York City together and into the same apartment just six months ago. I was thrilled to explore the new, exciting city. David was more interested in staying home to read. I wanted to go out to parties and restaurants. He told me how much he admired women who stayed home and cooked. I wanted to dive into my career. He was focused on his. In my effort to please, I kept pushing myself to be someone I wasn't.

"Like mother, like daughter." Stanley laughed, lightening the situation. "No way to turn your mom into a housewife. Good thing I like to cook."

It was a simple comment, but it signified an understanding and acceptance of Mom the way she was.

Mom never uttered a peep about my decision to move in with David, or to leave him. I should, at the very least, extend the same courtesy to her should she decide to live in sin with Stanley. It's not like I can argue, "You're too young, you don't know what you're getting yourself into."

I tune back into the conversation at the Thanksgiving table. By now my brothers and Erica have turned the turkey talk into a discussion of cooking a pot roast.

"How many gallons of gasoline would it take to launch a pot roast into space?" Enrico asks. "If it stayed in orbit for awhile, would the pot roast on the way back to earth burn up on reentry, or be perfectly cooked?"

I excuse myself from the dinner table. Enough is enough. I

can do without this incomprehensible, ridiculous chatter, and I need a moment of quiet.

I walk down the hall, turn the corner, and stop dead. Aaack! There, in the hallway before me are Mom and Stanley. Her back is against the wall, and Stanley is pressed against her, their arms clutching, their eyes closed, their lips locked. A sucking noise is coming from their deep-throated kiss.

I'm frozen. I'm entirely caught off guard, unprepared, and repulsed. I never even noticed they left the dinner table. I want to scream, "Stop!" but I don't have a chance. Stanley peeks open one of his eyes, sees me, opens the other, then gently pulls away from Mom. She opens her eyes, looks at him disappointed, sees me, and jumps.

"Oh, Cookie!" She's startled and embarrassed. She detaches from him, smooths down her skirt, and pats down her hair. "I didn't see you there."

"Didn't expect to see you there either," I say as I quickly squeeze past them down the hall. My eyes focus entirely on the bathroom door at the end of the corridor: safety.

I pull the bathroom door closed behind me, lock it, lean up against it. Uggg! A frightening thought flashes across my mind. Are they having sex? Oh, God. They must be. Why haven't I thought of this before? I have; I just repressed it. Ick! Mom and Stanley in bed together. I might be sick. Here comes a splitting headache. He must have some aspirin. I reach for the medicine cabinet, then quickly recoil. What if I see something in there I don't want to? Condoms? Would they use condoms? Of course not. They're too old for that. But what if they did? No, they can't. Am I going to need to talk to her about STDs, safe sex, and family planning? No, that's ridiculous. Family planning? Please, Daniella, get a grip! It's more likely he'd have Viagra in here, and she, a vial of her menopause medication.

Then, with all the drama and anticipation that might accompany a trip to a minefield, I brace myself, take a deep breath, reach for the medicine cabinet, and slide open the cabinet door. There! Before my eyes, all kinds of things: nose hair clippers, Pepto-Bismol, Tums, and a bottle of hair coloring. It's a beautiful sight. I never thought I'd be so happy to see a bottle of Mom's L'Oreal Brazilian Brown hair color. Emboldened and encouraged, I slide open the other side of the cabinet: Band-Aids, cold syrup, and a prized bottle of aspirin. I exhale.

I finally regain my composure enough to leave the bathroom and reenter the Thanksgiving dinner circus. Just as I'm about to sit down at the table, Erica turns to me, gets up, and says, "Come on, let me show you something."

Great. Whatever she's got to show me under a microscope, I'm pretty sure I don't want to see it. I politely follow. It's too early in our relationship for me to dish out attitude.

We clear dishes, then she smiles and motions for me to follow her into her childhood bedroom. She opens the white door and walks straight across the rose-colored carpet to the far corner of the room where she drops down on her knees in front of a dollhouse.

It's a magnificently crafted nine-room dollhouse that goes up just as high as my hips. I sit down Indian style on the carpet next to her. The dollhouse is a light-colored wood. The eaves on the roof have delicately hand-carved interlocking, swirling, S shapes cut out. There are miniature Tiffany-style lampshades hanging in each room, and inch-high Impressionist-style framed paintings on the walls. The furniture inside, in girly pastel shades, has been carefully hand-painted. A miniature man and woman stand at the kitchen sink, and a little girl doll sits in the toy room upstairs, playing with an even smaller dollhouse.

"It's beautiful," I say.

"Yeah. It was a family project. Dad helped with construction and electricity. Mom helped with decorating," she says wistfully. "Did you have a dollhouse?"

"Yeah. You could say mine was a family project, too," I answer.

We are both silent. I'm thinking about Dad. She's probably thinking about her mom. We give ourselves time to swallow our emergent tears.

"What does your house look like?" she asks.

"A lot like this. Just tinier," I answer. "I have the same copper pots and pans in the kitchen, a similar crib in the bedroom. But mine has some toys for boys in it, too: like mini trains and cars."

She flicks a miniswitch and poof, the lamp in each room of the dollhouse is illuminated.

"Dad insisted on giving this family all the amenities it would need, especially the electricity. That's the stubborn engineer coming out in him," she says. "Took him forever to do the whole circuit. Messing around with those microscopic electric wires almost sent him over the edge. I'm surprised he didn't install a garbage disposal."

We laugh.

Then she says, "I wish playing house as a child would have prepped me better for the real world." She repositions the man and woman to sit at the kitchen table.

We are quiet. Just as the silence is about to get awkward, she perks up and says, "And why aren't guys in real life as sweet, simple, and obedient as the boy dolls always were?"

"I've wondered the same thing myself," I answer. "Once, I got set up with a guy who looked just like a Ken doll. Problem was, he had the brain of a Ken doll, too."

Erica nods knowingly and bam! We connect. We're off, recounting worst date stories, dashed hope stories, and current possibilities. Turns out she does have a boyfriend back at the lab. "But it's still in the experimental stage." She laughs.

We marvel at how our parents found love not once, but twice, and wonder whether we'll be able to follow their example.

Fourteen

As if making it through the drama of Thanksgiving *à la nou-velle famille* (sounds like a new kind of French dinner dish) wasn't enough, on the way out of Stanley's house that night, Enrico, who never talks about his personal life, asks me if we could have lunch privately the next day. I look at him as if he's nuts. He responds with a nervous laugh.

"It'll be tough." I put out my hands and count off on my fingers. "I've got to help Mom with the music, dessert, flowers, and invitations. I'd love to, but I'm not here in California for very long, and you know how possessive Mom gets when I'm in town, always trying to squeeze in more time with me."

Enrico gives me a rare, serious look.

"It's important," he says. "Breakfast? My treat?"

"Okay, okay," I give in. "I'll work something out."

He smiles, relieved. "Thanks. Gotta run. See you in the A.M.!" He hops in Max's electric car, and they buzz off.

Weird. What does he need to talk about so urgently? Mom's marriage? His girlfriend Leslie? Are they breaking up? Is she pregnant? Are they getting married?

No time to worry. Mom's already whisking me back to her house in her car and yammering away about the busy day she has planned for us tomorrow. We have to swing by the stationer and approve the invitations, we've got a noon appointment with the pastry chef, and a three o'clock with the florist. All this plus post–Thanksgiving Day traffic, and Mom trying to be punctual. Sounds like fun.

"I scheduled it all in one day so we could do it together," she says.

"Sounds fine," I answer. "I'm just going to have breakfast with Enrico first, okay?"

She shoots me a suspicious look, then darts her eyes back to the road.

"I have no idea what it's about," I respond defensively.

"Just be ready to go to the city at nine-thirty, sharp," she insists.

Uh-oh. Mom is showing signs of turning into the scary creature I've heard about: a bridezilla.

At eight o'clock Friday morning, I'm seated across a rickety wood table from Enrico at one of Berkeley's small, hippie cafés. Enrico has a croissant and coffee, black. I've ordered a scone and mint tea, anticipating I will need calm, not caffeine, for the day ahead. Enrico makes nervous small talk. I smile along. What does he want to talk to me about? I have a potential bridezilla waiting back at the house, and I don't want to keep her too long.

Enrico senses my impatience.

"I'm a bit concerned about Mom's decision." He sounds

protective. "She's so vulnerable. I feel like this is all a bit rash, don't you?"

"Are you kidding me?" I ask.

"What?"

"She's bought the dress. We're shopping for her wedding cake and flowers this afternoon. She's practically living with him, and now you want to talk about this? Didn't we discuss this when they first got engaged?" I'm exasperated.

"Well, I feel different now."

"Look, from what I know of Stanley, it's not as if he's going to take advantage of her. And, anyway, we've already been over this. Enrico, there is nothing we can do about it. We've lost our window of opportunity to stop it. It's what she wants."

Enrico is easily convinced, which is entirely out of character. He usually puts up a fight until he wins, or until the other person is too tired to carry on with the argument.

"Well, if that's all, I'll be going now, can't keep a bride waiting." I lean over to get my bag.

"Uh, Dani?" Enrico asks timidly.

"Yeah?" I ask.

"There's something else." He's looking down.

"Speak, Brotha, speak!" I grow New York impatient.

"It's Leslie," he says.

I look at him questioningly. What about her? She's everything he's ever wanted in a girlfriend. She's charming, quick-witted, and cute. She's a politically active attorney who has exposed Enrico to a life outside of his lab that is more exciting than he ever imagined. Theater. Dance. Parties. She plays cello. She plays tennis. They've been dating for about six months. What's the question?

"What?" I tease. "Think you might make a big commitment soon? Like go for a weekend in Napa?"

Enrico smiles and loosens up.

"I'm just thinking things are going really well between us, and, well, we're thinking of making a big move," Enrico says.

Already? He wants to get married already? Don't we have enough to think about with Mom's wedding? And if that's what he's up to, he might as well just say it. I don't need a replay of the same oblique conversation I had with Mom a few months ago. Mom said she was doing "it" without saying what "it" was. Now Enrico's not even saying "it." Like mother, like son.

"I dunno. Whatcha talking about?" I play dumb.

"I'm, um, we're. Well, we've been . . . Leslie and I have been talking."

Fantastic! I have this super bright family that can convince anyone of almost anything, but is completely incapable of speech when it comes to articulating the *M* word. I nod to Enrico, encouraging him to keep trying with this one whole, big thought.

"Well," Enrico continues, "maybe commitment might be a good idea for us, too?"

I nod again. Stay silent.

"Why aren't you saying anything?" Enrico asks, exasperated.

"If you have any questions for Leslie, you're going to have to ask her, not me. You also might want to try and be a bit more committed and smooth in your delivery," I say.

"Yeah. Sure. Right," Enrico says dismissively. "But do you think it's a good idea?"

"Enrico, it's your life. I think it's great. But I don't know much about your relationship with Leslie. It's not like you tell me much. From what little I know, she's good news. And commitment's a good thing. Just think about all the good things Leslie could bring to the marriage. Heck, what Leslie could bring to the wedding."

Enrico is smiling more widely than my commentary merits.

"You wouldn't have to hire a musician for the wedding. She could be her own cellist," I say. "For that matter, she's a lawyer, maybe she could be her own justice of the peace." I laugh, knowing it's totally impossible but acting out the theatrics for Enrico anyway.

"*LESLIE: 'Do I, Leslie, wish to marry Enrico?'*
"*LESLIE: 'I do.'*
"*LESLIE: 'Do you, Enrico, wish to marry me, Leslie?'*
"*ENRICO: 'I do.'*
"*LESLIE: 'With the power vested in me by the state of California, I declare you and me, man and wife. You may kiss me now.'*"

Enrico is laughing too hard.

"It's not *that* funny," I tell Enrico.

"Yes it is," he says. "I'm not planning on getting married. Leslie and I are just thinking of moving in together."

"Huh?"

"Her lease is expiring, and we spend every night together. We might as well live together."

"Oh. Well, that sounds good. Why not? I like Leslie."

"But you had such a bad experience living with David."

"That doesn't mean it'll be bad for you. Everyone's different. I don't think you have anything to worry about."

"Really?"

"Really. Go for it. You have my blessing to live in sin."

"Thank you, saintly one," Enrico says.

"No problem. But I gotta go. Bridezilla's waiting."

"Thanks, Dani. Please don't say anything yet. We haven't decided for sure, and I don't want any unsolicited input from you know who."

"I won't tell Mom. Anyway, she has enough on her mind."

I get up to leave.

"Enrico?"

"Yes."

"Congratulations. I'm impressed."

"Thanks."

Minutes later, I'm in the car, racing to meet Mom. I'm honored that Enrico used me as a sounding board about Leslie. It's nice to have the trust of someone who is so intensely private. I'm happy for him but slip back into that familiar territory of feeling sorry for myself. Even if Enrico's only talking about moving in together, marriage will obviously be the next step. What if Enrico and Mom get married within the year? Just get my twenty-two-year-old brother engaged, too, and I'll feel like a complete failure. Then I'll be talking commitment, too, but maybe to an institution not a person.

I pull up in front of Mom's house, and she's already outside waiting. Her knuckles rap on the trunk as I try to park. She motions frantically for me to pop the trunk, as if there's a living being inside the trunk that needs out.

I pull the lever to unlock the trunk and get out of the car. I feel her high energy field as I approach. I give her a quick hug, help her put her things in the trunk, and return to the pilot seat for buckle up and liftoff. This is going to be quite a journey.

"Oh, Cookie. I'm so excited you're here." She slams the passenger door shut with unnecessary verve. "This is going to be SO great! Another mother-daughter adventure! We're going to take MLK to 80 then over the bridge and off on Front Street. What did Enrico have to say? We have so much to do today. We have to stop and get gas. Cookie. Why are you wearing black again?"

No need to answer, I know she'll keep talking to herself anyway. She immediately starts digging through her purse. "Dani. I have to take advantage of every minute with you. So, I brought a few wedding band tapes along. Klezmer music. They sound like my favorite groups, Oi-Va-Voi and the Klezmatics, but different. Do you mind listening? You can help me choose. Do you like klezmer music? I can't remember which one of you kids hated it."

That'd be me.

She pops a tape into the car stereo, and out pours a frenzied, upbeat melody of a clarinet with an accordion groaning, squeezing, and pulling in the background. I'm trying to focus on the road and keep the dissonant sounds from distracting me. Can the California Highway Patrol ticket me for "unsafe driving due to annoying passenger requests and irritating music"?

A violin pulls in tune with the melody, and a xylophone keeps tempo.

"The name of this band is Goldie's Yiddish Simcha band. I love them. Stan isn't such a fan, though. What do you think?"

I bite my tongue. To Mom these are the soulful sounds of our heritage, but to me it sounds like an elephant with a stomach disorder.

"I heard this great band in Chicago . . ." I start to recommend Big Rick and the Dyno-mites, and then stop myself. I remember my excruciating vision of sixty-year-old guests playing air guitars.

"Dani," I can hear in her tone she's already switching subjects. "I was talking with some girlfriends about your situation. We think we might have someone for you. Dinah's daughter's husband has a friend. He's a very accomplished doctor. At least that's what Dinah's son-in-law says. Only thing is, he lives in Washington. But we could probably arrange a meeting. And oh yeah, there's this other lovely man. He's a physicist. Works with Erica. He was over to dinner the other night at Stanley's with his girlfriend."

I interrupt. "With his girlfriend? You want to set me up with someone who has a girlfriend?"

"No. It's not like that. It's just that he reminded me of Stanley and was very sweet and smart," Mom backpedals.

Even better. Mom trying to set me up with a guy who reminds her of Stanley, but younger and with a girlfriend. Perfect-o.

She pops in another tape.

"Do you think this music works?"

I nod. "Better." Anything is better than discussing her arrangements for my betrothal.

"Oh, and I had another idea that my friend Jeannie told me about. Have you ever heard of that Web site J-Date? It's a Jewish singles Web site." An accordion groans.

Have I ever heard of J-Date? I've heard so many nightmares about that one Web site that I've sworn never to visit. One friend of mine met a guy through J-Date who thought because she was wearing a choker he should choke her. Another friend of mine kissed a guy she met on J-Date, to which he responded, "G'night Mom." That same friend was going to give up on J–Date but couldn't resist meeting one man with an incredible online profile. Turns out, he had stolen the profile, in its entirety, from another man.

"So," Mom continues, "my friend Jeannie logged onto J–Date for her daughter and started to pick out men for Elana. I thought maybe that was a little over-the-top, you know? Getting involved in her daughter's life a bit too much. Sending those men e-mails. But Elana wasn't doing enough to get herself out there. Shy girl. Anyway, so Jeannie played matchmaker for her own daughter online, and now Elana's gone out on three different dates! Pretty good, no?"

"No." Terrifying is what that is. I would rather join a convent than have my mom trolling ads on J-Date for me. I can just see it now:

MOM: *"Cookie! Look at this one. How about Ezra Silverman? Nice looking. From New Jersey, chemical engineer. Oh! And look, interests: acting and klezmer music."*

ME: *"He's six inches shorter than I am, and he weighs less than I do. It'll never work."*

MOM: *"Oh, Daniella, never say never. You should at least meet him. That wouldn't kill you, now would it?"*

ME: *"Possibly."*

"Where is the stationer?" I ask, trying to drive the conversation back to her wedding, not mine. I know she's just trying to help.

Within two hours, we've made it to the city, approved the invitations, picked out LOVE stamps at the post office, and looked at wineglasses for the ceremony. I'm tired and hungry.

"Now, it's time to get down to business, no goofing off," Mom says. "Onwards to Chez Josephine." Josephine is the pastry chef, and there's a lot of pressure on us to perform well at her shop. Our reputation is riding on it.

Here's the story. When it comes to culinary questions, Mom has a pretty spotty track record, and I follow in her footsteps. Mom has always had great contempt for anything related to cooking or kitchen. In fact, for the first ten years of my life, the running joke in the family was, "Yummmm, it smells good! The neighbors must be cooking."

Then one night, when I was about eleven years old, things changed. Dad returned from a scrumptious, food-filled trip to Italy with an agenda. He marched through the swinging door into our Texas kitchen with a cowboy swagger and ousted Mom from her spot before the stove. He pointed at the still swaying door and said, "Woman, out of the kitchen!" Mom was thrilled. That night, he took charge of dinner heroically, delectably, creatively, and enthusiastically. And from then on, the family meal at my house was forever changed. Dad reigned chief chef. Mom encouraged Dad, always hoping to extend her kitchen expulsion, never asking to be repatriated.

This left her utterly unprepared for Stanley and his passion for food and cooking. He took haute cuisine to a higher level and insisted on sharing his enthusiasm for the culinary arts with Mom. He refused to accept her food ambivalence. He cooked for her. Took her to fancy restaurants. Gave her "fun" jobs to do in the kitchen. He was relentless. He wanted her to enjoy food, and he decided if only she learned more and ate more, she would. Stanley fed her and fed her until she finally acquiesced. Now she knows *French Laundry* from *Chez Panisse* and her cheese grater from her mandoline. Still, you would never mistake her for a culinary aficionado.

As you might imagine, finding the right food for the wedding was a prized project for Stanley. He saw it as "fun" and "a great opportunity" for Mom to learn about fine cuisine. So, since the engagement, Mom and Stanley have been spending their weekends on a never-ending circuit of wedding banquet tastings: debating the subtle differences between this dill sauce and that dill sauce for the salmon. Or is the lemon-caper sauce better? And would a lime-cilantro vinaigrette on the salad make the meal too citrusy?

Despite her questionable taste in food, Mom has one undeniable strength: the sweet spot. For everything she doesn't know or appreciate about appetizers and main courses, she does have an inarguably strong instinct when it comes to cakes, cookies, and desserts. Mom proved her mettle when she introduced Stanley to her all-time favorite pain au chocolat from Chez Josephine.

"I've never had a chocolate croissant this good outside of France!" he said, impressed that she had discovered such a treasure. So, when it came to choosing a wedding cake, Stanley deferred to Mom's proven strength in sweets and superior aesthetic eye.

Mom and I pull up and park in a spot next to a Dumpster, behind Chez Josephine.

"Josephine only tells her favorite clients about this parking spot," Mom says proudly.

We enter through the back kitchen entrance. The smell of baking butter and cocoa lures us inside. There are three cake makers in the cramped, warm kitchen. Two men and one woman. One of the men is meticulously placing and spacing raspberries around the perimeter of a round cake, as if putting numbers on a clock. The other man, wearing black-and-white checkered ballooning pants and a red bandana on his head like a pirate, is dusting cocoa on top of what looks like a tiramisu. The woman has her head in a refrigerator.

"Bonjour, mes amis!" Mom greets the bakers in her impeccable French accent. They all look up from what they are doing to welcome us. *"Bonjour!"* they respond.

Josephine, a tiny Vietnamese woman, pulls her head out of the refrigerator and comes over to us, dusting her hands on her white apron. She glances my way and then leans in, gives Mom a kiss-kiss; this cheek, then that one. Mom introduces me to Josephine, who responds, *"Enchantée,"* and motions for us to follow her to the front of the bakery.

There, in the midday light, on the scuffed hardwood floors, there are dozens of exquisite French pastries and cakes in glass display cases. It's dreamy. Fruit tarts with concentric circles of divine glossy raspberries, blueberries, and strawberries. Mille feuilles with light, airy, crispy pastry dough dividing the smooth cream. Crème brulée with fragile, glasslike, caramel-transparent coating. We can't go wrong here. Not possible. Mom has my unconditional support in this department, whatever she chooses.

To the side, in a standing glass refrigerator, I see what we came for: towering sculptures of wedding cakes. One cake looks like smooth vanilla gift boxes stacked in a helix. Another consists of three circular cakes in tiers with brightly colored icing flowers blanketing the top of each cake. A third cake has a smooth, wide, rectangular cheesecake base with increasingly smaller rectangular blocks building up into an Aztec-like pyramid. They are all lovely.

Behind me, I look at Mom, who is busy chatting away in French with Josephine about the number of people on the guest list and whether cheesecake or chocolate cake is more appropriate. Mom makes eye contact with me and motions me over to sit down at the only table in the tiny bakery. It's a round, two-person, tiled café table with two white china dishes on it. Time for tastings.

In front of me and Mom are twin plates, each artfully prepared with half a dozen different sample wedges of cakes fanned out in a semicircle around the upper perimeter of the dish. A shiny, tiny silver spoon at the bottom of each plate looks as if it were set there as the handle of a fan.

The cakes range from the simplest white cake at three o'clock to a cheesecake-tiramisu at midnight, to a rich chocolate raspberry mousse cake at nine o'clock. We start with the white cake, which is light with a subtle vanilla flavor. Josephine stands over us, watching us. I fear she wants to have a detailed conversation about the ingredients in each cake, its preparation method, and its aesthetic merits. But Mom and I are not interested in discussing the specifics of each cake. We're too consumed with their tastes. And it helps that we came hungry.

As we approach the tiramisu, the flavors get increasingly rich. By the time we reach the raspberry mousse, we are both deep in a sugar buzz bliss. The indulgence of it all! Mom tries to maintain her composure and focus on the mission at hand, but an occasional giggle squeaks out. Her words from earlier, "our reputation," "no goofing" keep repeating in my head. Josephine can't see what's worth giggling about anyway, which makes our efforts to suppress the laughter even more difficult. I can see the edges of Mom's lips are turning up and quivering. The heavy creams melt and evaporate in our mouths. I'm transcending into an alterative, sweet, universe. Or, I'm just hungry after my morning adventures.

I must think about heavy, depressing things in order to stave off the sugar giggles. Here's something scary: maybe Mom and Stanley will make a big mortifying cake-cutting scene.

Hand over hand, they'll hold the shiny, silver cake server. Stop. Kiss for the picture. Click. Cut more cake. Stop. Smile at the camera. Click. Shove cake at each other, smile, camera click. Smear white icing and raspberry coulis all over each others' faces. Click, click. Icing in the hair. Click! The photographer gets overly enthusiastic with cake shots. Photographer encourages Stanley to lick the icing off Mom's face.

Yuck! Even pictures taken of the youngest, daintiest newlyweds doing that cake ritual look stupid. Unfortunately, those kinds of pictures do not improve with age(ing) newlyweds. I should relax. Mom and Stanley are way too old for games like that. Or are they? Frosting smothered all over Mom's face? Messing up her lipstick? Pictures of it? No way. More likely they'll put nice, bitc-sized pieces of cake on the end of silver forks and, in the most dignified way, feed it to each other, arms interlocked. I can live with that.

"So, what do you zeenk?" Josephine asks us.

"Mmmmmm," Mom and I say in sync, a dumb, giddy, happy smile on our faces.

"Good. *Très bien.* Now zee pastries. Vincent? Vincent! Could you pleaze bring out zee pastry dishes?"

Mom and I look at each other alarmed. More sweets? If we eat any more sugar, we may turn into diabetics. But when Vincent puts another twin set of plates fanned out with minia-ture pastries in front of us, we melt again, and miraculously, we make more room in our stomachs for them. We're defenseless. These pastries hit our soft sweet spot in a big way. Each dish has a mini everything: an éclair, a fruit tart, a napoleon, a crème brulée, a mille feuille, a lemon tart, a brownie. The petit fours are delicate, flavorful, and refined without being too heavy or too creamy. I'm a sucker for the napoleon and the fruit tart. Mom is gaga over the crème brulée and the éclair. Mom and I smile at each other and start giggling again. Not only have we shown our aptitude for gluttony, but it's been our job to pig out. We're like children with our hands in a bottomless cookie jar. Josephine can't see the humor in any of this.

I stand up, fearing there may be more sweets coming. I'm also afraid that if I look at Mom again, I might break out into an uncontrollable laughing fit. I pace around the café, reinspecting the cake and pastry offerings in the display cases. Mom chatters away with Josephine. Turns out that Josephine's sister, Claudine, has a catering service in the South Bay near Stanley's house.

I admire the cakes. They are so gorgeous and so delicious! But something's missing; I just can't quite figure out what.

"Why do you look so perplexed, *ma chère?*" Mom asks me.

"Oh nothing." I wave it off. "It's just. Oh nothing."

"What?" Mom persists.

"Okay, well, I feel like there's something missing from the cakes, and I don't know what it is."

Josephine dusts off her hands on her apron and carefully pulls open a drawer beneath the counter.

"Voilà!" she pronounces. "Noseeng iz misseeng! *Rien ne manque.* Ere are zee cake topperz."

Mom and I bend over and look inside. There, lying on their backs, lined up neatly next to each other on a bed of cushioned purple velvet, are dozens of miniature brides and grooms, destined one day to stand in regal pairs atop a tiered wedding cake. The little clay sculptures come in all shapes and sizes. Some are three inches tall. Other couples are five inches tall. And, this being San Francisco, there are figurines of two men in tuxedos holding hands. Two women kiss like winged angels in flowing dresses. There are black couples. Asian couples. Mixed couples. There is one bald groom wearing a Scottish kilt and argyle knee socks; his bride is a hula woman complete with bikini and grass skirt. I look at Mom and smile. She's speechless. There's even a dog figurine wearing a tuxedo.

I snatch one of the brides out of the drawer.

"Ne touchez pas!" Josephine cries out.

Too late, the bride's head falls off her shoulders and shatters on the floor under the counter.

Josephine shrieks.

"Oh my God she's lost her head!" I apologize.

Mom bursts out in uncontrollable laughter.

I look at Mom. I look at the headless bride in my hand, and I fall into the fit of laughter that's been building up for the past hour. Mom's crying and snorting. I try to collect pieces of the bride's head as I convulse in laughter.

Rigid Josephine even cracks a smile.

One of the chefs comes from the kitchen to the front.

"What's going on?" He smiles.

"The bride's cracked!" Mom squeals.

The chef shrugs, swats his hand forward, "We see that all the time!"

"Like this?" I wildly shake the headless bride in his face.

"Hey!" Josephine admonishes me. "Zey are very fragile dolls. Be careful."

Josephine, in her nervous way, wipes off her hands on her apron again and takes a deep breath. She takes the headless bride, thrusts it back into the drawer, and scolds me, "Forget zee head. I can put zee head back togezer later. But, you should know, zeez leetle statues are made by a famous sculptor in Marin County."

Mom and I try to focus. We don't look at each other for fear of another fit of laughter.

"Zee way he works iz, you zend him a picture of zee happy couple, and he makes a leetle one to put on top of zee cake." I can see the figurines of Mom and Stanley already. She with her curly, perfectly coiffed, light-brown hair. Holding a cell phone. He with a shock of silver gray hair and a bulging belly holding a spatula. It might be funny, but somehow, I have faith Mom and Stanley won't go for these cake toppers. They want people to laugh with them, not at them.

"What do you zeenk?" Josephine prompts. "Zee ozer alternative is to have another cake artist here in town make marzipan cake topperz."

Thanks, but no thanks. I don't really want to bite a bride's head off for dessert. Well, on second thought, it depends on the bride's behavior, really.

"*Je dois discuter les minisculptures avec mon Stanley,*" Mom answers. She must discuss it with Stanley. Mom turns her back to the sculptures and returns to oohing and aahing over the pastries and cakes. Mom can't figure out how to react to the tacky figurines without offending Josephine.

We head back toward the kitchen. Nothing has been ordered, but Mom really likes the chocolate-raspberry mousse cake and the idea of an assortment of pastries.

"I'd order now," Mom explains, "but I want Stanley's input. And, anyway, I want to meet your sister Claudine. I want to try her catering. Maybe we can have a sisters' team at the wedding."

"*Bien sûr*, of course," Josephine says, but she's peeved, obviously put off by our behavior. "We do weddings togezer all zee time. Maybe I can give you a discount." Josephine wipes her hands on her apron, hands Mom her card with Claudine's number written on the back, and the other pastry chefs nod good-bye to us.

Once in the car, Mom says, "Those figurines make me not want cake at the wedding."

"Don't worry. They weren't made for you anyway," I say. "I didn't see any couples in the drawer your age, did you?"

Mom warns me that the florist is eccentric with the potential to be prickly.

"Be careful about what you say to him, and be open-minded. He's extremely talented," she promises. "Just give him a chance."

We push open the glass door into the shop. Chimes tinkle.

It's a mellow place. Small. Narrow. Chilly. Fragrant. And, yes, the floral arrangements are extraordinary. The florist obviously has a distinct flair for mixing tropical flowers with bold, bright classics like roses and tulips. The exotic orchids he's cultivated at the entrance of the store are delicate, graceful.

"Fernando, hello? It's me, Maya," Mom announces her arrival.

Fernando pops out from behind a huge vase, clippers raised in the air.

"Maya. Aren't you just gorgeous today?" He stops and admires her. "You don't look a day over thirty."

Fernando is what comes to mind when people try to stereotype San Francisco's gay scene. He's pretty. He's flamboyant. He's eccentric. He's close to forty years old. He's wearing a shimmery purple shirt and slim black pants which highlight his sculpted body. He walks over with a limp wrist and looks me over.

"And this must be your daughter, Daniella. Or is it the other way around? ha-ha-ha. Ha-choo," he sneezes.

"Bless you. Nice to meet you, Fernando," I say.

"Thank you," he says dabbing his nose with a tissue. "I just think it's so adorable that your mom's getting married again, don't you? We don't see that too often. Just lots of high-maintenance first-time brides. You know, the Marina crowd? Ha-choo. Anyway. It's so great to work with an adult for once."

"Bless you," Mom says.

He looks me up and down again. I'm wearing boring black pants and a black turtleneck. "And what magnificent creative style *your mother* has."

Obviously, the sneezy Fernando thinks that as long as he flatters my mother, he risks nothing by insulting me. He's probably registered that I'm not wearing an engagement ring and therefore won't be dumping bags of money on his doorstep any time soon.

"Anyway, what are we doing here today, Maya? I just love that name." He grabs Mom's elbow and leads her deeper into the store. "We decided on the gerber daisies, right?" He wriggles his nose, holding back a sneeze.

"Right," Mom says. "I just wanted to get Daniella's approval and ideas on what we have planned."

"Okay, let's take a look." He grabs an enormous, heavy, midnight blue glass vase. He puts it on a worktable, and starts his art.

"The arrangement is about gerber daisies. That's what Maya wants. So we're ordering these gerbers from Southern California. Ha-choo! My pollen allergies get worse and worse every year. Anyway, I always like using local flowers. I love these bold colors for the gerbers: a nice fuschia, sunflower yellow, orange, red." He expertly stabs six different-colored gerbers into the green styrofoamy sponge at the bottom of the vase. "Then I recommend we mix up the bunch with some roses, all a bold red." He wriggles six roses into the green sponge. "See, now we have some uniformity."

I feel like I'm a student in a flower arrangement class.

He adds sunflowers and lilies.

"I thought you only wanted gerbers," I whisper to Mom.

Fernando shoots me a dirty look.

"Now, we need some fern leaves and more roses," he continues.

"Mom, don't you want to say something? Have him slow down?" I ask.

"If you have something to say, why don't you share it with the class?" Fernando chides me. His eyes are watering.

"Oh, I'm sorry." I lower my head in apology.

"So," he continues. "A few more daisies and some drooping ivy."

"Mom . . ." I nudge her. "Speak up, don't you want something simpler?"

Fernando looks straight at me, his tongue bulging against the inside of his cheek.

I smile at him, trying to recover from my interruption.

With a deep sigh, he continues to work.

I sneeze.

He glares at me. "Would you like to come back at another time?" he asks, exasperated.

"No, no. Please," I say.

He gives me a big, nasty, fake grin. I freeze and shut up and don't dare utter a peep until he's done, and an enormous, bright, mixed bouquet is towering in front of us.

"Something like that?" he asks, quite satisfied with his work.

"Yes," Mom responds, awed. "That's certainly original! Makes a big statement!"

I nod. It is a masterpiece in floral design. It's so striking in fact, a guest might miss the bride for the flowers. It's not at all what Mom had in mind. What she described to me was a subtle mix of pastel peachy pink orange gerber daises mixed in with some papyrus. A hint of baby's breath. That's it. No roses, no lilies, no ferns. Mom wants something simpler. This arrangement may be spectacular, but I'm sure it's ten times more expensive than what Mom had in mind.

"Fernando," Mom asks, pulling out her new digital camera, "do you mind if I take a picture of the arrangement? That way I can show Stan what you created? See what he thinks?"

Fernando hesitates, dabs his nose and eyes, then nods, standing proudly next to his arrangement.

Mom nudges me to go stand on the other side of the arrangement for the picture. Despite her new digital camera, she's still of the old "film" school, and can't waste a picture or pass up an opportunity to take a shot of one of her kids.

We both force a smile, obliging for the bride. Click. Mom has a quick conversation about how many tables there will be at the reception, how many arrangements, how much it will cost, and then we're done. On the way out, Mom looks back, waves, and says, "We'll call to make arrangements! Ha-ha." A not so funny pun to polish off the day.

In the car on the way home, Mom asks me what I thought of the arrangement.

"Well, it's quite, as you said . . . it well . . . It makes a big statement." I don't want to be critical.

Mom prods, "I know it makes a big statement, but do you like it?"

"Well, I don't think it's exactly what you had in mind. Didn't you just want two kinds of flowers? Could hardly see the gerber daisies with all the other flowers around. Seems like he's trying to get you to sign on for something that's more over-the-top and expensive than you planned. How much is it?"

Mom looks at me as if I've just cracked a secret code.

"Oh. I guess he never really gave me a firm price."

"Mom!" I can't believe her sometimes. "It's business, not friendship!"

"I hadn't really thought about it that way," she says. "I thought it just looked so nice. And the way he suffers from those flower allergies. It's awful!"

While she mulls, I think about Fernando's place. The orchids, delicate and simple, were easily the most beautiful flowers in the store. Refined, graceful. Each petal and branch seemed so deliberate. Like each stalk grew, trying to anticipate what its admirer would want to see. One potted orchid would be a stunning centerpiece for tables at my wedding. Just white.

Wow. This may well be the first time I've consciously thought about what I would want at my wedding. I've been so focused on finding the right guy, I haven't bothered to think about wedding party planning. Is there something wrong with me? I bet the wedding marketers of America would say, "Yes, there is something terribly wrong with her." The marketers would prefer that young girls start developing their wedding lust from the moment we can utter the words "I do." They want our desires for a fairy-tale wedding to be as strong as our pining for true love. And they hope that by the time girls are old enough to tie the knot, we will bring lifelong yearnings for wedding day frills to the altar; saying yes not only to the groom, but yes to the more expensive wedding dress, yes to the more elaborate floral arrangements, and yes, let it be top-of-the line everything! Can't skimp on the happiest day of your life!

If the wedding marketers were smart, they'd conspire with divorce facilitating industries (like the alcohol and sex industry) to break up marriages. That way, one woman would get married multiple times and spend for the happiest day of her life more than once.

One friend of mine was so influenced by the marketers that she bought her wedding dress years before she found a groom. She then had to hurry to find a groom before the dress went out of style. "I've got the dress, now I just need to find a groom to go with it! C'mon girls, let's go man shopping!"

Another guy I know bought his wedding bands and engagement ring years before finding a fiancée. He kept looking for a woman's finger to fit his ring.

Well, the marketers missed me. I've never even had a vision of my wedding. To me, musing about my wedding without having a fiancé is like going to a PTA meeting without having a child. I've never wanted to dress up like a typical princess bride. Not even when I was a child. For Halloween, I dressed up like a witch. Mom dressed up as a gypsy.

My parents never suggested that a big wedding should be a life goal. Sure, Mom and Dad encouraged us kids to strive for good, solid, loving relationships. Sure, we were raised to believe in marriage. But a big, white wedding? It didn't even hit the radar screen. "Life is full of more important things than a big party," was the message. Now, though, the message has shifted. "A big party is an important part of celebrating life." But the change in the message did not happen overnight.

At the beginning, Mom's bride-self poked her head out timidly. A few weeks after the announcement, Mom hinted to Stanley that it might be fun to have a big wedding.

"It could be fun, but would it be tacky for a widowed couple of our age to be celebrating like young people? What would people think?" Mom asked.

"People would be thrilled. It would be fun for everyone," he answered. "There's nothing tacky about it. What's the alternative? Go get married quietly and alone as if we've got something to hide?"

"But it's such a frivolous waste of money," she argued.

"And what exactly do you want to spend your money on now? You've bought a house . . . a few times. You've sent your kids to college. Now is the time to spend on us!"

"But we're semiretired," she protested.

"All the more reason," he said. "We have the time to celebrate."

"But, aren't we too old for these games?" she doubted.

"Maya," he said calmly, deliberately. "Last spring we went to a handful of weddings, right? And the brides and grooms weren't all spring chickens, now were they? Second weddings for our generation are mainstream by now. We just want to celebrate our marriage with our friends and family. No need to overthink it."

Mom still wasn't convinced.

"Well, I'll tell you one thing," he said. "If we're going to have a wedding, we're going to do it right. Down to the icing on the cake."

Mom finally came around to accepting the notion of indulging in a big wedding. She justified her decision by asking, "How often in life do you get to celebrate, I mean really celebrate?" She repeated this question so many times that eventually her repressed inner-girl bride let loose in full glory.

Fifteen

"I've got five minutes free, let's go," Jackie, another reporter for BizNews, says as she pokes her head into our broadcast booth at the NYSE.

"Okay, let's go." I push my chair and keyboard back.

We walk quickly to our spot on the balcony overlooking the NYSE testosterone pit. We come here between market updates and CEO interviews to deconstruct guys the way we would any good story. We review our conversations with men, pluck out the most salient sound bites, and try and make sense of the rest.

Jackie is a petite blond whippersnapper of a reporter with an acuity for finance that makes even the sharpest Wall Street men stumble over their words. She divorced her husband a few years back when she says he "failed to meet performance expectations." Jackie is a woman of action, impatient with anything less than the best.

"So?" she prods.

"It's Ruben," I tell her. "I'm kind of on the fence about him. He is so sweet and well-meaning, but his blue moods are really getting me down."

She nods.

"I just got back from California," I continue, "and watching my mom and Stanley together—they just seem so perfect for each other."

Jackie's eyes are locked on the floor of the Exchange, watching the men hum around like flies. She lifts her gaze and looks me hard in the eye.

"If Ruben were a stock, would you invest in him?" she asks.

"Uh . . ."

"Look. I've been tracking his performance. Sometimes he does well, but sometimes he's a big loser," she says. "Overall, you're able to maintain your initial investment, but are you seeing strong returns? Daniella, you need to invest in your future. How long have you been with him? Three months? Four months? Can't waste time with stocks that might cost you in the long run."

"But . . ."

"I've heard this kind of doubt from you before," she continues. "Either believe in him fully or cut your losses. Can't be wishy-washy."

"Yeah, but . . ."

"There are plenty of other guys out there. Look at me," she gives her blond hair a quick flip. "I'm booked solid this week. I've got three different dates this week: an M.D., a VC, and a Ph.D. It's just like the market, so many stocks to choose from. And not just one can reap rewards. There are plenty of winners out there."

"I guess so," I say.

"You know Ruben's fundamentals. You know his board of directors, you know his operating budget, you know his weaknesses and you know his areas for growth. Is he a growth guy, or has he already peaked?"

I know the answers, but I don't want to admit or accept them. I've invested a lot in him, and I can't quantify my emotions for him on a balance sheet.

"It's hard, Daniella. I know. But look at the bright side; there are so many other options out there. There are so many options right here," and she sweeps her arm from left to right, indicating the traders swarming on the floor.

"It's just so hard to give up, you know?" I say.

"Yes, but if you want a powerful merger, both partners have to be strong." She smiles, spins around, and leaves for her next update.

"Thanks," I call after her as she clicks in her heels back to the booth. She waves back at me without turning around.

She means business when it comes to relationships. And ever since her divorce, she's been flipping men like a day trader flips stocks. She's getting some short-term rewards, but what about long-term gains? Isn't that what we all want?

I don't have time to mull it over. I've got to rush over to Attorney General Eliot Spitzer's office for a press conference. But I hesitate. I take a good look at the men scurrying around the floor. Maybe I've been too hasty in dismissing the whole lot. There are so many of them. Maybe Jackie is right. At least one of these guys must be nice, intelligent, witty, and good for me. Right?

Doubt it. I know these guys. They're fun and quick, but they aren't my type. Too macho. Too money hungry. None too sophisticated. Odds are they'd be a bad bet for me. I dash out of the

Stock Exchange. I'm just not ready to call it quits with Ruben yet; I've invested too much, and the alternatives are bleak.

As I walk over to Spitzer's office, I justify my decision to stay with Ruben by reminding myself how much the single life stinks. Dating involves entirely too much time, energy, and disappointment. I've met so many men who are less than impressive. Just consider the gadget guys: Matt, Joey, and the Aussie.

I met Matt one warm, summer evening. I was with a group of friends having a picnic at an outdoor concert in Central Park. We spread out on blankets, sharing wine, cheese, the last rays of sun. Matt, a flirty redhead, asked to borrow my cell phone. I passed him my phone, then watched as he dialed a number, which made the black cell phone lying on the other side of his paper plate of cheese and grapes ring. He picked up the black phone, grinned at me, chuckled, "You don't mind if I save your number here into my phone"—he waved the black phone—"do you?"

"No, I don't mind," and I immediately saved his number in my cell phone under the name phonthief.

Then there was Joey the caterer. I met him at a bar one night where we were celebrating a friend's thirtieth birthday party. Joey, who had made the desserts for the party, had had a bit too much champagne. He was slurring—telling me a drawn-out version of his life story, with special details of his divorce, and the life story of each pastry he hand-crafted for the party. Another fruit tart story, and I excused myself to the bar to get a drink.

There, I saw an old friend, and we pulled out our palm pilots to beam each other our contact information. Joey the caterer came over, palm pilot in hand, and offered to beam me a list of New York's best restaurants. I accepted and reciprocated by beaming him a subway map. The next day, I found Joey's contact information and his bank account numbers in my palm pilot. Oh, temptation. All the geeky technology, cool clothes, and plane tickets I could buy with his mistake. But it hardly seemed worth it. I certainly didn't want to give him a reason to track me down. I deleted his information.

Then there was the tall, blond, charming Aussie. I melted when he spoke. Didn't matter what he said. His accent made him sound sexy and intelligent. I was entranced by his jewel-green eyes and his muscular forearms. I also enjoyed the occasional glimpse of his tight behind. All was well until he began sending text messages to my cell phone.

Beep-beep: *"got n-e time 2 c me l8r?"* he wrote.

At first, I was tickled by his clever one-liners. Cute. But cuter still if I heard him say it out loud.

"Yes, fcrse, wld luv 2 c u," I responded.

Then he grew more bold: beep-beep: *"U r l i need. Qt, I m ur mn."*

Good sense of humor. I encouraged it.

"sxy boy ur so fly, myt av 2 gve u a try," I sent a message back.

A few days and text messages later, I realized he wasn't trying to be funny. He was actually taking his poetry by phone seriously. Regretfully, the more he worked at it, the sillier, sappier, and more juvenile the messages became. And without the accent to assist the delivery, or the eyes to distract me from the message, I struggled to repress my laughter. Then, this came:

"sum luv 1,sum luv 2,i luv 1, n that sum1 is u"

I burst out laughing in the middle of the newsroom. Jackie grabbed for my phone, desperate to get a whiff of anything THAT funny. I clasped and rocked my cell phone close to my heart. The poor guy was so sincere! I couldn't show it. Although I really wanted to. The poor dear. It was bad enough that I was laughing at him, but to allow others to mock him would be just too cruel. This man thought himself a digital Shakespeare, a pioneer of prose. Eventually, the messages got so corny, I couldn't bring myself to read them any longer. When the Aussie realized his skills in virtual verse were unreciprocated, unappreciated, and unread, he set off to find someone who could grasp his true value.

"2 bad. Guess wznt bound 2 b. I lvd u, but u didn't c it n me" he wrote.

Ouch. Here we have all the technology in the world to help interpersonal communication, and yet the cell phone number thief, the palm pilot intruder, and the text message abuser ruin it.

For all their failings, the gadget guys amused me. They may have fumbled in their approach, but at least they were creative and imaginative. They were inventive, romantic, risk-takers who showed traces of IB. If I met these types, then I could probably meet other men who might show these IB qualities and (deliberately) make me laugh.

I arrive at New York State Attorney General Eliot Spitzer's press conference where a new, cute, male addition to the financial press corps signs in on the roster before me. In this new reporter, I see options, possibilities, excitement. Maybe I should give dating another shot. I could tell this new reporter how I went to a wedding where Spitzer was the best man. I could tell him how weird that whole wedding of power people was. We could laugh about the dry world of financial news. Maybe I need a break from Ruben. Maybe as Jackie said, I should cut my losses.

While the attorney general releases the latest news about another mutual fund investigation, I wonder how I should break the news of breaking up to Ruben. Should I tell him in a café? No. Too public. In my apartment? No, too private. The park? Possibly. But the bone-chilling temps aren't conducive to much discussion. Although, I could use the weather to my advantage.

The icy cold will prevent the painful conversation from lasting too long. Better to be brief, like these press conferences, so I don't get off message. I also must act fast before I lose my nerve.

That Saturday afternoon, Ruben and I are bundled and gloved walking through Central Park. My silence makes it obvious I have something to say.

"What is it, Daniella?" Ruben asks.

"Nothing," I answer, wanting desperately to chicken out.

"Come on, you don't just bring me here on a freezing winter day to tell me nothing. If there were nothing to say, we could be saying nothing in a warm place, cuddling inside."

He knows me. I love cuddling. I take a deep breath. The cold is sharp.

Ruben is silent, using the oldest reporter's trick in the world, knowing I'll talk if he doesn't.

"You know how much I care for you and admire you, Ruben," I say filling the silence. "I respect your ambitions. I love your charisma, your sense of humor. I love so much about you . . . But . . ."

Ruben is quiet.

"But, I feel like we're not the right fit long-term. You know. Sometimes things are just so rocky between us, and I feel like we're just on different paths—like this relationship shouldn't be so hard."

Ruben stops walking, and we face each other, standing next to a pond. He doesn't look surprised, but he's obviously disappointed. He looks at me and says, "I thought we were really growing together and could have a future together."

"I thought so, too. I really care for you. But there are too many disconnects. Between me and my job and you and your ambitions, we are growing more distant. Come on, you know it."

He nods.

My turn to be silent.

"Listen, Daniella, I think our relationship is good. I want to be in it. What can I do to make it better?"

I want to say, "Stop with the blue moods. Chase your dreams again. Rediscover that passion, that fire you used to have for living. You're bumming me out. Perk up for God's sake!"

But I don't say anything. I don't want to exacerbate the problem. He's already ashamed of his dark streak and work jealousies. The last thing I need to do is tell him to change it. And even if I did tell him, would he change? Could he?

"Nothing?" he asks.

I'm silent; I might cry.

"If you're unhappy, Daniella, and there's nothing I can do, it won't work. I know that much. I can't force it. I don't want to convince you to be in a relationship that isn't right. I wish you wouldn't end it like this, without giving me a chance to work on the problems that you see."

We're silent.

"Okay. Well that's really too bad," he says. "I'm going to miss you."

His maturity and compassion in responding to this breakup shows me he's more levelheaded than I gave him credit for. I might be wrong, but my instinct tells me I need a break.

I look at him. I don't say anything.

He stretches out his arms to hug me.

I fall into his solid embrace. I turn my face away from his so he can't see my eyes welling up. I'm going to miss this hug. I'm going to miss this security. I'm going to miss him. I pull myself away. We just stand there looking at each other, our eyes shining with tears. I can't say good-bye. Neither can he.

Finally, I say, "Talk to you later?"

He nods.

I hope he understands how hard this is. I want to say, "I really care for you, this really hurts." But I don't. Instead, we turn from each other and walk away separately, alone. I want to look back, but I resist.

Sixteen

Jackie is nodding that she's listening to me while she's looking at the computer and typing a script. I'm sitting at the Times Square office next to her, trying to tell her about the breakup with Ruben.

"The best way, to get over," she types a couple of words, "it," she gives me a quick glance, "is to get back in the market."

Her phone rings, she answers it with the headset on, her fingers still flying across the keyboard.

"BizNews, Jackie."

I study my cuticles.

She hangs up. "Diversify your portfolio, Daniella. Date lots of different kinds of guys and see which ones deliver," she says definitively and returns to her script.

That was sensitive, Jackie, thanks. She's not exactly subtle, but she's efficient. And she's right. That's what this whole breakup is about. It's about a chance to see if IB can become a reality.

On the way downtown to the New York Stock Exchange that afternoon, I try to squish into a packed subway car. A tall bald man inside the car with big brown eyes and a wide, warm smile pushes the crowd back half a step to make room for me. The doors slide shut, but the subway doesn't move. The edge of my bag is wedged between the doors, holding up the train. Together, we pull the bag into the car.

"Thank you," I say.

"My pleasure," he says in a deep voice and a foreign accent I can't place.

Diversify, Jackie's advice is fresh on my mind. So what if he's bald? He looks like he might be Jewish, and he's got nice manners. He's wearing a United Nations pass around his neck.

"You work at the UN?" I ask.

"Yeah, the Israeli consulate," he responds.

"Your accent doesn't sound Israeli," I say.

"I was born and raised in Italy."

Oh boy.

"My dad was born in Italy," I say. "I've spent a lot of time in Italy. And in Israel."

Five stops later, we've exchanged numbers.

"Great meeting you, Narciso." I smile and get off at the Wall Street stop.

Did I just meet IB? They always say you'll meet him when you least expect it. This is so serendipitous. What are the odds that we'd be on the same train, at the same time, in the same city? And just after I ended it with Ruben? I'm so hopeful.

Narciso does call, and a few nights later we go out for Japanese-Italian food. Over dinner, he's undeniably charming, accomplished, and intelligent. I think my search is over. He's a bit skinny, but I think he's cute. And I'm fascinated by his work at the United Nations, trying to improve global, social, and environmental situations. He said he was in "intelligence" when he served in the Israeli Army. He seems tough on the outside and soft on the inside. He's comfortable with the chopsticks. I'm smitten. Could I be over Ruben and onto the next so quickly? It's only been a week! That would be too lucky. I hope he'll want to get together again. I launch a full-fledged charm offensive for the rest of dinner.

"Me? I work in television." I reveal just enough so that he'll be curious to know more. I smile and laugh and let him talk about himself. I present my all-out best brainy-coy-flirty-mysterious combination, and miraculously, at the end of the night, he suggests we get together again soon.

A few days later, we're walking along Fifth Avenue. I'm a sucker for his Italian sense of style. I like the clothes and furniture designs he points out in the windows. I like his easy way of walking in his fancy Italian shoes and the way his tailored coat hangs on his broad-shouldered frame. His gray scarf falls just so around his neck. I'm cold, and we stop for an espresso. He orders, "One espresso, one cappuccino," in the accent in which they were meant to be uttered.

I'm tickled by his stories of his work in India, Israel, and Ireland.

"The second day at the consulate in Bombay, there was a power outage," he tells me. "And guess where I was? An elevator. The elevator grinds to a halt, the lights go out, it's sweltering hot, and I'm in a full suit on my way to my first meeting with the Indian consul in fifteen minutes. I'm sweating it. Then I hear a scraping noise and a grunt from the other guy in the elevator. And within a minute, he's managed to pry the door open with this metal rod. He was pretty bored by the whole event. Turns out power outages happen all the time. I learned right then how to pry open elevator doors."

The afternoon is fantastic, and I run home afterwards to call and tell Mom and my brothers about him. The clever conversation. The chemistry. His high-powered job. Our familiar, almost familial cultural background. "Do you think he might be the one?" Mom asks.

"Maybe." I try to contain my excitement.

I never told my family about Ruben, even though we were dating for almost six months. I worried they wouldn't approve given his age, career, and religion. And here, I'm telling all and we've only been out twice. There's nothing objectionable about Narciso.

Over the next few weeks, I have lunch with him at the United Nations, I hold onto his arm at a diplomatic cocktail party, he comes to drinks with me and my colleagues after work. I'm tempted to invite him to Mom's wedding.

"He's blue chip." Jackie nods approvingly over cocktails at our Times Square happy hour haunt.

Each time I see him, my feelings for him grow stronger. Does he feel the same way about me? He hasn't said anything to give me a clue. He hasn't even tried to kiss me. Just the formal air cheek-cheek, kiss-kiss. Should I tell him how I feel?

"Absolutely not," Jackie says. "It'll be the kiss of death to any budding relationship. Men like the chase too much. Once they know they've got you, they lose interest."

"Go for it! Tell him!" Mom recommends. I listen, even though I don't trust her interpretations of bachelor communications in Manhattan. "Go after him," she says. "That's just what I did with Dad and Stanley, and it worked for me!"

My impatience wins out over my better judgment, and one night, outside my apartment after a dinner in a small, Chelsea restaurant, as he is about to kiss-kiss me good night, I tell him, "I'm beginning to have feelings for you."

He smiles, hugs me warmly, pecks me on the cheek, smiles, and says, "Good night," as if he didn't even hear me.

I dismiss it. Maybe he has feelings for me, too, but is afraid to admit it. But the next day, he does not call. Nor the following. Nor the day after that. I jump each time the cell phone rings. I check my e-mail obsessively. Nothing. Has the secretary general of the United Nations tapped him to be a possible successor? Are terrorists holding his cell phone hostage? Did someone more important than me require his immediate assistance (i.e., God)? I come up with all kinds of possibilities and forgive him for each one. I replay our parting scene in my head. Why didn't I just say "Good night"? Has he met someone else? I'm afraid of the truth. And I can't risk calling him. I've seen the danger in reaching out to him.

After a week of fixating on Narciso, I begin to give up hope. Never again will I tell a man how I feel. Must make him fight for it. My sadness soon turns to anger. He didn't even have the courtesy, much less the courage, to say good-bye. Is that what they taught him about women in diplomat's school? Coward.

Now, each time I talk to Mom and my brothers, they ask me for updates on the diplomat. I change the topic. I try to direct the conversation elsewhere.

"Did you decide on the dill sauce or the lemon-caper sauce for the salmon at your wedding?" I ask Mom.

"Is this wedding planning driving you guys nuts?" I ask my brothers.

"What about the subway Israeli dude?" my brothers persist.

"Work is going very well," I answer. "Interviewed Bill Gates this week."

"But what about the UN guy?" Mom insists. She can't be bothered with corporate titans.

I finally answer with a dismissive, "Oh him? The diplomat? Nothing special."

I tell myself that I'm over him, but I still check my e-mail and cell phone hopefully. Jackie gets impatient with me.

"Move on!" She says. "Cut your losses."

I don't want to go out with anyone else. I want him. I want the diplomat.

Seventeen

You know things are bad when you're sitting on your bed, calling your ex-ex boyfriend. I'm dialing the number for the apartment he and I used to share in Brooklyn. Maybe, maybe he's changed. Maybe he's evolved from toad to prince since I last saw him a year ago. I press the familiar sequence of keys into the phone. Did I make a mistake when I broke up with him? Why did I end it? Such a sweet guy. On the third ring, he picks up. His voice, which has always sounded a little like a frog's, croaks when he answers. That voice is either endearing or annoying, depending on what kind of a mood I'm in. He's shocked that I'm calling after so long. His voice sounds sweet.

"I was just wondering if you might want to get together for a drink some night," I ask tentatively.

I hear him snicker-snort over the phone. The nerve. Jerk. I know exactly what he's thinking. He used to say the best time to ask women out was in December because that's when they're at their weakest. His thinking? "Women will say yes to almost anyone, because they can't bear the idea of New Year's Eve without someone to kiss."

"Sure, Daniella," he says, as if he knew this call would come, it was just a matter of when, "I'll e-mail you."

We agree to go out two nights later. Over the next couple of days, we exchange half a dozen e-mails about when and where to meet Thursday night. The interminable negotiating process reminds me of one of the reasons we broke up. He only wants to meet me at a location that is halfway between his law firm and my office. Or at a location closer to him. He wants to meet at a time that is convenient for him, and makes a few digs about my perpetual tardiness. We agree to meet Thursday night at an underground cocktail lounge downtown. I'm prompt, he's early.

From what I can see, he hasn't changed one bit in the year since our dramatic breakup. He's got the same wiry glasses and goofy smile. We hug. He still feels familiar.

Last time I saw him, we were in our shared bedroom, in our shared Brooklyn apartment. I was packing up my clothes to move out. He was sitting on the bed watching me.

"You aren't really serious about this, are you?" he kept asking as if my moving out was all a joke. His eyes were dry in denial, mine were wet with sad reality. Mom and Stanley came the next day and helped me move out.

Even after a year, our defenses are still up. We talk about mutual friends, work, and current events. The candles on the table soften our faces, and the liquids pouring down our throats ease the conversation. I tell him about my new responsibilities at work.

"But how'd you pull that off, Daniella?" he asks as if a merit-based promotion were out of the question. Yes, he tends to be condescending toward me, but overall he's sweet and flattering; the way I like to remember him.

I'm not ready to leap into talk about my love life, so I steer the conversation to family. I ask about his sister, his brothers. I ask about his parents. I tell him about my brothers and of course, about Mom's engagement. David says he's very happy for Mom. He knows all about second weddings. Both his mother and father remarried after they divorced. I tell David all about the wedding planning. The white dress. The flowers. The cake.

"Why aren't you married yet?" he asks.

I'm speechless.

"No one's asked?" he persists.

I'm shocked, mute.

"Someone got mighty close," he says sheepishly. It takes me a second to realize he's referring to himself.

What? He planned to propose to me when we were together! I had no idea. I thought we were always on the brink of breaking up.

I am softened by his words, and reveal to him that I'm dating, and that it's difficult.

"Want to go grab dinner?" he asks.

A big part of me wants to say "Yes!" It would be nice to fall right back into David, who knows me better than any man ever has. But that yes part of me shrinks into no as I envision the negotiations that will inevitably go into picking the restaurant. The table at the restaurant. The wine.

"Umm. I'd like to. But I can't. Thank you," I decline. I feel guilty for having even called him and stirred this up at all. "I need to get home—work tomorrow."

We leave with a hurried hug in the cold, our defenses back up.

The story of the "almost proposal" does not impress Jackie when I tell her about it the next day at work.

"An 'almost proposal'? Ha! That's as useless as 'almost pregnant,'" Jackie says while she slathers on foundation makeup in the ladies' room. "Either he did or he didn't. Either you are or you're not." She checks her watch to see how many minutes she has till she has to go back on air. She picks up her eyelash curler, closes her right eye, and presses her left eyelashes round. She then unclamps the scary silver device, bats her eyes, and then waves the eyelash curler at me as she speaks. "What you need is a good date. No more regression."

She presses her right eyelashes round.

"Look at me," she says. "I'm not lamenting men past, or my present single state. I'm going out there, doing something about it. I meet good men all the time. My whole weekend is booked solid. I'm going to the spa all day Saturday, then Sunday I have a brunch date with some guy my mom wants me to meet. I'm going to a matinee with John. Then there's a wine-tasting party Sunday night at my friend Dara's new apartment. Do you want to come to Dara's? She's got a lot of banker friends."

"Uhhh," I hedge. "I've got plans."

"Don't worry," she says. "I'll keep an eye open for eligible men for you, too." She runs out of the ladies' room, her hair brushes and makeup strewn across the counter.

The next Monday at work, Jackie tells me the buffet of men served up at Dara's wine tasting was not to her liking. But, she says, the night was not a total loss.

"I conferenced with Dara about you. We decided to leverage our network of friends and set you up on some blind dates."

"Blind dates?" I ask.

"Yes, but they aren't deaf or dumb, so you're sure to be heard even if you're not seen," Jackie jokes.

The men she sets me up with are not only the seeing, hearing, and speaking types, but they are some of the most over-achieving, aggressive, type-A New Yorkers I've ever met. One man is a partner in a law firm. Another, an emergency room doctor. Another, a successful entrepreneur. You get the idea. They're confident; accustomed to fighting for what they want and getting it. They come on strong, and they start the hunt immediately. My guard goes up just as fast. I don't want to be chased, I want to be understood, and so "extreme dating" begins.

Dates with these overachievers prove so demanding, rife with mental gymnastics and emotional contortions, that I imagine myself the athlete in the sport of "extreme dating." The men must see themselves as athletes, too, as they try to get through the intellectual, emotional, and physical triathlon that often accompanies dinner with me.

One night, I find myself at an underground champagne bar in Midtown with an investment banker. I ask him, "So, my mom's getting married for a second time. She's wearing a long, white dress. She's getting a band, a caterer, flowers. She's going all out. Do you think women's roles are evolving or revolving? Are we on the cusp of a new kind of retro-feminism? Why do you think young women are getting married later? Did your parents set a good role model for you in terms of marriage?"

Like the rest of these guys, he furrows his brow. He crinkles his nose and stretches his lips as he tries to search his big brain for the right answer. He smiles uncomfortably and laughs.

"So do you think the bond market will bounce back?" he asks.

Next! I respect a man who knows when he doesn't have answers. But the bond market as the alternative topic? No thanks.

My technique proves effective and efficient on most dates. I like the guys who crack through my game and make me laugh at my own seriousness. And I respect the ones who start digging into things they learned in their college sociology class. One man even minored in women's studies in college. Depending on how they respond to the questions (if they don't run away or walk out first), I can separate the boys from the men immediately and decide whether they merit the next leg of the challenge.

One Friday night, after a particularly exhausting cocktail party date with a venture capitalist, I am thrilled to get back home, alone. The party was the kind I used to fantasize about before I came to New York: the ritzy apartment with high ceilings, the fashionable people, the sophisticated conversation. But when I was younger, I didn't understand how much effort would go into attending these kinds of parties. I, too, have to get dressed up. My conversation must be sufficiently quick-witted to engage other guests. There are so many nights that I would just like to stay home in sweats, no makeup, no effort. But if I don't go out, I won't get a chance to meet IB.

It's been a long week of going out on blind dates, answering panic calls on Mom's wedding hotline, and working super hard. I'm wiped out. It's almost midnight, and I've just dropped my bag by the door of the apartment and kicked off my heels when my home phone rings. It's Narciso, the "diplomat." By now I've shortened his nickname to "the Dip."

It's been more than a month since we last spoke, and I'm shocked to hear from him.

"I'm in your neighborhood. Do you want a visitor?" he asks in the tone a waitress might ask, "Do you want decaf or regular?"

"Now?" I ask noting the peculiar timing.

"Sure," he says.

"Okay," I say and hang up.

What kind of a mess did I just get myself into? Nothing I

can't handle. The way I see it, there are two reasons for his call. (A) He wants to come over to apologize for the way he's treated me. (B) He has grand (but mistaken) ideas of hooking up with me tonight. Either will be entertaining.

The Dip arrives minutes later. I shove my bag and shoes out of the way and welcome him in my most lukewarm manner: a quick, weak hug with a light tap on the back. I offer him a drink; he declines. I direct him to a seat on the couch. I sit back in a chair across from him and fold my arms. I don't know what his night has been like up until now, but I've been whipping out one-liners all night at that cocktail party, and now, though I'm tired, I'm warmed up and ready to deal with the Dip, whatever he throws my way.

Since he doesn't begin our late-night rendezvous with option A, the apology, he must be angling for option B, the make-out session. I want option A, and unfortunately for him, he's trapped himself in my apartment.

"So, where've you been?" I ask sweetly, flirty, but firmly. "Why haven't you called?"

"I've been busy," he squirms. "I've had friends visiting from abroad."

Feeble. That's just not going to cut it, Dip. If God had called, I might have been more understanding, but friends from abroad? Please. I'm a journalist and I'm going to keep needling till I get the full story, so you might as well just dish it out now.

"Who taught you to kiss and not call?" I smile. "Did they teach you that in diplomat's school?"

"Why didn't you call me?" he asks.

"I would have," I say feeling cornered, "but I figure if you wanted to talk, you would've reached out." I regain some confidence. "What would you do in my shoes? I told you I was beginning to care for you, and you ran away. And now you tell me I should've called?" My voice is quavering in a way I didn't count on.

He's quiet.

"What's so bad about someone who tells you they care for you? Why are you so afraid?" I ask.

"I'm trying to work that out with my therapist right now," he says.

Ah. Good. At least that's one honest answer I can accept. But he still hasn't apologized for kissing and ditching. Even if he's not sorry for the way he treated me, I can tell he's beginning to be sorry he called tonight. And that's satisfying enough.

I needle and pester him until he's slouching and sinking into the couch like a scolded child. He looks pathetic. He's right where I want him.

"Narciso, it was so nice of you to stop by." I get up from the chair.

He looks disappointed and relieved. I walk over to the front door and open it. He peels himself out of my couch, comes to the door, nods his head once, and leaves.

Justice. I go to bed alone, but satisfied.

The sense of justice keeps me walking around with my head high for a few days. But soon enough, the contentment wears off, and the self-doubt kicks in. The Dip was the closest thing I've seen to IB in my life, and I kicked him out. Sometimes I wish I weren't so sensible. It would have been much more fun to go with his Plan B and, who knows? Maybe it would have led to something. Maybe I could have helped him overcome his commitment phobia.

"Nonsense," Jackie says over lunch in our Times Square cafeteria. She stabs at her salad. "No regrets, Daniella. That guy was a total poser. He had me fooled, too, and I like to think I have a good radar for men. My ex-husband excluded, of course. I thought the Dip was blue-chip. Wrong. Penny stock all the way."

She pushes the lettuce around the plate with her fork.

"You did the right thing. Now move on."

She's more cynical than usual.

"Everything okay?" I ask.

"Fine." She puts down her fork, looks up at the ceiling, and sighs. Her eyes look glassy.

"You sure?"

"Just getting tired of dating," she says.

"It's hard work."

"Yeah," she says looking dejected and disgusted. "I just thought that after I divorced, life would get better. That I'd meet someone better for me. I didn't expect to meet him right away, but I didn't expect it to be this hard. It's been two years, and by now, I've met about a quarter of the eligible bachelors in Manhattan. Three dates last week. Four dates this week. I'm just exhausted."

"Why not take a break from dating. A date-break?" I say.

Jackie doesn't seem to hear me, she just continues, "I can tell within minutes of meeting these guys whether there's a chance. And there's nothing worse than having to sit through some interminable dinner and entertain a man I hope I'll never see again. I just want to get married, settle down, and cook dinner for my husband. Is that too much to ask?"

"Nope. It's not. It's totally retro. But never mind. Maybe you should just take a step back from all of this. Take a date-break," I repeat.

"I would, but I can't. I don't want to back down from a challenge. If I just try harder, it'll pay off. I can't give up."

"I'm not recommending you give up," I say. "I'm just suggesting you slow down, take a few days off. A little vacation from dating work."

I can see tears forming in her eyes.

"Come on, Jackie. It's not that bad. Look on the bright side—at least you have a million dates. It will work out. Don't give up, just chill out."

"My makeup is running." She dabs her gray blue eyes with the cafeteria paper napkin.

I'm not getting through. I try another approach that she might understand better. "If you can't stop dating, at least try to date some of these guys more than once. Give them a chance. You know, like a stock. Even if you don't get immediate returns, they might be able to deliver long-term gains. Just give it some time."

"I just hate wasting time. I don't have time. I'm thirty-four years old. The bio clock is running out." Jackie looks down at her full plate of salad.

"Jackie. Your persistence will pay off. Just give yourself a break, and give these guys a chance." I start getting up.

"Don't hug me," she says, anticipating my next move. "It'll make me cry more."

I sit down.

Jackie's look of despair suddenly turns hopeful. "Will you help me?" she asks.

"Of course, anything," I say.

"Come with me to the Matzo Ball Thursday night."

"The Matzo Ball?" I shudder at the thought. "Are you sure?"

"Please?" she asks.

Every Christmas Eve, single Jews get out and party at Matzo Balls across the country. The idea is that since Jews aren't celebrating Christmas, they might as well get sloshed at bars and clubs, meet their mate, and eventually procreate.

"Come on. You don't have other Christmas Eve plans do you?" Jackie asks.

"How about Chinese food and a movie? That's a good Jewish Christmas tradition," I say. "It can be one of your nights off from dating."

"Please?" she asks.

I hesitate.

She looks at me with pleading eyes.

"Okay," I say.

"Thank you." Jackie looks relieved. "You're a good friend." With that she gets up from the lunch table. "Let's go, I have to do another update in thirty minutes."

That night I call Maxine.

"Jackie was so bummed out, I felt like I had to say yes." I explain the predicament I've gotten myself into. "But I really don't want to go to the Matzo Ball. I hate those singles mixers. I've got to get out of it."

"Why not go? What have you got to lose?" Maxine asks.

"Dignity," I say.

"Oh come on. Be like Jackie and get out there. It'll be fun. I wish I could go. I miss my dating days. It was so exciting. Now I just stay home feeding Lara and changing her diapers . . ."

I hear Lara crying in the background.

"You know what? I'll go with you," Maxine says. "Jon's got to work at the hospital Christmas Eve, and I was just going to get some Chinese food and rent a movie. I'll get my sister to babysit, and we'll all go out."

"I was actually trying to get out—"

"Absolutely. No problem. I haven't been out in months. I'd love to get dressed up and have a martini. A night out with the girls! Much more fun that being part of an old married couple!"

"But—"

"Not another word. It'll be awesome. Just like old times. You, me, Jackie, and the men of Manhattan. Watch out!"

Christmas Eve and I'm with Maxine and Jackie in Manhattan's meat-packing district for the Matzo Ball. The line to get into the club is long, with men in black leather jackets, slicked-back hair, and eyes that dart around. Most of the women are in high-heeled shoes, tight jeans, low-cut tops, and stick-straight hair. We're all freezing cold as we survey the scene.

"I miss this so much sometimes," Maxine says.

Inside, as the leather jackets and pretenses come off, the men prove to be more nebbishy than cool, and I am more at ease. Still, I feel kind of pathetic. But, if I think about it logically, I can find comfort. Consider this, self. If I've been pressured into attending this party, a man like me might also be here, having succumbed to similar coercion by his friends.

With drinks flowing, my guard comes down. One man approaches me, and I decide to give him and this whole event the benefit of the doubt. Maxine leads Jackie away. He's a tall, nice-looking man from New Jersey named Dave. He offers to buy me a drink. I thank him. So what if he's from Jersey?! Dave works in insurance.

I ask my best and only actuarial question.

"So, do you think it's fair to charge people who live in poor neighborhoods higher premiums than you charge people in wealthy neighborhoods?" I ask.

"Oh. Well. I haven't really thought about that. That's something a different division of my company addresses," he says. "I'm a mold expert."

"Mold?"

"Mold. You heard about the Texas mold crisis, right? People claiming their houses were destroyed by mold? Well, mold claims in Texas rose 1,306 percent in 2001. And as you might imagine, all those claims sent homeowners' insurance rates up . . . just shy of 41 percent."

Mold? My interest rate in Dave plummets.

"Rates up just shy of 41 percent," he repeats as if it'll have more impact the second time. He yammers on about premiums, and I tune out and start crunching my own numbers. If I give Dave 80 percent of my attention, the other 20 percent of my focus can go to balancing my pink Cosmopolitan drink in the martini glass.

Dave continues, "So, now the mold problem is spreading throughout the U.S., premiums are rising, and coverage is decreasing, causing a compounding effect. I went to the Casualty Actuarial Society's Seminar on Rate-Making in Philly last week . . ."

As Dave goes on about deductibles, the Cosmo balancing game steadily steals the show. A debate rages in my mind: What will be the best use of this drink? Playing balancing games with the pink liquid, or letting the Cosmo slide down my throat and alter my mind.

"So far, thirty-five states approved ISO mold exclusions . . ." he continues.

By now, the Cosmo's got 80 percent of my attention, Dave's got 20 percent. Dave, sensing my dwindling interest in the emerging frontier of mold, pulls out the big guns.

"I really think this whole mold issue needs to be depoliticized;

we need some market-based solutions to attract and retain insurers."

Will he sell me a life insurance policy that has a stipulation for death by boredom? I smile at him. I knock back half of the Cosmo. I sense he's on the verge of asking me about my insurance coverage, so I gulp down the other half of the drink.

"That's one heck of a wild story," I say, "but if you'll please excuse me, I must, must go find my friends. They're probably scouring the place looking for me now. Thank you very much for the drink," I tell him. "Good luck with the mold."

I comb the multiple rooms and floors of singles. Where are Jackie and Maxine? I dodge and swerve through the throngs of people, painfully aware that people are looking me over as I walk by. Fitting: the party is in Manhattan's meat market. Eventually, I find Maxine and Jackie talking to three men. They're all short, shorter than we are. Jackie is smiling a lot, and Maxine is tossing her head back laughing and flirting like I haven't seen in years. One of the guys is a middle school math teacher. Another is a banker. The third is a classical musician. Not bad. The musician grabs my full attention when he tells me about his favorite composers. I know so little about music, but would love to learn more. He plays the cello in a Manhattan quartet and teaches music at a New Jersey Jewish community center. Nice. We exchange numbers. He could be a friend.

Maxine and Jackie seem to be having a great time, but I feel nauseous at this party; as if I were a stock being bounced around the floor of the New York Stock Exchange. There are many potential bidders, but are any the right buyer? We mingle in the nightclub, looking each other over, trying to determine one another's value. I hate being sized up on the market. I'm sure my mom never went to this extreme to get a date. At last, the closing bell rings.

"I miss my baby," Maxine says. "Yeah, I'm ready to go, too," says Jackie. They are the best lines I've heard all night, and I've heard a lot of lines.

The next morning I wake up, triumphant. I look at myself in the bathroom mirror and say, "Congratulations, Daniella. You survived the lowest point in your dating life." Going to the party took a toll on my self-esteem. Last night, I branded myself first and foremost as "woman looking for love." I was not defined primarily as journalist, or friend, or daughter. I was not even funny, or smart, or even brunette first. I was single.

But I made it through the evening. And it was comforting to find that I was not alone in my single state. I'm inspired to do a little celebration dance, knowing I didn't destroy my dignity entirely and knowing I will never sink so low again. Gloria Gaynor singing, "I Will Survive" pops into my head. I turn my toothbrush into a microphone, the bathroom walls serve as backup, and I start to sing in my best Gloria voice, "*I've got all my life to live, I've got all my love to give, I will survive, I will survive . . .*"

Beep.

Ugh, the phone.

I lower my toothbrush from microphone position.

It's Jackie.

"I have something exciting to tell you," she says. "You know that guy Marc I was talking to last night? The math teacher? He just called me! Now you know me, I don't go for guys who are teachers. I like the more high-powered type. But he was so sweet. We even went to the same summer camp. He's not exactly what I had in mind, but there's something special about him. We're going out on Sunday afternoon!"

"I'm so happy for you," I tell her, rolling the toothbrush in my mouth now as if it were a cigarette.

"What about you? Anyone you want to see again?" she asks. Her voice is much more positive than it usually is.

"No."

"I'm sorry. But at least you had fun, right?" she persists.

"Yeah." Fun, in the masochistic sense of fun. What was undoubtedly the low point of my dating life may well turn out to be the end of hers. Go figure.

In the days after Christmas, I try to distract myself with work, but the markets are slow, and the CEOs are on vacation. So I catch up on one of the less glamorous parts of my job: combing through press releases. My e-mail and snail mail in-boxes are packed with dozens of unopened press releases. This tech company is introducing a new software suite. That oil company is spinning off one of its drilling units. As I'm sifting through envelopes in the mail room, I come across something strange and out of place. An envelope with a return address from the Jewish community center of Englewood, New Jersey. Not exactly financial news.

I open it up, and the title reads, "Musician Meets Reporter on X-mas Eve." What? I'm confused. It turns out to be a gentle, twisted reminder from the musician I met at the Matzo Ball. I read on. The musician, Seth Abramson, has cleverly crafted a press release describing our meeting and our conversation. It reads:

MUSICIAN MEETS REPORTER
ON X-MAS EVE

New York, NY—On what is considered one of the hottest nights of the year for the Jewish singles scene, there was a chance meeting at Manhattan's Matzo

Ball, of Seth Abramson, a musician, and Daniella Finzi, a reporter. After a brief and reportedly pleasant conversation, the two exchanged business cards.

Asked for comment soon after the meeting, Abramson said, "She seems nice to me. I'd love to get to know her better—perhaps over a nice piece of chocolate cake or a night of swing dancing." At this point it's "wait and see." Shares in SethAbramson.com surged up over 4.5% in after-hours trading on speculation that Finzi might take him up on his offer. Industry watchers were unreachable for comment.

Now this is original. It makes the cell phone number thief, the palm pilot intruder, and the text message abuser seem rather ordinary.

His press release version of our meeting makes it much more exciting than I remember. Still, I call the "contact number" listed on the press release and tell him how flattered and impressed I am with his writing. He "aw shucks" me. We arrange to meet "next year" for coffee. If he can replicate the wow factor of the press release on our first date, then he could have excellent long-term potential. Maybe, maybe I'll even have a date to Mom's wedding after all.

Eighteen

New Year's Eve, and my dates for the evening are Enrico and his girlfriend Leslie. They haven't moved in together yet, and as far as I can tell, they haven't talked about marriage either. They've come to New York for New Year's, and I've promised them an authentic Brooklyn experience at my friend Stefanie's party. It ought to be a lively crowd, considering Stefanie is a playwright, and most of her friends are musicians, performers, and theater types.

We walk through the beaded curtain into Stefanie's apartment. Stefanie has created a warm atmosphere in her cramped one-bedroom apartment with cinnamon-scented candles burning and big band music swinging in the background. The party is packed. I squeeze through the crowd and introduce Enrico and Leslie to people I know. Soon I realize they prefer to be left alone to coo over their champagne and themselves. So I leave them to it. Besides, I'm here to meet new people.

Stefanie calls me over to the kitchen where she's preparing to mix martinis. She's looking festive tonight. She's got glitter sprinkled across her face and tinsel in her cropped, orangey red hair. We haven't seen each other in awhile.

"Ruben and I broke up. I'm dating. And my mom's getting remarried," I tell her.

"Ah, the encore wedding, I know it well." Stefanie turns from the cupboard to face me. "Second or third?"

"Second or third what?" I ask.

"Second or third marriage for your mom?" she asks, facing me and leaning her lanky frame back against the counter.

"Second. Why?"

"The third marriage is easier than the second. By the fourth time," she swats her hand forward, "it's a piece of cake. But, I must admit, by then the novelty's lost."

She turns back around to face the counter and refocus on the drinks. She seems so matter-of-fact about it.

"How do you know so much?" I ask.

Stefanie's eyes are focused on measuring out gin in a shot glass and pouring it in the shaker.

"My mom," she looks up at me from the shot glass, "is a serial bride. On husband number four."

And I thought I was in an uncommon position.

"Did your mom have four big white weddings?" I ask, almost afraid to hear the answer.

"Depended on the husband." She dumps shots of vermouth in the shaker. "She wore white each time, but the ceremonies were all different. She eloped with my dad, her first."

She turns back to me and puts her middle finger to her chin and looks up, trying to remember how the next ones went.

"Number Two had just wrapped up a nasty divorce of his own, so we all went on a vacation to the Caribbean. I was like seven or eight years old. I just remember we were on the beach: me, my brother, Mom, Number Two, and a guy in Bermuda shorts with a bible acting like he was God. Mom got so mad at me for throwing sand in my brother's face," Stefanie says. She gives the metal shaker a vigorous shake. She opens up the top and takes a whiff of her concoction and crinkles her nose.

"I was in college for Number Three," she continues. "Mom called me sophomore year, saying she had met the man who was going to make up for her past mistakes. 'Not that your father was a mistake, honey.'"

Stefanie carefully pours the drinks into the glasses.

"I had to be part of the bridal party for Number Three," Stefanie remembers. "That sucked. I barely knew the guy, and I was still getting over her break with Number Two. I was smack in the middle of my combat fatigue wearing phase, and Mom insisted I wear a pastel-colored dress."

She holds a glass up to the light and looks at the liquid.

"Wedding number four wasn't so bad, except for the 'family moon.' That was just a few years ago," Stefanie remembers. "Mom, in her New Age phase, insisted that my brother and I go with the newlywed couple and Number Four's preteen twin boys on a bonding vacation—aka family moon—after the wedding. I still think my brother and I were brought along as babysitters. Why my mother chose the Caribbean again is beyond me."

She passes me a martini, lifts her mouth into a smile, and lifts her glass. "Here's to lots and lots of love in life."

"Cheers!" I answer, unable to come up with anything better to say.

We both knock back a big gulp of the drink.

"Drinks anyone?" Stefanie turns from me and calls out to the crowd over the music.

I'm afraid Stefanie's mother's marriages were the wrong

subjects to bring up. I do wonder, however, what her mom's hand would look like if she stacked divorce rings on her right hand the way I envisioned CEOs with broken marriages should. Maybe I should ask Stefanie about her own love life. No. Given her spotty record with men, I'm better off leaving it alone unless she brings it up. Perhaps I should try an easier topic, like say, the Israeli-Palestinian conflict?

A good-looking guy with curly black hair walks in and starts talking to Stefanie about their shared interest in African drumming. Better.

I slip away to search for Enrico and Leslie. I'm wishing I had a kissable date tonight. On second thought, given Stefanie's story about her mom, none may be better than many when it comes to men. "Less is more, more or less." I find Enrico and Leslie sitting on the bed with all the guests' winter coats piled up around them. They are deep in conversation. I say a quick "Hi," then duck back out to the main room. Enrico and Leslie obviously are fine.

Half an hour later, I am in a deep, dark conversation with a depressed poet. She's telling me how being broke, single, and in New York freezes her creative juices.

"And poets have shorter life spans," she says.

The party is hot, loud, and crowded, and I'm looking for an escape.

"Can I talk to you for a second?" Stefanie rescues me.

The poet looks dejected.

"It'll just be a minute," Stefanie reassures and pulls me over to a corner where we sit down on her couch.

"Listen, maybe I was a bit abrupt about all that mother-wedding stuff. I'm sorry," she apologizes. "It's just I'm a little jaded with encore weddings by now."

"I didn't mean to bring up a bad subject."

"Well, it's not really a bad subject. It's just I've thought about it a lot. And actually, here's how I see it. If my mom can get married four times and your mom can get married twice, then you and I can probably manage to get married at least once, that is, if we want to at all," Stefanie says. "I've spent a lot of my life married to the romantic notion of finding my one and only soul mate. But lately, I've been thinking there are many who can be a good fit. Maybe we should stop test-fitting all these guys to meet our soul mate criterion, and just take a risk. A leap of faith."

"Are you saying we should lower our standards?" I ask.

"No, it's just that a better marriage may be more like a partnership than a soul meeting. We should be open to men who don't fit perfectly into our romantic idealization of a soul mate. We could learn new things from someone who isn't perfectly in sync with us. Plus, if we wait too long looking for 'the one,' we might spend our lives alone. And even if we find the perfect soul mate, it could lead to disaster. Look at Sylvia Plath and Ted Hughes, I think they were soul mates, and she killed herself."

"Hmm," I mull. "But Plath was nuts."

Stefanie ignores my comment and continues, "My mom took chances on men. Maybe too many chances. But at least she can say she tried."

"Fair enough," I say.

We're both quiet.

"How about giving me a few tips about helping my mom through this whole wedding thing?" I ask.

"Oh, that's tough. It's hard to be a mother to your own mother. Especially when we don't have any experience. My mom employed me as a confidante when I was eight years old and she was getting remarried for the first time. Then, I didn't mind so much. But now I wish I had had more time to be a child. She still relies on me for all kinds of things. I remember just a couple years back when she was getting married to Jim, husband number four, she insisted I go shopping with her for the bra to go with her white wedding suit."

"Lovely. I have lots to look forward to. So what do you think all these encore weddings mean about marriage?" I ask.

Stefanie looks a bit sad. "Just because you get married and have a wedding doesn't mean its forever."

Stefanie looks far off into space.

"Well, what am I supposed to do? What am I supposed to do for her?" I ask.

Stefanie is quiet. Then she says, "Do for her what you want her to do for you."

Simple, yet so profound. She sits quietly for a minute then gets up, spins around, and rejoins the party.

I remain on the couch.

Midnight is approaching, and the party is getting increasingly animated. People are gathering around my spot on the couch to see the television screen across from me. I miss Ruben. I hope for electric love with Mr. Matzo Ball. I keep my eyes glued to the TV screen, waiting for the ball to drop in Times Square. I pretend I'm enraptured by Dick Clark. I keep looking straight ahead to avoid the intimacy of the soon-to-be-kissing couples. As the ball begins its drop, the party counts down in unison. We all chant, "Five! Four! Three! Two! One! Happy New Year!"

One. I need just one.

Nineteen

Now I'm part of the show in Times Square. I'm not just watching it as I was on New Year's Eve. My stock market reports and interviews air constantly on a five-story-tall screen in Times Square—right across from where Dick Clark dropped the ball on New Year's Eve. In fact, had I been working on December 31, his image and mine would have gone head-to-head.

Standing on the corner of Broadway and Forty-third Street, I look up at my image on the gigantic screen. There I am talking, talking, talking, but no one can hear me. Ironic, isn't it, that here, in the center of a city of eight million people, my head is huge, yet I haven't gotten through to the one person I really want to reach. And Mom, a widow, in a much smaller city, found her soul mate without any media exposure.

Well, I'm about to respond to a media inquiry. Tonight I'm meeting Mr. Matzo Ball. Could he be "the one"? Getting dressed for the date, I try to strike just the right balance between getting all gussied up (to show I made an effort) and giving off a relaxed look (to show I'm not too high-maintenance).

"You look nice," Mr. Matzo Ball says as we sit down in a neighborhood café. Nice? Did my dressing effort work? He has a friendly face and gives me a warm hug. We sit down. I really want to like him. I'm sick of dating. I tell him again how impressed I was with his press release.

"It was nothing," he answers. Within five minutes, our conversation defaults to conventional date questions: his family, my family, the chocolate cake, and our respective professions. I spare him the series of Mom marriage-feminism-evolution questions. There's no need. He's proven himself kind and humble already. Within half an hour, though, we hit that dreaded moment in which you either suffer silently or force conversation.

"This cake is delicious. So moist. I like the chocolate chips in it," I say. In fact, there might be one stuck in my back molar. Absently, I try to dislodge it with my tongue. As much as I want it, there just isn't any chemistry between us. We both do our best to string the conversation out further, but somehow, we've both lost interest in each other.

"So, I better get going," I say. "I've got to be at the Exchange at eight tomorrow morning." Once again I press the button for the work escape hatch. He asks for the check, and I try to pay. (I like to pay on bad dates so I won't feel obliged if he asks me out again. It also helps me keep track of my life. On my credit card statement, I can see an itemization of failed dates at the end of each month.) Mr. Matzo Ball insists on picking up the bill. A friendly kiss-kiss good-bye, and it's over. As is the case with so many media promotions, the hype was better than the event.

The Matzo Ball disappointment pales in comparison with what threatens to be an even bigger disappointment just days from now: my thirtieth birthday. It's hard to believe I've been on this planet almost thirty full years. With each year, I meet more and more men, which should, theoretically increase my odds of running into IB. Right? Wrong. With each year, I become more and more aware of what I need in a man, or as others might say, I become increasingly picky. I prefer "discriminating."

Rather than pity myself for being picky and turning thirty, I decide to throw myself a gigantic birthday bash. Heck, if I'm planning Mom's wedding, I at least deserve to plan my own party.

My birthday week arrives, but IB doesn't. Maybe he'll somehow appear at my party—invited to my apartment by a friend of a friend?

Meanwhile, Ruben keeps calling. He knows I feel vulnerable, and he wants to get together and talk. But I can't. It'd be too easy for me to slide back into his strong arms and familiarity. I don't even invite him to the party.

The theme of the party is an "international affair," and I've asked guests to bring food or drink from the city or country they call home. Many of my friends are foreign journalists who stream into my studio, arms full. A Swedish cameraman brings meatballs and lingonberry jam. A Dutch-Italian magazine reporter brings a salad of Dutch tomatoes and Italian mozzarella cheese. A radio reporter who grew up in Manhattan brings Park Avenue chocolate bars.

Leif from Fairway supermarket shows up and hands me two trays, one stacked on top of the other. "I wanted to bring you a full fish," he says flipping his hair back, "but I couldn't slip it under my shirt and get by the checkout clerks." The top tray is piled high with cookies, miniature cakes, and pastries. The bottom tray is packed densely with fine cheeses, meats, olives, crackers, fruits, and vegetables. Leif then hands a plastic Fairway bag to me and whispers in his deep voice, "This one's just for you.

Happy birthday." It's a pint of Ben & Jerry's Mint Chocolate
Cookie ice cream.

Jackie, still in her full TV attire and makeup bops in. She's
picked up a neatly packed white box of butter cookies from a
gourmet bakery downtown. "I was in such a hurry, I didn't have
time to make anything," she apologizes. "I didn't even have a
chance to change out of my work clothes. I was going to bring
Power Bars, ha, ha. You know they're just so efficient and power
packed, but I didn't think others would quite appreciate it. My
sweetie sends his best. He wanted to come, but he couldn't, had
to go to a school fund-raiser." She smiles, satisfied. "Isn't that
cute?"

The party grows increasingly lively as more guests stream in.
Music and words in multiple languages float through the air.
There's nothing quite like a bit of attention to make a gal entering her fourth decade feel better. Bachelors abound, but
none come close to IB. Or maybe I just don't see him. Maybe
he's here at my party, and I can't recognize him in one of my
old friends. I'm happily overwhelmed with emotion and affection but just sober enough to still feel lonely. I introduce one
person to another, "Juan, this is Kyoko, she brought sushi.
Kyoko, this is Juan."

"Here," Juan hands her a rectangular brownie with marshmallows, chocolate chips, and coconut strips on top. "Have a
toxic waste bar. I'm from Jersey." I pour drinks while continuing to keep an eye on the door, wondering if IB might miraculously walk in.

The music is alternating between salsa, French pop, and
African drumming—creating a good vibe—when the phone rings.

"Hello?" It's hard to hear, the party is too loud. It's Mom.
Mom, who has always claimed to be twenty-nine years old.

"These first thirty years together have been wonderful with you!" she shouts. "I hope the next thirty years are even better!"

"Thanks!" I yell back.

"Can't wait till you find someone as wonderful as Dad or the stupendous Stan to share your life with. It's going to make your life so much better."

"Thanks," I answer, although I find it totally grating that she compares husbands in the same sentence and then has the nerve to suggest that my life isn't good right now. "I've got to get back to my guests," I tell her.

"Wait, Cookie? I need to talk to you about something else," she says. "I need your help."

"Can it wait?" I ask.

"Yes, but . . ."

"Okay. What is it? Quickly."

"Well, Stan and I have decided to get hand-carved wedding bands. They're designed by one specific jeweler in Manhattan. The name is J. Walter. Do you know it? I know this isn't the greatest time to ask, but Daniella, could you help us find the artist's shop in Manhattan? I think he'll have more of a selection in his shop than what we can find here."

"Sure," I tell her. Could the question not have waited till tomorrow? "I've got to get back to the party now though. Good night."

First she tells me she doesn't need a ring or any symbol of commitment, and now she wants me to go searching for wedding bands? On my birthday? I decide right then, in the first big decision of my thirty-first year, that I don't need symbols of happiness: a ring, a dress, a wedding. Even if Mom succumbs, I won't be pulled into believing that those things will bring me happiness. I'm after happiness itself; no symbol will substitute.

Suddenly, the lights in my apartment go out. I run toward the light switch, only to feel someone else's hand covering it. Then I see it: a Ben & Jerry's ice cream birthday cake with three candles, one for each decade. The candle flames dance on top of the cake as the forty or so friends and friends of friends in my apartment sing "Happy Birthday" to me. I sing along. There's one distinct, rich, full-bodied baritone voice in the crowd that I don't recognize. Did one of my friends become a professional singer and neglect to tell me? Just as I'm about to blow out the candles, Jackie claps a hand over my mouth, and I get my answer.

The party goes completely silent as a blond stranger with the build of a football player belts out an operatic rendition of "Happy Birthday." His butter-smooth voice makes my skin tingle. I glance at my friends. They are equally stunned. He finishes, and I blow out the candles. A hearty round of applause follows. The stranger-singer and I make eye contact, and we both take a bow. How did this guy squeeze into my party without my noticing?

Incredible. See? When you have friends, and friends of friends to entertain you like this, finding a mate becomes less critical. Maxine, who is unlatched from her husband and daughter tonight, introduces me to her friend William, the baritone. She whispers in my ear, "He's single." Turns out he is a professional opera singer. New York City Opera, no less.

"I am so impressed," I tell him. "And flattered. Thank you! Do you often sing 'Happy Birthday' to strangers?"

We sit down on my orange, swiveling barstools.

"Only when the strangers also happen to be beautiful party hostesses. The pleasure was all mine," he says with his clean voice. He tells me about life backstage at the opera. He wows me with his stories of traveling the world to sing in French, in

Italian, in German, in Czech. It's so glamorous and refined. I'm intrigued.

I'm so captivated by William's stories that before I know it, it's one in the morning, and my friends are wishing me happy birthday and good night as they trickle out. Wow, time flies in your thirties. William and I exchange numbers as he leaves.

With my ears still ringing and my head still spinning with alcohol and overwhelming emotional intensity, I step over out-of-town guests who are sprawled out across the floor for the night and flop down on my bed. The party was great. That opera singer was a wonderful surprise. The apartment is a wreck. Tonight, the first night of my thirty-first year, I've got friends snoring and tossing in makeshift beds across the room, and I wonder, Is this the modern family? Friends close, family distant, soul mate optional? The youthful dreamer in me hopes the aging realist in me is wrong.

Twenty

My fourth decade starts with a song and continues with the drama of opera, literally. Two days after my thirtieth birthday, William the opera singer calls. He proposes dinner.

I say "Yes." He asks if I'd like to see him perform at Lincoln Center.

I say "Yes." He asks if I like opera.

I say "Yes," even though I slept through the only opera I ever attended. It's agreed then, Saturday night, I'll see him perform in *Carmen*, and then we'll go out for dinner. He refuses to tell me which role he plays.

That Saturday morning, Stefanie and I weave our way around SoHo looking for the J. Walter store, the jeweler Mom asked me to scope out.

"Thank you so much for coming, Stefanie. I owe you big time."

"No big deal." She smiles, her orangey red cropped hair all mussed up. She loops her arm in mine. "I wish I had someone to help me when my mom was getting remarried and remarried and remarried."

"Well, you're building good Karma. One of the world's most experienced daughters of the bride is helping me ring shop for my mom," I say. "What a way to start my thirty-first year. It doesn't get much weirder than this."

"Actually? It does," Stefanie says. "I'm hearing about wedding rings and engagement rings everywhere I go lately. I have this friend, Zoë. Zoë's always been a bit . . . shall we say, 'different' from the rest. Anyway, her boyfriend of five years finally got up the nerve to propose to her. He gave her this spectacular nontraditional engagement ring. It was a thin, rainbow band of gems: rubies, sapphires, emeralds, and diamonds. Well, Zoë loved him, but she didn't like the idea of a ring—too much of a symbol of social convention. So, she said yes to marriage with one condition. She wouldn't wear the engagement ring on her finger."

"Huh?"

Stefanie continues. "Most ladies want to show off their rock. But this one? She said she'd wear it only as a toe ring."

"What?"

"Can you imagine? 'Dear fiancé, I love you very much but I can't show the world that I'm engaged to you or some social convention. I'm going to wear this lavish token of your affection on my foot.'"

"Wow. How'd that work out?"

"Didn't. In the end, she couldn't handle the notion of marriage, and he was so insulted by the foot business, he broke off the engagement."

"What happened to the ring?" I ask.

"I guess he got it back." Stefanie shrugs.

"But then what? What do you do with a sapphire-ruby-emerald rejected toe engagement ring?" I ask.

"I don't know. Put it in a box in your closet as a token of your disappointment and dashed dreams? Get rid of it? Is there a resale market for rejected toe engagement rings?"

"Not that I know of." I ponder. "But then again, I've never been in the market for one. I guess you could Google it: www.rejectedtoerings.com?"

"What did your mom do with the wedding band and engagement ring from your dad?" Stefanie asks.

"She still wears the engagement ring from my dad. I don't think that'll ever change. But I don't know what she did with their wedding bands. Never really thought about it. What'd your mom do with her wedding bands?"

"She offered a couple of them to me, but I passed. I didn't want reminders of her various ex-husbands. But your situation is different. You should find out what your mom did with the band your dad gave her. Maybe she'd give it to you. You could wear it now. Stack it with other rings on your right hand? It's very trendy."

"And it might be the only wedding ring I ever get," I say.

"Oh come on, Daniella. Give it a rest. Woe is you. Dumping guys left and right and worrying about it? If you end up without a wedding band of your own, it'll definitely be your own choice. Anyway, you don't need to wait for a man or your mother to give you a ring. You can do it yourself. Haven't you heard? Lots of single women are buying themselves right-hand rings: independence rings. I saw it in *Vogue*."

"Independence rings?"

"They're all the rage. Women are wearing them on the

fourth finger of their right hands. Everyone's selling them: Chanel, Wal-Mart, the Home Shopping Network. They're usually lots of little round diamonds in an intricate design. The rings send out the message, 'I'm accomplished, I'm independent, and I'm single.' Of course, it's all just a marketing ploy by De Beers to sell more diamonds. But women are lapping it up.

"Daniella." Stefanie narrows her eyes and looks at me more seriously. "You do know De Beers is behind 'A diamond is forever.' You know it's just another marketing campaign to sell more diamonds, right?"

I give her a blank stare. She stops and looks at me.

"'A diamond is forever' is not some sentimental, emotional, or traditional expression. De Beers came up with the slogan to prop up prices. 'A diamond is forever' so that people won't trade in personal diamonds, flood the market, and bring diamond prices down."

"Really?" I ask incredulously.

"Really. Daniella, underneath all your sensible practicality, sometimes I think you're too romantic for your own good. Look!" Stefanie points. "There it is! The jeweler."

By now we're on a narrow, cobblestone side street. The storefront window is about eight feet long and four feet high, with one small display case inside. To the right of the window is a simple glass door, just two steps up with gold lettering on it reading J. Walter, Jeweler. Stefanie, her arm still linked with mine, pulls me up and inside of the brightly lighted shop. The jeweler emerges from a workshop in the back to greet us. We're the only ones in the store.

"Hello, ladies. How can I help you today?" Mr. J. Walter is wearing an apron and looks like a hippie Santa Claus.

"We're looking for wedding bands," I say.

"Really?" He raises his eyebrows and responds in a crackly teenager's surprised voice. The tone doesn't gel with his grandfatherly appearance.

"Okay. No problem. Come sit down." He directs us to a navy blue velvet–covered bench facing a glass-topped display case. Stefanie drags me over.

"We have beautiful rings for women." He sits down on the other side of the display case. He pulls out a tray of glimmering rings and sets it on top of the case. A dozen different delicately crafted gold and platinum bands shine at me. One has winding vines carved into it. Another has doves kissing.

The jeweler points to a series of bands with geometric shapes cut out. "These are really popular in commitment ceremonies," he says encouragingly.

I unhook my arm from Stefanie's.

"My mom told me all about your work," I say to the jeweler. "She saw it at a craft fair in San Francisco."

"Some of my biggest clients are from San Francisco. I'm pretty popular with that crowd."

What crowd?

"It is gorgeous," Stefanie tells the jeweler, inspecting the ring with geometric shapes. I nod.

"So, just the band? No engagement ring?" he asks. He shows us a series of solitaire engagement rings.

"No. No engagement ring. My mom and Stanley decided against," I explain.

He looks confused.

"Oh, they said there was enough of a commitment without the symbolism of an engagement ring."

He looks even more perplexed.

"I'm sorry, I'm not quite sure I follow," he says.

"The ring isn't for me, it's for my mom," I answer. "She's the one getting married. Her fiancé is a man named Stanley. My mom's in California and asked me to come here and take a look at your selection. She thinks you must have additional choices of rings that weren't on display at the San Francisco craft fair or in the catalog. She wants me to tell her whether it's worth her making a special trip to New York to buy a ring."

"Oh!" he says. "Now I understand."

Stefanie and I pick out the band we would want should we ever get married.

"Well, ladies, you know you don't need to wait for a man to get a beautiful ring. I've got these wonderful new right-hand rings." He pulls out a tray of sparkling rings. Each has half a dozen small diamonds on it arranged in abstract designs. "We're calling them independence rings." He smiles.

Stefanie and I exchange knowing glances. We admire the independence rings, take one last look at the wedding bands for Mom, inquire about prices, and thank J. Walter.

"My pleasure," he says, smiling as if entertained by the previous misunderstanding.

As we turn to leave, Stefanie loops her arm in mine again, gives me a kiss on the cheek, and with her best attempt at a sexy, flirty voice, and a wink back to the jeweler, says, "Come on, sweetie, let's go home," and leads me out of the shop.

The door closes, and we burst out onto the street laughing. I'm used to people mistaking me for the bride, but a lesbian bride? This is a first.

My afternoon as a presumed lesbian is followed by an evening of opera and a late night of drama. Sounds like a bad three-course meal, doesn't it?

Act Two of the evening is spent alone. I get dressed for the opera. Light blue cashmere sweater, long, fitted, straight black skirt, knee-high, high-heeled black leather boots. William has instructed me to pick up my ticket under his name at the box office at Lincoln Center. I walk proudly up to the ticket booth. "The name is William Henderson," I say, whispering as if I'm an opera insider, but loud enough so people can hear. The ticket agent slides the ticket under the window and squawks, "Next! Step up to the counter!" So much for royal treatment.

Instead of feeling like royalty, I feel self-conscious and alone. What's the big deal? I ask myself. I'm a grown woman. Thirty years old. Confident enough to be on my own at the opera. What's to be embarrassed about? That said, I do wish these other operagoers knew that I was actually on a date with an opera star. The usher directs me to the best seats in the house which are, of course, front and center. As I walk down the row, people have to stand up or turn their knees to the side to let me by. I'm making a spectacle of me "by myself." Uggh. I finally sit in the one lone available seat in the center of the theater and am relieved to be just another back-of-head to all the other operagoers behind me. On my right is a frail, petite lady who's so old she's almost dead. On the other side, a distinguished older gentleman with slicked-back silver hair. The rest of the crowd is closer to Mom and Stanley's age. If I'm at the opera doing something popular with her age group, what is she doing tonight? Out at a rock concert with Stanley waving her cell-phone light like a lighter?

I scan the audience in front of me: gray, bald, white, blond. Hey that baldie looks just like the Dip! It is the Dip! I gasp, triggering the old lady next to me to clutch her chest.

"Okay?" she crackles.

"Yeah," I choke. Four rows up and to my left, I see the silhouette of his lanky frame. He's laughing at something.

Unfortunately, I still find him attractive. I haven't seen him or spoken to him since his midnight visit to my apartment a few months back.

Maybe he's on his own, too? That could be interesting. The Dip leans over and whispers something to the blond, female back-of-head next to him. Gasp! The man on my left glares at me.

Mercifully, the lights go down, and the show begins. I can be by myself in darkness now and stop watching the bald-blond show. The heavy velvet curtain rises from the stage, and I soon get carried into the story. The opera is spectacular! Carmen steals the heart of the dim-witted Don Jose. Don Jose gives up everything for her. But then Carmen dumps him for—oh my God, it's William!—the dashing toreador. William's voice is rich, entrancing, and very masculine. I hardly know him, and yet I'm proud of him! Carmen and I simultaneously melt for the toreador as he whips his dashing red cape around.

Intermission. I don't move from my seat. I'd prefer to skip this break entirely. I'd rather just stay lost in the fantasy. I also don't want to make a sideshow of myself. I don't want to see the Dip. Rather, I don't want the Dip to see me alone.

Eventually, the lights dim for the final act, and I exhale in relief: I managed to escape notice by the Dip and the blonde. Onstage, Carmen escorts her beloved toreador, William, to a bullfight where he will gracefully dodge the raging bull. The brokenhearted Don Jose tracks Carmen down outside the bull ring and begs her to come back to him. She refuses. She says her heart is forever with the toreador, and Don Jose stabs Carmen to death as the oblivious crowd inside the ring cheers the toreador.

Wow. High drama. I love it! As the curtain comes down, I'm excited to go backstage to meet my date, the dashing toreador. Top that, Dip!

Act three begins as the toreador greets me most elegantly backstage. He escorts me to dinner at Fiorello's, an Italian restaurant across from Lincoln Center. On the way, we're stopped twice by people asking for William's autograph. At the restaurant, ten of his fans and friends stand up from one long table and clap as he walks in. He takes a bow. The restaurant owner sends over a bottle of champagne on the house. The drinks flow, the conversation flows, and I am thrilled to be part of the elite opera scene. Questions about the real personalities of the performers onstage fly across the table. We ask William about stage fright. William tells us about the mistakes in the show. It's a dreamy night, one of those "only in New York" evenings.

Reluctantly, I leave the lively conversation for a quick trip to the ladies' room. When I stand up, my head is light from champagne. I make my way to the back of the restaurant and there, before my eyes, an encore to the sideshow from earlier in the evening! The Dip is sitting at a table with Carmen and the blonde! Our eyes meet. I toss him a flippant smile that he returns with a stuttering hello. I keep walking. Do not stop till I'm in the safety of the ladies' room.

I want to splash water on my face, to wake me from this surreal dream. But of course I can't: running makeup isn't attractive to Dips or toreadors. Maybe if I stay in here long enough, they'll all go away. But the last thing I want is for the toreador to rescue me from the ladies' room. It would be chivalrous but embarrassing. And if the Dip is waiting on the other side of the door for me right now, I don't want to take too long. I can't have him thinking that seeing him affects me.

I straighten my posture, take a deep breath, and gird myself for whatever surprise may await me beyond the ladies' room door. I paste on a smile and push open the door with as much conviction as I can muster in my shaken, tipsy state. I look around, paw the wall for balance. Neither the Dip nor the toreador has come looking for me. Fine. I walk deliberately and briskly right past the Dip, Carmen, and company, who are laughing and deeply involved in conversation. I return to my seat of safety under the wing of the strong and brave toreador.

"Everything okay?" the toreador asks. "You look a little shaken up. Do I need to go wave someone away with my cape?"

"Oh, no. Thank you." I'm rattled and further undone that he can see I'm upset. "I'm fine." Although, it sure would be fun to watch the toreador use his red cape to make the Dip disappear.

The conversation at the toreador table resumes its lively tone, and I gulp back more champagne. I try to engage with the others, but I'm preoccupied. I hate to admit it, but I still like that jerk Dip. The Dip had an edge, a coarse humor but soft demeanor that captured my affection immediately. I thought we had so much in common, an inherent understanding. I mean how many Jewish Italians are there in the world? But then, the way he behaved with me was so low.

I wish the Dip would come visit my table or at least see me laughing and smiling with the toreador. But as night rolls into morning and the restaurant empties, I'm the one who spots the Dip walking out with Carmen. The Dip doesn't stop to say hello or make eye contact with me.

Then I brighten. He may be with Carmen, but Carmen ends up dead.

Twenty-one

Carmen may be dead, but I've failed to fall in love with the toreador. There is nothing wrong with him. He's kind. Handsome. Accomplished. And yet, somehow, even his magical capework fails to sufficiently enchant me. It's a damn shame, really. If I could just fall for him, my life would be a song. Ha. Ha. But it's not. Instead, I insist on searching for this ridiculous, romantic, IB. Is there an opera about chasing the imaginary?

Instead of opera, my life is like a haunted funhouse at a county fair, where I stand before mirrors, and images of Ruben reflect back. Everywhere I look and everything I sense reminds me of him. He's ubiquitous in this city. Massive posters of Ruben and the entire Live on Five morning team are plastered on the sides of buses and in subway cars. Promotions for his weather segments run on the JumboTron screen across from my office in Times Square. Even at home, it's as if he's calling me. Little mementos of our time together are scattered throughout my apartment: a screwdriver he brought over to help me fix the cables to my stereo. The Columbian coffee he likes is still in my freezer. My Live on Five keychain.

Not helping matters is the fact that Valentine's Day is fast approaching. I have to admit, I'm sucked into the Hallmarketing hogwash that is inescapable in February. It's in the stores. In the newspapers. In conversations I overhear. I know the card companies are just trying to make a buck. But their research teams of psychologists and marketers have done such a good job campaigning for love that I am pulled into their vortex of needing affection in February more than any time of the year. Even more than on New Year's Eve.

As Valentine's Day nears, I get more anxious about the prospect of spending February 14th at a bar or alone at home. Sometime after midnight, on the morning of the 13th, I wake up in a panic. I've fallen asleep on the couch watching TV. My defenses are down and my emotions well up as I envision my life in ten years.

There I am, forty years old, pregnant thanks to artificial insemination. Mom, at age seventy, is on to her third husband. My child is born without a father. But the baby has three grandfathers, and of the two who are living, none are genetically related to my baby girl. On a special trip to California to show off my new little girl, Mom gets all emotional as she rocks my baby.

Mom looks to her third husband and says, "Honey, should we tell her now?"

He nods.

"Daniella," she looks into my eyes earnestly, reaches across my baby, grabs my hand, and says, "we're pregnant."

"Pregnant?"

*"We're pregnant. I'm in my second trimester. The baby's due
October 7th. It's going to be a boy."*

I look at her in disbelief.

*"Dr. Chen and his technology made it all possible. Dr. Chen says
it's getting more common all the time. We just thought why
not give parenthood another whirl? We liked it so much the first
few times. Anyway, it'll give your little darling an uncle to
play with."*

Suddenly, the prospect of simultaneous motherhood for me
and Mom is making the idea of spending Valentine's night at a
dreadful singles bar party sound more rational. But I can't bring
myself to do it. The Matzo Ball must have done more damage
than I realized. Maybe some form of post-traumatic stress disorder?

I reach for the phone on the coffee table. I want to call Ruben.
But I shouldn't. Not if I'm trying to end it. And anyway, it's after midnight, way too late to be calling him. I put down the
phone. Oh, forget it. I pick up the phone. Who can be rational
at a time like this?

I dial Mom's number. It's only 9:45 at night in California.
Of all things, Daniella. Calling your mom two days before
Valentine's Day to ask for advice? Really, you should be stronger than this by now. Asking her what to do is almost as dangerous as calling Ruben directly. It's like opening a box to a
thousand more questions. But at least I'll get a reality check.
She'll still be on her second husband and I'll still be a mere
thirty years old.

The phone keeps ringing at Mom's house, but no one picks
up, voice mail. Strange.

Hang up, dial cell phone. No answer. Voice mail.

Stanley's house? Voice mail.

Maybe this is a sign: I shouldn't be discussing my love life with Mom, and Cupid is somehow protecting me. But then I begin to wonder. Where is she?

I sit up and call Enrico. Voice mail.

Try Max. "What's up, Sista-Sista?" Max asks in his typical breezy manner.

"Where is everyone?" I try to mimic his breezy tone.

"What do you mean everyone? I'm right here."

"Mom, Stanley, Enrico? Nobody's answering their phone." I'm now pacing around the apartment.

"Dude, Hawaii," Max says loosely.

"What Hawaii?" I stop pacing, I'm growing impatient.

"They're in Hawaii," he continues easily, as if he were saying, "They're at the grocery store."

"What's in Hawaii?" I persist.

"Beaches, palm trees, excellent windsurfing."

"Come on, Max, please?" I crack a smile.

"The soon-to-be marrieds have just left on their pre-mini-moon, to an island in the Pacific . . ." Max uses the game show host voice he perfected during the days of the Mock Mom's Dates show. The theatrics continue. "Stanley whisked Mom away on a surprise trip to Hawaii for Valentine's Day."

"With Enrico?"

"No. Not with Enrico, ya goofball. Enrico's at some stupid night school for driver's ed. Got a speeding ticket. Cop said he was doin' seventy in a fifty-five—"

"Max," I interrupt. "Honestly, not so interested in Enrico's driving record. What's up with the mini-moon lovebird trip to Hawaii?" Why didn't she tell me?

"Why you so worked up? They just took a long weekend.

That's what lots of couples do on Valentine's Day," he says matter-of-factly.

Exactly. That's what couples who are deeply in love and deeply romantic do. That's just the kind of thing IB would plan for me. It's not quite what I had in mind for Mom on Valentine's Day. I figured Mom and Stanley would, at most, have some low-key dinner. Maybe an "early-bird Valentine's special dinner." The End. But Hawaii?

"Dani?" Max asks over the phone. "Earth to Dani, you there?"

"Yup. I'm here," I answer. "Just thinking. Kinda out of character for Mom to spontaneously do anything. Don't-cha think?"

"Yeah, but Mom's been doing a lot of strange things lately. Cooking, exercising."

"Cooking?" I ask in disbelief. Mom never cooks.

"Yep. Cooking," he sounds disappointed. Mom cooking is not necessarily good news. "Listen. Dani, I'm tired. I want to go to sleep. Anything else?"

"No. That's cool."

I hang up with Max and immediately dial Ruben's number. This is an emergency. I could use a good friend right now. I know it's late, but maybe he'll understand. And if Mom can be impulsive, so can I.

"Hello?" Ruben is understandably cold and disoriented when I call. I've woken him up.

"Hi. I'm sorry I'm calling so late," I whimper. His voice warms up immediately, and he becomes irresistibly sweet.

"How are you?" he asks in his soft voice.

I'm on the brink of tears. I can hardly answer.

"Hello?" he asks gently.

"Hi, I'm sorry I called. I shouldn't have woken you up."

"No. No problem."

"I should go. I should let you sleep," I apologize again.

"What's wrong?"

I'm quiet.

"Do you want to talk?" His voice is so sweet, caring, forgiving.

"Yeah."

"Now?"

"Uhh . . ."

"How about tomorrow? How about we get a drink tomorrow?"

"I'd like that," I sniffle.

"Good. In the meantime, lighten up, Mo-Hon. Good night."

I smile. Mo-Hon.

I will not spend Valentine's Day alone or with a mass of lonely hearts. I will spend the evening regressing into a comfortable, old relationship. However bad Ruben is for me longterm, he sure makes me feel better short-term, and I immediately fall asleep.

Valentine's evening is wonderful in its familiarity. As we walk to the small Turkish restaurant we resolve to drop our hurt and doubt for the night. We agree to just spend the evening together, sharing a dinner table and conversation without any vast implications. We sit down at the table and very quickly we cross over the line from faint cheek-cheek hello kisses to hand-holding.

A red light flashes inside me warning me to slow things down. I'll just get sucked into this relationship again. But my rational red light is unplugged by my emotional green light that craves comfort.

After dinner he walks me home and without asking, follows me upstairs just as he always did. I do not stop him, even though with each step, I know I should. Inside, we sit on the orange swivel stools at my bar, holding hands and talking in hushed tones about how nice it was to spend the evening to-

gether. It's after midnight, and I know he needs to be at the station in four hours for the morning show. So when he gets up, I
presume he's leaving. Instead, he pulls me up from the barstool
and wraps his strong arms around my waist. He pulls me into
him and lifts my chin for a kiss. I can't find the strength to resist his sweet lips. I'm immediately covered with goose bumps.
I know I should stop, but my defenses are too run-down, and I
slip further into his comfort. But when his hands move underneath my sweater, I pull away.

"Ruben, I can't do this," I tell him.

The silence is uncomfortable.

"I understand," he says softly. "We'll ease into it this time."

This time? Oh boy. I should stop this for good immediately.

"Thank you," I say instead.

He gives me a big bear hug, presses a kiss into my cheek, and
then holds my cheeks in his hands, looks me in the eyes, and
says, "Mo-Hon, I'll call you midmorning, after the show." Then
he leaves.

I wave good-bye and close and lock the door. I lean my back
against the door and slide down it till I'm crumpled, sitting on
the floor, my head collapsed on my knees. I'm flattened by
Ruben's intensity all over again. Tonight was all fun and good
until he said "this time." I sit there on the cold floor for a while,
conflicted. I want to start over and I want to flee. Eventually I
drag myself to my bed.

When the alarm goes off a few hours later, I'm in a panic.
Last night was suspended in time, but now I wonder again, is
Ruben the one for me? What am I going to say when he calls me
later today?

I don't have space to think about this. Rather, I don't want
to make the space to think about this. I have to get to work.
He's on air right now. I have to be on air in a couple of hours.

When I walk onto the floor of the New York Stock Exchange, I sense a volatile session. The Dow and the NASDAQ are jumping in and out of positive territory. They're directionless. They're unpredictable. They're strangely in sync with my heart fluctuations.

If I were to plot today's market activity and my romantic volatility, they would be strikingly similar: bouncing, horizontal zigzag lines with no end in sight. If Mom had a chart for the past year, it would look like a smooth and steady stock climb: starting in the bottom left-hand corner zooming up straight to the top right. How nice that would be: start at the bottom and gradually, predictably move your way up to something better.

Between reports on the floor of the Exchange, I sit in my windowless, closet-sized booth at the New York Stock Exchange and draw a nine month chart of my relationship with Ruben: highs, lows, and splits. Hopefully, I'll be able to glean some new information from the chart that will help me predict our future relationship performance. Just as I feel like I'm about to figure something out, my cell phone rings.

Mommobile.

"Hi Mom, back already?" I ask in a "thanks for ever telling me you were gone" tone. "How was Hawaii?"

"Dani? Cookie? Hi. I'm in Hawaii. It's great. Love it. Having so much fun. Went snorkeling this morning."

The phone reception is crackling. Snorkeling? Maybe I've misheard her.

"You went snorkeling?"

"Yeah! Beautiful fish!"

"You got your hair wet?" I tease, but deep down I'm frightened. If she is letting her hair get wet, it's symptomatic of something much bigger than I imagined.

"Oh, Cookie, of course I got my hair wet. And it was great! Incredible coral. I feel so rejuvenated. Oh, and we're having the most divine food and great drinks! Mmm. Love the mango juice."

Mango juice? Mom hates mangoes. Too sweet. What kind of drugs does Stanley have Mom on? Does he have any extra for me? What has this man done to her that she's spontaneously jumping on airplanes, getting her hair wet, and eating mangoes?

"Cookie?" she continues in a more serious tone. "I need your help again."

What could she possibly need from me that she can't get from him and Hawaii?

"I was wondering if you might be able to come to California. I have some more wedding details to take care of. I could really use your help."

"Aren't you vacationing in Hawaii? What details? Why are you worrying about all this right now?"

"I don't really want to get into the details. The wedding is just sixteen weeks away! Can you come?"

"Sixteen weeks is a long time. When do you need me?"

"As soon as you can make it," she says.

I look down at the romantic volatility chart on my desk and trace its ups and downs with my finger.

"I'll come." Running away from the Ruben problem seems a serendipitous quick fix. "This weekend."

"This weekend? Terrific!" She's overjoyed. "I'll call from Hawaii today and make appointments in San Francisco for this weekend. I'll be back in the Bay Area Thursday."

I look down at the chart. There's going to be a gap in the Ruben volatility chart.

Twenty-two

The jet propellers slam into reverse as the wheels burn tarmac in San Francisco. I'm relieved to have escaped New York and the Ruben question. And anyway, who could be so cruel as to turn away her mother in a time of need?

Mom picks me up at the airport, and before I even close the car door, she launches into the agenda for the next forty-eight hours. Her eyes are darting from the road to me and back to the road as she drives. The words "swatch," "shoes," and "tuxedo" fly from her mouth. Her high energy level is like a jump into cold water, even after thirty years. But something feels different about her today. No. Something looks different. The hair is the same light brown. She's tan from Hawaii. And, her teeth. It's the teeth! They seem whiter. In fact, they seem unnaturally white.

"Mom, what's going on with your teeth?"

"Nothing. Just teeth." She smiles, taps her pearly whites together a few times and launches back into planning.

"You're bleaching them!" I smile.

"Am not."

I narrow my eyes and look at her.

"Okay, so I am. Just trying to look my best for the big day. Anything wrong with that?"

"No. But if you bleach them any more, your wedding dress is going to look dirty by comparison. Any other prettying up planned?"

"No."

"No?"

"Well, yes."

"Well?"

"Oh, it's nothing much, just a little change."

"Mom, what is it?"

"Oh, it's not that important. Anyway, so the shoes I'm looking for—"

Oh no, she's not going to get away with switching the subject on me, that's my specialty. I wonder if Stanley is the brains behind this makeover plan.

"What are you going to do or have done?" I persist.

"This Bay Area traffic gets worse and worse all the time," she says, glancing over her shoulder to check her blind spot.

"Mom?" What's to hide? Is Stanley encouraging liposuction, Botox, or collagen injections? How dare he. "Mom? He's not pushing for plastic surgery or anything is he?"

"Oh, no!" Mom says, acting just as outraged at the idea as I am.

"So what is it?"

"Earrings."

"What?"

"Stanley thinks I should get my ears pierced," she says.

Ears pierced! I've been telling my mom forever that clip-ons look like garbage. But she's always stubbornly resisted getting her ears pierced. The only thing she's ever updated in our discussion of ear piercings is her excuse for avoiding it: "What if someone pulls on the earring and rips my ear? What if it gets infected? What's wrong with clip-ons?" Now, one request from this guy, and she plans to get holes punched in her ears?

"Ears pierced? Already?" I tease. "Any other surprises?" I wonder what else he's talked her into that we kids haven't.

"No, no more surprises," she says. "But if you'd go with me for the piercing, I'd really appreciate it. Oh! And I can't wait for you to meet Trey."

"Trey?"

"Yeah, Trey. You know Trey. My personal trainer," she says as if everybody knew.

"Trey, my personal trainer?" What is going on here? My mother does not cook. She does not get her hair wet. And she certainly does not exercise with a personal trainer. Who is this woman who looks like Mom but is acting like someone else? I didn't even think "personal trainer" was in her vocabulary.

"But you've never worked out in your entire life!"

"Well, if Stanley's dieting for this wedding, I figure the least I can do is some toning."

Isn't that quaint? They're getting in shape together.

"You'll meet Trey tomorrow, seven A.M. Fridays it's thirty minutes cardio, usually on the bike, and thirty minutes muscle toning."

"What bike?" Mom doesn't ride bikes.

"Oh. I didn't tell you? I got a stationary bike in the garage. Right in front of the TV."

Mom is not a TV-watching, stationary-bike riding, ear-piercing, tooth-whitening cook. Am I even in the right place? I need reassurance. I look at the pedals in the automatic car. Her right foot is on the gas, her left foot hovers above the brake, ready to screech to a stop. Yep. It's Mom all right.

"Trey might be able to show you a few good Pilates moves," Mom says.

Great. Mom and Pilates. This is going to be a long weekend.

The doorbell wakes me up Friday morning at 6:55. Mom peeks her head in my room on her way to answer the front door. She's wearing black spandex tights, a snug-fitting pink T-shirt, and sneakers. I rub my eyes. I must be dreaming. She's never worn spandex in her life. She's never been relaxed enough to be seen in a T-shirt. And she's always said white sneakers are tacky.

"Wake up, Cookie! Get out of bed. Come downstairs! Meet Trey," and she disappears from the bedroom door.

I hide my head under the covers. I hear a deep, male voice and my mom's high-pitched giggles.

I need a personal trainer to help get me out of bed.

Alas, Trey's tied up at the moment, so I'll have to be my own personal cheerleader. First, take a deep breath and reveal the head. Good, Daniella. Then the shoulders. Rest. Breathe. It's not so overwhelming. You can handle this. Sit up, nice and easy. That's it. So what if she's wearing pink? Turn sideways, drop feet on the floor. So what if she has a personal trainer? Rest. So what if she looks great in spandex? Head back on pillow.

Finally, I coax myself out of bed. I put on one of Mom's old, floral, quilted house coats over my flannel plaid pajamas. I'm so glam. I arrive in the basement just in time to see Mom lying on her back and Trey stretching her straightened leg toward her upper body. Trey is gorgeous! Long brown hair, brown eyes, and a tanned, rippling body. Of all the trainers in the world, my mother picked him? Nice, Mom, nice. He must be a model or actor supporting himself as a personal trainer.

"Hi, Cookie," Mom calls from her position on her back. "This is Trey. Trey, my daughter, Daniella."

"I've heard so much about you," Trey says, looking at me while holding Mom's ankle with one hand and bending her knee with the other. "You're out in New York. A weather reporter, right?"

Weather, traffic, business, who cares? Here's a guy who's so good-looking, I just want to agree with him. On everything. He could have said, "You're a veterinarian, right?" and I would have wanted to bark yes.

"Your mom is a very energetic woman," he says, as if this is news. "And she is going to be in the best shape of her life for her wedding. Right, Maya?"

Oh, pu-lease.

"That's right," Mom chirps.

"I'd be happy to work with you while you're out here." Trey looks me over.

I look him over and admire his hard body. Is my trip really only three days long?

"Thank you. But I'm only here a few days, and Mom's got me running around plenty. Pleasure to meet you, I've got to go, big day ahead."

"Pleasure to meet you," he says while pulling Mom's arm way back as she lies on her side, cheek squashed to the floor.

"Cookie?" she halfway groans and yelps in pain. "First stop—shoes."

Gotcha.

• • •

Mom is marching around the shoe section at Nordstrom's holding the swatch of wedding dress fabric down next to each different pair of shoes to see if the shades of ivory match.

"Ivory shoes? It's so silly to buy this color," Mom says, showing signs of being the levelheaded woman who raised me. "They self-destruct. I'll only be able to wear them once, and then they'll be destroyed." She holds a shoe up and inspects it. "But I guess if there's any time to wear ivory shoes, now is my moment." As she peruses the options, she explains that she wants to look good and be comfortable. When I pick up a pair of low-heeled ivory pumps and show it to her, she looks at me in disdain.

"I want something comfortable, not geriatric!" She rolls her eyes.

Okay. Just trying to help.

As we're sitting in those comfortable department store chairs waiting for a salesperson to bring out shoes, it occurs to me that the men in the wedding party probably need more help getting ready for the ceremony than Mom does.

"So, what's the stupendous Stan going to wear?" I ask, thinking of the tacky maroon polyester blazer he wore over Thanksgiving. Stanley had said, "it's cardinal red, like the color of Stanford University," where he works. Another time, I saw his university pride stretched proudly across his belly. He was in his garage, wearing a too tight Stanford Linear Accelerator T-shirt pulled like a drum taut over his paunch with jeans that were hiked up above his waist. Seems his fashion sense is defined entirely by school spirit. Will he wear a maroon tie and cummerbund to the wedding? Yikes.

"Funny you should ask." Mom drops her voice and gives me a serious look. "I hate to say it, but he doesn't exactly have the best fashion sense."

Aha! Stanley isn't perfect after all.

The saleslady comes out with half a dozen boxes of shoes and sets them on the floor in front of us.

"Thank you," Mom nods to her then turns to me. "Well, I gently suggested that if I was going to wear a special white gown, he might consider wearing a tuxedo." She steps up and into a pair of shoes. "He said he had a tuxedo already, just had to find it." Mom sits down and looks at me. "Of course it was the tuxedo he wore when he married Miriam thirty years ago. Well, that obviously made me uncomfortable, but I didn't really want to say anything."

She inspects her foot as she flexes and straightens her toes in another pair of ivory pumps.

"So, he found the vintage tuxedo in mothballs in the back of his closet. It reeked!" Mom tells. "It had bell-bottoms, a huge lapel, and surprise, it didn't fit. Just a tad too tight. I was so relieved. Now we could buy or rent a tuxedo a bit more modern. Well, turns out, the tuxedos for rent were . . . I don't know, what is the word? Cheesy? You know the polyester kind? And, the guy trying to rent the tuxedos was pushing colored or printed bow ties and cummerbunds."

Mom turns back to the shoes, opens another box, steps into the pumps, twirls around before the mirror, and comes back. I can tell from her face she doesn't like the shoes and is getting impatient with shoe shopping. She sits down next to me again.

"Anyway, so I didn't like the tuxes they had for rent. And I didn't like the sales guy catering to Stan's taste. So I suggested we look at the tuxes for sale. Of course those tuxedos were much better quality. Fine light wools, beautiful tailoring. But Stanley wasn't sold. He thought he might as well rent, because it was going to be a one-time event. But then . . ." Mom turns to me and with a sparkle in her eye says, "I told him, 'You'll use the tux again. Our kids will get married sooner or later.'"

Right. I guess "sooner" applies to my brothers or my new stepsister. "Later" most likely applies to me. I can only hope IB shows up before I go gray.

"So, he tried on a few tuxes," she explains, "and we picked out a beautiful tux for him. It'll go to the tailor two weeks before the wedding when he's lost all his weight. That diet is really working for him."

Mom leans over for another look at the shoes. I give the thumbs-up on two pairs. She's still not convinced.

"I'll just buy these four pairs here, put it on a card," she explains, "then return the ones I don't like."

Good to see Mom's lifetime commitment to sensible spending vanish in the shoe department.

We're walking in the mall, and Mom squeezes my arm as Anne's Jewelers comes into view. We're on our way to getting holes in Mom's ears. She made me wait till I was sixteen to get my ears pierced, and now at sixty she's going take the leap herself. I'll be the experienced one holding her hand.

"Will it hurt? How can I keep my ears from getting infected? What kinds of earrings should I get?" she asks nervously as we walk through the mall toward the jewelry store.

"It'll be relatively painless, easy to care for, and any earrings will be fine," I reassure her.

Anne's Jewelers is one of those generic mall stores with fluorescent lights, red carpets, and dozens of glass display cases. We walk in and see a handful of teenage girls leaning over a display case oohing and ahhing over silver heart-shaped pendants. A saleslady in her twenties approaches us.

"Good afternoon. Can I help you with something?" She's wearing a name tag that reads Stacy, but no jewelry.

"Well," I explain, "my mom here would like to get her ears pierced. You do that, right?"

Mom tries to look calm, but Stacy picks up on her squeamish vibe.

"Sure. I've been doing piercings for well over a year. You've got nothing to worry about," Stacy says in a matronly tone. "Usually I pierce for teenagers and newborns. Adults are a piece of cake—although I don't see it too often."

Mom nods, still wary.

"You're going to just love having pierced ears," Stacy says, swatting her hand forward in conviction. "Sometimes, people get their ears pierced, love it so much, they get addicted to piercings. Oh, and tattoos. Lots of my friends started with two holes, then went to three and couldn't stop. People just get hooked on body art. You know, a ring here, a tattoo there. You'll wonder why you didn't do it earlier."

Serial body artists. I'd forgotten about them. They aren't just teenagers. In fact tattoos, or as the cool people call it, "ink," are becoming more popular among the senior crowd. I have a distant aunt who at age seventy-one, got a tattoo to celebrate the birth of her grandson. It's a little heart tattooed on her left shoulder, with the word "Grandma" printed on the arrow piercing the heart.

"Hope you don't mind me asking, but why are you getting your ears pierced now?" Stacy asks.

"I'm getting married," Mom says.

"That's great. Congratulations. Never too late to try all kinds of new things. Speaking of . . . you know tattooed wedding bands are all the rage right now . . . just a band tattooed straight onto the ring finger. Nothing says forever like a tattoo!"

"Oh," Mom says.

Maybe encouraging Mom in this ear-piercing endeavor was

a mistake. In her current state of bridal bliss, she's highly impressionable. She's already done the tooth bleaching, the getting into shape, the cooking. What's to keep her from going to town with holes and ink?

She could start with the ear piercing. Then add a third hole for kicks. Then (as she's always been fascinated by multicultural customs) she might go for a Hindu-like gold nose ring. Perhaps she'd add a Mayan-style serpent wrapped and tatooed around her upper arm. A wedding band tattooed on her ring finger. She'd insist the whole thing would look cool with her bare shoulders in the wedding dress.

"Cookie? Cookie?" Mom rouses me from my panic fantasy. "Pearls or gold posts?"

"Pearls! Pearls!" I say.

She points at the simple, conservative pearls in the case, sits down in the piercing chair, squeezes her eyes shut tight, and waits for the needle to stick.

Twenty-three

On the red-eye back to New York Sunday night, I realize I must end it with Ruben. And we never even got back together! It's the third time I've found myself flying back to a man I'm not sure about. Why, oh why did I have to get so weak on Hallmark hell day? If I make a step-by-step plan for this breakup, write down every word I need to say and rehearse it, it might go more smoothly. I'll try to explain my ambivalences without hurting his feelings any more than I already have. I'll tell him he hasn't done anything wrong. That I'm just not ready for a relationship. Or, this relationship. No, "a" relationship is better. I've got to see him in person.

Monday night, back in my apartment, I pick up the receiver many times and then put it back down. Finally I muster the nerve to call him. He answers in an unemotional tone. We make small talk, but it's awkward.

"How was your trip?" he asks. "Your mom?"

Blah, blah, blah.

"Maybe we should get together . . ." I suggest.

He cuts me off. "Daniella. I know what you're thinking. I can hear it in your voice. I can read your actions. Not hard to figure out what another emergency trip to California means for you and me. Valentine's was a lapse. I know it. Got it. That's okay," he says coldly. "But I don't think we should see each other or talk anymore. For a long time. Good luck with your mom. Good luck with your career. Good-bye."

Good-bye? That's it? Not "let's discuss it?" That's harsh. Last time we broke up, he tried to get me back. He called. He sent me letters. I felt guilty. But somehow it seemed easier, like we were easing out of the relationship.

This cut-and-dried "it's over" approach is an abrupt jolt of reality. He's given up on me. I understand. He's right. It's the best way to handle this. Probably the way we should have done it before. But does it really need to be so drastic?

At least this clean break leaves me where I want to be. Free, open, and available. I am back in a familiar space. Strong, independent, accomplished woman of the twenty-first century. Unambiguously single.

No one will want to hear every nitty-gritty detail of my life (except Mom). Who will know if I had a bad day? Who will be there to make it better?

I will not have a date for Mom's wedding. I don't even have a dress for Mom's wedding. Of all things, I should at least be able to find a dress. The dress doesn't require emotion or commitment.

Beep.

Oh, God. Phone anxiety. Is it Ruben? Who is it?

Beep.

Phone says, "Momhome."

How does she always manage to catch me at my most vulnerable moments? Maternal instinct. Or maybe it's the rule of probability: I'm having more vulnerable moments, and she's calling more often.

Beep. Beep.

She probably just wants to know whether my flight back was okay.

Beep. Beep.

"Hello?" I answer.

"Cookie?" she sounds really weak.

"What's wrong?" I ask.

"Uhh . . ." she sounds disoriented.

"Mom?"

"Uhh . . ."

"What's going on?" I prod.

"Ummm, my face hurts."

"What?"

"My face hurts . . . You used to be a health reporter . . . microdermabrasion?"

"Microdermabrasion?"

"Yeah, and chemical peels?"

"Did you have microdermabrasion?"

"Yeah."

"Microdermabrasion shouldn't hurt, but the chemical peel can," I say in my best doctorly bedside manner. "Is it stinging?"

"Yeah. It's stinging."

"Where are you?" I ask.

"Lying on my back on the living room rug. I'm fanning my face. What else can I do? I didn't think it was going to burn like this!"

"Mom, put some ice on your poor face."

"I have ice on it. But it's barely helping."

"What were you thinking?"

"I just wanted to look good for the wedding." She sounds ashamed. "I didn't want to do Botox or a face lift. So I thought this might be better. But they didn't say it would hurt so much."

"Tylenol."

"What?"

"Take some aspirin or something. That could help, too."

"Okay, I just don't want to get up right now. It burns too much."

"Mom. You. Are. Beautiful. You don't have to do any of this stuff. Just be natural, and stop worrying. It's the worrying that ages us. Didn't you always tell me that a smile is the best makeup? Your youth is in your charm. You shouldn't suffer for this wedding."

"I know," she says. "It's just the magazines. The books. Everyone looks so beautiful. So young."

"They *are* young!!" I'm mad at Mom for hurting herself. I'm mad at the dermatologist for letting her do this. I'm mad at those stupid magazines for preying on the young, the old, the impressionable.

"I know. I just thought. Well, I just hoped . . ."

"Mom," I say sternly. "Next time, call me *before* you do something like this. Not after!"

"Okay, okay," she says sheepishly.

"I mean why not go to a sauna? Get a facial? Take a soy bath? Try something natural? How about sunblock? How about makeup? There are a million things you can do before you go slathering chemicals on your face and submitting to some machine designed to scrape and scratch at your face. How do you look, anyway?"

"A little raw. A little red. The doctor says it'll look better in a couple of days. I don't want anyone to see me like this. My face is too sore. It's just so tender. Like they took a layer of my skin off."

Are you kidding me?

"They did take a layer of your skin off." C'mon, Miss Ph.D. "That's what it was all about."

"I guess so," she says.

"Mom. You'll be fine. Get some ice. Get some aspirin. Tell Stanley what's happened, and let him come take care of you. He needs to love you in sickness and in health, no matter how sick you look or act."

"He can't see me like this."

"Mom!"

"Okay, okay," she whimpers, exhausted, "I'll call him."

"Okay," I say. "Call me later."

We hang up. Technology better be advanced thirty years from now so I don't have to suffer chemicals, knives, or skin-blasting tools to maintain a youthful complexion. Better yet, society will have evolved enough in thirty years' time to respect the beauty of age and the wisdom that comes with it. If all else fails, I have a plan. I'm just going to put on some weight. I'll eat and eat until fat fills up my wrinkles.

Ruben. Back to Ruben. Maybe in thirty years' time, there will be some kind of surgery or treatment to rid me of the pain of emotional roller-coaster relationships. If it were available today, I'd climb onto a gurney immediately and put myself first in line for the doctor's knife. Right now I'd go. I mean it. Doctor, take the pain of failed relationships and loneliness away. Please. Surgery, drugs, therapy. I'll take it. Yeah, so it sounds a bit like a lobotomy. But it'd be different. I hope.

If only I could think of something easier, more immediate, a little escape with instant gratification to ease the pain of Ruben's abrupt breakup. I don't smoke. I don't do drugs. Maybe I should.

I'll call Stefanie. She'll know what I'm going through. She was such a good girlfriend when we went ring shopping together. Last time I talked to her, she had just broken up with her boyfriend, and her mom's fourth marriage sounded shaky.

"Stefanie?" I tell her about Ruben breakup number two and California trip number three.

"You've got to be kidding me," she says. "You're worried about a sorry life after breaking up with a crack weather reporter? Come on, give me a break!"

Recently, she's become increasingly pessimistic about marriage. Now she even claims to love the single life. Yeah. Right. Sure.

"You're still worked up about your mom getting married before you? Please. Marriage is so old school. So retro. Look where four weddings got my mom. Nowhere. I'm quite fine without it, thank you. And you will be, too."

"I don't feel better," I tell her.

"You know what I do when I'm feeling like shit, Daniella?"

"What?"

"Retail therapy."

"Retail therapy?"

"Retail therapy."

"Well, I'm glad you can get such a quick fix, but I hate shopping," I remind her.

"You should give it a chance," Stefanie continues. "We ended up having fun finding that wedding band for your mom, no? Anyway, I could use some retail therapy myself, and you'll be my excuse. Let's go. Tomorrow. We'll get something nice for you. Not for work. Not for the wedding. Not socks. Not another wedding band for your mom. Not an independence ring. Just something nice for you. Whaddaya think?"

"Stefanie, I have to go to work tomorrow. I've got to be at the Exchange. It's Tuesday. We don't all have a flexible writer's schedule."

"Blow it off, Dani," Stefanie insists. "How old are you? How many kids have you got? Mortgages? You don't even have a dog. Not even goldfish to take care of. Take advantage of it. Lighten up!"

"I don't want to go shopping. It'll just stress me out. It'll just remind me that I don't have anything to wear to her stinking wedding," I say.

"Fine!" Stefanie counters. "We'll be productive. We'll get you one fine dress that'll make you feel foxy at the wedding. It'll be for you. Not exclusively for the wedding. Purple? Backless? Frontless? Foxy and frontless?"

"Stefanie, that's not exactly proper wedding etiquette."

"So many hang-ups, Dani. Get over it! Who cares about proper etiquette? Trust me, after my mom's four weddings, I can tell you it makes no difference. Anyway, what do you think women were fighting for in the sixties? For us to follow men's rules of correct etiquette and femininity? Hardly. Daniella. Get a girdle or get a grip. Let's go downtown first thing tomorrow morning and take care of this dress bit. It'll be entertaining."

"Let me think about it," I tell her. "I'll call you back."

"Don't think too hard." She hangs up.

Retail therapy. Hmm. It worked when I was in high school. Maybe it could work again now. I know, I know. I hate shopping. But I do need a dress, and I haven't even had a moment to find one because I've spent so much time on Mom's dress. Okay, okay. Maybe I don't have a dress because of a wee bit of procrastination. All right, fine. I admit. Maybe I don't have a dress because of a subconscious resistance to Mom getting remarried.

But give me a break, please. How would you feel? Do you know what an appropriate dress for the daughter of the bride looks like? I still don't know after months of being one. I still don't even know what my roles and responsibilities are for the actual wedding. Despite going to bookstores, libraries, and surfing online, I still can't find an etiquette guide for the daughter of the bride. Not even *Daughter of the Bride for Dummies.* I'm just making it up as I go. As a strong, independent, accomplished woman of the twenty-first century, I should, at very least, be able to tackle the dress task.

I e-mail a note to my boss requesting a personal day. I call Stefanie.

"You're on," I say. "But remember, we have to get a dress. No messing around."

"Fine," she says. "I won't let anything get in the way of finding a dress: nothing will creep in or distract us from our mission. No mission creep."

"Fine. See you at eleven tomorrow morning, Broadway and Prince."

At nine-thirty Stefanie calls.

"You out of bed?" she asks.

"No. I don't feel so well," I hedge.

"Bullshit. Don't mess with me. You know I'm taking time out of my valuable and limited writer's schedule to meet you." She hangs up.

No chance to protest. I stay lying in bed, depressed, thinking about Ruben. Then I become more rational. If I don't find a dress now, I'll have to do it later. At least if I go today, Stefanie can distract me. But why bother dress shopping at all? I have plenty of dresses here in the closet. I don't really need something new. On the other hand, who knows? Maybe I'll find a dress so fabulous that it'll make me feel fabulous inside. And I already "wrote" in sick to work. Might as well take advantage of it. Fine. I coax myself out of bed, into the shower, into some clothes, onto the subway, and downtown to meet Stefanie.

Stefanie raises her left hand as if taking an oath when I see her.

"I, Stefanie Rose, to the best of my ability, promise to uphold the responsibilities of preventing mission creep. I will not let anything derail, distract, or sidetrack from 'mission find Daniella DOB dress,' So help me God, amen."

I smile hello.

"But first, I just want to take a quick peek into this kitchen store around the corner," she says. "You don't mind, do you?"

"You're fired! You are mission creep personified." I laugh.

"So, was California that bad?" Stefanie asks as we walk toward the kitchen store.

"Let's just say I'm grateful to live in New York. One weekend on the West Coast reminds me how valuable distance from family can be. But now I'm back here dealing with breakup number two with Ruben, and it's no vacation. He just said, 'Good-bye, have a nice life.'"

"So?"

"Well, it's what I wanted, and it's right, but it doesn't make it any easier," I explain.

"Get over it! Dwelling on it won't improve anything. How hard could it be?" Leave it to cynical Stefanie with her spiky, orangey red hair to yank the heartache and emotion out of the experience.

"You should feel lucky, Daniella. You'll be over Ruben the split second you meet someone new. And knowing you, you could meet someone this afternoon. The question is, Miss Picky, is any man good enough for you?" Stefanie opens the door and walks into the kitchenware store.

"I'll just be a minute," she says as she starts to caress a blue wineglass on the very first display shelf. "You know, Daniella, you're pretty lucky. At least you don't have to help your mom pick out china patterns for her bridal registry."

Stefanie's right. It could be much worse.

"And you don't have to organize a bridal shower for her. Do you? I had to go to one for my mom. It was a champagne brunch for her wedding to hubby number three. If your mom decides to have one, you could give her a set of these wineglasses. Aren't they pretty?" Stefanie then starts walking to the back of the store. "Oh, they have an excellent knife collection here! Come. Take a look at these ceramic knives."

I follow her, but I'm hung up on the bridal shower bit. Have I shirked my responsibility? Should I organize a bridal shower for Mom?

All those ladies over at the house on a Sunday morning wearing pastels, floral prints, and matching sweater sets. They gush "my son" this and "my daughter" that. One lady bounces her four-year-old granddaughter on her knee. The ladies congratulate me on Mom's remarriage, tell me how hard my father's death was, and ask me about my love life.

"Tick, tick, tick," they remind me of my biological clock.

As the bubbly flows, they get increasingly tipsy. Their perfectly applied lipstick gets on their teeth. The top layers of their sweater sets come off with each hot flash.

Mom sits in a high-backed chair with a mountain of pastel gift boxes at her feet. The dozen ladies sit around the coffee table, mimosas in hand. Underneath the satiny ribbons and printed wrapping paper, Mom finds a cappuccino maker. A heart-shaped waffle iron. A pair of candlesticks. All of the gifts are luxuries, Mom already has all the household necessities. The requisite oohs and aahs are followed by the "thank yous" and "you're so thoughtfuls."

Another round of mimosas. Mom reaches for a slim, rectangular, shirt-sized box. The ladies giggle, whisper, and fan themselves. The attached card says something about "spicy." Mom looks at me. I am mortified, but I nod "go ahead."

Mom lifts the tape off of the pink wrapping paper, lifts the top off the box, unfolds the pink tissue paper inside, and her eyes bug out. Her face turns red, and she quickly closes the box.

"C'mon. Don't be shy," the ladies egg her on. "We're old enough to handle this." Giggles and whistles drown out the classical music playing in the background. Mom, half-embarrassed, half-thrilled, looks at me for permission. I nod okay again. I have to. And out from the box comes the skimpiest, laciest, silkiest purple g-string teddy I've ever seen. Mom holds it up to herself, unable to suppress her smile. Then she stands up, holds the teddy to her torso, and starts prancing-dancing through the room, kicking the boxes, wrapping paper, and tissue paper that litter the floor into the air. Someone throws confetti on her. The cameras flash, the ladies clap, smile, and throw their heads back, laughing.

A scraping sound brings me back into reality. Stefanie's trying the knife sharpener. I wince.

"What's wrong?" Stefanie asks, putting down the knife and sharpener.

"Nothing, just thinking about the bridal shower thing."

"Truth is," Stefanie says, leading us out of the store, "your mom doesn't need a shower. You need a shower."

I look at her skeptically. Do I smell?

"An unbridal shower," Stefanie says. "A shower where you go to Barney's or Bloomie's, pick out your favorite outfits and register for them. Then your friends buy them for you and give them to you at a party."

She pulls at a lock of her red hair and contemplates.

"Sounds good," I say.

"An unbridal shower makes more sense, presuming you're still bent on attracting and marrying a man," she says. "If you're single, and you want to attract a man, awesome clothes can help do the trick. Heck, you could even put lingerie on your unbridal shower registry. What better way to keep your allure high than with a silky number? Once you've got a man, you don't need that sexy teddy anymore. You can wear washed-out cotton briefs and bras for the rest of your life. Now's the time to put a teddy to use," she says.

"And, it's more practical to have a shower while you're single," she continues. "Once you have a man in your life, you have dual incomes, you have more disposable income. By then, you don't really need a shower. Now, while you're on your own, is the time you need the most help. Not after you've found your mate, presuming again that finding a husband remains important to you."

"Great idea, Stefanie. Makes sense. Gifts without legal documents signed or strings attached? Sounds just the way things should be. Go ahead, throw me a shower. I won't resist."

"Ha! I'd love to, but we don't have time right now, do we? Don't we need to find you a dress for the wedding?" Stefanie says.

"That's what I thought," I say, and we head for the trendy boutiques.

The dresses I pull off the racks are evidently the result of my passive-aggressive state of mind: a bright polka-dot dress with a

Flamenco flair; a lace and acid-washed denim dress that looks like something Madonna wore in the eighties; a plain, conservative black dress.

"That black one looks like a mourning gown," Stefanie says.

"So?" I ask petulantly.

"Maybe you and your new stepsister should wear matching dresses," Stefanie torments me. "Fuschia, ruffled, tea-length and taffeta?"

A couple hours into the mission, I find one acceptable dress. It's even cute. It's a fitted, spaghetti-strapped cocktail dress with a knee-length A-line skirt. It's white with a pattern of delicate black roses that look as if they were painted by hand all over the fabric. I buy the dress when I see its magnificent return policy — sixty days and money back.

What would a dream return policy say if attached to a guy?

Take him home. Try him on. Try him on with different shoes and hairdos. Does he need accessories to look good? Does he really fit? Does he accentuate your best features or detract from them? Does he make you look better or worse? Does he make you feel fat? Does he make you feel younger? Is he scratchy or uncomfortable in any way? Or is he smooth and supple against your skin? Is he restricting or too loose? Any elasticity? Is he functional or just a guilty pleasure?

Take him out on the town. Is he versatile? Can he go to many different events, or is he only good for one kind of gathering? Can you run with him and play? Or is he only good for a formal sit-down meal? Do your friends like him? Does your family like him? Look at him over and over.

Is he interesting? Well-tailored? Was he made by good designers? How does he respond when you spill something on him? Does he resist stains or absorb them?

Any problems, and you can get your money/time back, no questions asked.

I clutch my shopping bag (with the black-and-white cocktail dress and fabulous return policy in it) as Stefanie and I press on with the dress mission. We're walking up Broadway when we stop dead in our tracks. Tents and Timberlands on display in the window of an outdoor sports supply store call our names like Sirens beckoning Odysseus. The mission creep alarm wails, warning us we're veering off course. We ignore it, unable to resist the allure of the sleeping bags and camping stoves in the store window. We look at each other. We know we will surrender to temptation.

We walk in and squeal with excitement. This is the closest we've come to the great outdoors in awhile. The fleece jackets, the hiking boots, the water sandals! Stefanie is immediately drawn to a corner bursting with first-aid kits. She's planning a trip to Africa and is captivated by the kit that contains sterile syringes and a "do-it-yourself epoxy dental-filling kit."

I'm looking for a compass. No reason. I just think they're cool. The idea of a device that tells you where you are and how to get where you need to go seems priceless. After some tinkering and testing, I orient myself toward the camping food section. The air-light, airtight, freeze-dried "dinners" packed in shiny silver wrapping are intriguing. It's what astronauts eat while traveling in outer space. Maybe I'll take a few home in case of a future dinner emergency. I could even serve them at a dinner party.

"It's the very latest in trendy cuisine," I would tell them.

The freeze-dried Neopolitan ice cream sandwiches look good.

"Hey, Stefanie, hungry?" I toss a shiny bag of "food" toward her.

She catches it, inspects the label.

"Nope, don't like chicken teriyaki. Prefer the beef stroganoff," and she tosses it back.

But a cute salesman intercepts, snatching the "chicken teriyaki" midair.

"The albacore tuna and cheese noodle casserole is the best," he says. "You ladies planning a camping trip?"

I stare at Stefanie. Stefanie's going to have to talk about her Africa trip. Ain't no way I'm telling him we're actually dress shopping for my mom's wedding. I haven't been camping in three years.

"I'm going to Kenya in June," Stefanie picks up the cue. "I've survived New York; now I need a Darwinian adventure outside the city."

While she's talking, I check out the man, whose name tag reads Chad. He's got longish strawberry-blond hair, green gray eyes, and he hasn't shaved in a few days. His muscled neck suggests a beautiful body hiding under his forest-green fleece. I'd like to believe it's from kayaking or chopping firewood.

"The epoxy in the dental kit makes it a really good value," he says. "Last thing you want in Africa is tooth trouble. I just got back from Tanzania. You don't want to skimp on the first-aid kit. And you've got to be really careful with the water. Have you seen our new portable water filtration system?" Once they cover the benefits of the water filtration system, he engrosses her in a conversation about mosquito netting and zip-off pant-shorts.

While Stefanie's trying on zip-off pants, Chad helps me. I tell him I'm looking for a compass and a Swiss Army knife. I explain I want a simple Swiss Army knife. Like the one Dad had. You know the kind; corkscrew, two blades, a can opener. Chad knows exactly what I'm looking for.

"But can I show you a few other knives, too?" Chad asks. He sets four other knives on the glass counter, each one more elaborate than the last. He explains each model until finally he arrives at the SwissChamp XLT.

"Just take a look. The SwissChamp XLT knife has fifty functions, including four blades, a nail file, and a fish scaler with hook disgorger. I wouldn't feel safe in the wilderness without it." Of course I don't need all these gadgets, but I pay attention because I like them, and I want to make Chad happy. Stefanie comes out of the dressing room in the zip-off pants. Her right leg is in full pant, the left leg zipped off into shorts.

"What do you think?" she asks. Chad and I give her the thumbs-up.

Half an hour later, Stefanie and I are walking out of the store smiling and waving good-bye to Chad. Both of us have Chad's business card, but he didn't ask either of us for our numbers. Our wallets are lighter and our shopping bags heavier. I bought two Leatherman knives (for my brothers,) a simple compass, and the SwissChamp XLT. Stefanie bought the top-end first-aid kit, a water filter, the mosquito net, and the zip-off pants, too. Ahh, retail therapy.

Outside, Stefanie dutifully tries to lure me into another dress shop. "If we find the right dress, you won't have to go shopping anymore."

I convince her (which isn't hard) that I've already got one acceptable dress in the bag. More importantly, it'll be much more interesting to navigate our way to a lunch spot using the new compass than it will be to endure another dress boutique. We can even use the SwissChamp XLT to cut sandwiches or pop the cork off a bottle of wine. She pretends to raise a white flag in defeat. Mission creep again proves stronger than we are. We unwrap the compass, laughing at how utterly useless it is in Gotham. A couple bucks gets you much farther in this city.

What I really need is a love compass. Unfortunately, that's not for sale.

"So, what's the hurry to get married anyway?" Stefanie asks as we sit down for lunch. Stefanie rifles through her first-aid kit.

"I mean there's no reason for women like us to get married anymore. It's such an antiquated institution. We're professional women. We can support ourselves. We can have kids without getting married. Hello? What do you think artificial insemination is all about?" Stefanie inspects the do-it-yourself suture set. "Truth is, I figured I'd be divorced by now, not married. The institution of marriage is like slavery. Who needs that?"

Okay, Stefanie's being a little extreme, but I'll go with it.

"Married people live longer, healthier lives," I try. "They have more sex."

"Yeah, yeah, yeah," Stefanie concedes. "I admit, there are some perks. Like the bachelorette party. Your mom is going to have a bachelorette party, no?"

"I don't know." I shudder at the thought.

"Oh, she should definitely have one!" Stefanie says. "Can't you just see your mom and her pack of sixty-year-old girlfriends roaming drunk, tripping, and singing through the streets of San Francisco?"

No, I can't see it.

"Just think: they're in their skimpiest outfits and highest heels swinging miniature plastic penises on keychains in the air, singing, 'Girls just wanna have fun.' They're wearing feather boas and glitter makeup, and they're sucking down cigarettes."

"I've got the picture; you can stop now," I say.

But Stefanie continues. "They'd end up at some foul hole-in-the-wall club with your mom dancing and grinding on the bar in her miniskirt whirling the boa as the barflies egg her on."

"Enough!" I insist.

"Ooo . . . sorry, I didn't think you were so fragile," Stefanie snaps back.

I think to myself, *I didn't realize you were so shattered.*

Twenty-four

The frenetic scene on the floor of the NYSE is an oasis compared to my personal life. At the Exchange, I report on companies. I have no emotional attachment to them. I watch the markets fly and dive. I cannot influence them. As I work, I define myself as an individual. I don't rely on a man to help define me. I am proud of what I accomplish on my own.

One early afternoon, the markets are slow, and I'm so comfortable, I'm actually bored. I'm standing in my camera position on the floor of the Exchange mumbling words to myself, trying to memorize my lines. But it's difficult today. The content is just so dull. I'm fidgeting with my clip-on microphone when Scott, the producer in London, dials into my earpiece.

"Perk up, lady," he says into my earpiece. "You're looking sleepy on the preview monitor here in London. Is it really that dull?"

"How could you tell?" I give a weary glance up at the camera and go back to tinkering with the microphone on my lapel.

"Find some energy. You've got thirty seconds to air."

"I'm looking," I say, not even bothering to look up at the camera.

Then, from deep within the crowd of traders, a young messenger emerges, makes a bee line straight for me, places a trading slip in my hand, and disappears back into the buzz. Hmm, nice surprise. This note might spice up my report. Traders often pass me news tips or opinions scribbled onto these two-by-three-inch trading slips, which I then relay to viewers.

"Drinks? 4:30? Delmonico's? Josh," it reads, in straight and small handwriting.

Josh? Who's Josh? I'm confused. This is not broadcast material! I look up, around, no recognition from anyone. Is this meant for me? Then to my right, a clean-cut trader with dark brown hair smiles straight at me. This is Josh? I can feel my face flush.

"Anything good on the note?" Scott asks. "You're blushing. You've got fifteen seconds."

I fold up the note. Fold up the personal part of my brain and smooth out my market news notes on the clipboard in front of me and focus. Three-two-one, the camera's hot. I roll into a report on the latest mutual fund investigation. I talk about the day's consumer confidence survey. I talk about a new twist in a proposed telecom merger.

"Back to you, Tony, in London," I hear myself toss to the anchor. I feel myself smile good-bye as I fold up the market notes.

"Good cover, Daniella," Scott says dryly. "Must've been one hell of a note . . . you were talking at lightning speed, and your cheeks are bright red. Next time, share it with the class. We could all use a little thrill. See you in a couple hours."

I smile back at him through the camera and then switch off my microphone and earpiece. Smart-ass.

Now, unfolding the note. Who is this Josh? I can feel him looking at me. I'm embarrassed. What am I supposed to do with this? Part of me is flattered, part of me is flustered. He's probably just making professional contact with me. That's right. This is probably an invitation for a business cocktail. Business cocktail. Nothing wrong with that. No professional space violation. I look up at him, he's looking at me. He smiles and waves me over to his post. I double-check that my microphone and my earpiece are turned off. I don't want to broadcast this conversation, nor do I want Scott in the London control room to make any commentary in my earpiece. I step out of the camera's field of view and over to Josh's post.

"Hi." Josh's voice is rough from yelling trading orders all day.

"Hi," I squeak back. My smooth, controlled, broadcast voice, gone. I'm unnerved by the unconventional way he's approached me, and confused, because I don't know what he's after. The NYSE is my professional turf, and he's disrupting the strictly professional understanding here that I so cherish.

"Slow market day, huh?" His blue eyes concentrate so hard on me through his glasses I squirm inside.

"Yeah," I say, relieved that the conversation is simple.

"Are you up for drinks after work?" he asks, his eyes darting to the trading screen in front of him, then back to me.

"Sure." I'm awkward. Too many people can hear us. I'm sure the guys around us are already gossiping—what's more fun than gossip on a slow market day?

"I gotta run."

"Okay." He smiles. "See you later."

"Bye."

I dart off the floor, hugging my clipboard flush to my chest. This was a less than auspicious beginning. The way he looked at me makes my skin crawl. I'm in for one long, awkward cocktail this evening. Can I get out of it? I wish, but I'm not willing to cross the floor again to renege. I wish I had said no. But I felt I had to say yes the way he was boring down on me with his eyes. All right, so it's just one hour of my life. One hour I'll never get back!

As the market's closing bell approaches, I grow increasingly resentful about meeting him. The intensity of the way he looked at me creeps me out. I cake on what feels like another two inches of foundation and powder for my closing report. Why am I so hostile? First of all, I'd just rather go home. Secondly, I feel like my little oasis, my rare haven where business forces personal life to the fringe, has been invaded by a traitor, er . . . trader. The NYSE has always been a place where I said I'd never find a date, and surely not a mate. And now, what's his name? Josh? Jackie would laugh. "You're destined to end up with a trader," Jackie always says. "It's always the guys you never suspect that get ya!"

This is probably not a date. It's probably just a business cocktail. To think otherwise would be presumptuous. Really, Daniella, I tell myself, there is no reason to get so worked up. He probably wants to talk shop. Maybe he wants to become a commentator on our TV program, *Pulse*. Or maybe he, like many other traders, wants to give me flack for my comments last week. Well, he can stop right there. When I predicted computers would replace human traders at the NYSE, I meant it, and I'm not retracting it. It's already happening. That's just the nature of trading today. And why was he narrowing his eyes at me that way? Does he have a problem with me, or a problem with his vision?

I blot my lipstick on a tissue, grab my microphone and earpiece, and rush out to our balcony camera position for the closing bell report. The floor of the Exchange below is already emptying out. I flick on my microphone, put in my earpiece, the hot, white lights go on, and three-two-one, I'm up.

Seven minutes later, I'm done with my report for *Pulse*, and I'm back in the office, cursing under my breath about these drinks with Josh. I wipe off most of the powder and eyeshadow I just put on my face. The makeup that makes me look decent on air makes me look like a prostitute in person.

When I arrive at Delmonico's, Josh is waiting for me at the oak bar. I hardly recognize him. He's not wearing his trader's uniform: that baggy, ugly, dark brown mesh jacket with the name of his company monogrammed on the breast pocket. Instead, he's in a fresh, royal blue shirt and pressed khakis. Cute, but let's make this snappy.

He looks at me without blinking, gives me a disarming smile, then gets up to greet me, putting his cheek to mine and kissing the air near my ear. Shiver. Smells good. Without asking, he takes my shoulder bag, heavy with newspapers, makeup, and a water bottle, and sets it down below the bar.

"Taking a big trip somewhere?" he asks.

"No." I laugh. "Just my daily luggage."

He helps me onto the barstool.

"You look nice without that tangle of microphone wires and that clipboard full of secrets. You aren't hiding any recording devices on you, are you?"

"No recording devices. Just my brain, complete with selective memory."

I order a beer. I guess I've been duped into a date, not a

business cocktail. I ramp up my efforts to be obstinately difficult and provocative to shorten our visit.

"So, what's it like to be an insider at the NYSE, a member of that bastion of male, white power?" I dig.

"Fine. I know how privileged I am," he says easily. "I don't know if things will ever change dramatically, but we are making inroads. A few women on the floor. A few men of color."

He pauses. Thinks. Looks hard at his beer. Takes a sip.

"But anyway, it's pretty irrelevant," he continues. "All of us traders are going to be replaced by computers anyway, it's just a question of when. And electronic transactions will balance the playing field. There are too many agreements and understandings between members of the club right now. Computers will give everyone equal trading opportunity."

Can't argue with that. It is uncanny, however, how much his comments sound so much like my commentary from Wednesday's edition of *Pulse*.

"So where can I see you on TV?" he asks. "I've looked, but I've never been able to find you."

Huh? He's never seen me on TV? He's not just regurgitating what I said on TV? Suddenly he doesn't seem so creepy. In fact, it's pretty impressive to meet a guy who can envision, accept, and talk openly about the gloomy fate of his own career.

"We're in Europe and Asia, mostly, but we're also on Channel 57 cable here in the city," I answer.

I probably shouldn't stereotype him, but I do. And, as it turns out, he's about as typical as traders come. He's from New Jersey. He went to Rutgers. He played football in high school and now he likes to watch it. He lives within five miles of his family. He's a Springsteen fan, even likes to play guitar and sing. Good money drew him to Wall Street. I was right in my stereotype of him, but I was wrong to think it would make him unattractive.

I get to the bottom of another beer then ask, "So, was there something in particular you wanted to talk about?"

Josh is unruffled and continues to look at me with a bold stare.

"I just thought it would be nice to know the person behind the no-nonsense business reporter," he says softly but directly.

I smile. I like his honesty. I also am beginning to like that intense look from his deep eyes. There's something profound about him, I just can't pin it down. The cocktail invitation leads to a dinner invitation, and surprise, I accept immediately. We follow the maître d' into the dark dining room. More oak panels, heavy curtains, and multiple oil paintings of landscapes, hunting scenes, and dead birds.

"So . . ." The maître d' scoots my chair in as we sit down to dinner. "We've been working on the floor next to each other for two years. Why haven't we ever talked?" I ask.

"Uh. Let's see," he says. "You never give any trader the time of day unless he's got news you can use."

"Oh," I smile at his friendly jab.

"Wine?" he asks.

"Sure. You choose."

The wine arrives and he toasts, "To new friends in old places. *L'chaim.*"

This guy is toasting in Hebrew? He's Jewish?

"L'chaim," I say and slowly take a sip of wine to absorb the surprising information.

"So. Two years, we've been working next to each other," I say.

"Yep, two years."

"Why now?"

He gives me a devilish look.

"Actually, ever since you started coming down to the floor, I was interested. But. Well. Don't take this the wrong way. You seemed a little standoffish. Aloof. Cold. Ice princess—"

"I get the idea." I laugh.

"Then today . . ." and he cracks a smile.

"Today what?" I smile, too.

"Today, you know how it was so slow on the floor? Well, Tim, one of the other specialists at my post, dared me to ask you out. He knew I'd been watching you."

"What'd you win?" I flirt back.

"Dinner's on Tim tonight."

"Filet mignon, then," I say, "and a bottle of Dom Perignon."

The conversation flows freely the rest of the night. It's punctuated with deep laughs, clever repartee, and unexpected soulful silences. I like his playfulness. I also dig his raw honesty. He isn't trying to impress me or flatter me. The way he looks at me is the way he thinks: directly. Either I like him the way he is, or I don't. He's not going to make himself into something he isn't. He's unapologetic.

I'm also a sucker for his scratchy, commanding voice. It's totally enchanting when he uses it to say soft things. He suggests we share a hot fudge brownie sundae for dessert. Mmmm.

All of a sudden, it's nine P.M., and he's got to catch the train back to Jersey. We've spent almost five hours together. Impressive.

He puts my heavy bag on his shoulder and walks me up to Wall Street, which is mostly deserted by now. This place, which I've always associated with cold work and buzzing business, suddenly seems dancingly romantic. We stop at the mouth of my subway station, and he tells me in that scratchy-soft voice that it's been nice getting to know me.

"You, too," I say.

Then, just as I think he's going to lean in and kiss me good night, he gives me a strong, firm hug.

"See you tomorrow at work?" he asks. "Maybe we can do this again sometime?"

"Thank you, yes."

He hands me my bag, and I turn and float down the stairs to the subway. How sweet he is! What a gentleman! What a surprise! A clever, blue-eyed trader complete with chivalry, charm, a brain, and breadth. It was so easy to be with him. He's a clear thinker, doesn't overanalyze things the way I do or Ruben does.

As I stand on the subway platform waiting for the train, I imagine how great it will be to see him again. On our next date, will we go back to Delmonico's, or will we go to the Wall Street Kitchen? Maybe Chinatown or Little Italy.

Then, just as the subway car screeches around the bend and into the station, a shooting panic strikes me. "Maybe we can do it again sometime?" What exactly did he mean, "maybe"? *Maybe* could mean *maybe not*. Oh, Daniella. Give it a rest. You like that he doesn't overanalyze things, so why don't you just relax yourself.

I step in the subway car and the doors slide shut. If this had been a business cocktail, it would have been hard to report the results to a boss. Josh and I certainly didn't close any deals or agree to any collaboration. I left with a good feeling and a big, fat maybe, but I'm not sure what he was thinking. That said, the foundation was definitely laid for some sort of partnership, but how far that joint venture extends is anyone's guess. Overall, I was not disappointed. The meeting definitely beat expectations.

Twenty-five

The morning after the Delmonico's date, I've dressed in one of my best suits. I also put on my makeup carefully to look good for him. Within seconds of arriving on the floor of the Exchange, a runner delivers a trading slip. I open it eagerly.

"Good morning," it reads in Josh's small, straight handwriting. "Glad to see the good ol' boys club let you in again."

Smart-ass.

After my live shot, I stop by his post.

"Hi," he says, giving me that unnerving look coupled with his sexy voice. "Are you busy tonight?"

We go out that night and almost every night after. For three weeks: a virtual eternity by New York City dating standards.

I've gotten into the habit of visiting him at his post after every opening bell report. My pretense is to ask him a pressing business question.

"The consumer confidence figure was better than economists

predicted, so why is there so much of a sell-off?" I ask Josh with my flirtiest eyes.

Our conversations standing at his post are always short. Usually less than two minutes. We're both pressed for time, and neither of us wants to bring attention to our private lives. That said, we can't resist saying hi and giving each other secretive looks. His deep stares, which used to creep me out, now have me hooked. And, to be honest, we do get a little thrill out of having a covert relationship within the confines of the Exchange. Dozens of video cameras bolted to the overhead balconies that wrap around the perimeter of the Exchange peer down on the trading floor like Big Brother. The cameras can capture our interactions, and the video can be bounced, beamed, and satellited to most anyone, in any control room on the planet. And yet, we push our luck, talking face-to-face daily despite and because of the possible consequences.

Before I talk to Josh, I'm always careful to switch off my earpiece and microphone, so that even if our pictures are somehow exploited, our words won't be. But, just as a safety measure, and just for fun, he's started calling me by my initials: DAF—which could also be a company's stock ticker. I call him by his initials: JET. Josh Eric Traub. Or sometimes JETCo.

Sometimes, our fear of being discovered manifests itself creatively, and we succumb to our cheesy impulses. We talk in our own private code that both sounds like business and sounds more racy than our relatively chaste relationship. "JET's performance beat expectations overnight," wink-wink or, "A lot of activity in after hours for DAF."

Overall, I spend less time trolling the wires on my computer in my NYSE booth, and more time gathering my news on the floor. By talking face-to-face with different traders it won't look like I'm giving JET special attention.

All my extra trading floor chitchatting is giving my reports more of an insider's flavor. And Josh's little market tutorials along the way are building up my knowledge and confidence. My boss says I seem more energetic, upbeat, and tapped into the floor scene. He says I've really got the "pulse" on the Exchange, and it's working well on air. My calculation? Date Josh = improved job performance.

Outside of work, Josh is improving my life, too. He is very supportive as I negotiate Mom's nonstop barrage of wedding questions.

"How long should the cocktail hour last? Should I give guests specific seats at tables, or should I just give them a table number and let them arrange themselves?"

"Just one decision at a time," Josh says. "Don't try to figure it all out at once." He introduces a level of simplicity and levity into the whole Mom scenario that makes it more palatable.

JET is also proving to be incredibly sensitive, nurturing, and tender. I've gone down to Jersey with him twice now on weekends, and he's lavished me with his home cooking and expert barbecuing. We've gone hiking, bird-watching, and picnicking down at the shore. I get to use my compass. It's a delightful escape from the city and a fitting way to welcome spring. And being with JET is so easy. No deep, dark sides (so far.) No career competition. He's just calm and even-tempered.

I wonder if Josh would want to come to Mom's wedding with me. Things are going so well, and he's so kind, I'm sure he'd oblige. But there's no need to rock the boat or rush anything. It's also late to be bringing him into the mix. I want to get to know him better before exposing him to my family and vice versa. Even though it's been three weeks already, it has only been three weeks.

I offer Mom little dribbles of information about Josh so she won't be surprised if he comes to her wedding. I know he's not the intellectual, worldly kind of guy Mom would like for me, but she's supportive anyway. And she likes that I've found a Jewish guy to date.

Sunday night, Josh and I decide to rent a movie and order Chinese take-out at my house. We settle on *Jerry Maguire*; enough chick flick for me with a sports element for him. Just as we're curling up together on the couch in my apartment to start watching the movie, the phone rings. It's Mom, and she desperately needs to talk to me right away.

"If this is about the dress, or any other wedding trivia, Mom, it can wait," I say firmly.

"It's not," she says. This time her tone is not panicked and high-strung; instead, she sounds hollow and sad.

I raise my index finger to Josh, indicating I'm going to be a minute. I cover the mouthpiece of the phone.

"Go ahead with the movie," I whisper. "Yes, I'm sure. This sounds like it's going to take awhile."

"Can I help?" he mouths.

I shake my head no and gently caress his cheek in thanks. I can handle this. By now, I have plenty of experience.

"Go ahead, Mom, what is it?"

"Well, it's about the wedding," she says.

I roll my eyes. What a surprise.

"Stanley and I are having, well, a difference of opinion about something," she says.

I'm shocked. Stanley and Mom—the perfect match? Stanley who can do no wrong has a different opinion from Mom? Not possible. Not acceptable.

"Is it about the flowers or is it about the wedding cake?"

"Neither," she says.

"Well, what is it?"

"It's about toasts," she says.

"What toast?" I rewind my mind to the dinner menu. Did they decide on the bruschetta after all?

"You know, toasts, what you say before you drink the champagne," she says with no sense of humor whatsoever.

"What's the problem with toasts?" I ask.

"Well, that's just it. I don't see a problem with toasts. He does," she says.

I'm perplexed. This is a new one.

"He just doesn't like them. Doesn't want them. Insists we not have them at the wedding. And I think the toasts are the best part. It's when you get to hear what people are thinking about. It's what distinguishes one wedding from another. It's what makes our wedding ours. It puts everything in perspective and makes it special. Gives the event context."

I couldn't agree more. Toasts are one of my favorite parts of the wedding. And I've even been looking forward to toasting Mom and Stanley myself. I've been thinking about what I might say ever since Jen and Jason's wedding in Chicago.

"I just feel like I've done so much for him," she goes on. "I've made so many sacrifices already for this silly wedding. And who needs a big wedding anyway? For that matter, who needs to be married?" She's angry.

I want to stop her.

"I can function just fine without a man. I'm sixty years old. I know who I am. I have a career. I have successful, wonderful children. I don't need a headache from an eccentric man without a sense of humor!"

"What do you mean a man without a sense of humor? You told me it was his laughter and levity that drew you to him!" I remind her.

"Well, this is different. And it's not like he's the only guy on the planet for me. If I can find him, then I can surely find someone else who might be a better fit. Think about it. I'm in shape. I'm smart. I'm sane," she argues.

Sane? That's debatable.

"He's pushing me to the limit. I gave up on having the table arrangements just the way I want. The main courses, the beef tenderloin and the pan-seared Pacific salmon are his choices, not mine. And I gave in to the Cabernet when my instinct said Merlot. But this toast bit? It's too important. And I'm sick of compromising. I'm beginning to feel like we have so many differences. I mean if we can't agree on wine, then how are we going to agree on anything else? Your father wouldn't have insisted on so many things. And he certainly wouldn't be afraid of a toast. What kind of man fears toasts?"

Her voice is cracking. She sounds deeply disappointed and exhausted. This is not the cheery Mom of the last few months.

"Okay Mom, relax. Take a deep breath," I say in my "I'm calm and in charge" voice. Then I repeat to her the concepts Josh used to soothe me, "Let's take this problem apart and see if we can work it out." If she gives up her convictions about love and marriage, it may well undermine my already fragile hopes for them, too.

"You know what, Daniella?" she's on a tirade. "I don't even want to handle it. He's so stubborn. If he can't be flexible on wines and toasts, what kind of a future can we have together? I don't want to fight for the rest of my life. I'm too old for that. I want someone who can understand me and accommodate me. Not some uncompromising control freak! I've tried. I even suggested a limited number of toasts. He said no way. No toasts. Can't do it. Won't."

Mom is exasperated.

"I just wonder if we're the right match for each other," she goes on. "Maybe I got into this whole wedding thing too quickly. Maybe I just got carried away. Maybe I was just vulnerable and impatient. You know? Maybe I'm making a bad decision. Taking you kids through all this. Maybe I just need more time to think about whether this is a good decision or a knee-jerk reaction to avoid being alone."

I guess she had been listening to our concerns after all—she's just a bit late in registering it. By now, she's convinced me that Stanley will be a good husband for her.

"Come on, Mom," I manage to slip a word in. "Every couple has a few disagreements along the way. It's just a matter of how you handle them. And I know you can. Both of you are intelligent and rational. And you are both pretty stubborn. So he's gotten his way on a number of things, but haven't you had your way, too? And haven't you agreed on a lot of things?"

"Yeah, I guess so. On a few tiny, little things."

"I think you've had your way on most things, no? What about the band? And the chuppah?"

"No, he had his way with the chuppah," she pouts.

"But didn't you say he had a good point when he suggested birch instead of bamboo? More sturdy or something?"

"Yes. But we're talking about toasts. It's what people remember, it's what's important," she says.

"Yes. Okay. But what about the wine? Are you really crushed without the Merlot? Is it really a deal breaker?"

"No, it's okay." She sounds resigned.

"And how important is chicken or beef?" I ask. "Chicken or beef?" I mimic an airline attendant.

"Beef," I can hear her saucy smile. "I have a beef with him. And for the record, chicken was never on the menu; neither of us wanted it."

"Ah? So you did agree on a few things. No chickens. Mom,

don't forget, you're the one who found the caterer. You outdid Stanley in his own department. You got Josephine and her sister Claudine to do the food. That was a biggie."

"Yes," she says softly. "But this toast thing. It's too much. It really is. Toasts are too important to give up."

"I agree they're important, but calling off a wedding over it is a bit of an overreaction, no? Mom. Maybe he can get over his toast fright? A little therapy? I don't know . . . a toastmasters meeting?" Mom does not laugh.

"What is he afraid we might say?" I ask. "What if we give him advance printed copies of our toasts and give him censorship power?"

"Tried to, won't budge. I'm telling you," she says. "He won't change his mind."

"Well, can you live without it?" I'm feeling like a mother. "You have been so happy since you met him. Are you forgetting your trip to Italy? Are you forgetting the romantic dinners? Are you forgetting how lonely you used to be? You don't really want to give it all up over a few toasts, now do you?"

"Maybe," Mom says.

"And Mom, he's a good guy. He loves you very much. He even schlepped my stuff out of the Brooklyn apartment to Manhattan to show you he cared. A guy like that doesn't pop up every day."

She sniffles.

"Look, I think you might be getting a little tired and worked up over everything," I say while actually thinking she is severely overreacting and needs to take a chill pill.

"Maybe," she repeats, childlike.

"Listen, I support you whatever you want to do." I try to calm her. "But please, take some time, step back before making any rash decisions. This whole wedding thing has been very exciting, but it's been stressful, too. You're juggling all kinds of things. Trying to make yourself happy, Stanley happy, your guests happy. It's a lot to balance. You may have already made the big decision to get married, but all these little decisions add up, too. Think about it: every day, it's something else: the appetizer, the table seating, the song list. And those are the small questions. Think about the posthoneymoon phase. Where are you going to live? How are you going to live together? It's a lot to handle all at once. Maybe this isn't about the toasts. Maybe it's about the overall stress?" I suggest. "Sleep on it. Please, take some time to reflect before you decide anything."

"Maybe," she sniffles again.

"Mom?" I ask in my most stern, no nonsense tone.

"Yes," she sniffles again.

"Yes, what?" I ask, demanding she respond in a complete sentence, the way she did with me growing up.

"Yes. I will sleep on it before I do anything," she gives in, responding in a complete, affirmative, sentence, the way she trained me to answer her.

"Good. Now, are you going to be okay?" I ask more gently.

"Yes." She sighs. "I'll be okay."

"Anything else? Dress okay? Fernando, Josephine, Claudine behaving?" I ask trying to lighten the situation.

"It's okay, it's all fine," she says softly. "Thank you. Go back to your movie."

"Call me in the morning?" I ask.

"Okay," she says. "Bye."

"Bye." I hang up.

No way is she going to call this thing off. I won't let her. It's too good. Hearing her sad like this emphasizes how happy she's sounded by comparison since meeting Stanley. He's been making her laugh. He's been cooking for her. With all the time they've spent together already, they're effectively married already.

If I could invoke parental privilege now the way she used to with me, I would. I'd say, "You're getting married to Stanley." And if she asked why, I'd say, "Because I said so."

And anyway, as independent as she may be, emotionally she does need someone to look after her and care for her. My brothers and I managed to give her the attention she needed in the past, but really, life is much easier with Stanley in the game. And Stanley has been doing a marvelous job.

"Well, that's a new one," I turn to Josh. "Mom's getting cold feet."

"Not so new." Josh pauses the DVD and sits up, giving me his full attention. "People freak out before big weddings all the time. My sister had a fit a month before her big day. I thought she was going to call the whole thing off. She was in tears. Planning what to do with the unused dress. Planning for a miserable spinster life."

"What were they arguing about?" I ask.

"I forget. Centerpieces maybe?" He smiles.

"Centerpieces?" I ask. "That's really something. I mean how would Cupid feel knowing that a centerpiece broke up his hard work and true love?"

"He'd probably turn a poison arrow on himself. Wait. First he'd aim it at the marketing machine behind the whole wedding industry." Josh laughs. "Maybe Cupid's first target would be De Beers, for profiting off love."

Ah! Here's a man who was listening to my ranting about De Beers and the commercialization of love last weekend. I could just kiss him for understanding! And, all this coming from a Jersey boy who makes his living off corporate America? Impressive.

"Don't ever let me fight about centerpieces or toasts," I plead.

"Okay." He smiles and pulls me down next to him on the couch.

Twenty-six

"I'm still angry," Mom pouts when I call her from my booth at the Exchange the next day.

"Well, did you talk about it with him?"

"Nope. He called. But really? I have nothing to say. I've tried everything and unless he's going to budge, I'm not budging either."

"You know you only have eight weeks till the wedding."

"What wedding?"

"Oh, come on! Am I going to have to fly out to California and sit down and talk to the two of you?"

"Nope. We'll just wait till he comes around."

"But, Mom, if he hates toasts as much as you say he does, is it worth it? I mean, even if he does give up and let you have your way, do you really want him *that* unhappy at his own wedding? The toasts aren't going to mean anything if he's uncomfortable."

"Well, then he needs to get comfortable. How was the movie

last night with Josh?" she asks, switching the subject. "Seems like you've been spending an awful lot of time together recently."

"Fine."

"When do I get to meet him?"

"At your wedding maybe, if you have one."

Mom is silent.

"Hello?" I ask, annoyed.

"Hello," she says.

"Listen, Mom, I have to run down to the floor and do my report. The markets are dropping big time today. Rumor has it, traders are edgy about the uncertainty of your wedding, and they're selling off in sympathy."

"Ha!" she snorts.

"Ha!" I say. "I suggest you go talk this out with your sons, your friends, or God forbid, your fiancé, before you pull the plug on this deal."

"We'll see."

With that, I grab my remote microphone and earpiece, turn them on, snatch my script off the printer, clip the script onto the clipboard, and rush down the back steps to the floor. Frazzled, I take my place in front of the camera, breathe, and concentrate hard on explaining why the treasury secretary's comments on the dollar are dragging down the markets. Miraculously, I make it through the report without any major gaffes. I exhale, but my shoulders and neck are still tight. I stop by JET's post.

"Good morning," he says. "Nice red suit. How's the MOM-STAN merger going this morning?"

"On the verge of collapse," I say. "Didn't you know? That's what's driving the sell-off today. Global stability is contingent on this merger working out, and with all this uncertainty, no one's buying."

"Ohhh," JET smiles. "Now you're the one giving me the scoop on what's moving markets. Very nice."

JET leans over and whispers to me, "I want to kiss you."

I blush and smile. That was bold.

"Me, too, and maybe more." I wink. "Mmm . . . last night."

"The pleasure was all mine," he says. "Hey babe? Just chill out. It's all going to be okay."

I want a big hug from him right now, but instead, I flee the floor.

Back in the booth, I watch the tickers. The markets are sinking lower and lower. We may be headed for a triple-digit loss for the day. I can't do anything to stop the market sell-off, but maybe I can prevent Mom from a precipitous self-inflicted crash.

Time check? One hour before my next report. Time to try a brand-new approach to family therapy. I'm going to tap new resources.

"Erica?" I call my stepsister-to-be at her physics lab. Erica and I haven't had much contact through this whole wedding planning business, but when we have talked, she's been friendly.

"Yes. Hello? Can you hold on?" she answers.

I hear whirring sounds in the background, the phone on the other end drops, then the receiver finds its way next to something with a ticking sound. Maybe this wasn't the best idea.

"Hello?" Erica asks.

"Hi. It's Daniella. How are you?"

"Fine, fine. I'm in the middle of soldering umpteen leads onto this distributor panel."

"Erica?" I interrupt gently. I don't have much time. "I'm sorry to be short, but I have something kind of important to talk to you about."

"Okay, what?"

"Well, I hear your dad really doesn't like toasts."

"Right, well it's all part of his diet. No carbs. What's the issue?"

"Toasts. As in speaking-champagne-wedding toasts."

"Oh," Erica understands. "He hates toasts. So?"

"It's just that, well, my mom really likes them. And, she really wants people to give toasts at the wedding."

"It'll never happen," Erica says matter-of-factly. "Now, why are you calling?"

"I'm calling about the toasts," I repeat firmly. "The wedding may not go on without them."

"What? What are you talking about?"

"Erica, my mom is really upset about the toast ban. Really upset."

"How upset?"

"Let's just say . . . It's kind of . . . Well, if we can't get past the toast problem, we're all going to have a lot more problems."

"Look, Daniella. My dad just hates them. I can see him bending on a million things, he already has, but this one? No way. Anyway, what's the big deal? No one is going to miss it."

"Yeah, they'll miss it. I'll miss it. My mom'll miss it. It is the best part of the wedding." I'm irritated. "It's what distinguishes one wedding from another. Gives the guests context and gives the wedding meaning. It's what draws people together."

"Hey, wait a second there, Daniella. Really, it's not the best part of a wedding. The best part is when the bride and groom say, 'I do' and kiss," Erica says assuredly.

"Okay, whatever." I look at my watch, we don't have time to argue. "We have to take care of this. Now, is he superstitious about toasts? Is he afraid someone will say something embarrassing? How can we help him get past this?"

"Daniella, he's not going to get past this. Just accept it. He's not going to budge. If you want to help, tell your mom to get over it."

"Get over it? Why don't you tell me why she should get over it? Give me one reason, and make it a good one, and unless—"

"When my mom and dad married, the toasts were about being together forever. Didn't happen—did it? Good enough?"

"Oh, I'm sorry. I didn't know. I'm so sorry," I say.

"Yeah, okay," Erica says. I hear something ringing in her lab. "Gotta go."

"I'm sorry," I try again.

"Forget it," Erica says. "I mean it. Just forget I ever said it. Bye."

I hang up and hold my head. Way to push it, Daniella. Way to take advantage of her goodwill. My shoulders and back are unbearably tense. I take a deep breath. I need to relax. I need to call Mom. Erica and I will be able to work this out. I need to untangle and unclip these annoying wires for the mike and earpiece and get them off of me.

"Oh, no!" A panic pang shoots though my body. My remote mike has been switched on this entire time. Anyone in any of those TV control rooms around the globe could have heard me lose my temper over toasts and then sound like a world-class jerk.

Then I get a sick feeling. My mike has been on since my last report. Anyone could have heard what JET and I said at his post. Oh God. What did we say? And we were trying to be so careful. Who was listening? Was it just the guys in the control room at the NYSE? Did my boss hear? Did his boss hear? Did the control rooms of all the major broadcast networks overhear our sweet nothings? What did we say? I so deserve this. That's what I get for mouthing off to Erica and trying to keep something secret from Big Brother Stock Exchange. What did I say to JET that might have revealed our romance?

Then I look at the clock. I have a report in less than twelve minutes, and I've got to get prepared. I can't call Mom. No time. I check the markets. Still selling off. Down over 175 points. Yikes!

I print some headlines out. Put on some lipstick, and rush down the stairs to the floor, turning the dreaded mike and earpiece on again. As I'm navigating through the sea of frantic traders on the floor, Scott, my producer, who's sitting comfortably in the London control room, begins teasing through my remote earpiece.

"Hey there, Daniella. Running to meet your bloke on the floor? Mmm? Snog a bit between reports? Why didn't you tell us about your mum's wedding? Sounds like you've got your work cut out for you. You know the wedding toast was a French tradition? At least that's what I heard. Blasted French. Always making things more complicated. I think the old French tradition was to put a piece of toast at the bottom of the couples' wineglasses. The person who reached their toast first would rule the family. Maybe your mum's hubby is afraid she'll outdrink him!"

"Hardly, Scott." I weave and bump my way to my camera position. "Nice ideas. And as much as I'd like to hear the history of French toast, we've got a newscast to do, and if I'm not mistaken, this is one of the biggest market sell-offs we've seen this year."

I arrive at my position on the floor and look up into the camera.

"Right," Scott says in my ear. "One minute to air. Your mike sounds good. Take two steps back. To the left. Okay, forty-five seconds."

I shuffle through my papers, put them in order, and three-two-one, roll into my market update: "Another bleak employment report coupled with those earlier comments on the dollar from the treasury secretary is making the markets queasy, triggering a massive sell-off . . ."

And just as I'm hitting my stride in the report, Scott says in my ear, "Fifteen seconds till you see your bloke, wrap it up."

"Back to you, in London." I manage to end my report, smile, and sign off.

"Good work," Scott says.

"Oh, Scott, dear?" I keep looking up at the camera so that he can see my smile has turned sour. "Could you please refrain from teasing me while I'm doing a live market update? It's a tad distracting."

"Right-o, mate," he says, and I switch off the mike and earpiece immediately.

I walk over to JET's post to tell him we've been found out.

"Bad news," I say. "There's been a leak." I point to my earpiece and microphone. "Forgot to turn them off after my last report."

"Ahh? Uhh. Uh-oh. Hey, babe, don't sweat it." Josh's attention is entirely on the computer screen and the massive sell-off under way rather than on the broadcast of our romance or my hot-headed conversation with Erica.

"Everything okay?" he asks automatically even though I can see he's just trying to be polite and maintain his dignity as he loses his shirt. His eyes are glued to the screen. His fingers are madly punching the keyboard in front of him.

"Yeah. Everything's okay. Except the MOM-STAN merger is on the verge of collapse."

"Huh?" he says.

"Ten cents for twenty thousand," a trader yells.

"Ten cents for twenty thousand," he shouts around me. "Take it."

"Talk to you later?" I say.

"Sorry," he takes a second to look at me directly, then, "Anyone else, ten cents at twenty?"

"Good luck," I say and dash off the floor. I hope he's going to be okay.

Back in the closet office I check that my mike is turned off. I call Mom repeatedly, only to get her voice mail over and over again. Why won't she pick up? I need to talk to her about toasts before she sets Stanley off. Erica told me to forget she said it. Does that mean I'm not supposed to tell Mom why Stanley's antitoast? I check again that the mike is turned off. I'm sure my boss is going to call me any minute and scold me for dating a trader. Am I going to get through to Mom before she calls off the wedding? Is Erica going to get through to Stanley and report on my bad behavior? I check that my mike is turned off. No one calls. No boss, no Mom, nobody, except Scott the producer who wants to plan our coverage of the day's sell-off for the *Pulse* report. By now, Scott can't be bothered to dish out any teasing. He's too consumed with the market's dive. Reminder to self: next time I do something embarrassing or incriminating, choose a busy news day, like this one, to draw the least attention.

After work, I call Mom from home and finally, I get through.

"Mom! How are you? Everything okay? Where have you been? Why haven't you been answering your phone? Did you talk to Stanley?"

"Shhh," she says calmly. "Everything's fine. What's wrong, Cookie?"

"Nothing. Listen, you gotta cut Stanley some slack on the toast thing. I mean Enrico, Max, and I can toast you guys privately and be done with it. He has good reasons."

"Oh yeah?" she asks.

"Yeah, but I'm not sure I can tell you," I say.

"Right. Listen, Cookie, I don't have time to play games right now. Stanley's on his way over."

"Please don't do anything you're going to regret," I warn.

"I won't, Cookie. Trust me. And stop worrying so much. I'll be fine. I'm an adult. Gotta go."

"Mom?"

She hangs up.

I want to call Erica and apologize, but bringing it up might make it all worse. I dial JET's cell phone.

"Hey hon," he answers. "That was a heck of a day."

"You're telling me, I'll never forget it, and it could get worse," I warn.

"What do you mean? The markets are closed," JET says.

"I mean my mom's wedding in crisis, I've alienated my stepsister-to-be, and our sweet nothings have been broadcast to the world!"

"Ohh," he says. "Well, FYI, the markets really collapsed today. Might have a tad more of a world impact than your mom's wedding or our relationship broadcast."

"Right, JET. But you know as well as I do that at the opening bell tomorrow, all you trader types are going to say, 'The sell-off brought prices back down to a bargain level, and now it's time to buy again.' The markets will recover tomorrow, if not the next day. But my mom, my stepsister, and our reputation may not bounce back so quickly," I say emphatically.

"Settle down DAF-fy. I think you're getting a bit ahead of yourself. Everyone was paying attention to the markets today, and no one was really listening to our sweet nothings. Did you notice? People lost piles this afternoon. Anyway, we were talking in code, no?"

"No." I answer. "I'm sorry. No need to stress you out further. You probably had a hellish day. The tech sector got slaughtered. How are you?"

"I'm fine. Listen. Your stepsister is going to get over whatever you said. And about your mom, relax," he says softly. "She's going to be okay. Sometimes, we just have to let them make their own mistakes. Daniella, you can't help her with everything. At some point you are going to have to let her go."

"It's just so hard," I answer. "I don't want her to make a mistake."

"I know, I know. But, DAF, you've got to let her go."

The markets open with a burst of buying the next morning, and my mom appears on the way to a recovery of her own.

"I'm emotionally spent over this whole toast thing," Mom says more calmly over the phone as I listen from my booth at the New York Stock Exchange.

"But you haven't called off the wedding?"

"No, I haven't," she says, sounding sheepish. "Stanley brought me yellow freesias last night and explained why he hates toasts. I felt so bad for pushing the toast issue. He didn't want to talk about it much, but he told me enough. I guess Erica told you, too. You know, you should go easier on Erica. He said if I wanted toasts that badly, then I should have them. He said he'd get through it somehow, and he just wants me to be happy. And I started crying and he started crying and I told him I don't really need toasts. I can live without them. I just want him to be happy."

"Good," I sigh in relief.

"And we started to plan our honeymoon to Russia and the Czech Republic and France, oh it's going to be so great!"

"Well I'm glad it all worked out so well," I say.

"Yeah," she sighs in relief. "Me, too. Let's not talk about toasts again. Okay?"

"Sure," I say.

"Cookie?" Mom changes her light tone to a more serious tone. "One of the most important things to look for in a mate is someone who can compromise, someone who can communicate, and someone who can help you laugh at yourself."

"Thanks," I say. Was I not just saying something along these lines yesterday?

Mom's storm has passed just as quickly as it appeared.

"So, is Josh going to come to the wedding?" she asks.

"I don't know yet. I gotta go do a market update. Talk to you later?"

"Okay," she says. "Thanks."

I exhale. She was fine after all. The wedding show is going on.

Twenty-seven

Now, should I invite JET to the wedding or not? I have to
make up my mind pronto. Sure, Mom would like to meet him.
And yes, it would all probably go just fine. But (of course there is
always a *but* when it comes to me and men) even though we're
getting along really well, I'm not sure what's going to happen
next. I don't want to scare him off by enveloping him into my
family too quickly. The whole introduction to the family thing is a
big commitment. And at Mom's wedding? That's pretty loaded.
At this age, if you bring a date to a family gathering, you might as
well say, "Get to know this one. He may be with me for eternity."

And I don't know if JET's the right guy for me. I mean, I
hardly know him. It's only been three weeks. His calm, cool,
measured approach to things is good for me. But where is his
passion? I haven't seen that yet. And he's not that creative, intellectual type I've been looking for. We haven't talked about a

future together or anything. We've just been enjoying the present. It's been so light and easy.

What if he comes to the wedding and everybody loves him and starts asking questions about when we plan to tie the knot? Or worse, what if they don't like him, and I have to defend him when I'm not convinced of him myself?

Finally, there's something else in the back of my mind which I'm not proud to admit. As much as I like Josh, my eyes and mind are still wandering. Part of me thinks I should appear unattached at Mom's wedding. Of course I'm not going to meet IB among the senior crowd. But I might meet the father, mother, or boss of a really nice guy. It'll be easier for me to explain to people that I have come to the wedding alone rather than deal with the questions of whether Josh and I are serious.

One afternoon, after work, Josh and I are walking down Wall Street together. We're both heading to the same NYSE media function. We've become more comfortable as a couple in public now. And Josh's public profile has grown. He's become quite the stock market pundit lately: he's done the TV circuit a couple of times, waxing about exchange rates, interest rates, and corporate scandals. I've helped him with his TV delivery, and he's been performing beautifully. I'm so proud of him.

Tonight, though, I must talk to him about Mom's wedding. And I have to talk to him now, because once we walk into the party, we won't be able to have a private conversation. The timing is less than ideal, I know. I know. But I've put this conversation off for far too long, and if we don't talk now, I don't know when we'll have time alone again.

"Josh, can we stop for a minute?" I ask. I'm using my low, "I've got something important but hard to say" tone of voice.

"Sure?"

I take his hands in mine.

"Josh, it's about my mom's wedding."

"Shew," he says relieved. "I thought you had something really heavy to tell me. I'd be happy to come with you. No problem."

"Well, here's the thing." I look at him. He looks so cute and sincere. I hate to deliver bad news, especially when it's born of my own neurotica. He looks at me, concerned.

Deep breath, Daniella, plunge.

"I don't know if . . . I think it may be better if . . . would you mind if . . . Josh, I think I should go to my mom's wedding on my own." There. I said it. Oh no. I hate that hurt look on his face. I should tell him exactly what I'm feeling, but I'm afraid it will hurt him more.

"It's just that I don't want to put pressure on you. I don't want you to have to deal with my entire family. And I don't want you to have to give up your work and your softball games and everything for me and my mom's wedding," I try to explain.

"I'd be happy to come. Really. No skin off my back," he answers.

"I know. You are so good. I just don't want to put you in any position you don't want to be in."

"What are you talking about, Daniella?" I can't pull anything over on Josh. "You know I'd be happy to come," he says. "There isn't anything I've got to do here that is more important than you are."

"You are too good," I tell him.

"Tell me what this is really about," he persists.

"I did."

"I don't think so," he says. "I think this has nothing to do with me. It's about you. Why not just say it instead of beating around the bush? You aren't ready for me to meet the family."

"No, it's not that. It's just that I need to give my undivided attention to my mom," I try to explain.

"Right." He doesn't buy it.

"No, come on. Really, it might be awkward. You know how those family things can be," I try.

"Daniella. Just play it straight, please. Tell it like it is. You aren't ready to have me there yet. I understand. It can be a lot of pressure," he says. "But don't tell me it's about me when it really is about you."

It would have been better if he'd been angry, but instead he's sympathetic, and he's calling my bluff. Maybe that's why I like him so much. There's no bullshit with him. Maybe I should invite him to the wedding. Maybe I do want him next to me in all of the pictures—maybe I won't have to push him to the sides in pictures so he can be cut out if we break up. Anyway, there's always Photoshop.

"I guess I'm just not ready," I concede. "And to introduce you to my family before I'm ready might hurt our relationship."

"Better," he says. "That, I can live with. You know, Daniella, sometimes I think you're not ready to settle down and get serious. You're just too busy being you. I don't hold it against you, but it's like you don't have space to think about me. You're too busy chasing dreams of perfection. Makes it hard to grow a relationship."

Am I that transparent—or does he just understand me better than anyone else?

"Yes, you're right, again. I'm so sorry. I just don't want to hurt you."

It's times like this when I like Josh most. He forces me to face who I am. Perhaps I am too selfish, too closed off, too immature to know the difference between dreams and realities. He pushes me to be more than I am. To grow and expand in ways that scare me.

Josh leans over and gives me a peck on the cheek.

Now why did he have to be so sweet? I feel like such a jerk. He just handled that situation the way IB would. Understanding, sympathetic, disarming. He loops his arm in mine, smiles, and leads me into the party without saying a word.

Twenty-eight

I'm on a plane, on my own, again. If Josh was hurt by my decision to go to the wedding solo, he didn't show it. He didn't try to convince me to bring him, and he didn't make me feel guilty. He just let it be. If Josh were on the plane next to me right now, we'd be laughing and holding hands, a team. Partners.

It's going to be all couples this wedding weekend. Enrico and Leslie are coming, and Erica is bringing her genius boyfriend, Ross. Erica seems to have either forgotten how tactless I was in pressing the toast issue, or she was just preoccupied with other things when I last spoke to her. Well, I didn't remind her about the toast conversation and laughed along with her when she complained that her biggest challenge with her boyfriend was dragging him out of the lab and getting him in presentable clothing for the wedding. At least Max is easing the social pressure on me. He's been teasing that he's going to bring his wind surf board as his date.

"It'll look wicked cool in front of guests and in pictures," he said. "Surf board, mother in white wedding dress, what could be more ordinary?"

Touch down San Francisco Thursday morning, and I brace myself. This is the fourth and final wedding-related visit. Even though we've made plans, backup plans, and backup, backup plans, I know the last few days before the wedding are still going to be a sprint to the finish line. It will be a test of my patience, planning, and commitment to Mom. T-minus three days till Mom and Stanley's W-day.

Mom is completely wired when she greets me at the airport.

"Dani. I'm so excited you're here. This is going to be great," she says as I slam the car door shut. "We have so much to do before Saturday. Is it okay if we don't go straight home yet? I have some last-minute details."

She screeches out of the arrivals pickup lane, and I fasten my seat belt and take a deep breath. There's a wild bride at the wheel.

"I've got to get a nice pair of hose to wear," she chatters as she drives. "I want to pick up this lipstick color that Dinah swears by. It's called Cha Cha Cha by Estee Lauder. Do you know it? It's a reddish color. You wear a lot of makeup on TV. What do you think? Should I try something new? Coral tones or red tones? I think coral. I've always done pink and starting on red tones now would be a massive change. I don't want to look like a tart, but I figure I'll pick up Cha Cha Cha anyway. What have I got to lose by trying it?"

"Do you think there will be enough flowers?" she asks.

"Yes," I try to calm her. "But if you're worried, the bouquets we carry can also double as table centerpieces."

"How can we ensure the dress is pressed perfectly when it's time to walk down the aisle?"

"We'll buy a portable personal steaming machine," I assure.

"I'm worried the guests won't like the play list of songs we decided on."

"We can always change the play list last minute," I respond.

The next few days are a frenzied blur of errands, cleaning house, and trips to the airport to pick up friends and relatives. Friday morning is my only opportunity to slow down; I squeeze in an early morning jog. Go figure. Running to slow down. At eight A.M., I arrive at the Inspiration Point path at the top of the Berkeley Hills. This is where Dad was running when he collapsed of a heart attack. I sit down on the gravel path to warm up. I stretch my legs out into a pike position and reach for my toes with my unadorned hands. I have running shoes to allow me to get places fast, just no rings or rocks to keep me bound to anybody or anything. Will the running shoes ever come off?

As I start jogging, I wonder what Dad would tell me about my wandering, unattached self.

"Keep wandering until you find a reason to stay put," he would say. "Just because Mom is getting attached now doesn't mean you need to. You are different people. She may need more tradition to feel comfortable. As long as you feel free as a wanderer, you shouldn't rush anywhere unless it makes your journey even more pleasurable."

I keep running.

Friday afternoon: the nuptial manicure/pedicure. I never get my nails done (not a huge fan of having people fawn over my fingers and toes). But the manicure/pedicure is as much a part of the American wedding as the groom and the bride feeding each other cake. My past experience with bridal spa days has been good. It's always the same: a gaggle of girls giggling as we primp all day to be on parade for the princess party. The facials, the massages, the nails. But this time, there is no gaggle of girls, it's just Mom and me.

The Korean nail salon is just another nondescript shop in a strip mall. Fluorescent lights and poison-smelling polish aggravate the senses as we walk in. The bright white walls are decorated with long, thin shelves of neatly organized nail polish bottles in a rainbow of pinks and reds. Sung Eun, who has her American clients call her Song, rushes over as Mom walks in. Mom is here every other week because only Song can make the works of art that Mom demands on her hands and feet.

"Speshl akayshin? Weddin weeken, yes?" Song asks.

Song guides us to the pedicure thrones, and her colleague, Dawn, another tiny Korean woman, motions for me to remove my shoes. With the speed and ease of experience, Mom takes off her shoes and sets her feet into the pool of warm water. I watch carefully, then manage to mimic the delicate dip. Song and Dawn motion for us to lean our heads back into the headrest to relax while they slowly massage our feet. Mom rests her head for a few seconds, then pops upright. I keep my head cradled in the headrest and give her a "just relax" shrug. Song, sensing Mom's jumpiness, speeds up the foot massage and tries to distract Mom with conversation about the weather. Mom gives short answers. Song rubs Mom's feet vigorously with the pumice stone. Mom shifts in her chair. She has too much on her mind to even discuss small things. In fact, knowing her, the small talk is more aggravating for her than silence. By the time we're sitting across from Song and Dawn at the twin manicure tables, Song has given up on trying to talk with Mom. Instead, she looks at my bare hands.

"Where your husband?" she asks.

"Not here," I answer.

"He coming?" she asks.

"Yes. Coming," Mom says, smiling. "He's coming. Just not here yet."

Twenty-nine

A nondescript Chinese food restaurant in a Silicon Valley strip mall is where we're heading for Mom and Stanley's rehearsal dinner. Enrico keeps his left hand on the steering wheel as his right hand pokes and swats at Max and at the car stereo. My brothers are play-fighting over whether to listen to the car radio or CDs. I'm in the backseat hoping the headlines tomorrow don't read, "Three Siblings Die on Way to Mother's Rehearsal Dinner."

I've been to the Golden Palace, once before with Mom and Stanley because it's one of Stanley's favorite restaurants. But it's not exactly the most romantic place in the world. It's got low ceilings, mauve cloth napkins, and red silk flowers in white porcelain vases on each table. But Stanley's been a regular there for years, and he loves the food, and the restaurant owners love him.

It's still strange, though, that Mom would agree to have one of the biggest parties of her life at the Golden Palace, considering she doesn't like strip malls or sterile-looking Chinese restaurants. The Mom I know insists on restaurants with great ambience and charm. But in her role as fiancée, Mom has an alternative personality designed to make Stanley happy.

"It's such a little thing," she had said. "And anyway, who doesn't like a good Chinese banquet?"

Yet, I'm still surprised. With all of her changes, I feel like I'm the old dog learning new tricks, not her.

In the backseat, I study my nails. Elegant, polished, out of character for me, but a nice change. I assess the dress I'm wearing. It's a multicolored, body-hugging, cap sleeve, knee-length, knit print. It's a miracle I have a dress on at all, considering the torment that went into finding attire for the wedding weekend. The dress shopping escapade with Stefanie was just the beginning of what dragged into weeks of trying to find the right wedding weekend wardrobe. As I looked for the right dresses, I found myself carefully checking return policies and collecting half a dozen different options. When it finally came time to pack, I still couldn't decide which dress would be best for the rehearsal dinner and which would be most appropriate for the wedding. So I put five different dresses in my suitcase, tags still hanging from three of them.

This morning, I still hadn't made up my mind which dress would be most appropriate for the big banquet night. Sedate? Sassy? Sexy? Mom surprised me with an incredibly efficient wedding-related decision; she picked out this dress in ten seconds flat.

"It's modest but also sexy and unique," she said.

I can't help but see the whole dress searching and picking process as an apt metaphor for my dating life: I collect many (with return policies) but can't decide on one. Would Mom be capable of choosing a man for me if I brought home five packed in a suitcase? Would she be able to find the wonderful details or the flaws?

In the front seat, the music fight dies down and a lively debate about aerodynamics has taken hold, again. I tune out, and wonder how our family life might change after tomorrow. Stanley's already changed Mom, mostly for the better, with a few exceptions, dinner parties at the Golden Palace among them.

Around Stanley, Mom shows her most charming, witty, and intelligent self. She is more flexible, accommodating, calm. She is also strangely deferential to him. Once, she even asked him what she should order for dinner! Mom has always been a no-nonsense, take-charge woman, and now, she's happy to go with Stanley's flow. Is Mom forever changed? Or is this a premarital metamorphosis, and she'll revert back to the mother who raised us next week?

Has Mom changed him? I don't know him well enough to sense a difference. But I know Mom's managed to loosen his grip on his maroon blazer, and she's coaxed him into trying restaurants with better décor than the Golden Palace. Are all these changes what people are referring to when they talk about the transformative power of love? Or is it deeper?

The three of us arrive together in the brightly lighted parking lot. Once out of the car, I fix Enrico's collar. Enrico pats down Max's hair, and Max says he doesn't like my purse. I swing my handbag at him, laughing.

My brothers and I decided not to bring dates to this event. The three of us figured it'd be simplest if we just tackled this one together.

The first person we see is Erica, with her boyfriend, Ross. They're walking in from their car just as we are. In other circumstances I might be annoyed that she brought a date, but I can't blame her. She doesn't have brothers or sisters with whom to share this situation. Tonight she is disarming, offering a warm hug and bubbly nervous chatter as we all head toward the restaurant entrance. She gives us a "this is going to be fun" glance.

And with that look, I sense for the first time that my brothers and I have a new, opinionated addition to our team, not an intruder.

The second Mom sees us, she runs over, lavishes us with kisses and hugs, and immediately starts introducing us to her new friends and reintroducing us to her old friends. Since all of her friends are here and none of mine are, then at my wedding will it be all my friends and none of hers? There are about fifty people in the private party room. Most of them are in their fifties, sixties, and seventies, with silver, dyed, or no hair. I imagine this scene looks a lot like a faculty party, with the only difference being that some of the normally disheveled professors combed their hair and are wearing ties. Mom stands out. She looks much more stylish than the rest. She's wearing a sleeveless, off-white, silk top and matching slacks. It is elegant and chic, but too subdued for the exuberant woman inside.

"We've heard so much about you!" the friends say to me and my brothers.

"Yes, I'm the one who works in TV in New York. Yes, they're the scientists. Of course, we're thrilled for our mom. So pleased to meet you."

"Of course, we remember you from when we were growing up," we say. I shoot a quick look at Erica, who is laughing and confident as she introduces herself and her boyfriend around.

I make my way over to talk with my aunts, my father's younger sisters. They have literally traveled across the world for the wedding. One has come from England; the other, Amelie, came from Israel. Amelie is the one who introduced my mom to my dad so many years ago. My aunts' familiar faces are reassuring. They look like my dad. I know they've come here to support my mother. But I also think they've come to represent my father. Even though it's difficult to move on, they say it's good for all of us. If they can see the positive aspects of the union, then certainly I can do the same.

Despite our best plans to sit together, Mom separates the siblings. Each of us is directed to sit at a different table so we can play host to the guests. At my table, I try to understand what Stanley's physicist friends are working on, while Enrico and Max meet some of Mom's college roommates.

The restaurant owners bring the food into the banquet room. They make great overtures to Stanley about how happy they are to share this occasion with him and his lovely bride. I was expecting New York style Chinese take-out food. Instead, massive platters designed to look like peacocks and dragons decorate the tables. The other guests are as delighted by the food presentation as I am. We clap and say "Wow" as each additional platter splashes more color across the tables.

It's all going much better than I expected until a man stands and taps his fork repeatedly against his wineglass. My brothers and I shoot glances at each other across the room. This looks an awful lot like the beginning of a toast. The party quiets down, and everyone turns their attention to Joe, the hefty man who is towering above everyone with toasting tools in hand. Stanley, in a light, humorous manner, asks him to please sit down. Joe, one of Stanley's oldest friends from Brooklyn, laughs. No way will he sit down.

"I've got to make a toast, Stan-man," he says in a booming voice. "That's what these occasions are all about."

My brothers and I shoot glances at each other, this could be ugly. A crash and burn toast?

"Come on, Joe. Please don't," Stanley asks.

Joe teases, "What, are you afraid? I must say something. I have too much good material on you, old man."

Stanley, in an uncharacteristically stern voice says, "Joe, please sit now. I do not want any toasts."

Mom looks worried. Joe looks peeved.

"Come on, folks, don't we want to toast the bride and groom?"

The room full of brilliant academics is stumped. Can't come up with an equation to sort this one out. There are a few timid claps and cheers in support of Joe's toast, but otherwise the room is awkwardly tense and quiet.

Joe opens his mouth as if he's going to say something, but then looks around, hesitates, knocks back a gulp of wine, and sits down without a word.

Stanley offers up one of his signature full-bodied laughs. Mom's furrowed brow disappears, and the face of a joyous bride returns. The guests are at ease again, carrying on their esoteric conversations as if nothing happened.

No one else dared toast the bride and groom the rest of the night, and the party was a success. But later that night, after the party, as I'm in the backseat of the car on the way home, I wonder what people would've said had they been allowed to toast.

"What is it about Stanley and toasts?" Max reads my mind, but he doesn't know the full story. "I would have liked to hear from Mom and Stanley's friends. I would've liked to toast the newlywed couple myself. Maybe I'll confront Stanley about the 'no toast' rule. Don't we all deserve an explanation? I mean who is Stanley to override our constitutional right to freedom of speech? Is he hiding something? Could a ribbing be so grating it would've ruined his evening? Maybe Mom was right to consider calling off the wedding because of the toast prohibition. Can't he just explain his toast fear?"

Enrico says sternly, "Do not say a word."

"Don't worry. I won't say anything this weekend," Max acquiesces. "But we'll get him back. He'll be making toasts at our weddings."

Thirty

Eight o'clock in the morning, and Mom is rapping on my bedroom door.

"Cookie! Cookie! It's finally here."

What? I'm groggy, deep in a sleep fog. Oh, yes. It. W-day.

"Good morning Mom-Bride," I answer.

She pushes open the door. She's wide awake, looking remarkably refreshed considering she probably hasn't slept much. She sits down on the bed beside me as she did when I was a little girl and rubs my arm.

"Cookie? Are you awake yet?"

"Getting there," I answer. "How are you?"

"Wonderful. Nervous. Giddy. Excited," she says, brimming with anticipation.

"Sounds good."

She's quiet.

"Is something wrong, Mom?" Now she has a distant look on her face.

"Nothing."

"So, what is it?"

She stares into her palm hard.

"Mom?"

"Cookie. I have something for you."

"Okay."

"And I think Dad would want you to have it, too."

"Okay."

She looks into her hand, and I see she's wearing the wedding band Dad gave her. She hasn't worn it in years. She removes the simple gold ring and puts it in my palm and closes my fingers over it.

I sit up in bed.

"Are you sure?"

"Yes, Cookie. I want you to have it."

I look at it and slip it on my right hand, fourth finger. It fits perfectly. Just the way it fit Mom.

"Enjoy it." She smiles and pats my fist, running her hand over my finger with the ring on it.

"Thank you."

"You're welcome," she says.

Then, in a quick upshift to avoid getting too emotional too soon, Mom leaps off the bed.

"Come on," she claps. "Get up. Hurry up! We have a lot to do."

Ten minutes later, I've got my face washed, my teeth brushed, and Mom launching a million and one questions at me. Which pair of hose? Which lipstick? Is this bracelet better or that one? I can almost see the nervous energy coming out of her fingertips and charging her frizzy hair.

She's got three different bras laid out on her bed. "Which one will be the best?"

"How would I know?" I ask. "You have to try it on, see what feels and looks good."

"Okay, later, I'll decide later. I'll just throw it in the bag for now," she says and, without missing a beat, "What do you think about the shoes?" she asks pointing to the three pairs on the ground.

"Which ones look best? Which will be more comfortable?" She's just chattering away about what's dashing through her mind, not really interested in actual answers. Her anxiety is just pouring out of her mouth.

She starts to hyperventilate.

"There's nothing to worry about," I tell her. "These are normal prewedding jitters. I've seen this before. It's how all brides are before their weddings," I embellish. "Everything will be just fine.

"Why not sit down and take a few deep breaths?" I suggest.

Not a chance. She's already running frantically around the house, dumping different tubes of lipstick into her makeup bag and stuffing different pairs of panty hose into her dressing bag. Off to the side of her bed, something silky, white, and lacy is dangling from another smaller bag. I register that it's something she'll wear for her nuptial late night, and I ignore it.

I toast a bagel for her and make her some mint tea. I want her to eat and drink to calm her nerves. And I want it, too. If I'm calm, she'll be calm and vice versa. I implore her to sit down, "Just two minutes, please." She sits on the edge of a chair at the breakfast table and nibbles on the bagel. She deliberately shows me she's taking a few sips of tea, and then she's off, running around the house again.

"Which dress should I wear?" I turn the tables on her.

She focuses on the options laid out in a row on my bed: the flowing pink floral printed dress? My simple blue sheath? That black-and-white floral printed cocktail dress I bought in SoHo with Stefanie a few months back? She points at the black-and-white dress. "It looks special," she says and promptly moves on to the next task. I guess that grueling day I skipped work to shop with Stefanie was worth it after all.

By midmorning, we put the multiple bags packed and bursting with options in her trunk. We hang her dress across the backseat of the Honda. She's incredibly tense, and we bicker about who will drive.

"I'm driving to the ceremony site," I insist. "Otherwise I won't get in the car. It's nonnegotiable." She's way too bride-wired to get behind the wheel.

She finally gives in and lets me chauffeur. I drive us down the same highway she was driving up when she initially announced her engagement nine months ago. This time we are driving toward his house, not toward Mom's house. This time, I'm in charge of the car and my mother.

About twenty minutes into the drive, Mom's nerves completely overtake her mouth. She's lucky if she can form a complete sentence before jumping onto the next thought.

"I hope Fernando remembers I want the blue vases not the . . . Josephine's daughter has a really bad cough . . . I think I said ten tables of ten each . . ."

Her chatter is increasing the tension in the car. Or maybe this is just Mom's way of relaxing. Maybe if I told her stories, the way Dad told me bedtime stories as a child, it would distract her and calm her. What stories to tell? Aha! I'll tell her about my dating life in Manhattan. Those stories never fail to entertain.

I envision myself sitting on a red carpet in the children's section of a library reading stories to a group of second graders. I use a calm, elementary school teacher voice and begin telling deranged, modern, urban fairy tales. I start with *The Cell Phone Number Thief of Central Park.*

"Once upon a time, in a land far, far away, past the Sierra Nevadas, there lived a fair maiden in Manhattan . . ."

Mom is captivated by the story.

"This fair maiden was on a quest to find her one true love, her knight in shining armor, and she wouldn't settle for anyone but. She braved the darkest bars in Manhattan, the worst movies ever created, and poisonously bad food on her quest . . ."

I manage to keep Mom absorbed in the story all the way to the last line.

". . . and the fair maiden kept his number locked in her cell phone under the name 'phonthief' forevermore."

"Another story," she asks.

I tell her *The Dip, the Toreador, and Carmen.*

"And from his place under the stage lights, the toreador magically waved his red cape, at once capturing the heart of Carmen and Daniella. But alas, their affections were ever so fleeting . . ."

I cap off story hour with *The Grocery Store Guy and the Floppy Fish.*

Mom's formerly frantic mind-set morphs into irrepressible laughter. The sight of this character, *Little Mom Wild Bride,* doubled over in hysterics next to me, triggers a laughing fit in me, too. Honking from the angry driver behind forces me to pay attention to the road. Mom soon replaces her girlish laughter with philosophical musings. Together, we consider the fairy tale she is living. We marvel at how Mom and Stanley, both widowed, and both approaching their seventh decade, found each other and fell in love.

• • •

Mom's frantic mind-set rears its head again as we pull into the parking lot of the wedding site, the Stanford University Faculty Club.

"Everything will be fine," I say. "I'll take care of everything, don't worry," I say as a wave of anxiety washes over me. I've never seen this club before, and I'm not sure I'm up for the task.

"Okay, so first things first." She marches in. "Let's do a full tour of the space and the preps." She completely ignores my efforts to relieve her of responsibility and stress.

I follow her into the building, which is nothing special. But the courtyard, where the ceremony will take place, is. We enter from the back. The floor is made of smooth, terra-cotta, Spanish tiles. I slip off one of my sandals and run my foot across the cool tiles. Lush, tropical plants grow all along the courtyard's perimeter. Large oak trees hang over and shade the stucco wall enclosing the front side of the courtyard. The weather is a little chilly and overcast.

A skeleton of what will become the chuppah, the Jewish wedding canopy, is also at the front of the courtyard. The chuppah looks naked, lonely; it's just a barren birch branch frame in the shape of an eight-foot-square box. To my left, dozens of white chairs are folded and leaning against the wall.

The right wall of the courtyard is made entirely of clear glass and also serves as one side of the adjacent atrium-like reception room. Through the glass wall, we can see the reception room is entirely empty but for a few folding tables leaned up against the walls.

"Nothing's ready!" Mom cries, panicked.

"It's only eleven in the morning. Nothing should be ready. You aren't getting married for another five hours."

"But what about Fernando and Josephine and Claudine? Shouldn't they be here already?"

"Their call time is noon. I'm sure they'll find their way here," I assure. "They do this every weekend."

"Right." Mom swallows.

"Let's go find your dressing room so we can put your stuff down," I suggest.

The dressing room is ascetic, functional. There's a full-size bed (for fainting), a dark wood standing closet (for hiding), a sliding glass door out to a garden (for running away), and a large mirror with a vanity in front of it (for reality-checking). A private bathroom (for getting sick) is off to the side.

By the time we've brought in and arranged Mom's various bags of marriage materials and tools, it's noon. I take a quick shower, dry my hair, pop into my printed cocktail dress, and slip on my black strappy heeled sandals. I then efficiently and expertly apply my makeup. (All those hours spent putting on makeup for TV are coming in handy after all.) By the time I'm ready, Mom is just coming out of the shower in a white terry-cloth robe. Her hair is swept up in a towel, no makeup, no jewelry, no shoes.

"You look great!" she says to me. "Cute dress! Perfect choice for the daughter of the bride."

"Thanks. It was easy," I say.

She grins, registering my sarcasm.

"I'll check on things in the reception room while you get ready," I tell her.

"Wait, I'm coming!" she says.

"No. Right now your job is to put the 'beautiful' in 'beautiful bride,'" I say firmly.

"Wait!" she yelps. "I need your help before you go out."

Bras. Bras and shoes. We hadn't resolved those questions yet. Unless I want to see her loose and barefoot in a few hours, I'll stay to help.

The dress is hanging to the right of the mirror. I go to unzip it from the clear, plastic bag it's wrapped in.

"Wait! Are your hands clean?" Mom asks.

"Yes, they're clean," I say automatically as I did a hundred times as a child growing up. "But I'll wash them again."

"I'll do it." She unzips the bag and lifts the dress out.

The dress looks more beautiful than I remember. It's so pure, youthful, smooth. We stop for a moment to admire it. It is elegant. Then Mom, in her corsetlike bra, bows her entire upper body toward me as if she's Japanese and puts her arms out straight forward, her elbows covering her ears. I lift and slide the dress over her head and arms and she stands up, the dress falling gracefully into place. She turns her back to me so I can button, hook, and lace her into the corseted top. I then sit down on the fainting bed as she twists and wriggles her dress into place. Finally she turns toward me.

"So? Do I look okay?"

Her torso is trim and shapely. Her waist looks tiny, and the skirt balloons out just enough to give a light, fairy sense.

"The dress looks spectacular on you," I say, as opposed to "You look spectacular." She's going to have to put on makeup and do her hair before she gets the full "you look spectacular" comment from me.

She insists on trying on the two other bras with the dress. As she squeezes into each corsetlike bra, I lace up the back of the crisscross corset top and think *You've come a long way, baby* since those zap action, loose, braless, feminist days of the sixties. I assist her patiently as she searches for perfection. The bras all support her beautifully and follow the line of her top perfectly.

"Just choose the one that feels most comfortable," I tell her, and she does. I hope when I'm on the brink of sixty, I'll look as trim and fit as she does.

Next, shoes. She tries on three different pairs. Like mother, like daughter. Every option open until the last minute. All of the shoes are elegant. But one pair stands out from the rest. It's got the highest heel of the three, and it has a subtle, shimmery, Cinderella-like slipper quality.

"You might as well go for it," I tell her. "This is a once-in-a-lifetime experience . . . or more."

She looks at me.

We both smile.

"I'm just going to put the other two pairs in the minifridge here in case your feet overheat and hurt and you need new, chilled shoes for dancing." It's an old trick I use if my feet get sore while I'm at work.

She then changes back into the robe, hands me the dress to hang up again, and sits down on the stool in front of the mirror to begin with her hair. She didn't want a professional hair-dresser's help.

"It would be frivolous," she had said. "And anyway, I know how to do it the way I like it, I have the most practice."

She holds the blow dryer in her left hand and the rounded brush in her right hand, straightening and curling her hair the way she always has. Meanwhile, I steam her dress. The high-pitched wail of her hair dryer reminds me of mornings, growing up in Texas, when she would get ready for work and I would get ready for school. I've witnessed this noisy routine hundreds of times. It used to drive me and my brothers batty. Now the sound is soothing in its familiarity.

"I'm going to take a look around," I yell over the sound of the dryer.

"Okay." She waves me away. "Come back soon."

"Okay." I motion with my hands.

By now, the courtyard is undergoing a transformation. The

white folding chairs have been neatly set up in ten rows of ten seats facing the front of the courtyard. The rows are divided down the middle, creating an aisle that leads to the chuppah. I look up. The clouds are clearing out. The sky is a bright blue, and the temperature has warmed up. It's almost seventy degrees. There is a gentle breeze.

A tall, muscular man I don't recognize is standing near the chuppah, his back to me. I straighten my posture, smooth down my dress, put on a smile, and glide down the aisle, poised, my eyes focused on him.

Smile and step. Smile and step. Back straight, I practice.

I arrive at the chuppah. He sneezes.

"Hi, Fernando," I say.

He hardly turns around. He's too busy expertly weaving, winding, and wrapping garlands of flowers and greens around the chuppah's birchwood frame.

"Oh, hello there, Daniella," he mumbles and half-smiles, half-nods. He's standing on a chair with the stem of a light pink gerber daisy in his mouth. He takes the daisy from his mouth and pokes it into one of the garlands on the chuppah. He steps back and down off the chair to evaluate his work. Sneeze. He reaches up to straighten the lacy, white cloth that is serving as the chuppah's canopy. He steps back again. He turns a red rose so it directly faces what will soon be the audience. He turns a yellow tulip so it's opening up a bit more skyward. He stands back to admire his work.

"Voilà!" he says, hands on hips, satisfied. There are so many colorful daisies, roses, lilies, tulips, irises, baby's breath, and vines of ivy wound around the chuppah you can barely see the birch frame beneath.

"Bravo," I say. The floral garlands dip and drip all over the frame. It's much more elaborate than Mom envisioned. I re-

member her saying, "Simple, elegant, exposed birch." I also remember her saying, "Gerber daisies, papyrus, nothing else."
But I'm not about to tangle with Fernando. Anyway, it's too
late to change. Asking him to adjust his masterpiece would be
like asking Mark Rothko to add a touch of pastel color to one
of his paintings.

"What a nice surprise," I say.

"Well, I'm glad Maya's daughter likes it," Fernando says in
his typical patronizing manner. "Off to put the finishing touches
on the bouquets now, ta-ta!"

I follow him as he strides into the reception area, where
enormous flower arrangements tower above the dozen, round,
white cloth–covered dinner tables. The arrangements are made
of the same multicolored flowers as the chuppah garlands.
Gerber daisies, roses, tulips, baby's breath, irises, lilies, and ivy
burst and overflow from enormous blue glass vases. Only one
problem. Mom's going to hate it. She's going to pitch a fit because the guests won't be able to see each across the tables—the
flowers are too big and smack dab in the line of sight. I must do
something, but I hesitate. I don't want to make a scene. And
Fernando seems ready to snap each time he sees me. But I gird
myself. Better he hear it from me now than in an hour from Mom.

"Fernando? Fernando." I approach him as he's hunched over
a table arranging what looks like the bouquets we'll be carrying.

"The centerpieces are fabulous, joyful, and beautiful all at
once. But . . ."

"Yes, dear?" Fernando's tongue bulging the side of his cheek,
a quick flick of his eyes at his watch. "Is there a problem?"

"Well, um, it may be a bit difficult for guests to see each
other through the arrangements."

"Ha-choo! Uh-huh," he says, making no effort to hide his
irritation. He returns to his bouquets.

"Well," I use my sweetest voice, "is there anything you can do about it?"

"Not at this very moment," he says. "As you can see, I'm a bit busy with things that *aren't* finished yet."

"Okay," I switch from a sugary-sweet approach to a cheap, forbidden, journalistic trick. The leading question. I like to call it affirmative questioning.

"So you *will* be able to fix the problem before my mother sees it then, yes?"

He rolls his eyes, hesitates. "Yes, I'll look into it."

Works like a charm.

"Thanks." I smile back. "She'll be here in about an hour to check on things."

He doesn't acknowledge he's heard my thanks. Fine. Be that way. I spin around and leave to check on the band.

The band is setting up onstage on the other side of the room. In front of the stage is the dance floor, and then the tables are arranged in a semicircle around the dance floor. The band of middle-aged men calls itself the Renaissancers.

"They don't do klezmer, they don't do country (Stanley's favorite), and they won't be memorable, but they'll be perfect," Mom had said. "They'll provide music but won't take the spotlight. And anyway, I like their name."

Okay. So, they aren't surefire rockers like Big Rick and the Dyno-mites, but the Rennaisancers are more comfortable. More . . . age appropriate, shall we say?

"Are you guys all right?" I ask the man with the shiny bald head and the goatee who's in charge of the band. He's squatting down next to the amplifier unwinding a cable. "Need anything? I'm the bride's daughter."

"Well now," he puts down the microphone cable he's uncoiling and stands up.

"Isn't that something." He looks me over. "The daughter of the bride. Don't get to see that too often. I guess we'll have to perform well tonight if we want to be asked back for your wedding."

I smile back and think, *Don't count on it*. I'm not getting married imminently, and if I were, I certainly wouldn't need a band of reborns. Anyway, I'd want Big Rick and the Dyno-mites at my party. And don't look me over like that.

"Right. Let me know if you need anything." I smile and spin away from him to check on the table settings and the food.

The catering staff is buzzing about, folding the white cloth napkins and setting the silverware and the various glasses in place. I hear Josephine and Claudine barking orders at their staff from the kitchen. I peek into the narrow kitchen and see the two sisters focused and looking seriously at something on a chopping counter. I'm about to offer my help when I flash back to the incident at the bakery with the shattered bride head. I better stay out of Josephine's way this time.

Anyway, I should report back to Mom-Bride by now. I'm sure she's getting antsy.

"Knock-knock, can I come in?" I ask outside the bridal dressing room.

"Sure."

I push open the dressing room and shriek. Mom is sitting primly before the mirror in her robe calmly drinking coffee out of a small white china teacup. Her dress is hanging precariously close to her.

"What are you doing with coffee in here?" I leave for just a few minutes, and look what happens. I scan the room for other hazards, like red wine. "You spill it on your dress, you're toast. Not champagne-cheers-toast. Trouble toast."

"No big deal," she waves me off. "I've been drinking this

stuff for over forty years. I think I can handle my coffee, Cookie."

"Okay," I say in my don't tell me I didn't warn you voice. I suddenly remember an article in one of those bridal magazines— "Don't forget your W-day emergency kit," it said. "Pack superglue to reattach beads that fall off. And remember Wite-Out in case you need to dab it on an unsightly stain." At the time, I thought the article was inane.

"How's everything looking out there?" Mom asks. She's much more calm and poised than she was earlier. Maybe all the excitement and stress has worn her out.

"Great. Just great. The whole cast of characters is here: Josephine, Claudine, Fernando, and the Renaissancers. The chairs are set up. The chuppah is dripping with flowers. The dinner tables are ready to go, complete with napkins, silver, and glasses. The band seems to be making itself comfortable onstage."

"Any problems?" she asks.

"No. No problems," I say. "But you should know, Fernando has gone a bit overboard with the flowers. The chuppah and the arrangements are a little more elaborate than you wanted, but it's beautiful. Striking."

"I could've guessed as much. He never listened, that guy. I'll have a word with him if I don't like it. For now though, makeup. I need help."

I take her makeup bag, which is the size of a checkbook, and empty it on the vanity. Out falls mascara, eyeliner, blush, and three different lipsticks. That's it. Mom's never worn much makeup. My cosmetics case, the size of a football, is bulging at the seams. From it, I unload the brushes, foundations, powders, blushes, eyeliners, tweezers, lipsticks, lip liners, and glosses I've learned to use over my eight years on TV.

I tilt her chin toward me and sponge on liquid foundation.

"It's cold," she whimpers.

"Stop squirming."

I'm careful to apply the liquid foundation uniformly all over her face. It's strange to look at her skin so closely. I never have before. Her forehead has faint creases. I can't help but think that my brothers and I are responsible for many of these lines. I smooth them over with pats of base powder.

"Suck in like a fish," I say as I brush blush high on her cheekbones.

"Look down." I brush eye shadow on her lids. The sad lines around her eyes must have formed after Dad died.

"Look up." I apply eyeliner and mascara with precision.

As I draw on her lip liner, I see smile lines and laugh lines around her mouth that she's deepened since meeting Stanley. I apply her lipstick, gloss, blot it, and smile. A touch more here. A touch more there and "Voila!" My makeup artistry gracefully accentuates her beautiful face of stories, wisdom, and experience.

When she turns back toward the mirror and gazes at the woman looking back at her, she's genuinely surprised. Her youth is apparent in her shocked smile.

A knock on the door, and her girlfriend, Dinah, doesn't wait for a response to fly into the room, giddy and bubbly.

"Gosh, I had hoped you'd like Stanley when I introduced you, but I never imagined it would be this great!" Dinah starts. "Seeing you, Maya, reminds me of my daughter's wedding last summer. And my own wedding thirty-five years ago. I love weddings. I am so happy for you. You know, according to Jewish law, the person who introduces a husband to his wife or vice versa gets a free ticket to heaven. I'm in great shape. This'll be my third successful setup. I've got a good afterlife in store."

"Could you help me with my dress?" Mom asks.

Dinah falls silent. We both stand upright at attention; helping

Mom with her dress is one of our biggest responsibilities. The dress is steamed and ready to go.

"Let me wash my hands of any makeup," I say, anticipating Mom's clean concerns.

Mom takes off her robe, revealing her corsetlike bra and slip beneath. She bows to us Japanese style, and we carefully slip the dress on over her head, her hair, her makeup. Not a hair is mussed, and no makeup is smudged. Dinah and I look at each other in self-congratulation. We turn her around, and she stands ramrod straight as we button, hook, and lace her into the dress. She's just turning around to admire herself in the mirror when there's a knock on the door. Before we have a chance to say anything, Stanley pops in. He's in his tuxedo, ready to go. He's calm, jovial, and delighted to get a glimpse of his bride in her gown before the ceremony.

"Get out!" Mom half-protests, half-flirts, "Bad luck!"

He looks her over. He makes no sound. But we can see the wonder on his face. His eyes are saying, *How could I be so lucky?*

"Okay," he clucks. Then he plants a kiss on her cheek and trots out of the room.

A few minutes later, there's another knock on the door. I rush to the door before another person has a chance to burst in unannounced. I peek my head out. It's Enrico and Max. They look dapper, confident, and older in their tuxedos; like men from a *GQ* magazine, not like my brothers.

"Picture time," Enrico says. "Let's go."

"But we're not ready," I protest.

"Well, hurry up! The photog says we're starting in five minutes."

"Okay, we'll try. Now go away, we have work to do," I tease.

Mom, Dinah, and I immediately launch into a tizzy of activity. The hair dryer's wailing, hair spray is squirting, and lips are stretching for one last gloss application. Five minutes later, we're racing out the door. We're halfway down the hall when Mom yelps.

"Jewelry! I forgot to put on jewelry." She spins around to head back to the room.

"And what about something old, something new, something borrowed, something blue?" asks Dinah as we chase Mom down the hall. "Did you forget that, too?"

"No," Mom calls from inside the room. "No time for superstitions right now. Where's my jewelry box?"

We're back in the room turning things over wildly, tissue paper from shoe boxes flying through the air, lipsticks rolling off the vanity. Where is that silver jewelry box?

"You have to do something old, new, borrowed, and blue," Dinah insists.

Mom is not responding to Dinah. Mom's too focused on finding her jewelry box.

Rap, rap, rap. There's another knocking at the door.

"Come on, ladies," Max tries to hurry us up. "It's picture time!"

"Mom, we'll find it later." I unhook the choker of pearls from around my neck. It belonged to her mother. "Put this on." I hold it out in front of me. "It'll work well."

Mom hesitates, then puts her back to me and bends her knees so I can drape the string of pearls and fasten it around her neck. She still has the pearl earrings in that she bought when she had her ears piereced.

"Great, it's something old!" Dinah says, then searches frantically around the room. "Now something new, something borrowed, and something blue."

Mom looks at herself in the mirror and straightens the necklace quickly, and without skipping a beat rhymes,

"This necklace is old and borrowed, this dress is new, I don't have anything blue, so this will have to do!"

With that, she makes a break for the door, but she trips.

"Oww!" she shrieks.

"What? What?" I run over to her side.

"Darn it! Stupid princess slippers," she moans. "I stubbed my toe!"

She kicks off her shoe and alternately hobbles around and holds her right foot in her hands like a flamingo in a white dress.

"How?"

"My heel caught on all this stuff all over the floor," she says agitated. She kicks a piece of tissue paper angrily in the air with her stubbed toe.

She leans against the closet, head down.

"Sit down. Sit down."

"Nope. Can't ruin the dress." She purses her lips and steels herself. "One minute, I'll be fine."

She puts pressure on her toe.

"Well, at least now I'll have something blue!" she says.

Then, in a flash, she's rushing-hobbling down the hallway toward the garden behind the faculty club.

"Slow down," I insist as I try to catch up with her. "You don't want to hurt yourself again."

"You'll ruin your dress," Dinah warns as we chase her through the courtyard. Mom glances at the chairs, the chuppah, the flowers, as she races forward, but she makes no face, and doesn't slow down till she's in the back garden.

Everyone's waiting in the back garden when we arrive. Stanley, Erica, her boyfriend Ross, Enrico, Leslie, Max, and Dinah's husband.

"Slow down, speedy," Stanley says to Mom as she rushes up to him and gives him a peck on the cheek. "The photographer's not ready—he went to get something out of his car. You look so fresh-faced and rosy-cheeked." Stanley smiles and motions for her to step back so he can look at her.

"Well, I've got to look good for these pictures," Mom says. "I'll never look this young again."

Stanley chuckles, admires her, sighs, and shakes his head. My brothers, Erica, and the rest gasp with oohs and aahs. Everyone fawns over Mom, and I size her up from head to toe. Everything about her looks fantastic. Not bad work, Daniella, if I do say so myself. Is her toe still throbbing?

Now for a better look at my brothers. They look sharp, almost unrecognizably debonair. It's the first time I've seen them in tuxedos since their high school proms.

"Nice threads, guys." I give them the requisite teasing pushes on the shoulders. I give Enrico's girlfriend, Leslie, a quick kiss-kiss.

Then Erica, my soon-to-be stepsister, gives me a big, gentle hug.

"Nice to see you. You look great," I say. I give her a look and gesture that questions the history of the simple flowing navy blue skirt and blouse she's wearing.

"It was my mom's outfit," she explains. "Was her favorite."

I pause, not knowing what to say.

"Nice to see you again," Ross says.

"And you," I say. Erica looks so comfortable with Ross. Do I look as awkwardly single as she looks contentedly coupled?

No time to ponder. The photographer rushes up. Ross and Leslie finish their quick hellos and then take their cue and duck out of the shot. Part of me wants to go with Ross, Leslie, Dinah, and Bob behind the camera so I can be a spectator to this moment, not a participant. Instead, I watch them as they watch us assemble. Despite having spent my entire professional life in front of a camera, this is the most surreal experience I've ever had in front of the lens. The photographer instructs us to turn this way and inch that way, look here, tilt your head . . . snap! The photographer captures the six of us together in one shot; our first image as a new family.

Thirty-one

"It just won't do," Mom tells Fernando as she inspects the table centerpieces. She's trying to keep her irritation under control, but she's impatient. We have less than an hour before guests start arriving.

"The flowers are extraordinary," Mom says. "But they're just too tall, smack-dab at eye level. No one will be able to see each other across the table."

"But . . ." Fernando protests.

"Frankly, I'm disappointed in you," Mom cuts him off. "I'm sure you'll be able to sort this out. You have an hour. Do something. I don't know. Change the arrangements? Make them smaller? I want people to be able to see each other." With that, she turns on her heel and marches off with her skirt and me trailing.

Mom heads over to the kitchen area, where she makes eye contact with Josephine and Claudine. Josephine looks up from a pot, and in one nod tells Mom that everything is under control. Mom nods in return, appreciating the efficiency of Josephine's gesture. We then head outside to survey the courtyard again. The chairs remain evenly lined up next to each other, but now they've been opened up into a flattened V-shape facing the chuppah.

"Wow," Mom says admiring the chuppah. "This is not at all what I had in mind, but it is spectacular." The chuppah is heavy and dripping with flowers. "I didn't want roses and tulips and all these other flowers, but I have to admit, it is a real work of art."

She looks at it. "I guess sometimes you get less than you want, and sometimes you get more than you could ever dream of." She sighs, trying to accentuate the metapor.

"Yeah," I say. More than you can dream of sure would be nice. But not everyone gets that lucky. "Good enough" is going to be good enough for me.

I lead Mom back to the bridal ready room and leave her there with Dinah so she can do a last-minute touch-up, and I can start receiving guests. I hunt down my brothers to back me up on this job. They are hunched over, hiding out in a corner by the kitchen, fidgeting with their digital camera.

"Come on, Enrico and Max," I tease. "We have a mission to accomplish. Guests need you handsome men at the door to set the tone for this glamorous event."

They smile and reluctantly oblige, slowly peeling their reedy frames from the two chairs. We know what we have to do. Guests have already started to trickle into the courtyard.

Erica and Ross are already there chatting with a gray-haired couple. Erica sees us and introduces us. "These are Maya's kids: Enrico, Max, Daniella." We smile and shake hands. Erica, sensitive to boundaries, isn't introducing us as stepbrothers or -sisters yet. We reciprocate and introduce her as "Erica, Stanley's daughter" to the people we know.

We are all on our best adult behavior, but I wish there were a kids table in the kitchen area where I could just hide out and flick uncooked macaroni at my brothers. Enrico offers his arm to a frail guest who claims to remember him from when he was just five years old. She leans on Enrico as he slowly leads her to her seat. "I'm the oldest of the three kids," Enrico gently reminds her.

Younger, more bouncy friends of Mom's and Stanley's gush over us, asking how we're doing, congratulating us, wondering what our plans are. I haven't seen some of these people since Dad's memorial service, and it's strange to see them again at another life event.

Then, from out of nowhere, the rabbi taps me, my brothers, and Erica. "It's time to sign the ketubah," he whispers softly in our ears.

Already? It's all happening so quickly, and it's so major. I'm to go get Mom and escort her to the small anteroom. Erica goes to get her dad. I thought I was ready, but now I'm not so sure. I managed the flowers, the band, the caterer, and the table arrangements just fine. But the ketubah? That's commitment.

The ketubah is a legally binding marriage contract. It brings thousands of years of Jewish tradition into the agreement. The ketubah is the real deal. In fact, many experts say that once the couple signs the ketubah, that's it, they're married under Jewish law. No looking back, and no need for any further ceremony.

When I walk into the bridal ready room, Mom is fussing with her hair.

"Oh, Cookie. What are you doing here already? What do you think of my hair? This way or that?" She fluffs it up and then pushes it down a bit.

"Either way. Better decide," I say. "It's time for the ketubah."

She takes a deep breath. "Already?"

"Yup." I take in a deep breath.

She gives Dinah, who has been the lady-in-waiting for the past hour, a "this is it" look. Dinah gives her the "everything's going to be fine" smile. Mom fidgets with her hair one more time. Brushes on a whisp more blush. Checks her teeth for lipstick, and then looks at me.

"Let's do it," she says.

I offer her my arm, and off we go. Dinah follows behind, making sure Mom's dress doesn't snag on anything or trip us up along the way.

We are the last to arrive in the anteroom, a remarkably plain space. Dinah's husband, Bob, is standing, talking with Erica. The rabbi and Stanley are sitting at a small folding table in the center of the room, looking at papers spread out on it. My brothers look nervous, like security guards with arms folded, standing together in tuxedos with their backs to a wall of dark books. When Enrico and Max see Mom, their nervousness morphs into shock. Stanley's eyes grow wide.

Mom looks absolutely stunning with her bare shoulders, slender arms, and practiced posture. She is smiling and staring straight at Stanley. Sure, we all just saw Mom an hour ago for pictures, but this time it's different. She's here to take the somber oaths of matrimony. The frantic, nervous energy she had earlier has dissipated into a calm, confident aura. Erica and I look at each other and exchange a knowing smile. Somehow, this woman in a white dress is more familiar, less overwhelming to us than she is to the men. Perhaps it's because we can imagine ourselves wrapped in white one day, too. We are sisters in understanding.

The simplicity of the room makes Mom stand out more. The space is austere, just a few bookcases and white walls. It's insulated from the trappings of the modern wedding. There are no flower arrangements, bands, or caterers. Here, nothing has been bought for the occasion but the clothes we're wearing. Here, the focus will be on commitment. Here is private. Here is pure.

Stanley and the rabbi rise to greet Mom. Stanley probably wants to kiss her but thinks better in front of the rabbi. Instead, Stanley hurries to her side and offers her his arm. She takes it slowly and gracefully, and he guides her as she floats across the room and into a chair at the table.

Rabbi Tennenbaum is round, cheery, and a good twenty years younger than the bride and groom. Stanley and Erica have known Rabbi Tennenbaum, or Rabbi T. as Erica used to call him, since she was twelve years old, studying for her Bat Mitzvah. Rabbi T. officiated at Miriam's funeral. Rabbi T. is new to me and my brothers but has a comforting presence.

Rabbi T. sits down on one side of the table, next to Mom and Stanley, and directs Dinah and her husband Bob to sit down across from them, on the other side of the table. We kids stand in a circle around the table, looking over the shoulders of the "grown-ups."

The room falls quiet, and after a solemn silence, Rabbi Tennenbaum, in a warm and earnest voice, says, "Welcome."

We smile.

"Now," he continues. "This is a special occasion. Rarely do I get a chance to share wedding wisdom with couples who have more matrimonial experience than I do."

We laugh nervously.

"Today, we are here to celebrate," Rabbi T. continues. "In this vast, complicated world of possibilities, disappointments, and challenges, it is an absolute wonder that two people can meet, fall in love, and commit to spending their lives together. When that amazing luck happens once, it is phenomenal. When that serendipity happens twice, from a wellspring of tragic loss, it is an absolute miracle. Stanley, Maya. You both experienced the joy of good marriages. You both know the profound pain of losing your spouse."

Mom and Stanley look at each other sadly with total comprehension. The rabbi looks around the room, making eye contact with each of us.

"Your grieving for Miriam and Giuseppe will never end," the rabbi says tenderly. "Their passing left a sadness, a gaping hole in your lives. And while that void will be forever present, Maya and Stanley, today you are building something new. A new commitment. A new attempt to find wholeness again in a new person, a new relationship. Today, you are moving on and allowing for joy and renewal."

"For the children here, watching your mom or dad get remarried may in some ways feel like a second loss," Rabbi T. continues. "But try to envision it as an addition. Jewish law says, 'It is not good to be alone.' And I think Giuseppe and Miriam would agree. If they could, I imagine they would encourage you all to go ahead with your lives, discovering and creating the most profound happiness possible, be it with another person or not. Move forward confidently, knowing your memories of Miriam and Giuseppe will forever be strong and bright."

With that, the rabbi looks around at each of us. Then he begins to chant an achingly beautiful mourning prayer for Dad and Miriam. It is an intense, yearning chant that pulls a chord which resonates in the hollowness deep within me. Mom was deeply submerged in that hollow nightmare when Dad died. We all were. Now she is emerging. There in silence, we swallow hard to hold back tears. Mom's eyes look distant. Stanley is looking down, biting his lower lip.

"Now," the rabbi says in an upbeat tone. "The ketubah. Anyone any good at reading Aramaic?"

We all laugh, not because it's funny but because we desperately need some comic relief.

"We are soon going to sign the ketubah, the Jewish wedding contract. Its origins date back to the first century, when this scroll proved that the groom had paid for his bride, and that he would look after her. Traditionally, it was written in the legal and technical language of our ancestors, Aramaic. Nowadays, though, it's often written in Hebrew, just like this one is. The ketubah, gratefully, has evolved in other ways over time. It now takes into consideration more modern understandings of love and commitment. At its core, it remains a legal transaction, but by now we've added a bit more egalitarianism and romance to the mix." He winks.

The rabbi unrolls the ketubah scroll slowly. The top half of the scroll is inscribed with a mystical text of black, dynamic, Hebrew calligraphy. The bottom half of the scroll reveals an English translation of the text, also in calligraphy. Below the text are blank lines waiting for signatures to validate the document. In the bottom corners of the scroll, two tree trunks are painted in vibrant watercolor. They grow and wind gently up the side borders of the scroll into branches that unite as one large, beautiful mass of leaves, fruits, birds, and twigs at the top border.

"Now, would anyone here like to read the Hebrew text aloud?"

We all look at each other and laugh nervously. We can all recite and write the Hebrew alphabet, but read it? No way.

"The text on this ketubah ties us to our ancestors. It is similar to what they signed when they married one another. While you may not be able to read this aloud, the translation below in English explains that this is a promise, a covenant between Stanley and Maya, to protect and respect their relationship and each other in the context of a profound history."

"Instead of taking the traditional text, because obviously, Maya cannot be sold, and even if she could, Stanley couldn't afford it—Stanley and Maya have chosen to take ideas from the old text and add and adapt some new ideas."

Ah! How very progressive! Mom didn't tell me about that.

With that cue, Mom and Stanley begin to read the English text on their ketubah in sync.

"We shall treasure and respect each other with honor and integrity as we create a future together . . ."

I try to focus on the words.

"May our lives be intertwined as long as we live . . ."

"May the two of us be one in tenderness and devotion."

They look deeply at each other as they come to the end of each sentence. The gravity of the words and solemnity with which they take these vows is palpable.

Then, a strange sensation washes over me and tingles my skin. I feel Dad's presence in the room with us. It's as if Dad is putting his warm, strong arm around my shoulders assuredly. Patting me gently. Squeezing my shoulder. Looking me in the eyes and smiling at me, saying, "It's okay. This is good. Mom will be happy. It will be good for all of you kids. Just go with it. Don't worry about me. I'm fine. You go ahead with your life. I want you to be happy."

"That we will make our world stronger through the bonds of each other and our families . . . We joyfully enter this covenant and solemnly accept its obligations," I hear Mom and Stanley say.

My eyes well up in joy and pain.

Mom and Stanley squeeze each other's hands.

The rabbi chants a cheerful matrimonial prayer.

Then he is silent.

He slides the ketubah in front of Mom and Stanley.

Each one of us kids holds our breath and holds down a corner of the scroll which would otherwise roll up. Mom inhales, and deliberately signs in Hebrew and then in English. Stanley scribbles his name in English and Hebrew in an easy, practiced autograph. Then Bob and Dinah sign as witnesses. The rabbi, in a way that he has done a hundred times, signs his name and then looks up.

"Mazel tov!" he pronounces. "You are officially married! Husband and wife."

Mom and Stanley hug. Mom laughing and crying, sniffles, "I can't start crying already, it'll mess up my makeup."

We all laugh and hug each other.

The rabbi smiles. "Okay, now for the grand entrance. Dry your eyes, the show must go on."

Seconds later, I'm peeking out into the courtyard, watching, as the rabbi waddles towards the chuppah. The guests are shifting in their seats, peering over their glasses, waiting eagerly to witness the celebration of this new beginning. The clouds have cleared entirely by now, and the temperature has crept into the midseventies. It has turned into a mild, perfect California late afternoon.

The string quartet begins playing. Bob and Dinah are off, confidently, proudly, walking arm in arm down the aisle before we've even gotten organized. The parade has begun. New family, places, please! Quickly. We shuffle. My brothers, Erica, and I line up to walk our parents down the aisle.

Erica makes the bold first move. Arm looped with her father, they start slowly, deliberately down the aisle. The fragile musical strings yearn and pull and bend. The guests crane their head around to see their entrance. Stanley, in his new tuxedo, moves with the confidence of experience. Erica, wearing her mother's outfit, falls in step with her father. She is cautious but poised.

Once in front of the chuppah, Erica stops, kisses her father on the cheek, gives him a squeeze on his forearm, turns to the right of the chuppah, and takes her place next to Dinah, facing the audience.

My turn. The music does not slow, I cannot pause. If Erica can do it, so can I. I take a deep breath, link arms with Max, and follow in their path. My feet are not heavy the way they've been at other weddings. They are so light, in fact, that Max tugs on me to slow down. He whispers, "A procession, not a sprint." My body feels weightless, and I feel a smile stretch across my face as I respond to the guests smiling at me. All of a sudden, we're in front of the chuppah, and Max is nudging me to take my place next to Erica. I go to my spot and turn to face the guests, who are already twisting around to face the back of the courtyard, anticipating Mom.

We wait.

And wait.

The music stretches and strains in harmony and discord.

At last, Mom appears. A collective gasp. She looks that beautiful. She waits at the end of the aisle, and everyone admires her. Her tight white bodice. Her tanned bare shoulders. Her graceful poise. Her flowing white skirt. Her dancing eyes. Her blissful smile. On cue, Enrico begins to guide her steadily, slowly toward the chuppah. She is radiant, youthful, and walks with the certainty of a mother. All eyes are glued to her every step. She looks calm, yet exuberant. In an instant she is standing before the chuppah and the rabbi. Enrico leans in, kisses her on the cheek, presses her hand in his, gives Stanley a solemn stare, and slowly leaves her at Stanley's side. Enrico almost reluctantly takes his place next to Max and Bob.

The strings quiet, and the rabbi begins speaking. His mellifluous voice floats through the air, creating an embracing sound canopy over us and all the guests. Mom and Stanley stand side by side underneath the elaborate chuppah, looking attentively at Rabbi T. and occasionally darting glances at each other, confirming that the other is still there. The rabbi explains that the chuppah represents a new home, a new beginning, and a sacred place because of the bursting energy of love within it. He chants a prayer over the wine, and Mom and Stanley drink carefully out of a shared cup. The air is still, silent, almost holding its breeze out of respect for the ceremony.

"The wedding ring; a band, a complete circle, represents the wholeness achieved in marriage. The circle represents many things, a sign of perfection, completion, safety, woman," I hear the rabbi say.

Mom's face looks unbelievably innocent as she points her right index finger toward Stanley. Stanley places the ring I worked so hard to find on her finger.

The rabbi asks Mom and Stanley to again read their ketubah aloud for the guests. The harmony of their combined voices is mesmerizing.

"Lives intertwined as long as we live . . . that the two of us become one in tenderness and devotion . . ."

I glance at the guests, who are on the edges of their seats, completely absorbed in the ceremony. Some ladies clutch white handkerchiefs. I turn Mom and Dad's wedding band on my finger, trying to stave off my own tears.

Then my attention shifts back to the rabbi. I hear the words "Giuseppe, Miriam, loss, pain, love, renewal." And I can't hold it back anymore. I twist my ring, and I am crying. It is so beautiful. It is so hopeful. It is like the first wedding ever.

"I am my beloved, and my beloved is mine," I hear Mom and Stanley say in harmony.

My eyes are flooding. My brothers and I look at each other through shared wet eyes. We silently, simultaneously, wish Mom a happy future full of love and fulfillment. A fleeting tinge of parental concern sweeps over us, and suddenly it's done. The wineglass is shattered. We've married her off.

Thirty-two

The band strikes up the celebratory "Simin Tov and Mazel Tov" music, and the guests start clapping and chanting, "Mazel tov," congratulaions! Mom and Stanley reluctantly unlock their lips, eyes, and hands from one another. I stop crying and start clapping with everyone. The breeze that had held back during the ceremony exhales gently through the courtyard as if patting us all on the back, saying, "It's okay. You can breathe now."

Mom is beaming. I'm exhausted, but I can't exhale yet. We still have the reception ahead. I wipe away the makeup which is surely smearing beneath my eyes, and focus. In the receiving line, I kiss, shake hands, and thank the guests. All the while I'm preoccupied, hoping all the elements of the party fall into place.

From out in the courtyard, I can hear the band playing The Beatles' "She Loves You . . ." inside the glass reception room. It's festive without being raucous. Perfect. "With a love like that, you know you should be glad . . ." the Renaissancers sing.

I flash back to my panic fantasy of the senior crowd getting down, and heart attacking to "Born to Be Wild." How could I have been so neurotic? Where is that Dr. Rosenfeld, anyway? Ah, over there. Nice to know, just in case.

Soon enough, we're in the reception room. The first thing I notice are the centerpieces. Fernando has somehow managed to hang the dozen centerpieces from the rafters on garland ropes like floral chandeliers. The arrangements of dripping daisies, vines of roses, and ivy hover gracefully, about four feet above each table. They are fantastic. A true work of art and genius. I see Mom in a group of friends pointing at the floral chandeliers and covering her mouth in amazement at how clever Fernando has been. He has really outdone himself. I see him in a back corner, transfixed by his own brilliance. I make eye contact with him, raise my hands, and clap gently so he can see how impressed I am. He smiles back, looking proud and exhausted. His body convulses in a sneeze.

I walk back toward the kitchen to get a closer look at the tower of pastries Josephine has artfully constructed. Another garland of daisies and roses and baby's breath encircles each tier of pastries. There is no white frilly wedding cake. No horrible bride or groom statuettes on top. Just an exquisite selection of delicate French pastries. Oh, how I love Josephine's mille feuilles. And the mini–fruit tarts are so festive. The tops of those éclairs are so smooth and chocolaty. I look around and behind me. I snatch one and pop it in my mouth. Who cares? It's sublime.

To the left of the pastry table is another table crowded with dozens of uncorked bottles of wine. I pick up a bottle of red and inspect it. Yes, after all the debate, I think this Australian Cabernet-Shiraz will be excellent. Not that I really know the difference between one or the other. But it will be excellent because that's what they chose.

The waiters are racing around the room, setting perfect-looking appetizers on tables. I'm staring hard at the appetizers, trying to remember what Mom and Stanley finally decided on. "Timbale of roasted corn mousseline, foie gras with brandy sauce, and potato crusted day boat sea scallops. Voila!" Josephine whispers in my ear, anticipating my question.

"Magnifique!" I respond.

The room is humming with conversation and laughter. The guests are engaged in conversation. If the Dip were here, he would have wowed guests with his job title, then offended them with his personality. Glad he didn't come.

The band transitions from "Bridge Over Troubled Water" into "Love and Marriage." If William the opera singer were my date, would he have volunteered to get up onstage and belt out his best Sinatra "I Get a Kick Out of You" or "I've Got You Under My Skin"? He could have melted the guests with his smooth voice. But that might have detracted from Mom and Stanley's spotlight. Better without him.

Ruben might have stolen the show, too, without trying. No matter how highly intellectual this crowd, confronted with Ruben in the room, they would have been mesmerized by his stories of reporting weather from the eye of the storm. It's better that he's not here.

Now Josh might have been a different story. He definitely would not have been the focus in the room. More likely, he would have quietly sat in the background and listened. He would have asked me every half hour if everything was okay and whether I needed anything. He would have helped me evade questions about my marriage plans. He would have understood the Jewish elements of the ceremony. He would have whispered jokes in my ear, not to the crowd.

This reflection brings me to a refreshingly new concept. Maybe I've been looking for the wrong IB. Maybe rather than searching for overaccomplished charmers, I should date more reflective, sensitive men. The kind of man who is big inside but isn't a grand entertainer.

Even I'm not putting on any show myself right now. I'm not presenting for TV, or acting to make good impressions. I'm not using makeup to cover up. I am not pretending anything. I am sincerely happy for Mom. Tonight, the spotlight is on her, and she is glowing.

The room shares a communal laugh when the band begins to play The Beatles' "When I'm Sixty-four." Mom and Stanley hurry onto the dance floor where they spin and laugh together. Their friends immediately join them; their grins wide and bright, remembering when the song first came out. The clarinet, piano, and light percussion infuses the room with a cheerful ambience as everyone sings along, "Will you still need me, will you still feed me, when I'm sixty-four?"

It's incredibly sweet. I sit down at a table with my brothers and my cousins, and realize there is no great drama here tonight, just good, honest fun. No one is mistaking me for the bride. Not even in my imagination. If I happen upon Mom and Stanley kissing, I won't be revolted. If Erica talks incomprehensible physics to me, I won't be surprised. This is just a well-behaved group of adults savoring this exquisite moment of joy. And, no one is daring to make a toast.

Then, just as I'm settling in, thinking how well everything is turning out, Stanley stands up and clinks his fork against his glass. No way. My brothers and I shoot disbelieving glances at each other. This is outrageous. Stanley raises his glass.

"I want to thank you all for coming here tonight to share this celebration with us. *L'chaim*. To life," he says, laughing, takes a sip, then sits down, and gives Mom a peck on the cheek.

I raise my glass to my brothers. "To life's surprises," I say.

The Renaissancers kick into playing "Hava Nagila," the traditional Jewish song of celebration. My brothers pull me out onto the dance floor, which is already spinning with the senior crowd, including Dr. Rosenfeld. Enrico clutches my left hand and Max clasps my right as the accordion pulls and the clarinet blows. My brothers grab hands with other guests to dance the hora, and we form a massive circle that revolves along the perimeter of the dance floor. The music picks up speed, and a smaller circle forms within the bigger circle, rotating the opposite direction. We're all doing some form of skipping, stomping Israeli dancing.

Mom and Stanley break off and spin each other around with crossed outstretched arms in the center of the two circles. They clutch each other's hands together like children in a playground, just the two of them, as the two circles revolve around them. The music speeds up into an almost feverish pace, and Enrico and Max drag me and Erica into the center where we create a third ring. We clasp hands with our parents and spin round and round, laughing and dancing, the six of us in our own orbit.

When the music finally slows down and releases us from the frenzied dancing, we splinter off the dance floor, our heads still pressured and spinning from the wild rotations. I realize with relief that no one tried to lift Mom and Stanley up in the chairs.

The main course, "your choice of beef tenderloin, pan-seared Pacific salmon, or vegetable strudel," is served, and people get quieter. I'm hungry, but I don't want to eat. Too much emotion. Too much stimulation.

I excuse myself from the table, leaving the salmon untouched. My brothers nod at me, their mouths grinning full. Outside in the courtyard, it is quieter. The chuppah is still standing, gorgeous in all its floral splendor, but lonely again. Some flower petals and leaves are scattered across the courtyard. The sky is clear, and the stars are bright on this cool night. Dad would have been happy for Mom, for all of us right now.

"Stop worrying about me," he would say. "Enjoy yourself. Moments like this deserve to be celebrated. They are too rare."

"Daniella?" I hear a deep, confident, male voice behind me. My heart skips a beat. IB?

I hold my breath and turn around, only to see one of my mother's friends. It's Danny.

"Congratulations," he says. "You did a great job, and you look beautiful."

"Thanks," I say, trying to hide my disappointment.

"Where's your date?" he asks.

Here we go again. I'm finally making peace with my perpetual single state, and some friend of Mom's needs to know about my personal life.

"I didn't want to bring a date," I say.

"Good." He winks. "Because I've got someone for you to meet. He's a prince. Like no one you could imagine."

"Oh yeah?" I smile. "Try me."